KRISS

THE GIFT of WRATH

AN ONI PRESS PUBLICATION

KRISS

THE GIFT of WRATH

WRITTEN BY
TED NAIFEH

ILLUSTRATED, COLORED, AND LETTERED BY
WARREN WUCINICH

EDITED BY ROBIN HERRERA
DESIGNED BY KATE Z. STONE

onipress.com
 facebook.com/onipress
 twitter.com/onipress
 onipress.tumblr.com
 instagram.com/onipress

@tednaifeh
tednaifeh.com

@warrenwucinich
warrenwucinich.com

First Edition: September 2019

ISBN 978-1-62010-661-7
eISBN 978-1-62010-662-4

Library of Congress Control Number: 2019931470

1 2 3 4 5 6 7 8 9 10

PUBLISHED BY
ONI PRESS, INC.

JOE NOZEMACK
founder & chief financial officer
JAMES LUCAS JONES
publisher
SARAH GAYDOS
editor in chief
CHARLIE CHU
v.p. of creative & business development
BRAD ROOKS
director of operations
MELISSA MESZAROS
director of publicity
MARGOT WOOD
director of sales
SANDY TANAKA
marketing design manager
AMBER O'NEILL
special projects manager
TROY LOOK
director of design & production
KATE Z. STONE
senior graphic designer
SONJA SYNAK
graphic designer
ANGIE KNOWLES
digital prepress lead
ROBIN HERRERA
senior editor
ARI YARWOOD
senior editor
DESIREE WILSON
associate editor
KATE LIGHT
editorial assistant
MICHELLE NGUYEN
executive assistant
JUNG LEE
logistics coordinator

CHAPTER ONE

THE GIFT OF WRATH

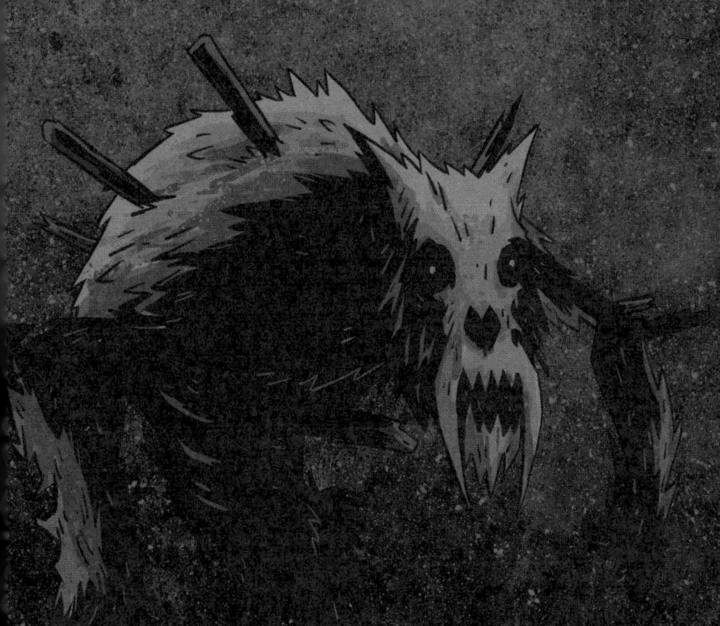

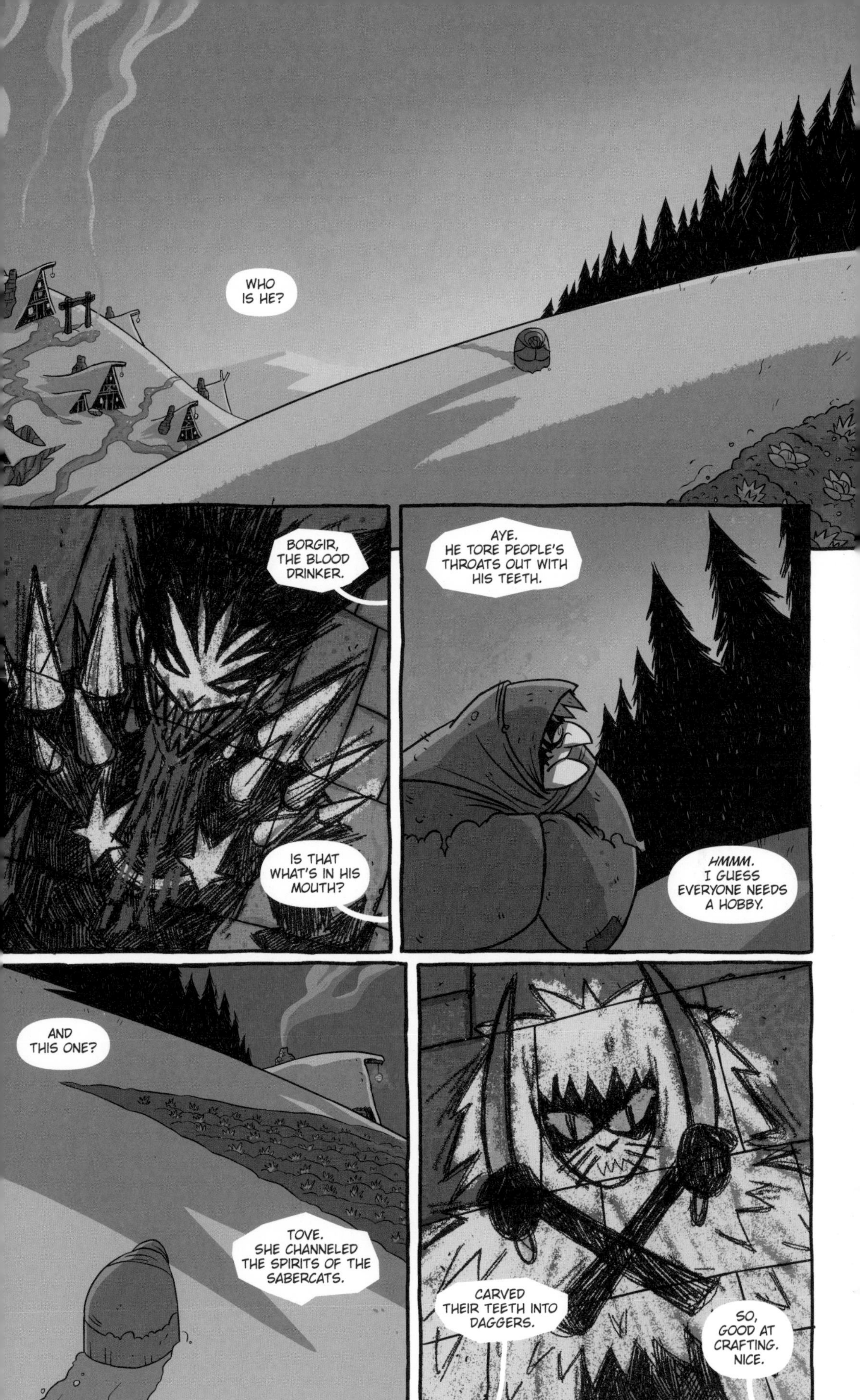
WHO IS HE?
BORGIR, THE BLOOD DRINKER.
AYE. HE TORE PEOPLE'S THROATS OUT WITH HIS TEETH.
IS THAT WHAT'S IN HIS MOUTH?
HMMM. I GUESS EVERYONE NEEDS A HOBBY.
AND THIS ONE?
TOVE. SHE CHANNELED THE SPIRITS OF THE SABERCATS.
CARVED THEIR TEETH INTO DAGGERS.
SO, GOOD AT CRAFTING. NICE.

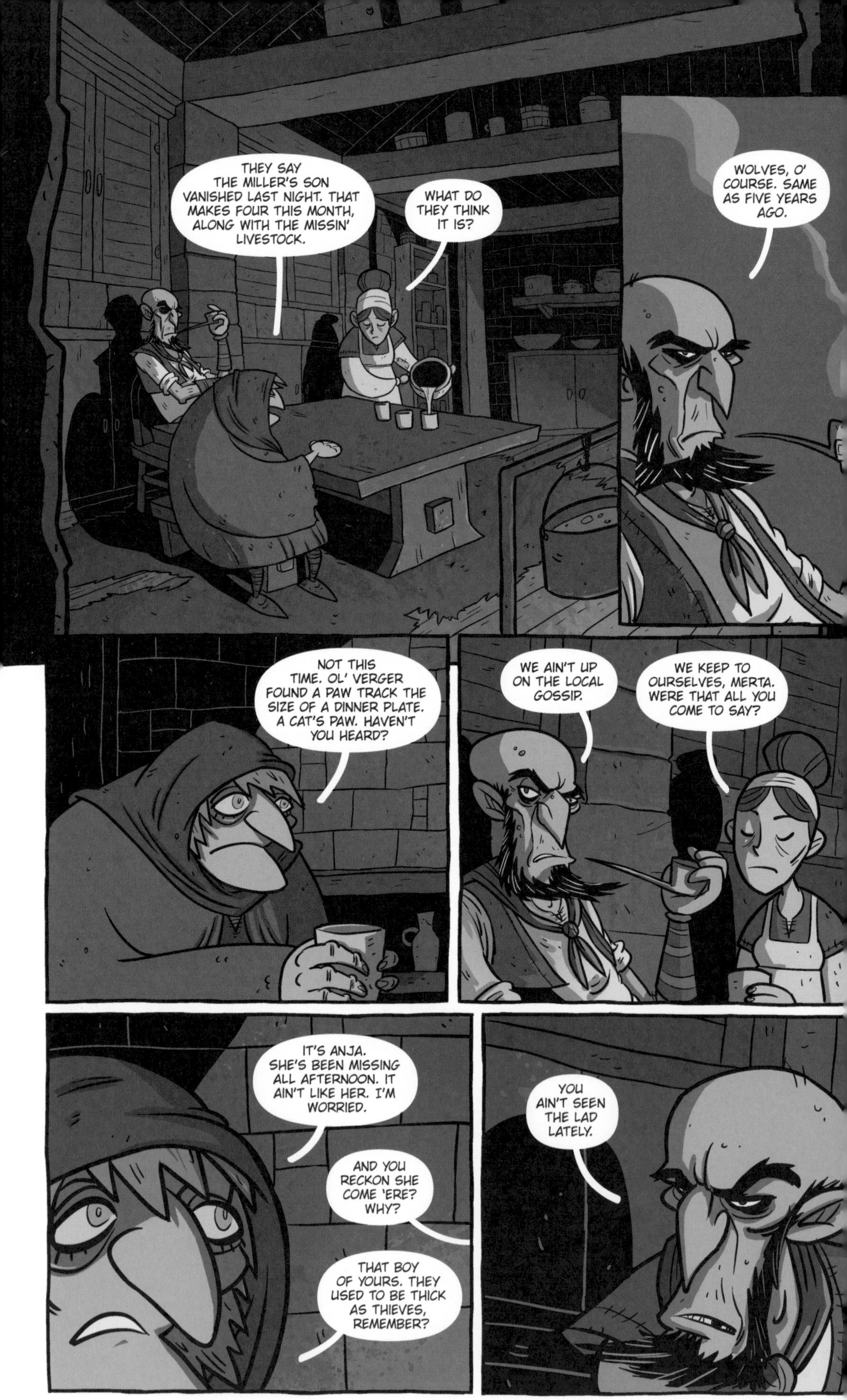
THEY SAY THE MILLER'S SON VANISHED LAST NIGHT. THAT MAKES FOUR THIS MONTH, ALONG WITH THE MISSIN' LIVESTOCK.
WHAT DO THEY THINK IT IS?
WOLVES, O' COURSE. SAME AS FIVE YEARS AGO.
NOT THIS TIME. OL' VERGER FOUND A PAW TRACK THE SIZE OF A DINNER PLATE. A CAT'S PAW. HAVEN'T YOU HEARD?
WE AIN'T UP ON THE LOCAL GOSSIP.
WE KEEP TO OURSELVES, MERTA. WERE THAT ALL YOU COME TO SAY?
IT'S ANJA. SHE'S BEEN MISSING ALL AFTERNOON. IT AIN'T LIKE HER. I'M WORRIED.
AND YOU RECKON SHE COME 'ERE? WHY?
THAT BOY OF YOURS. THEY USED TO BE THICK AS THIEVES, REMEMBER?
YOU AIN'T SEEN THE LAD LATELY.

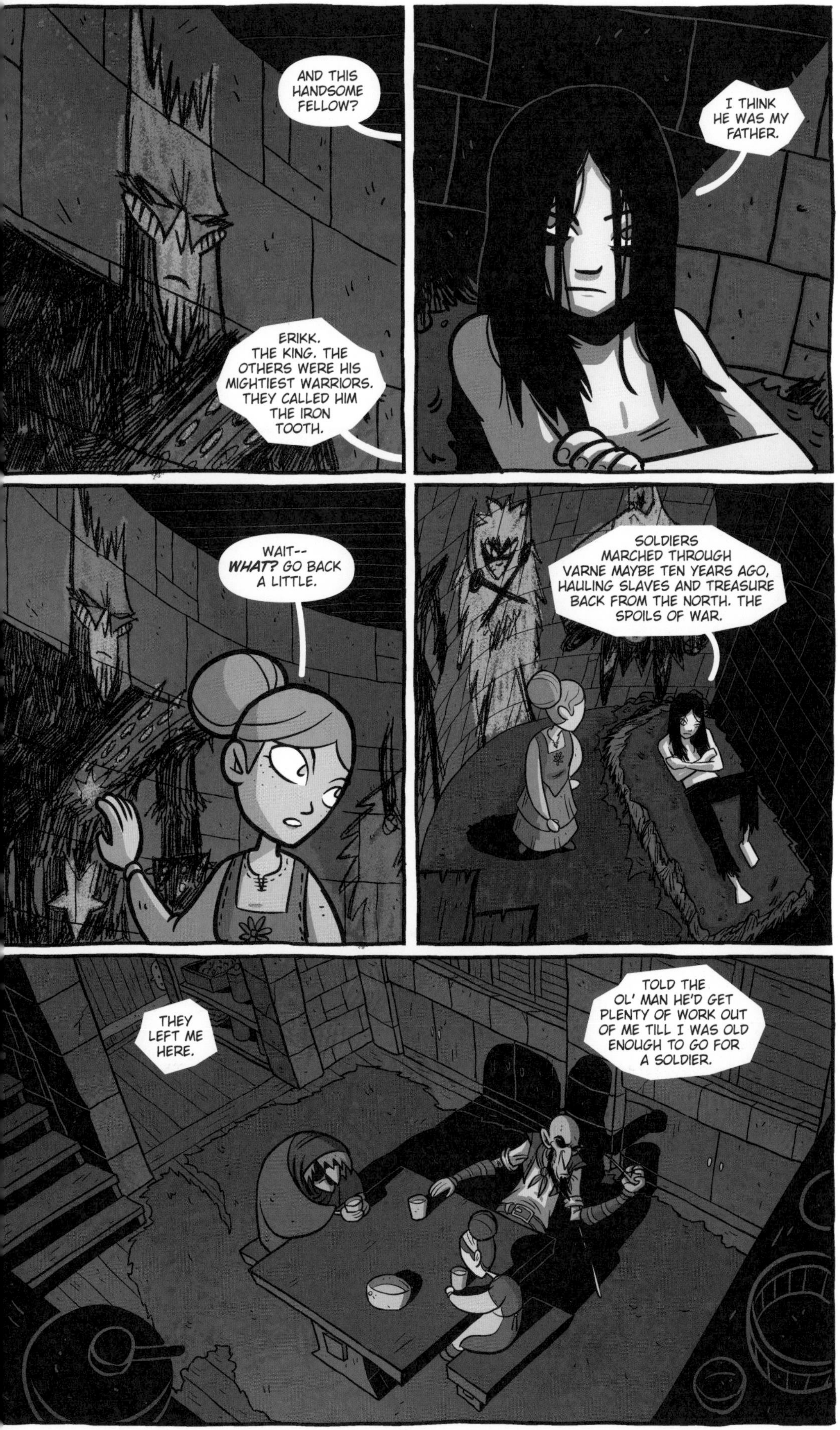
AND THIS HANDSOME FELLOW?
I THINK HE WAS MY FATHER.
ERIKK. THE KING. THE OTHERS WERE HIS MIGHTIEST WARRIORS. THEY CALLED HIM THE IRON TOOTH.
WAIT-- WHAT? GO BACK A LITTLE.
SOLDIERS MARCHED THROUGH VARNE MAYBE TEN YEARS AGO, HAULING SLAVES AND TREASURE BACK FROM THE NORTH. THE SPOILS OF WAR.
THEY LEFT ME HERE.
TOLD THE OL' MAN HE'D GET PLENTY OF WORK OUT OF ME TILL I WAS OLD ENOUGH TO GO FOR A SOLDIER.

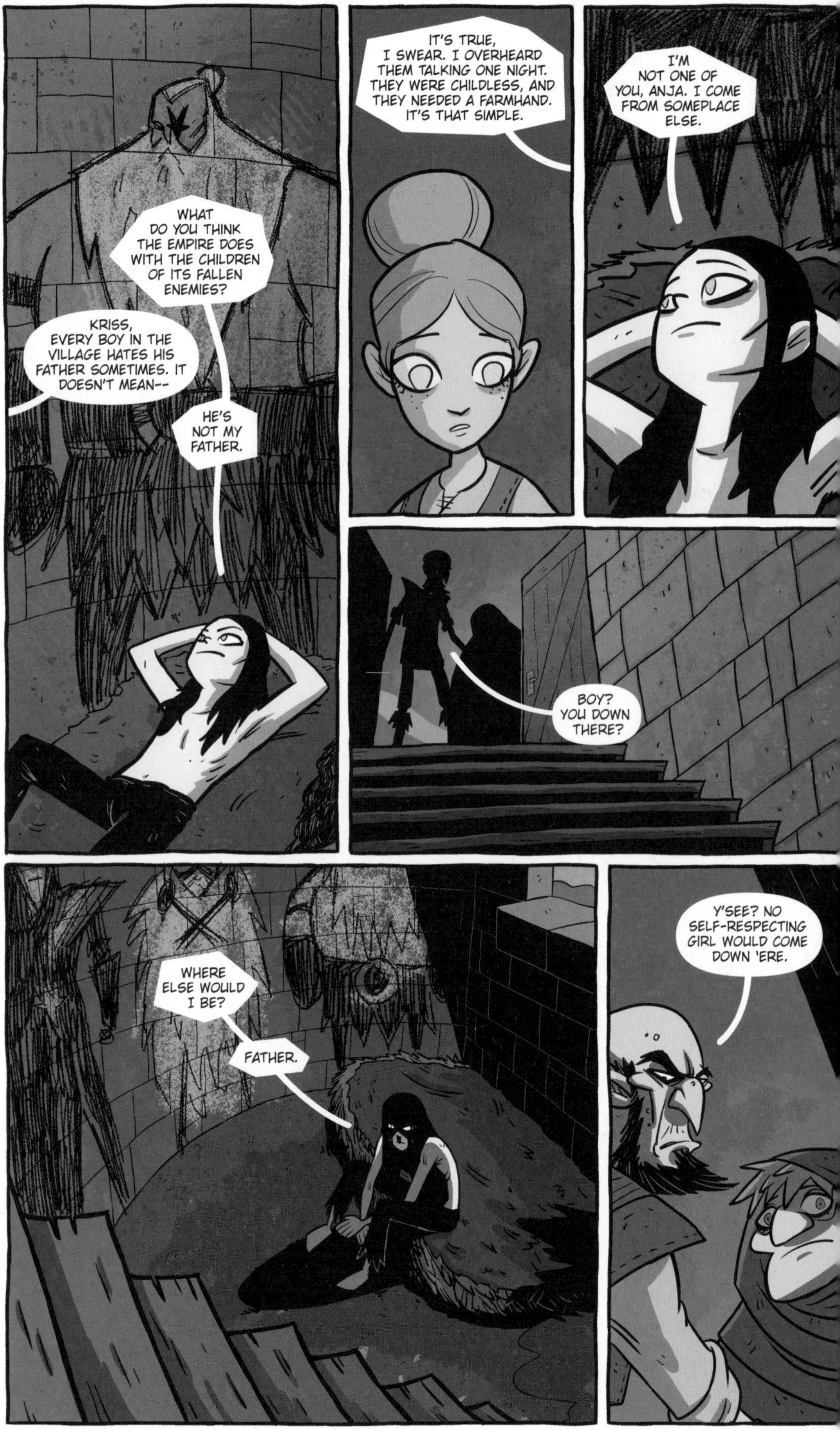
WHAT DO YOU THINK THE EMPIRE DOES WITH THE CHILDREN OF ITS FALLEN ENEMIES?
KRISS, EVERY BOY IN THE VILLAGE HATES HIS FATHER SOMETIMES. IT DOESN'T MEAN--
HE'S NOT MY FATHER.
IT'S TRUE, I SWEAR. I OVERHEARD THEM TALKING ONE NIGHT. THEY WERE CHILDLESS, AND THEY NEEDED A FARMHAND. IT'S THAT SIMPLE.
I'M NOT ONE OF YOU, ANJA. I COME FROM SOMEPLACE ELSE.
BOY? YOU DOWN THERE?
WHERE ELSE WOULD I BE?
FATHER.
Y'SEE? NO SELF-RESPECTING GIRL WOULD COME DOWN 'ERE.

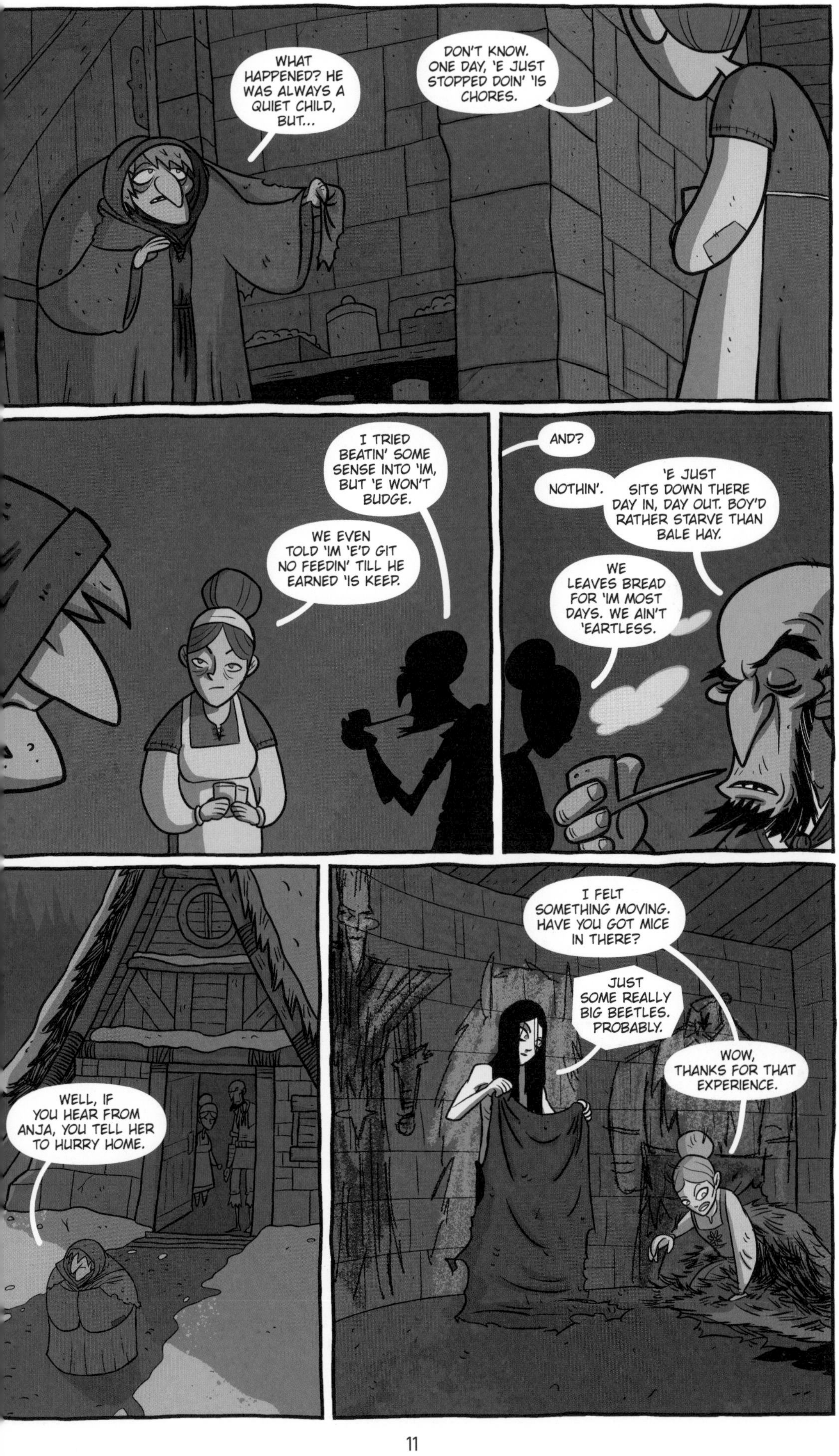
WHAT HAPPENED? HE WAS ALWAYS A QUIET CHILD, BUT...
DON'T KNOW. ONE DAY, 'E JUST STOPPED DOIN' 'IS CHORES.
I TRIED BEATIN' SOME SENSE INTO 'IM, BUT 'E WON'T BUDGE.
WE EVEN TOLD 'IM 'E'D GIT NO FEEDIN' TILL HE EARNED 'IS KEEP.
AND?
NOTHIN'.
'E JUST SITS DOWN THERE DAY IN, DAY OUT. BOY'D RATHER STARVE THAN BALE HAY.
WE LEAVES BREAD FOR 'IM MOST DAYS. WE AIN'T 'EARTLESS.
WELL, IF YOU HEAR FROM ANJA, YOU TELL HER TO HURRY HOME.
I FELT SOMETHING MOVING. HAVE YOU GOT MICE IN THERE?
JUST SOME REALLY BIG BEETLES. PROBABLY.
WOW, THANKS FOR THAT EXPERIENCE.

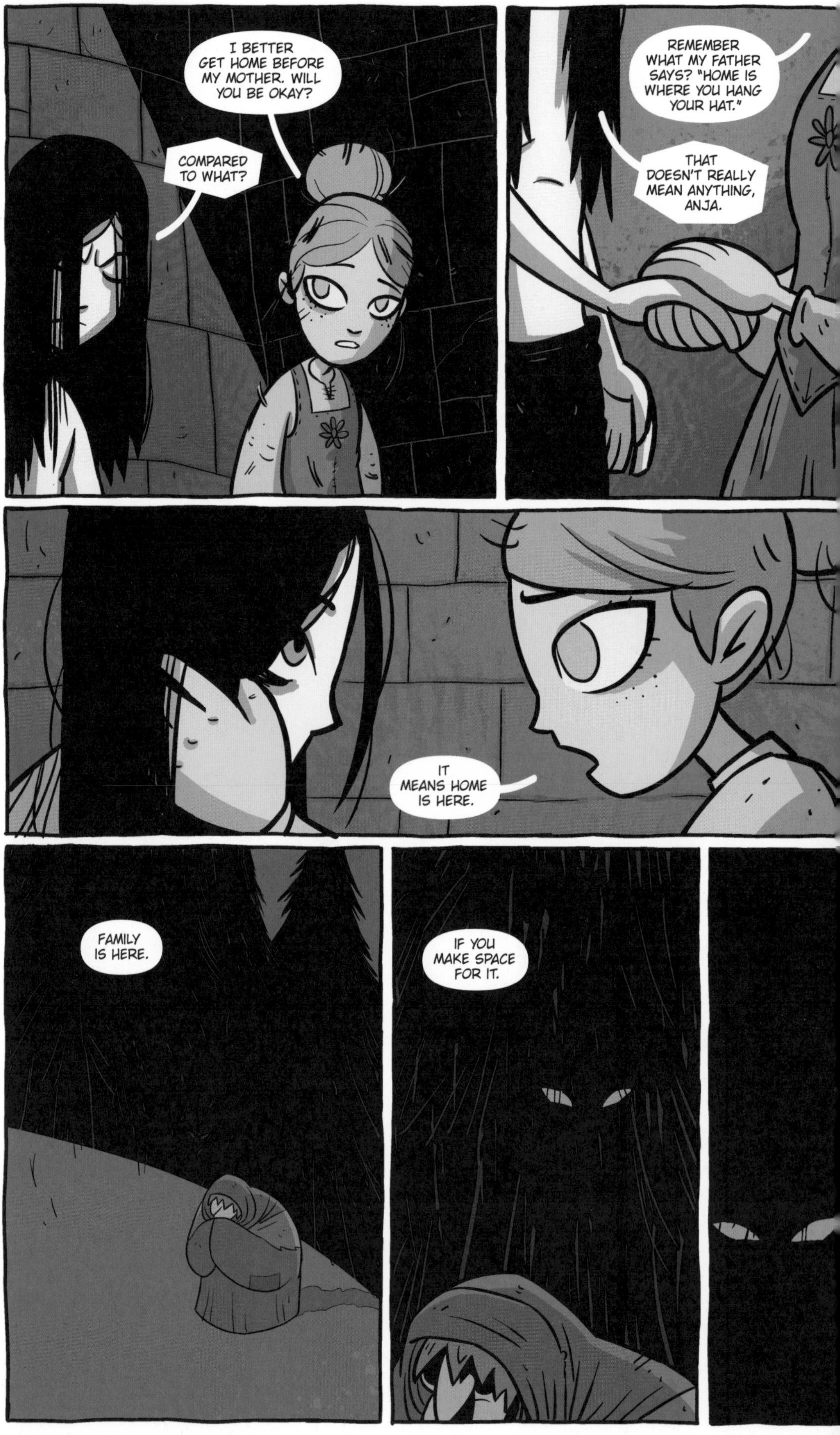
I BETTER GET HOME BEFORE MY MOTHER. WILL YOU BE OKAY?
COMPARED TO WHAT?
REMEMBER WHAT MY FATHER SAYS? "HOME IS WHERE YOU HANG YOUR HAT."
THAT DOESN'T REALLY MEAN ANYTHING, ANJA.
IT MEANS HOME IS HERE.
FAMILY IS HERE.
IF YOU MAKE SPACE FOR IT.

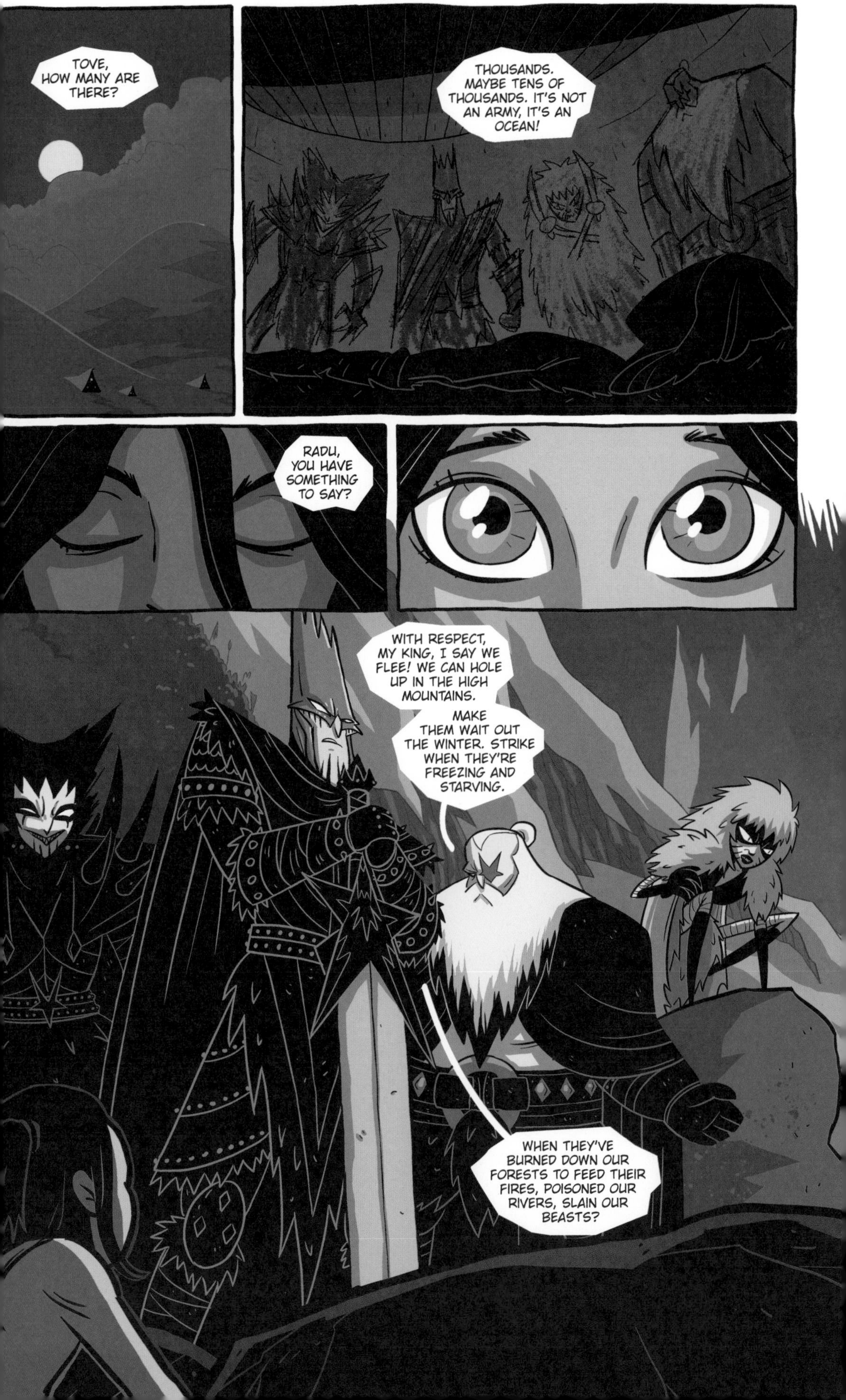
TOVE, HOW MANY ARE THERE?
THOUSANDS. MAYBE TENS OF THOUSANDS. IT'S NOT AN ARMY, IT'S AN OCEAN!
RADU, YOU HAVE SOMETHING TO SAY?
WITH RESPECT, MY KING, I SAY WE FLEE! WE CAN HOLE UP IN THE HIGH MOUNTAINS.
MAKE THEM WAIT OUT THE WINTER. STRIKE WHEN THEY'RE FREEZING AND STARVING.
WHEN THEY'VE BURNED DOWN OUR FORESTS TO FEED THEIR FIRES, POISONED OUR RIVERS, SLAIN OUR BEASTS?

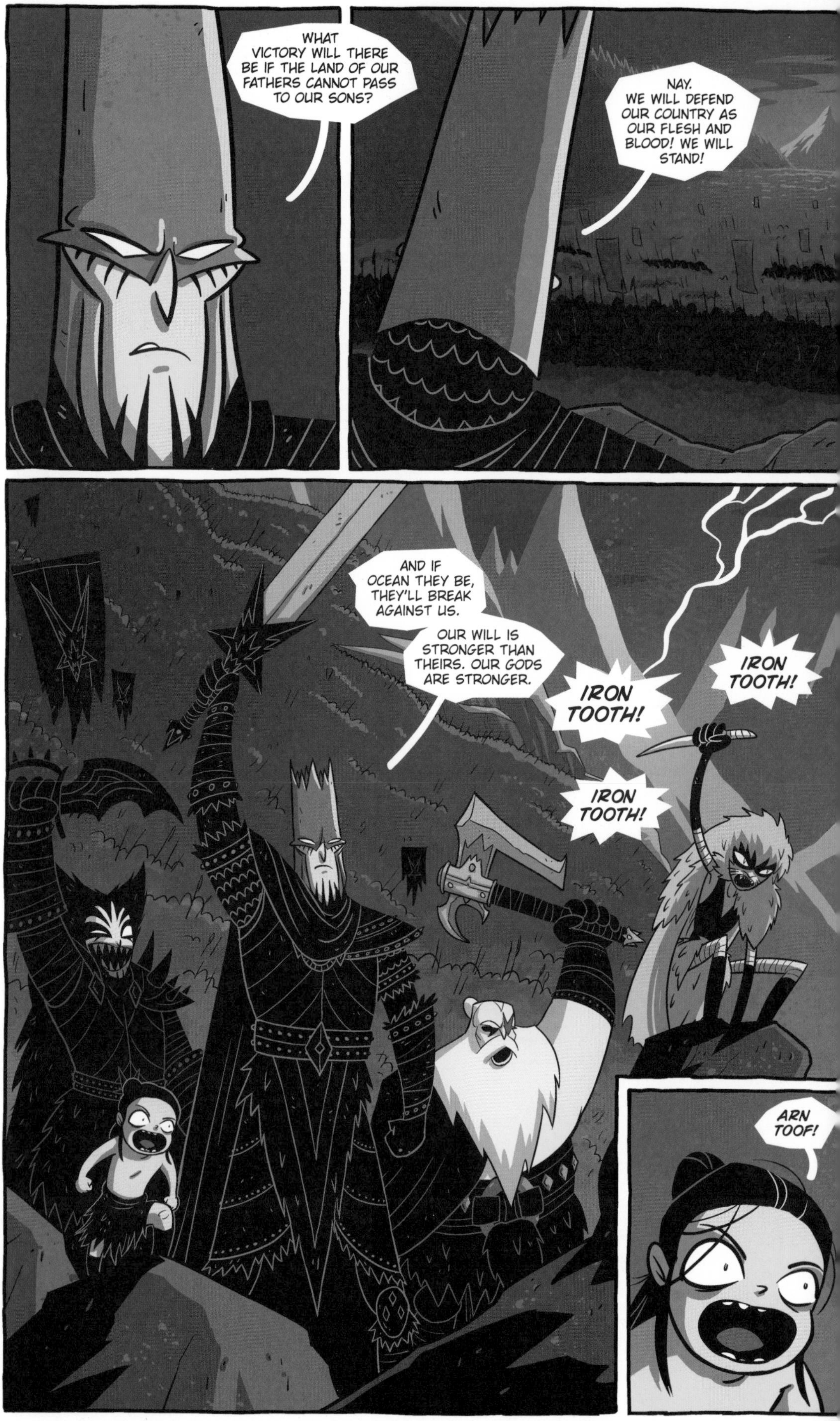
WHAT VICTORY WILL THERE BE IF THE LAND OF OUR FATHERS CANNOT PASS TO OUR SONS?
NAY. WE WILL DEFEND OUR COUNTRY AS OUR FLESH AND BLOOD! WE WILL STAND!
AND IF OCEAN THEY BE, THEY'LL BREAK AGAINST US.
OUR WILL IS STRONGER THAN THEIRS. OUR GODS ARE STRONGER.
IRON TOOTH!
IRON TOOTH!
IRON TOOTH!
ARN TOOF!

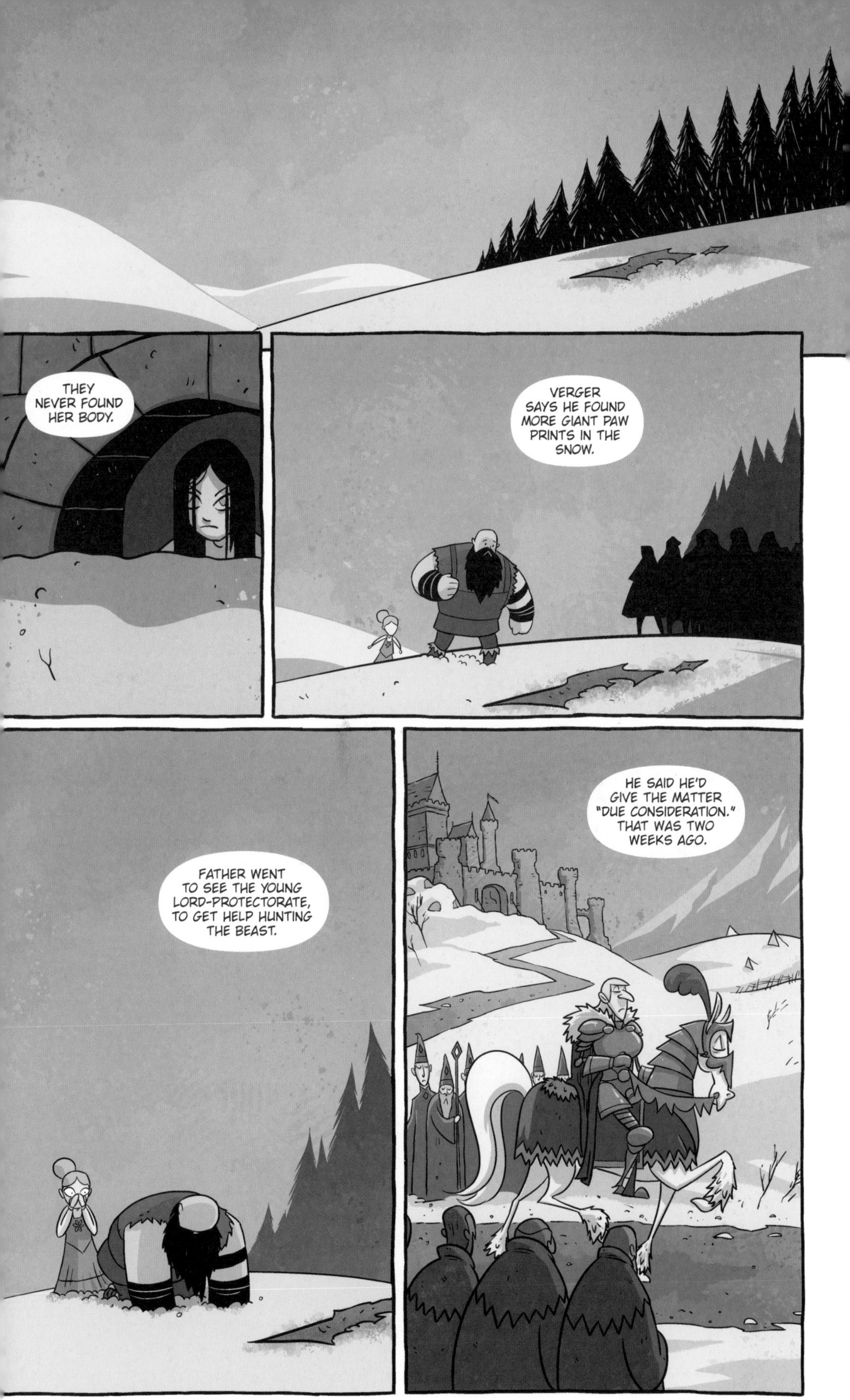
THEY NEVER FOUND HER BODY.
VERGER SAYS HE FOUND MORE GIANT PAW PRINTS IN THE SNOW.
FATHER WENT TO SEE THE YOUNG LORD-PROTECTORATE, TO GET HELP HUNTING THE BEAST.
HE SAID HE'D GIVE THE MATTER "DUE CONSIDERATION." THAT WAS TWO WEEKS AGO.

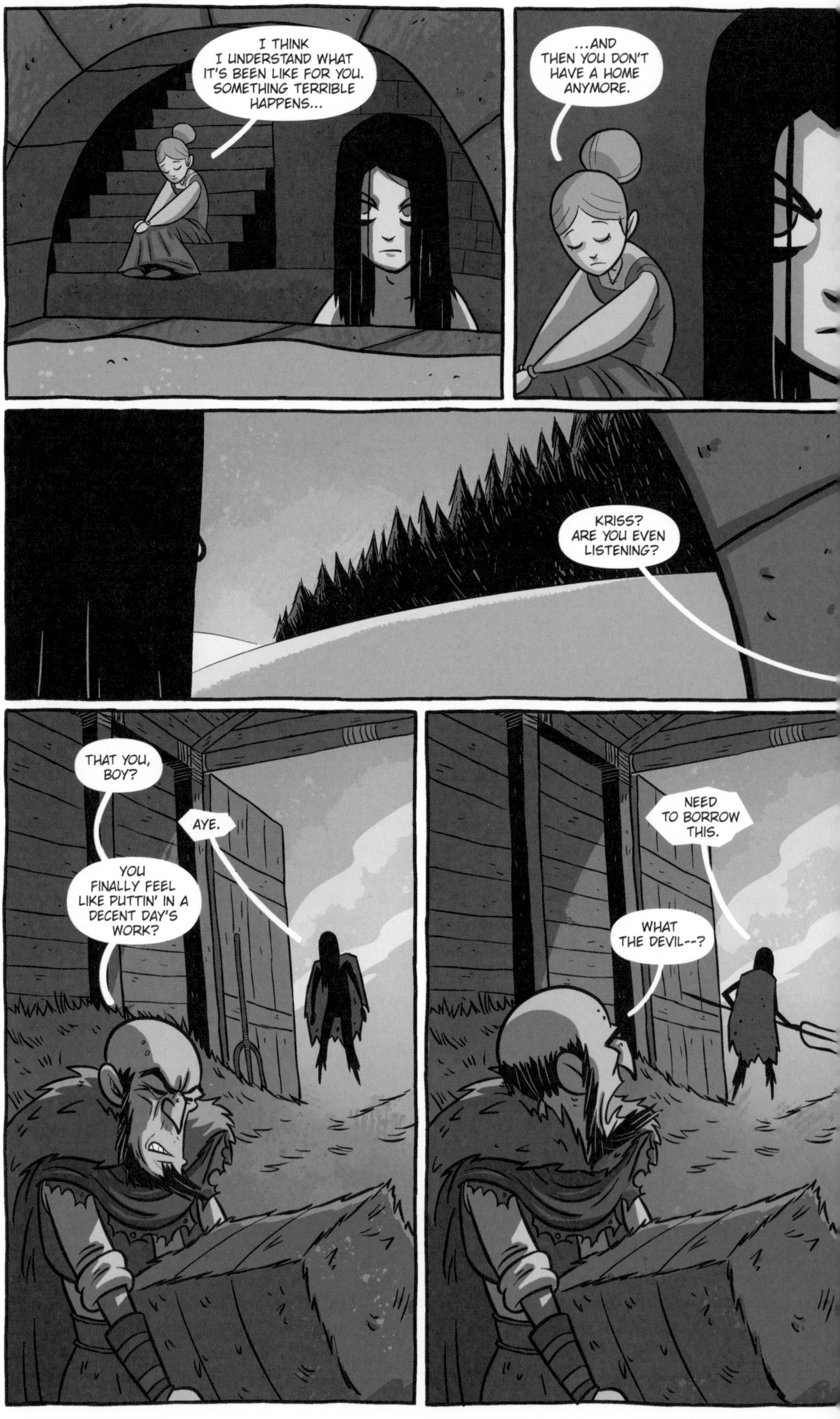
I THINK I UNDERSTAND WHAT IT'S BEEN LIKE FOR YOU. SOMETHING TERRIBLE HAPPENS...
...AND THEN YOU DON'T HAVE A HOME ANYMORE.
KRISS? ARE YOU EVEN LISTENING?
THAT YOU, BOY?
AYE.
YOU FINALLY FEEL LIKE PUTTIN' IN A DECENT DAY'S WORK?
NEED TO BORROW THIS.
WHAT THE DEVIL--?

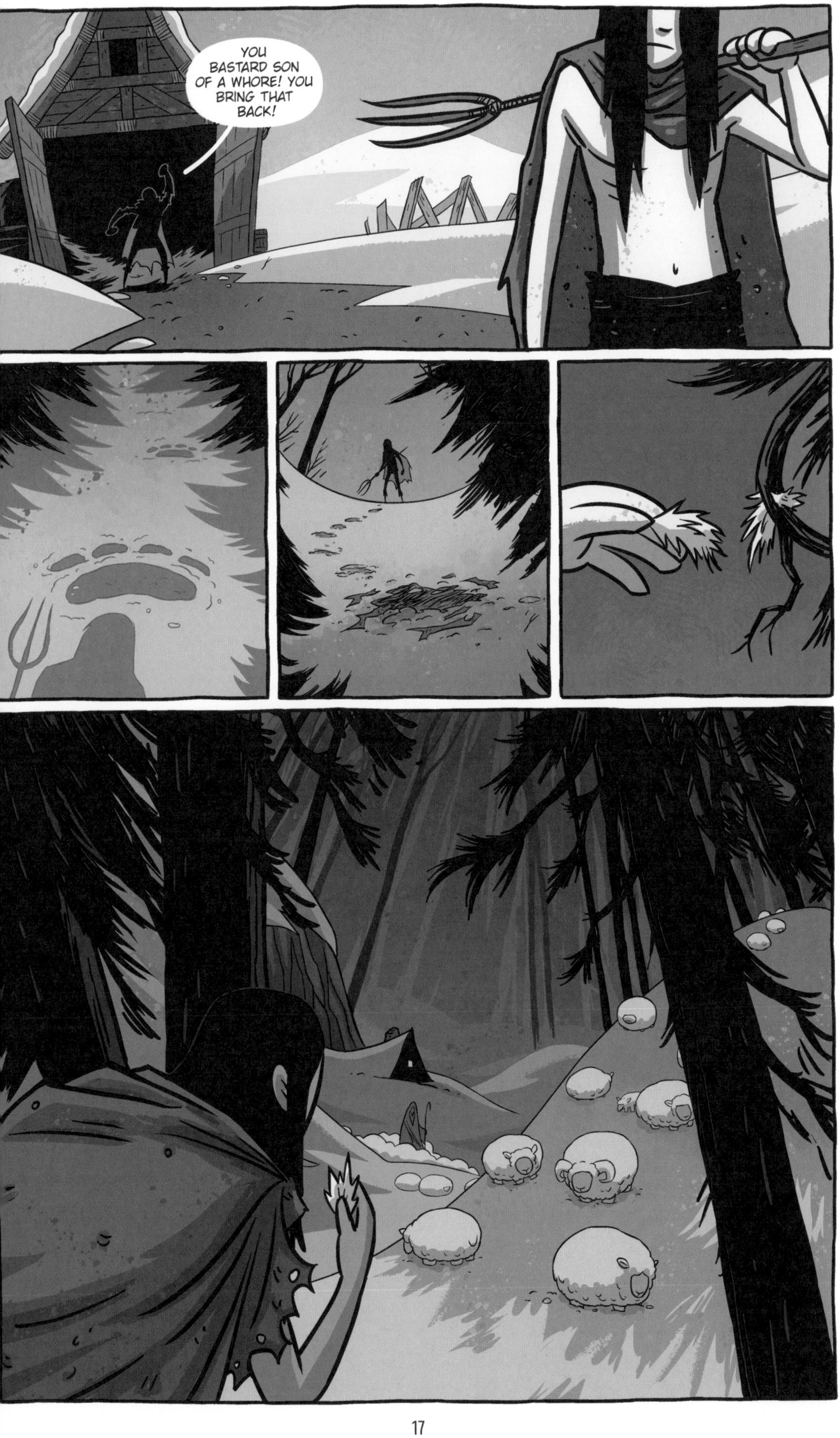
YOU BASTARD SON OF A WHORE! YOU BRING THAT BACK!

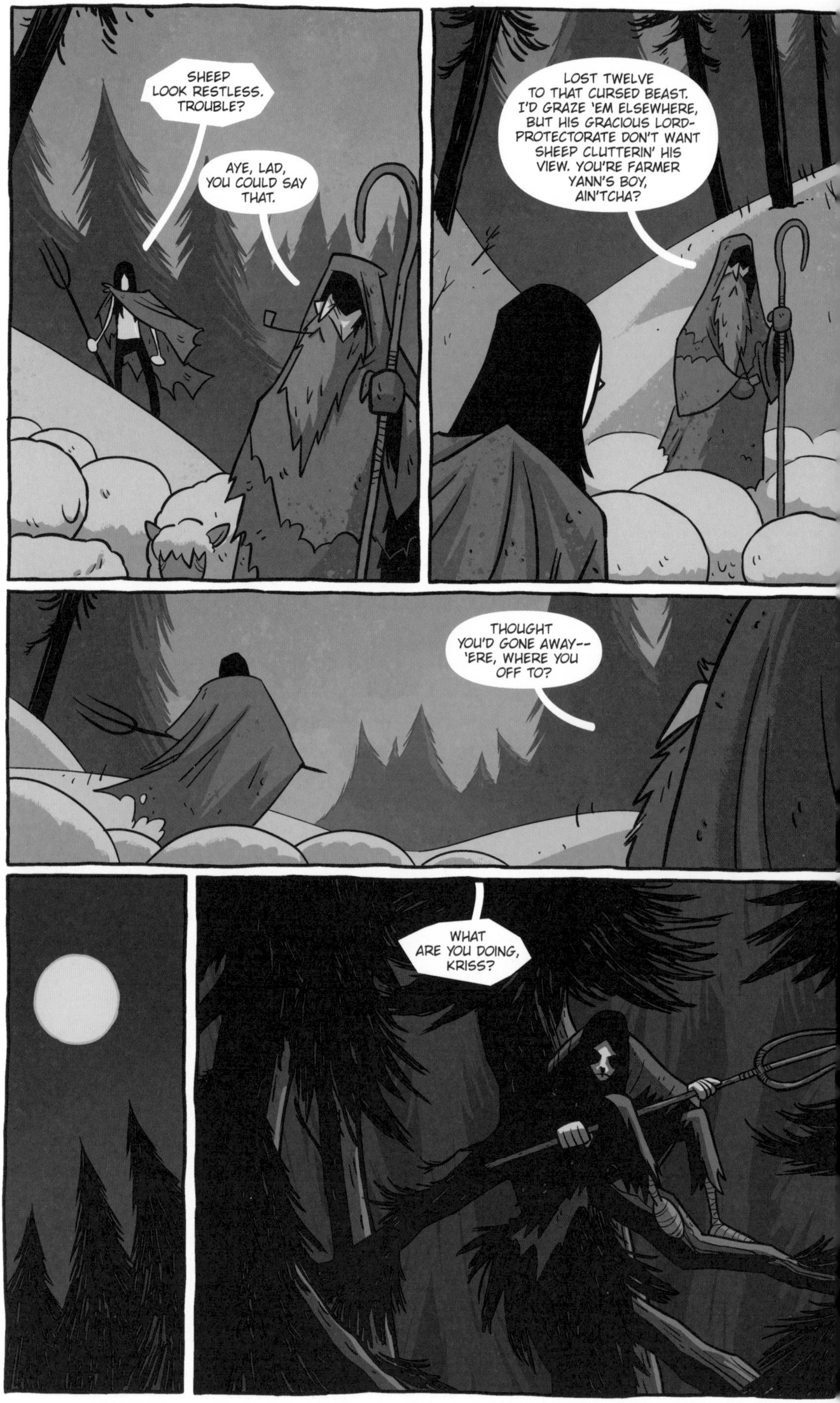
SHEEP LOOK RESTLESS. TROUBLE?
AYE, LAD, YOU COULD SAY THAT.
LOST TWELVE TO THAT CURSED BEAST. I'D GRAZE 'EM ELSEWHERE, BUT HIS GRACIOUS LORD-PROTECTORATE DON'T WANT SHEEP CLUTTERIN' HIS VIEW. YOU'RE FARMER YANN'S BOY, AIN'TCHA?
THOUGHT YOU'D GONE AWAY-- 'ERE, WHERE YOU OFF TO?
WHAT ARE YOU DOING, KRISS?

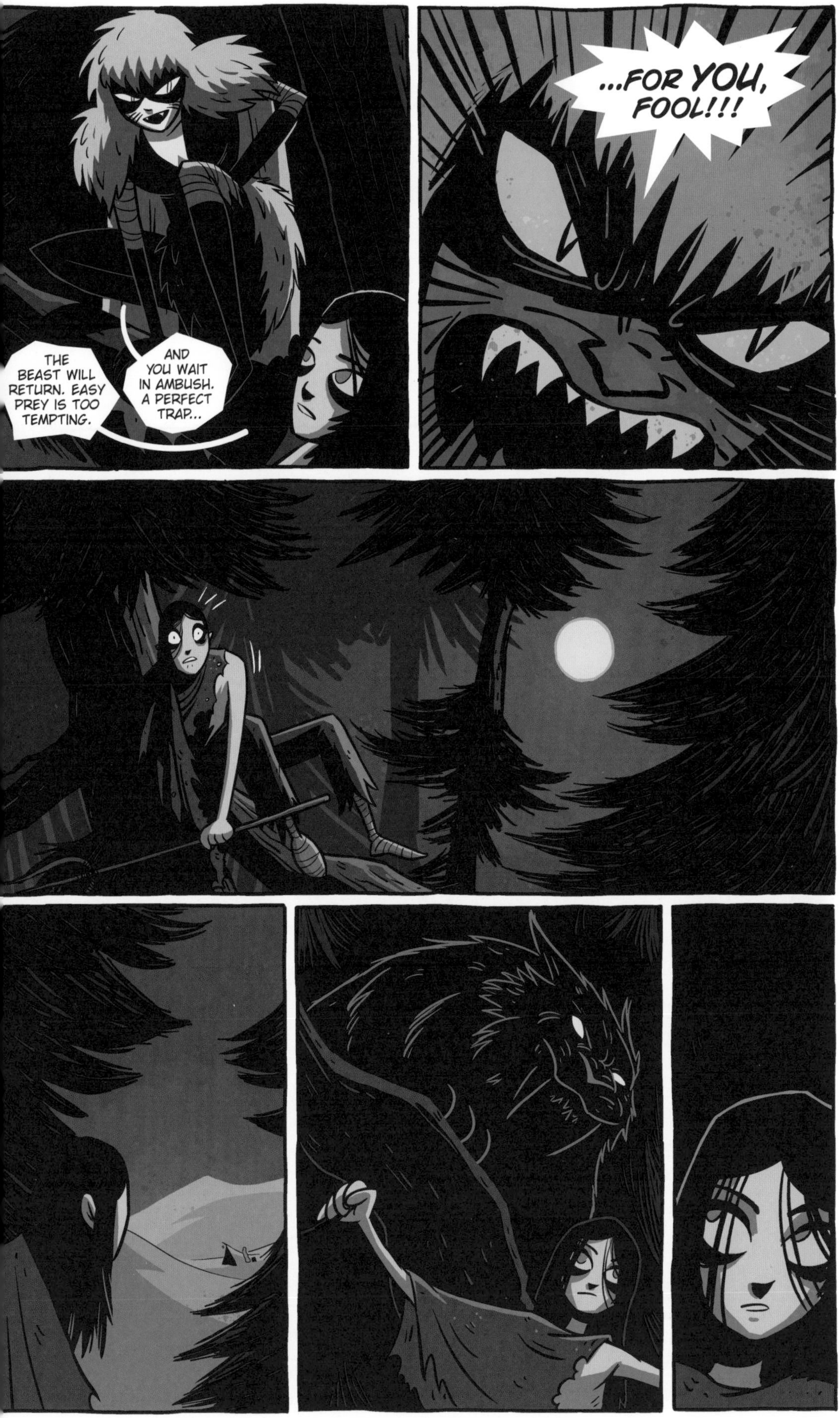
THE BEAST WILL RETURN. EASY PREY IS TOO TEMPTING.
AND YOU WAIT IN AMBUSH. A PERFECT TRAP...
...FOR YOU, FOOL!!!

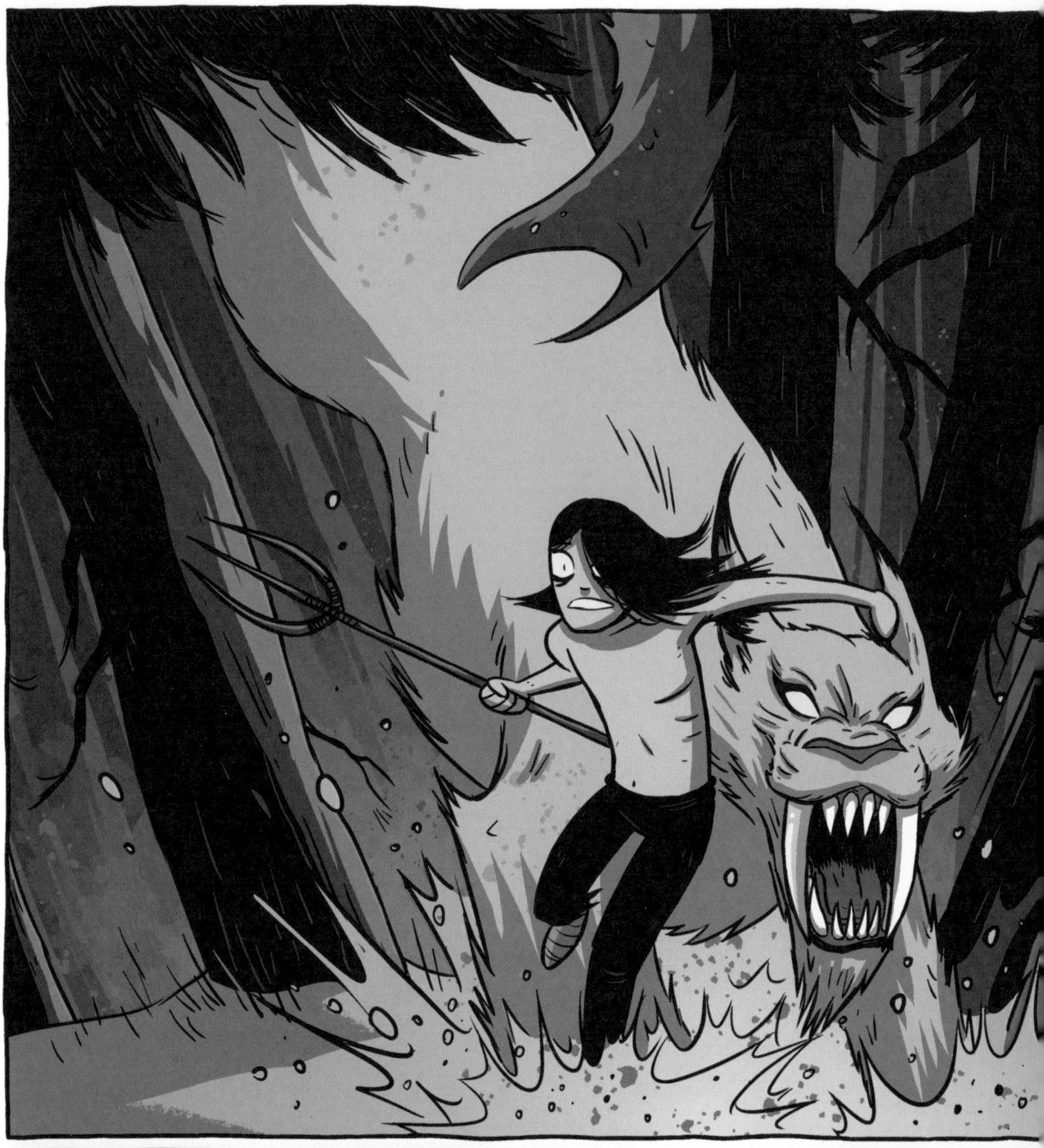

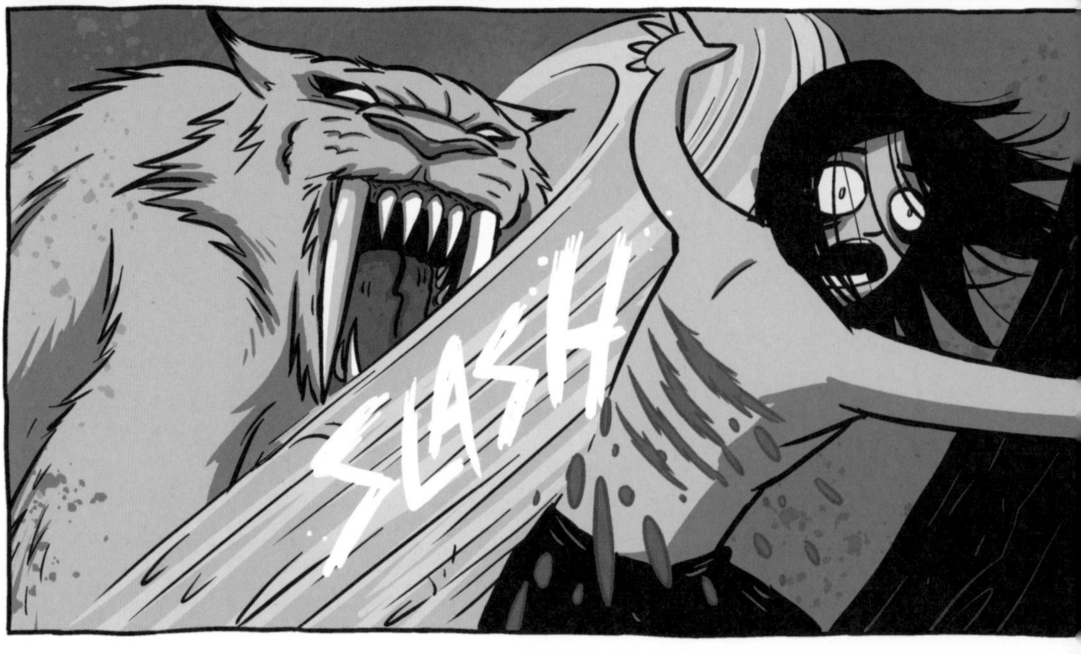
SLASH

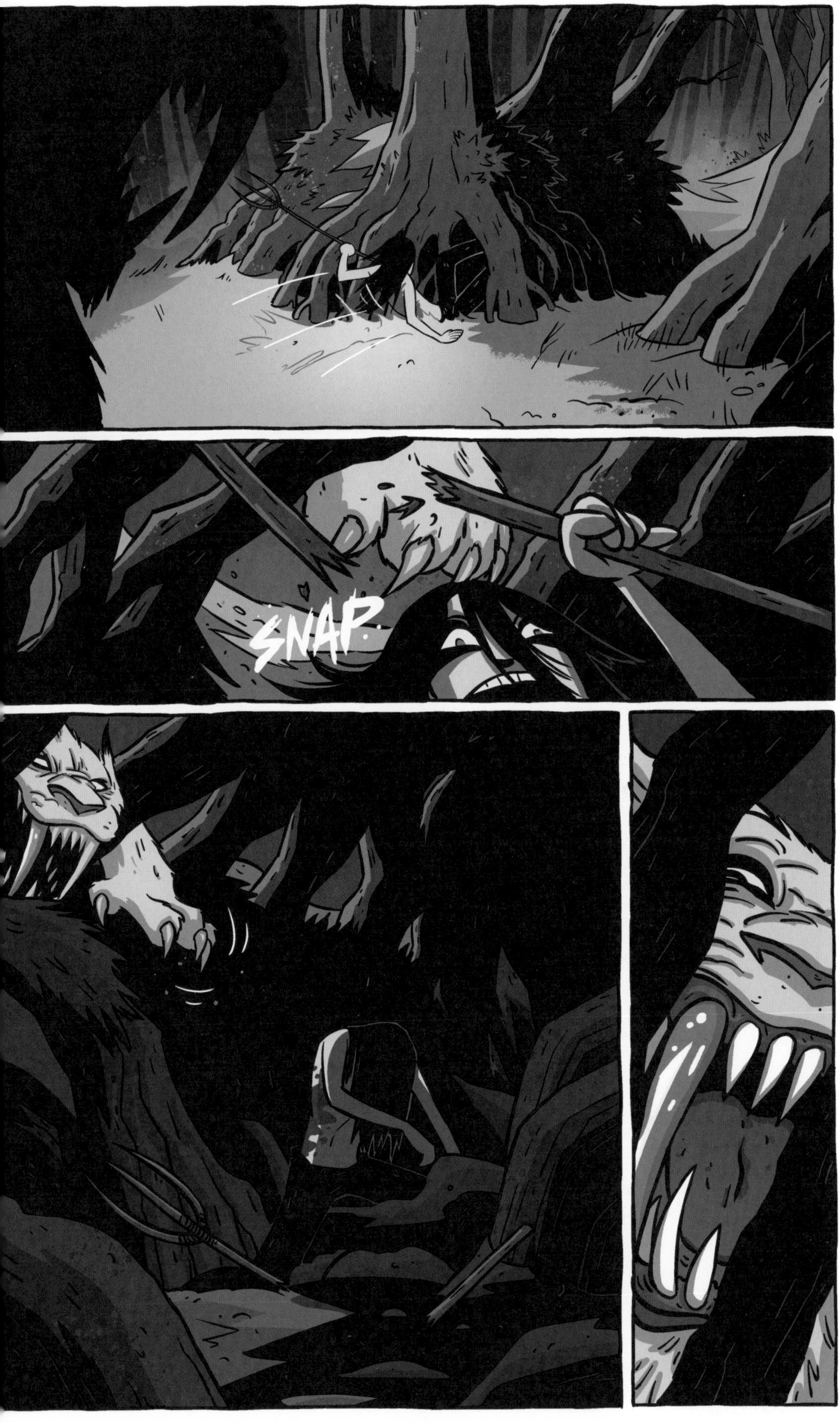
SNAP

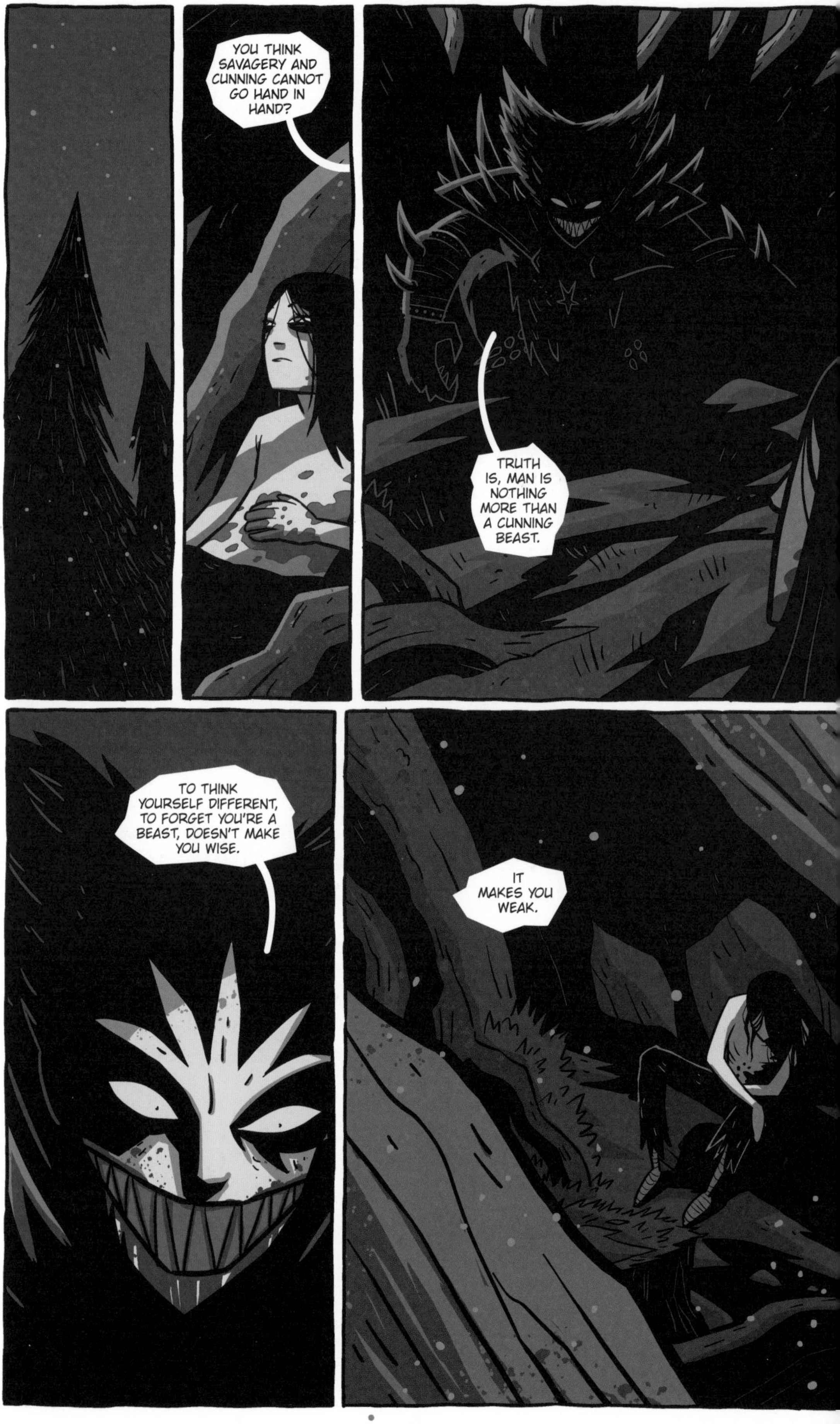
YOU THINK SAVAGERY AND CUNNING CANNOT GO HAND IN HAND?
TRUTH IS, MAN IS NOTHING MORE THAN A CUNNING BEAST.
TO THINK YOURSELF DIFFERENT, TO FORGET YOU'RE A BEAST, DOESN'T MAKE YOU WISE.
IT MAKES YOU WEAK.

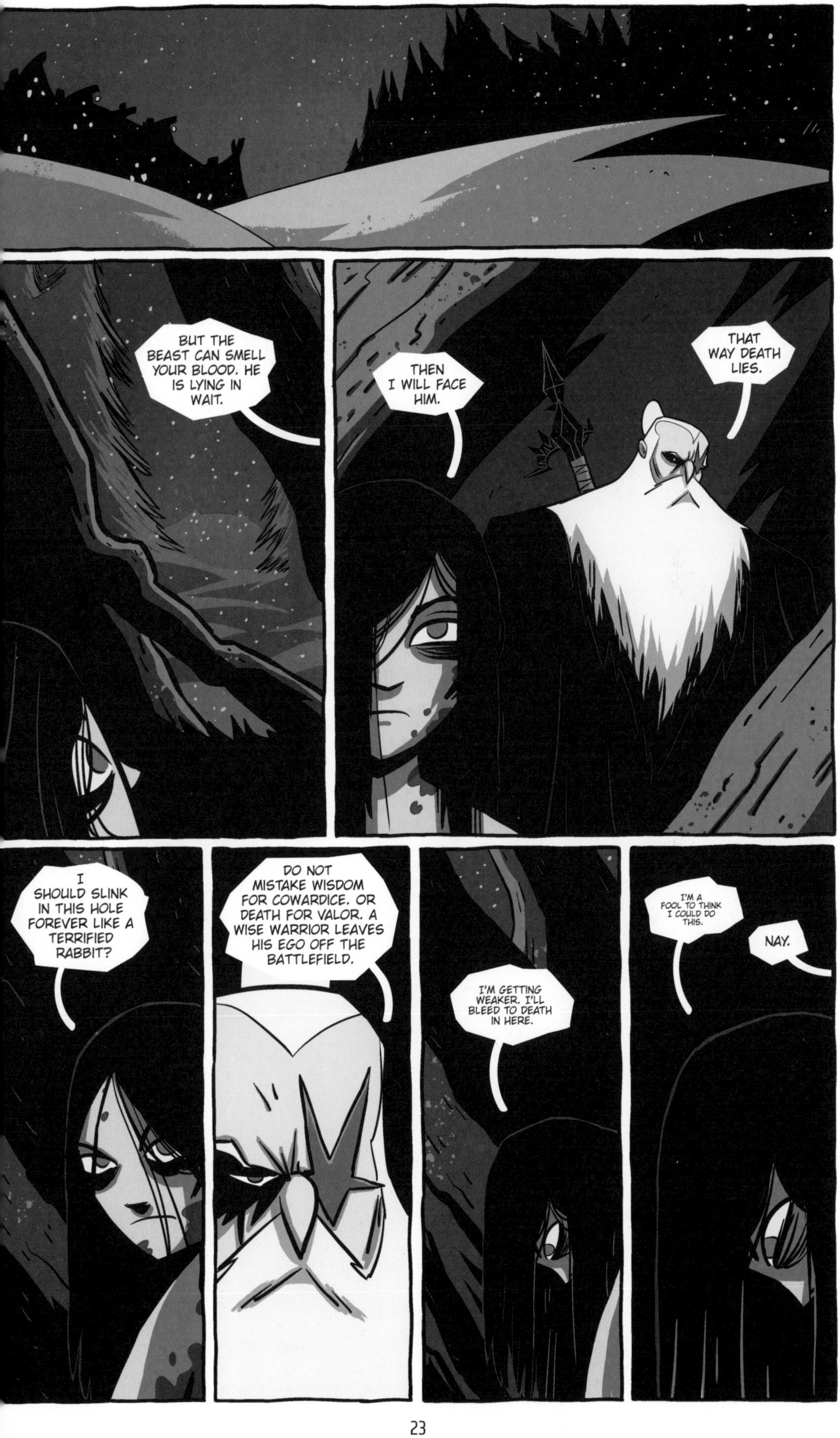

BUT THE BEAST CAN SMELL YOUR BLOOD. HE IS LYING IN WAIT.
THEN I WILL FACE HIM.
THAT WAY DEATH LIES.
I SHOULD SLINK IN THIS HOLE FOREVER LIKE A TERRIFIED RABBIT?
DO NOT MISTAKE WISDOM FOR COWARDICE. OR DEATH FOR VALOR. A WISE WARRIOR LEAVES HIS EGO OFF THE BATTLEFIELD.
I'M GETTING WEAKER. I'LL BLEED TO DEATH IN HERE.
I'M A FOOL TO THINK I COULD DO THIS.
NAY.

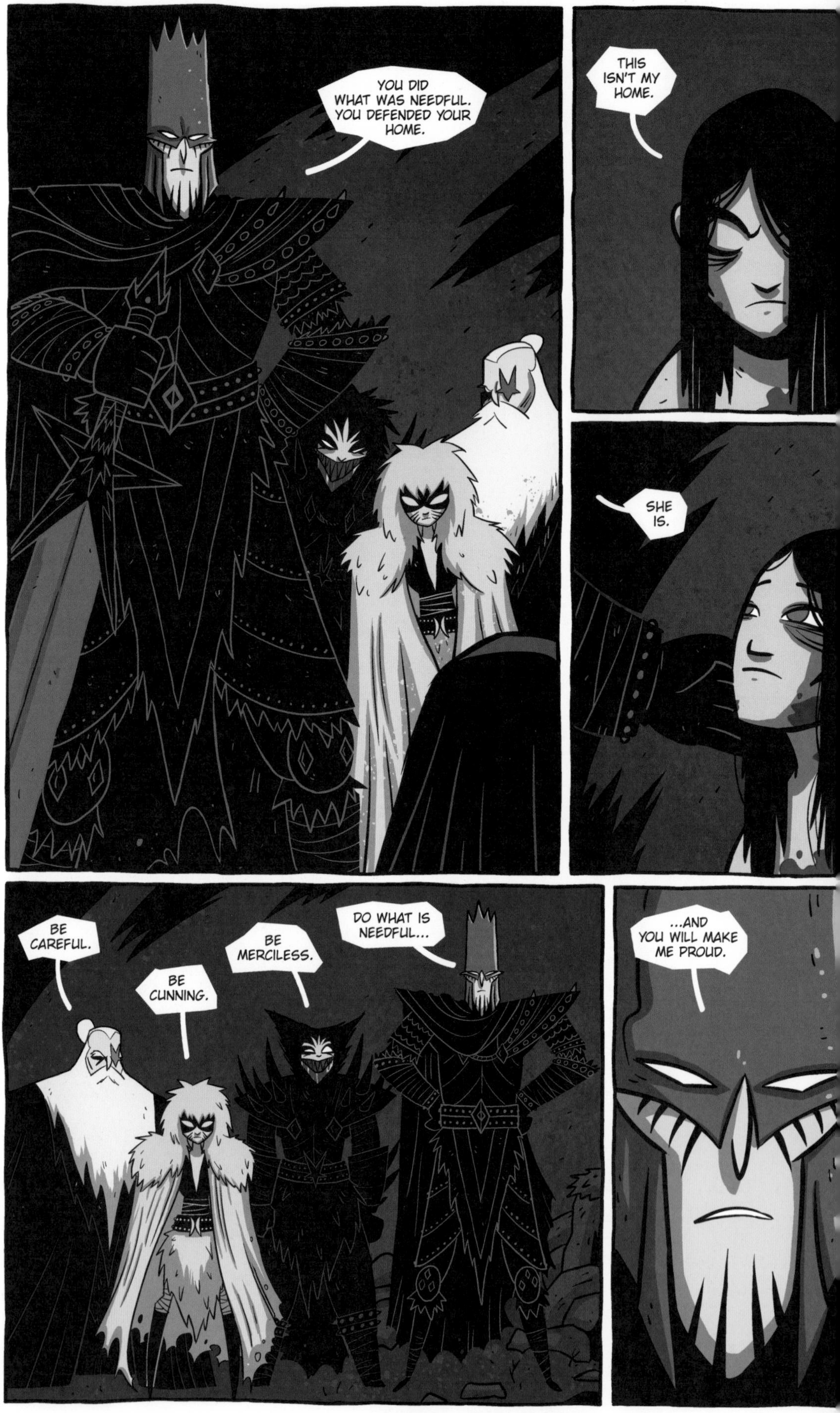
YOU DID WHAT WAS NEEDFUL. YOU DEFENDED YOUR HOME.
THIS ISN'T MY HOME.
SHE IS.
BE CAREFUL.
BE CUNNING.
BE MERCILESS.
DO WHAT IS NEEDFUL...
...AND YOU WILL MAKE ME PROUD.

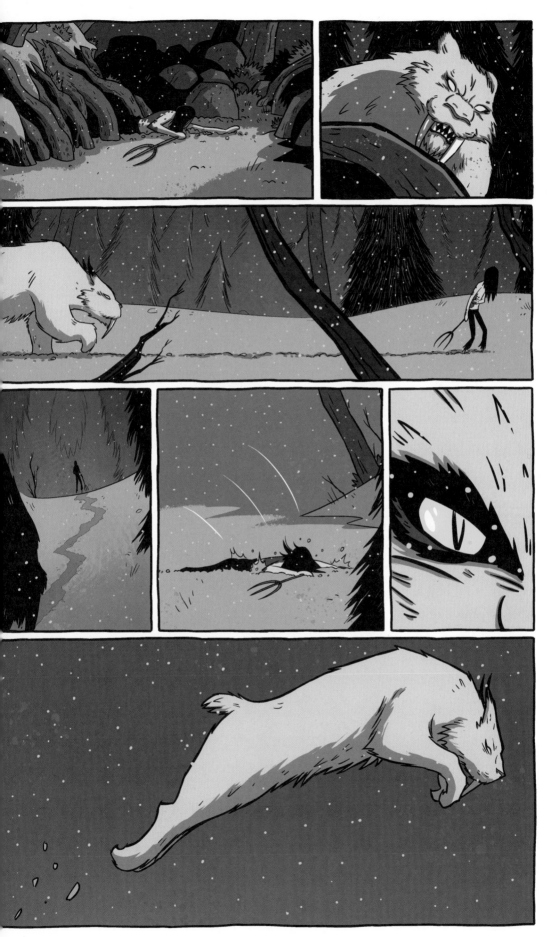

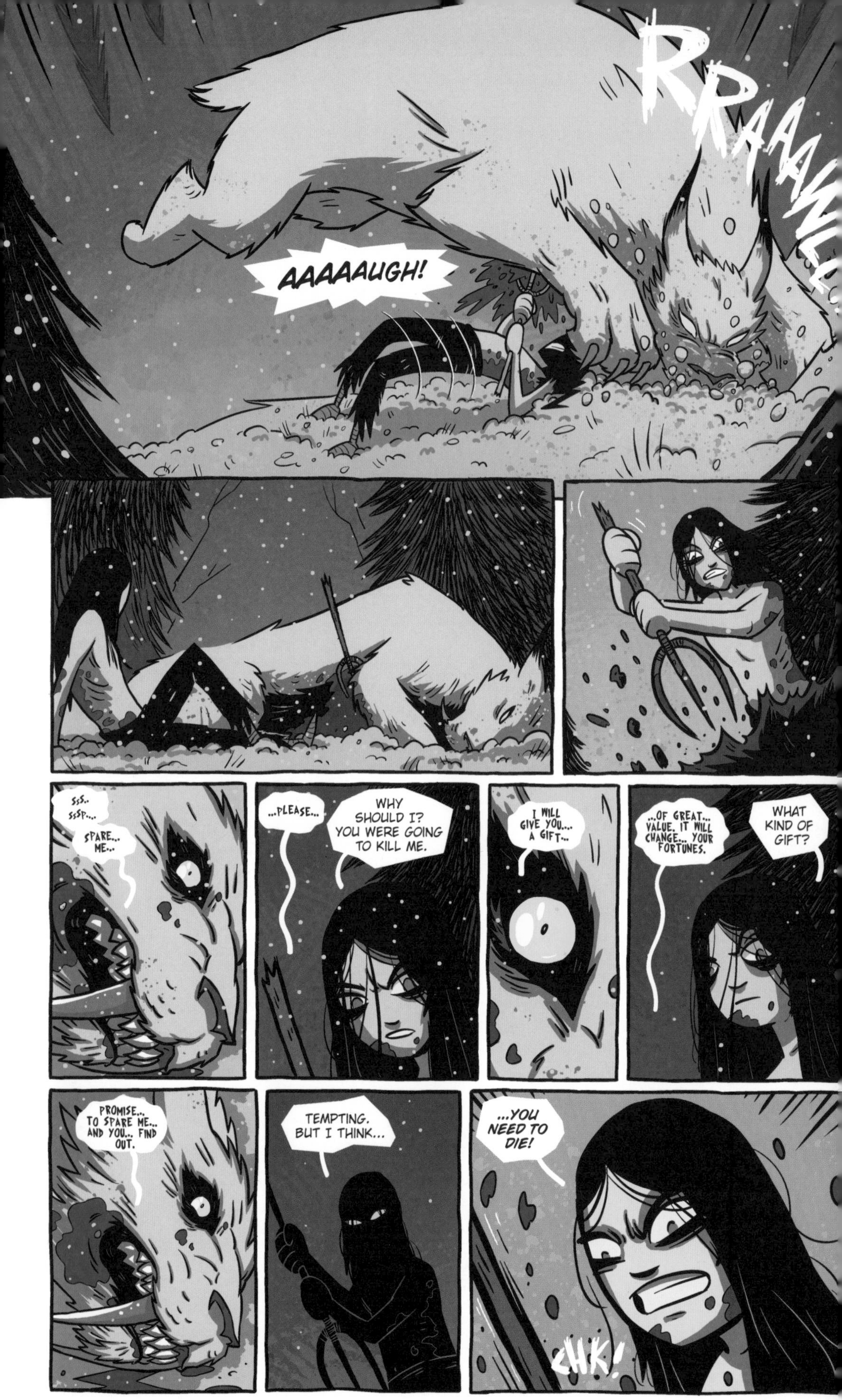
RRAAAWLL
AAAAAUGH!
SSS.. SSSP...
SPARE... ME...
...PLEASE...
WHY SHOULD I? YOU WERE GOING TO KILL ME.
I WILL GIVE YOU... A GIFT...
...OF GREAT... VALUE. IT WILL CHANGE... YOUR FORTUNES.
WHAT KIND OF GIFT?
PROMISE... TO SPARE ME... AND YOU... FIND OUT.
TEMPTING. BUT I THINK...
...YOU NEED TO DIE!
CHK!

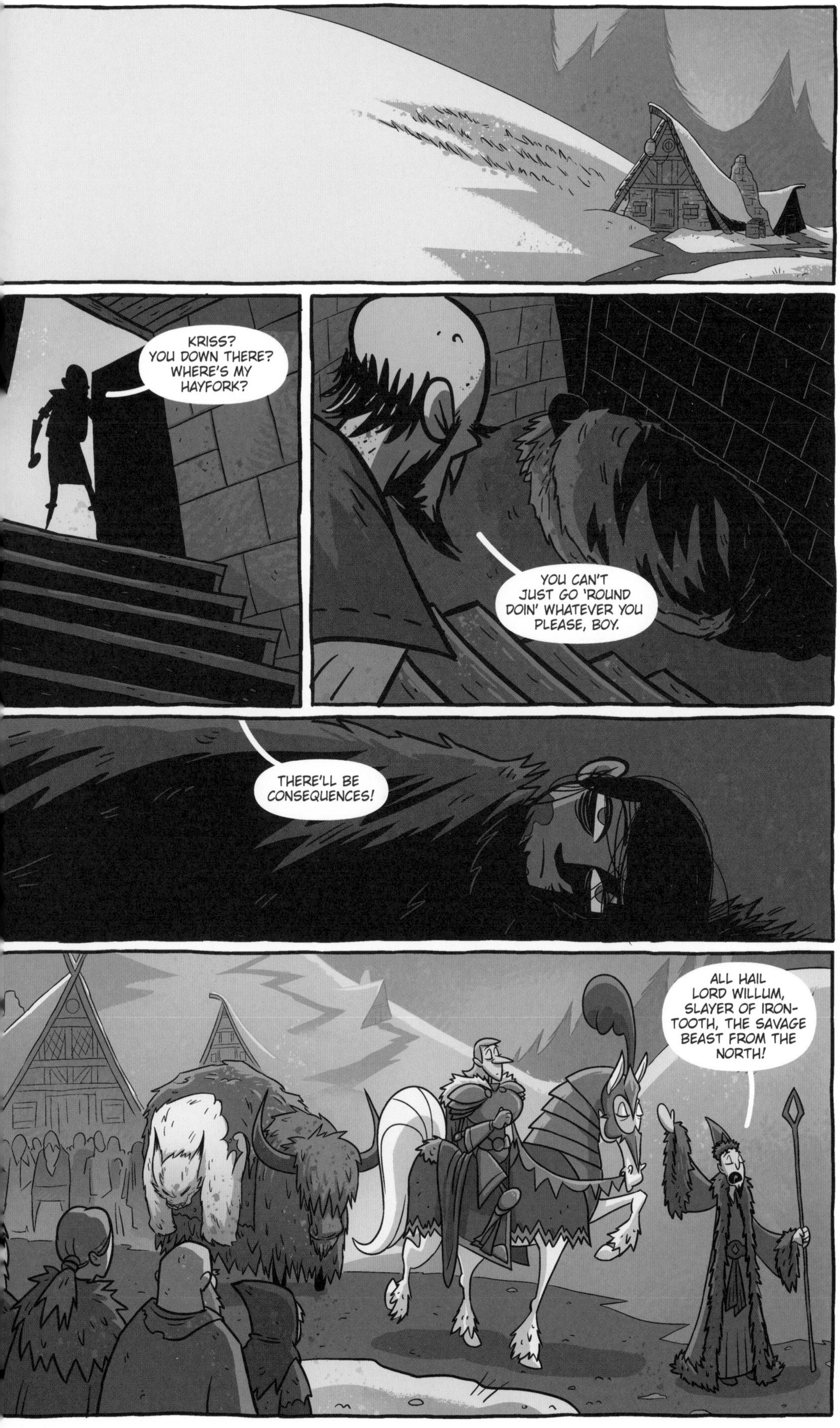
KRISS? YOU DOWN THERE? WHERE'S MY HAYFORK?
YOU CAN'T JUST GO 'ROUND DOIN' WHATEVER YOU PLEASE, BOY.
THERE'LL BE CONSEQUENCES!
ALL HAIL LORD WILLUM, SLAYER OF IRON-TOOTH, THE SAVAGE BEAST FROM THE NORTH!

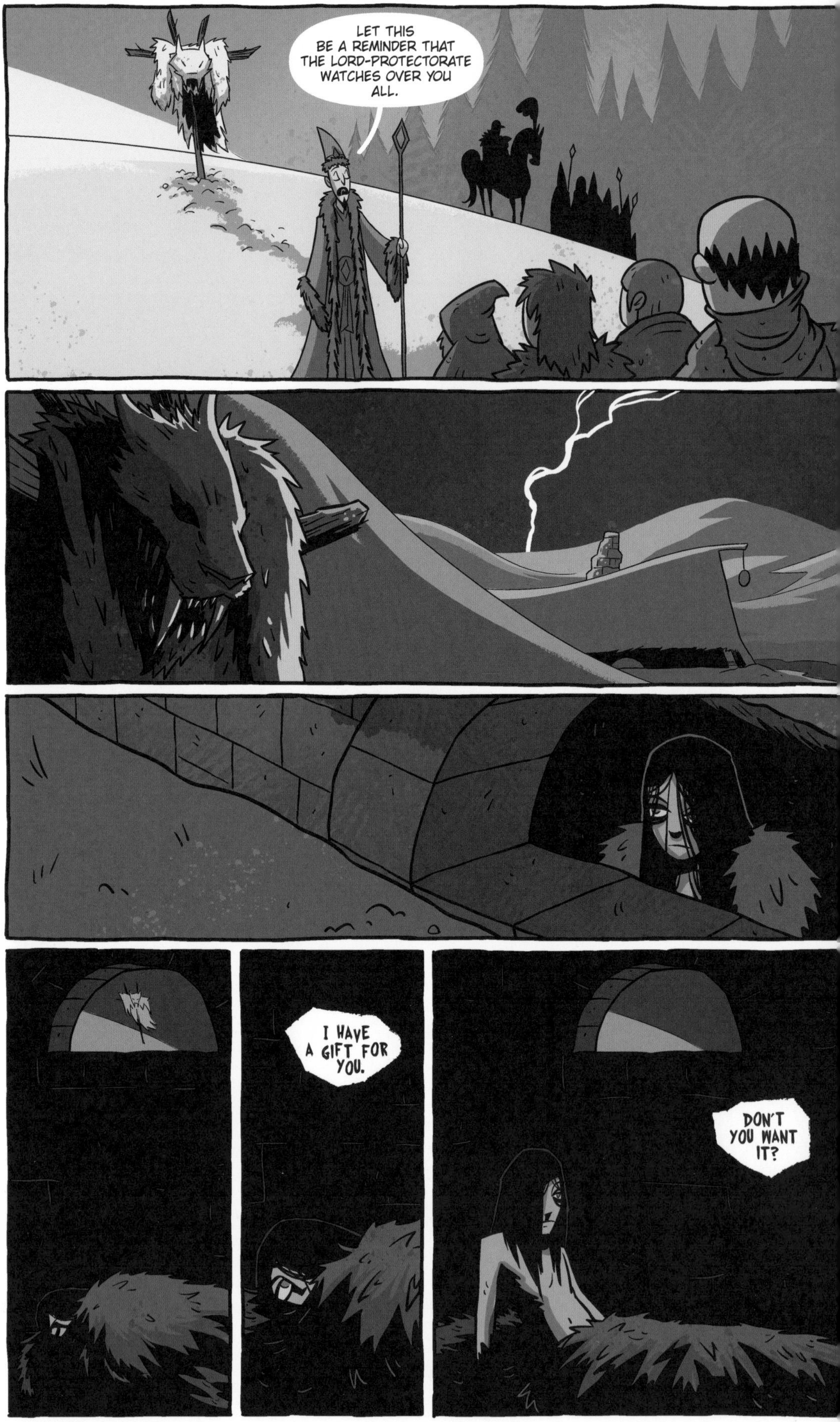
LET THIS BE A REMINDER THAT THE LORD-PROTECTORATE WATCHES OVER YOU ALL.
I HAVE A GIFT FOR YOU.
DON'T YOU WANT IT?

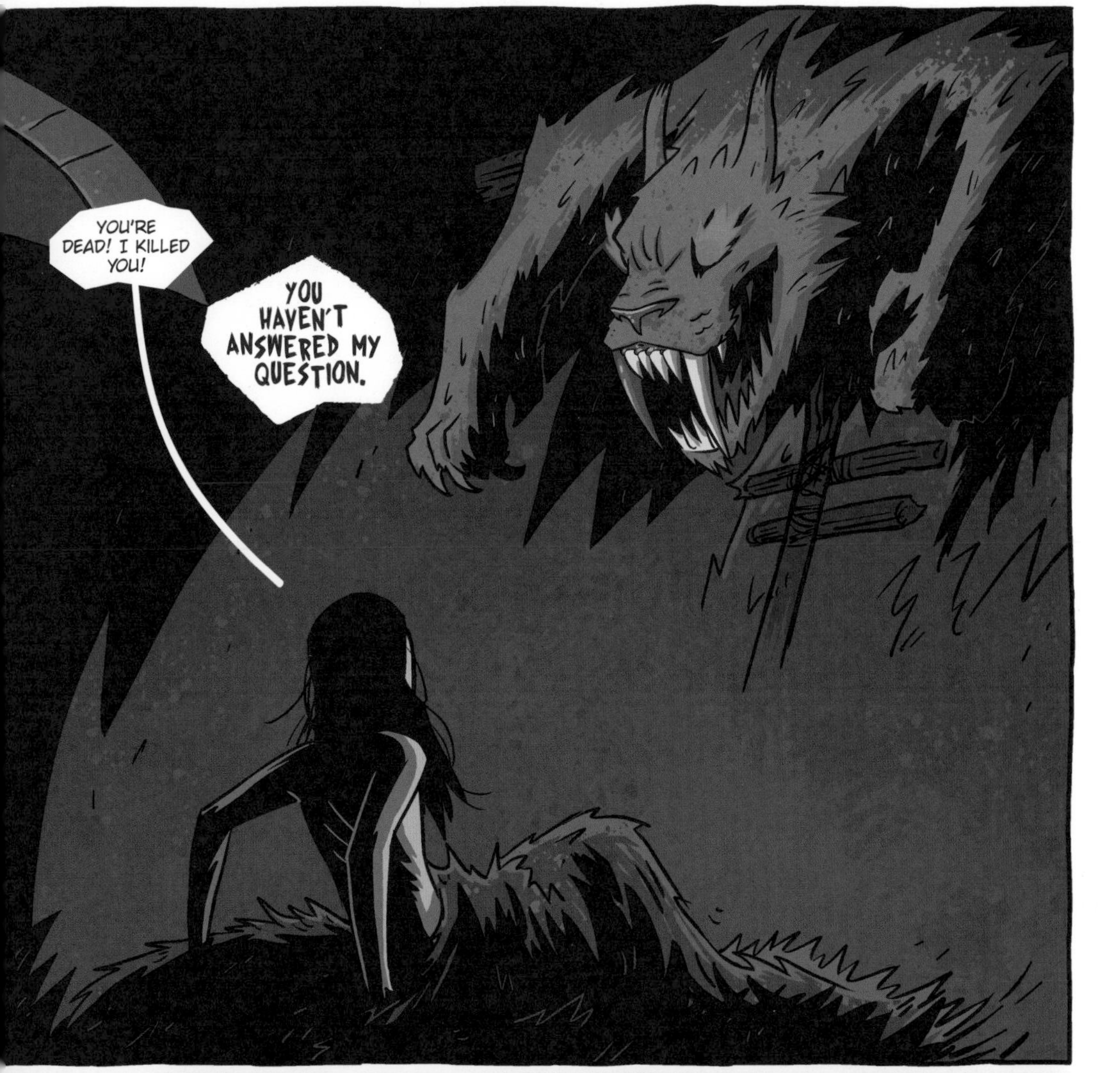
YOU'RE DEAD! I KILLED YOU!
YOU HAVEN'T ANSWERED MY QUESTION.

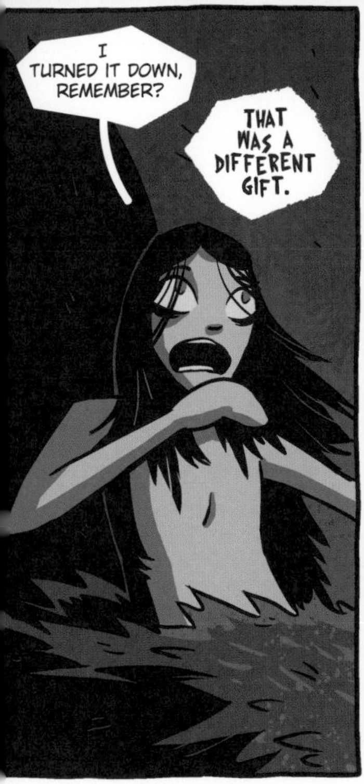
I TURNED IT DOWN, REMEMBER?
THAT WAS A DIFFERENT GIFT.

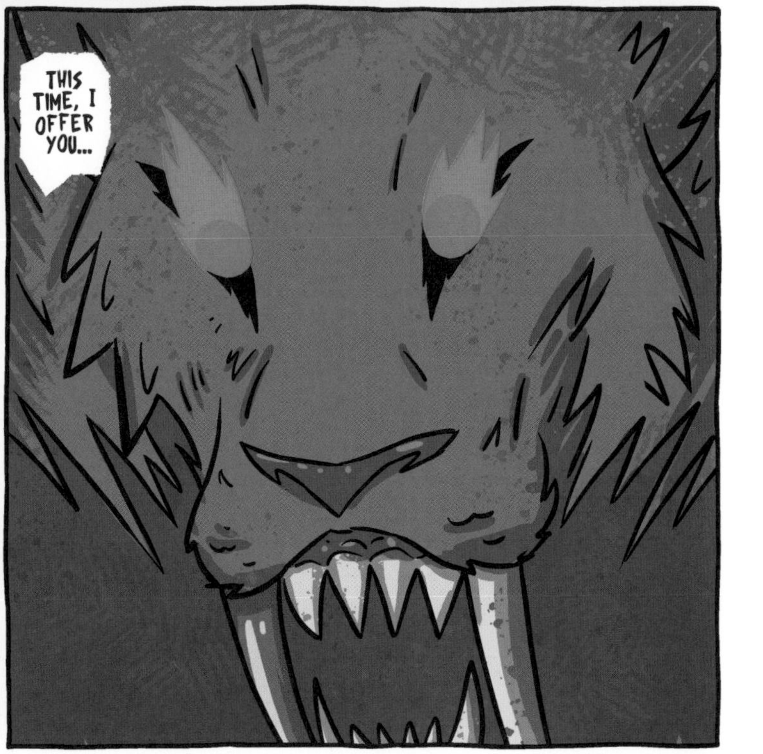
THIS TIME, I OFFER YOU...

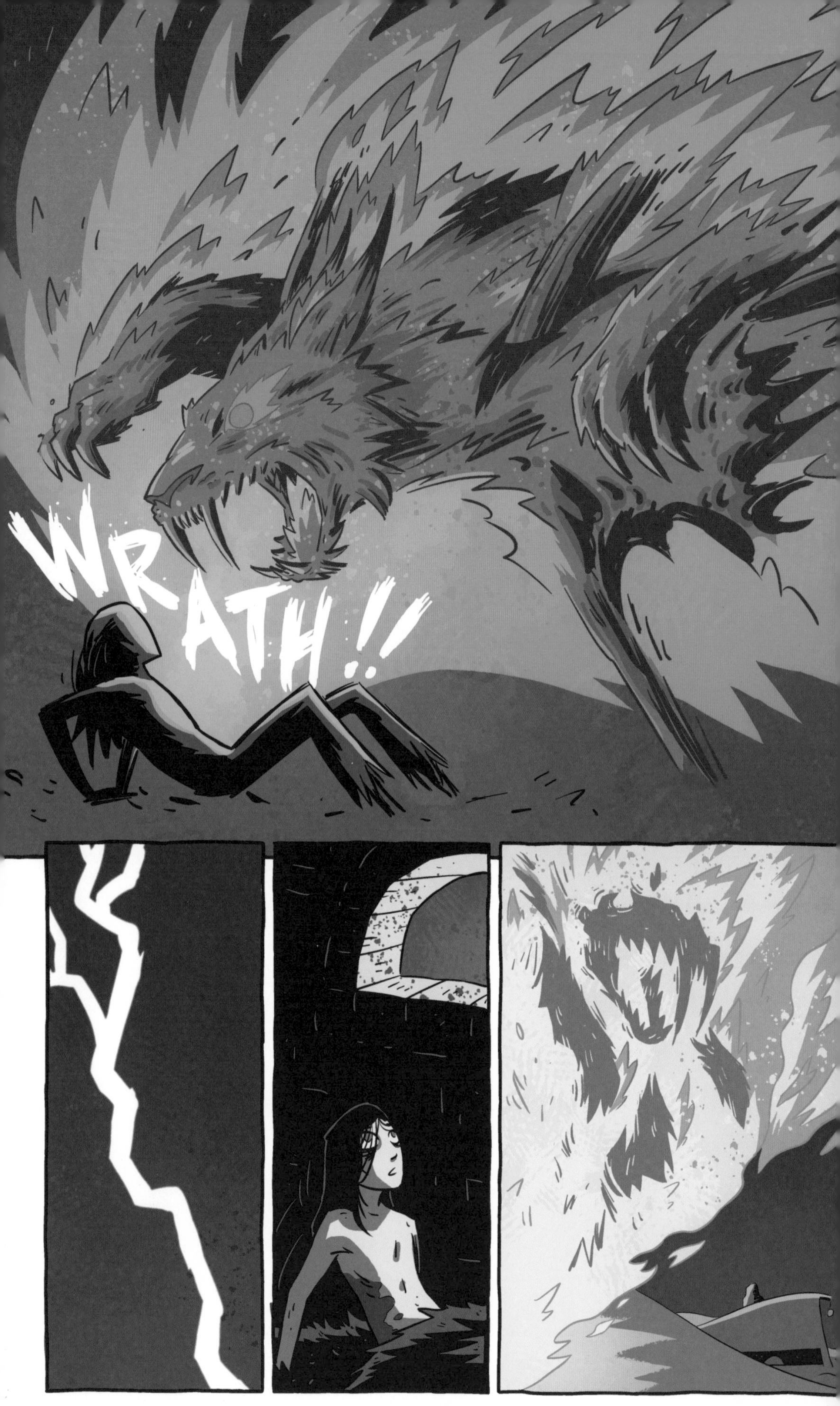
WRATH!!

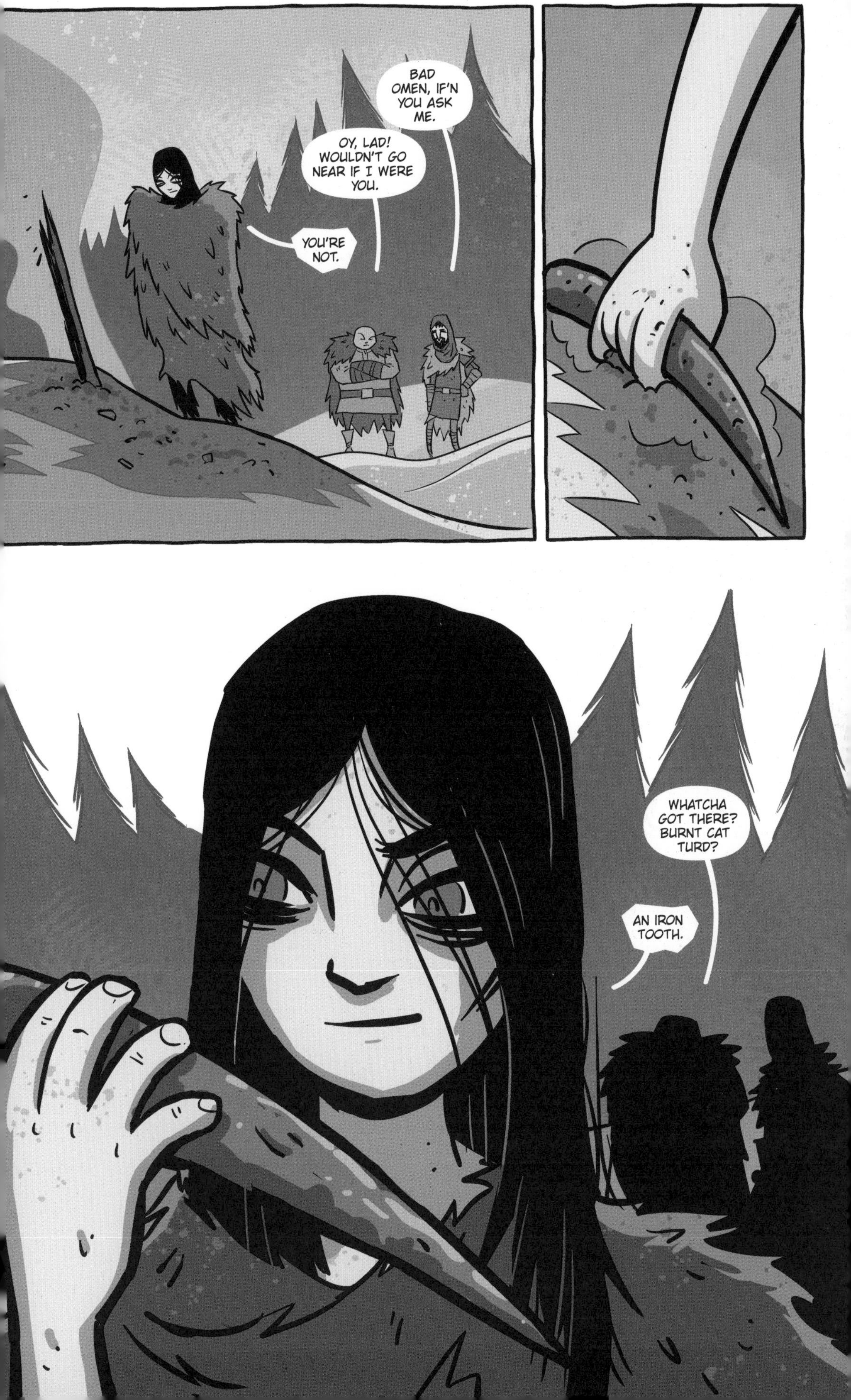
BAD OMEN, IF'N YOU ASK ME.
OY, LAD! WOULDN'T GO NEAR IF I WERE YOU.
YOU'RE NOT.
WHATCHA GOT THERE? BURNT CAT TURD?
AN IRON TOOTH.

CHAPTER TWO

THE LOVE OF IRON

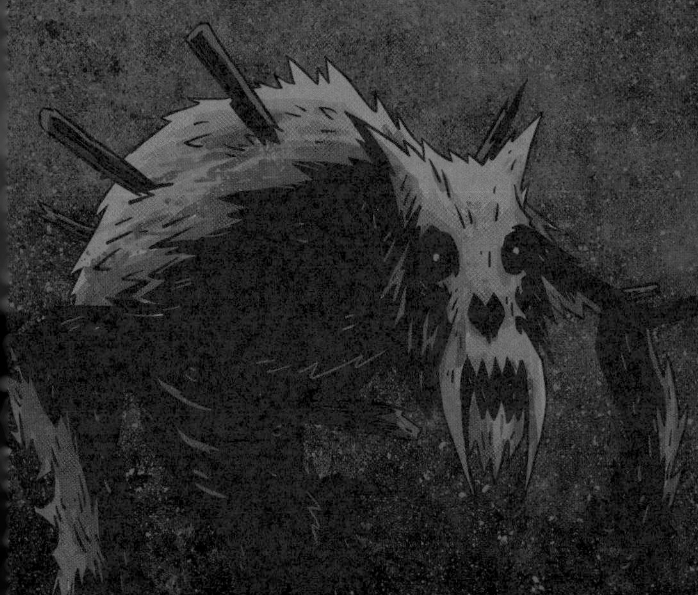

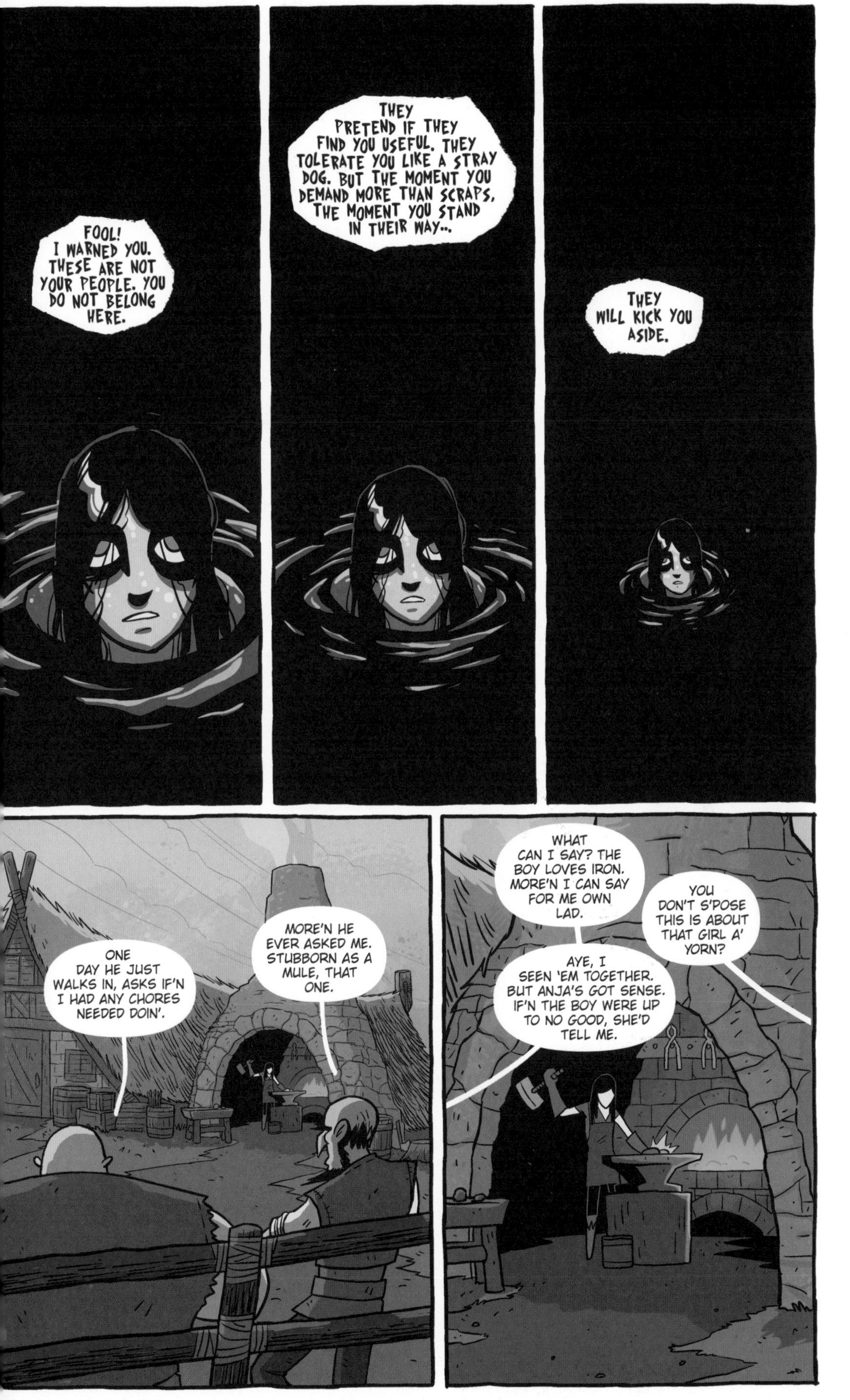
FOOL! I WARNED YOU. THESE ARE NOT YOUR PEOPLE. YOU DO NOT BELONG HERE.
THEY PRETEND IF THEY FIND YOU USEFUL. THEY TOLERATE YOU LIKE A STRAY DOG. BUT THE MOMENT YOU DEMAND MORE THAN SCRAPS, THE MOMENT YOU STAND IN THEIR WAY...
THEY WILL KICK YOU ASIDE.
ONE DAY HE JUST WALKS IN, ASKS IF'N I HAD ANY CHORES NEEDED DOIN'.
MORE'N HE EVER ASKED ME. STUBBORN AS A MULE, THAT ONE.
WHAT CAN I SAY? THE BOY LOVES IRON. MORE'N I CAN SAY FOR ME OWN LAD.
YOU DON'T S'POSE THIS IS ABOUT THAT GIRL A' YORN?
AYE, I SEEN 'EM TOGETHER. BUT ANJA'S GOT SENSE. IF'N THE BOY WERE UP TO NO GOOD, SHE'D TELL ME.

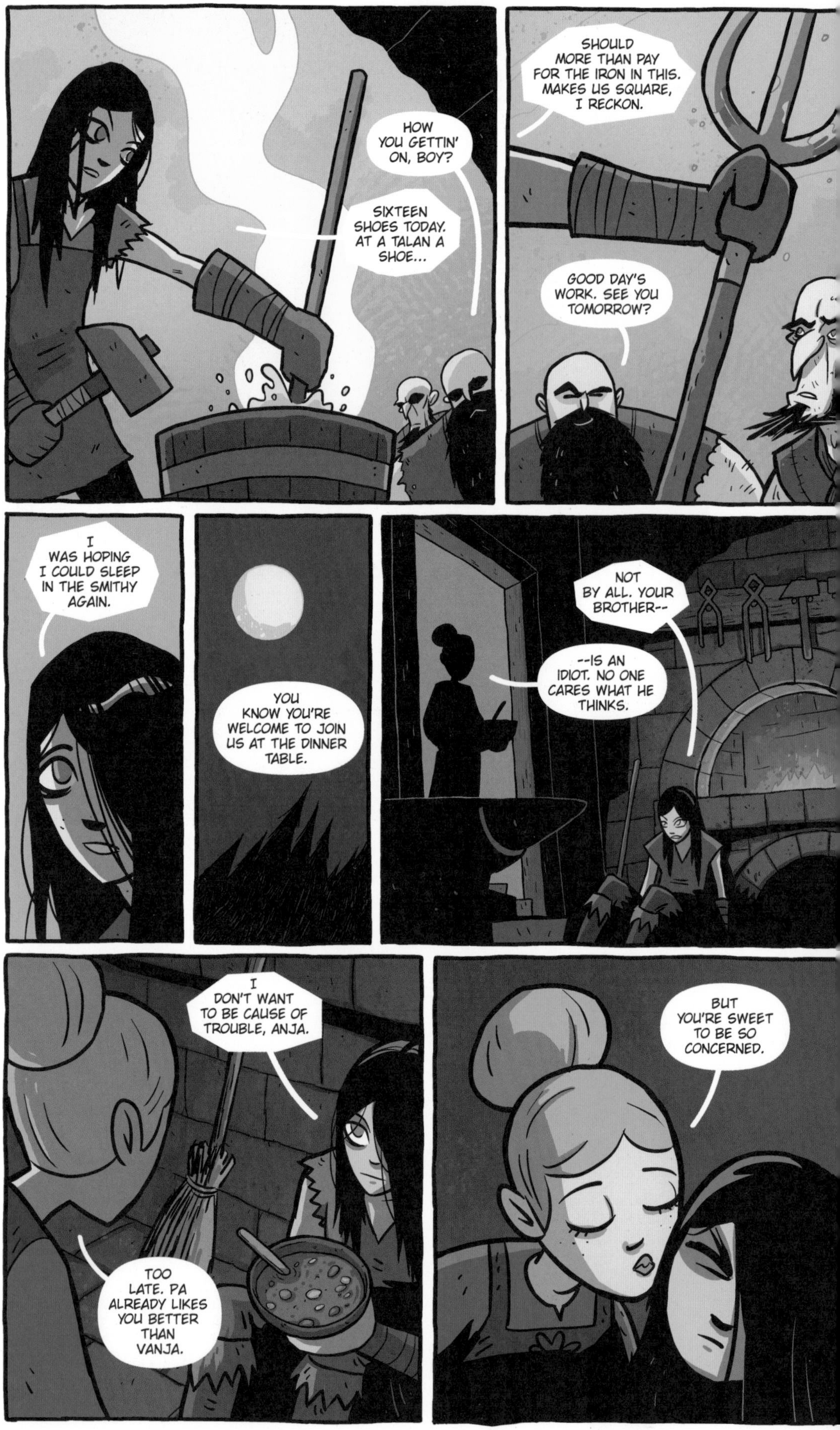
HOW YOU GETTIN' ON, BOY?
SIXTEEN SHOES TODAY. AT A TALAN A SHOE...
SHOULD MORE THAN PAY FOR THE IRON IN THIS. MAKES US SQUARE, I RECKON.
GOOD DAY'S WORK. SEE YOU TOMORROW?
I WAS HOPING I COULD SLEEP IN THE SMITHY AGAIN.
YOU KNOW YOU'RE WELCOME TO JOIN US AT THE DINNER TABLE.
NOT BY ALL. YOUR BROTHER--
--IS AN IDIOT. NO ONE CARES WHAT HE THINKS.
I DON'T WANT TO BE CAUSE OF TROUBLE, ANJA.
TOO LATE. PA ALREADY LIKES YOU BETTER THAN VANJA.
BUT YOU'RE SWEET TO BE SO CONCERNED.

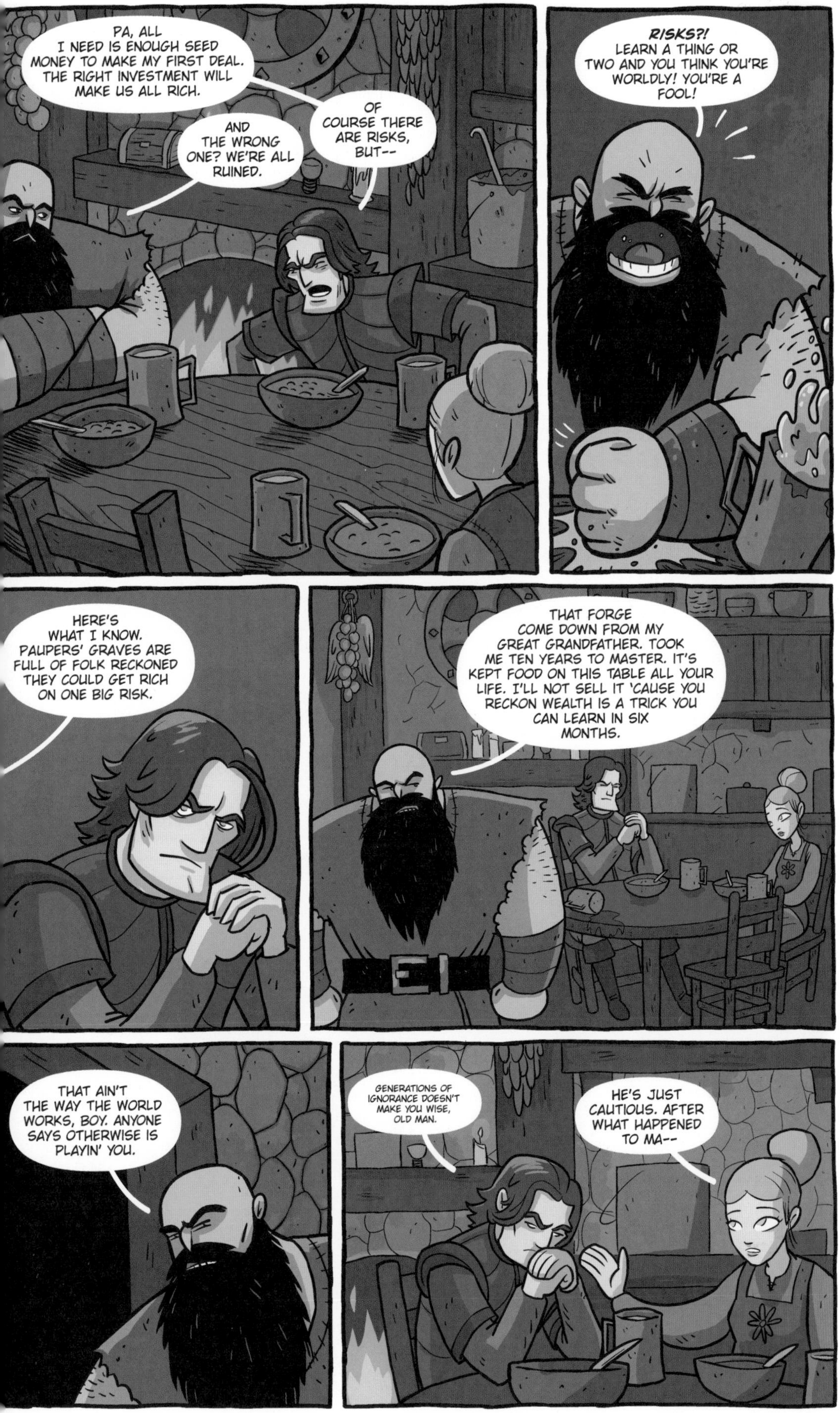
PA, ALL I NEED IS ENOUGH SEED MONEY TO MAKE MY FIRST DEAL. THE RIGHT INVESTMENT WILL MAKE US ALL RICH.
AND THE WRONG ONE? WE'RE ALL RUINED.
OF COURSE THERE ARE RISKS, BUT--
RISKS?! LEARN A THING OR TWO AND YOU THINK YOU'RE WORLDLY! YOU'RE A FOOL!
HERE'S WHAT I KNOW. PAUPERS' GRAVES ARE FULL OF FOLK RECKONED THEY COULD GET RICH ON ONE BIG RISK.
THAT FORGE COME DOWN FROM MY GREAT GRANDFATHER. TOOK ME TEN YEARS TO MASTER. IT'S KEPT FOOD ON THIS TABLE ALL YOUR LIFE. I'LL NOT SELL IT 'CAUSE YOU RECKON WEALTH IS A TRICK YOU CAN LEARN IN SIX MONTHS.
THAT AIN'T THE WAY THE WORLD WORKS, BOY. ANYONE SAYS OTHERWISE IS PLAYIN' YOU.
GENERATIONS OF IGNORANCE DOESN'T MAKE YOU WISE, OLD MAN.
HE'S JUST CAUTIOUS. AFTER WHAT HAPPENED TO MA--

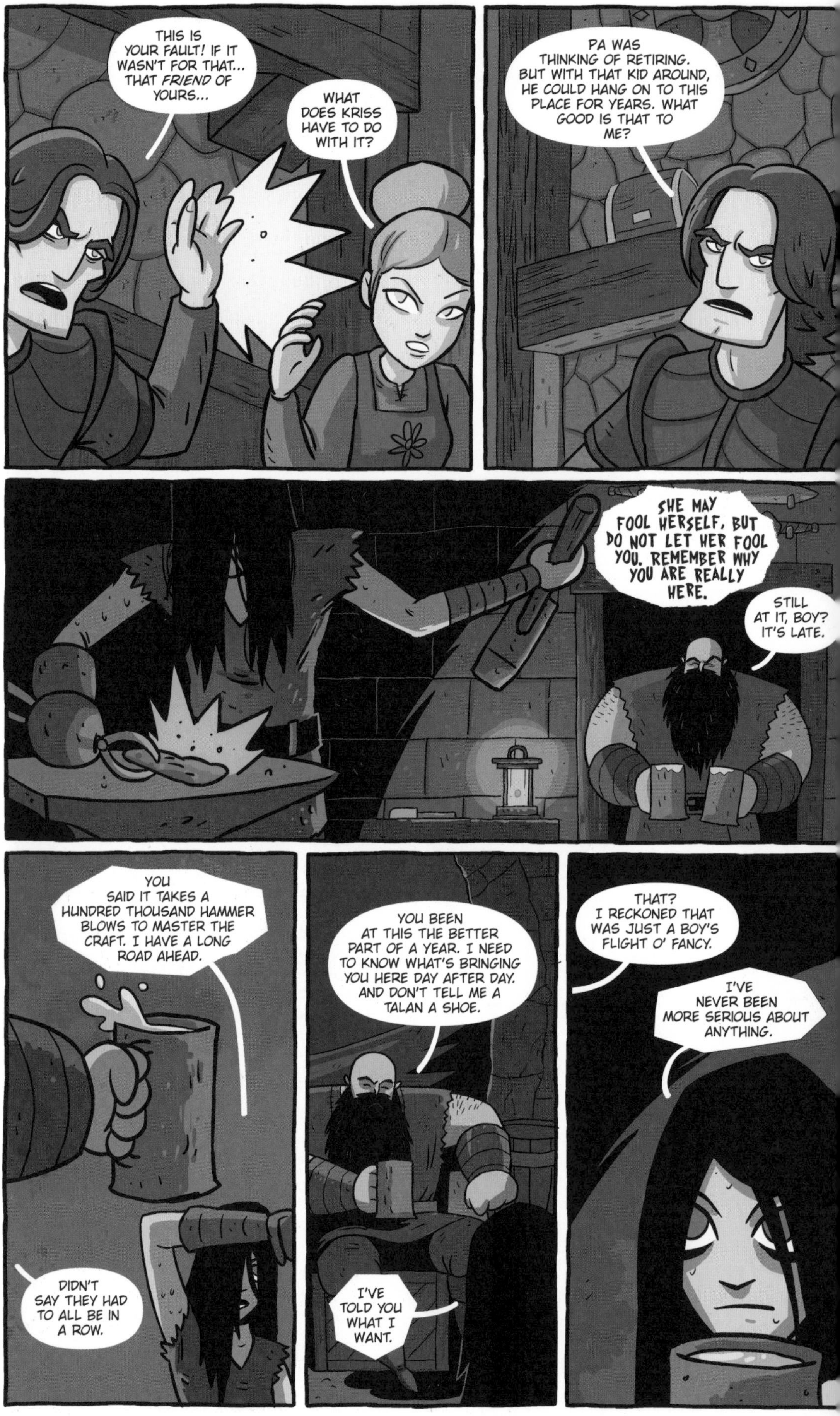
THIS IS YOUR FAULT! IF IT WASN'T FOR THAT... THAT *FRIEND* OF YOURS...
WHAT DOES KRISS HAVE TO DO WITH IT?
PA WAS THINKING OF RETIRING. BUT WITH THAT KID AROUND, HE COULD HANG ON TO THIS PLACE FOR YEARS. WHAT GOOD IS THAT TO ME?
SHE MAY FOOL HERSELF, BUT DO NOT LET HER FOOL YOU. REMEMBER WHY YOU ARE REALLY HERE.
STILL AT IT, BOY? IT'S LATE.
YOU SAID IT TAKES A HUNDRED THOUSAND HAMMER BLOWS TO MASTER THE CRAFT. I HAVE A LONG ROAD AHEAD.
DIDN'T SAY THEY HAD TO ALL BE IN A ROW.
YOU BEEN AT THIS THE BETTER PART OF A YEAR. I NEED TO KNOW WHAT'S BRINGING YOU HERE DAY AFTER DAY. AND DON'T TELL ME A TALAN A SHOE.
I'VE TOLD YOU WHAT I WANT.
THAT? I RECKONED THAT WAS JUST A BOY'S FLIGHT O' FANCY.
I'VE NEVER BEEN MORE SERIOUS ABOUT ANYTHING.

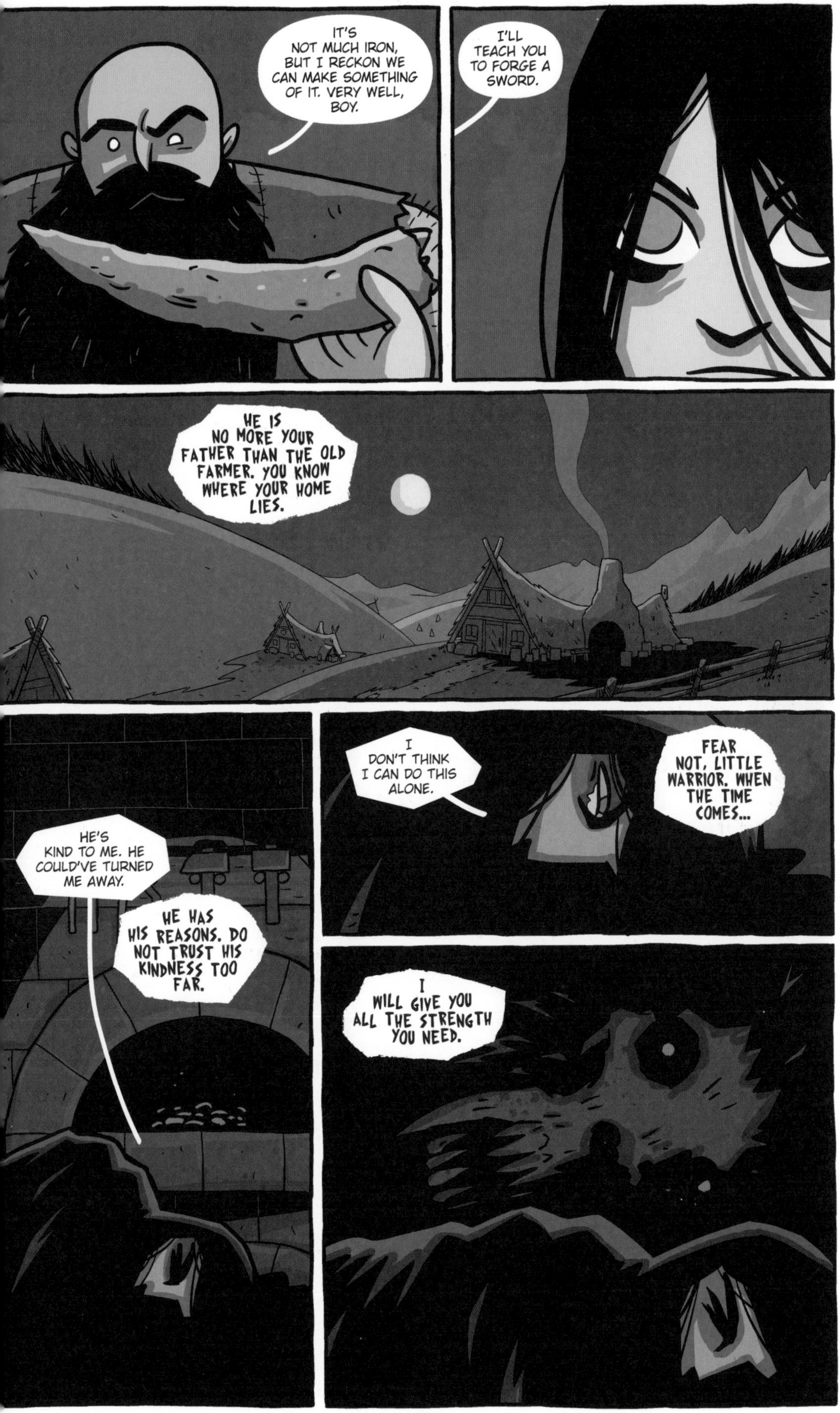
IT'S NOT MUCH IRON, BUT I RECKON WE CAN MAKE SOMETHING OF IT. VERY WELL, BOY.
I'LL TEACH YOU TO FORGE A SWORD.
HE IS NO MORE YOUR FATHER THAN THE OLD FARMER. YOU KNOW WHERE YOUR HOME LIES.
HE'S KIND TO ME. HE COULD'VE TURNED ME AWAY.
HE HAS HIS REASONS. DO NOT TRUST HIS KINDNESS TOO FAR.
I DON'T THINK I CAN DO THIS ALONE.
FEAR NOT, LITTLE WARRIOR. WHEN THE TIME COMES...
I WILL GIVE YOU ALL THE STRENGTH YOU NEED.

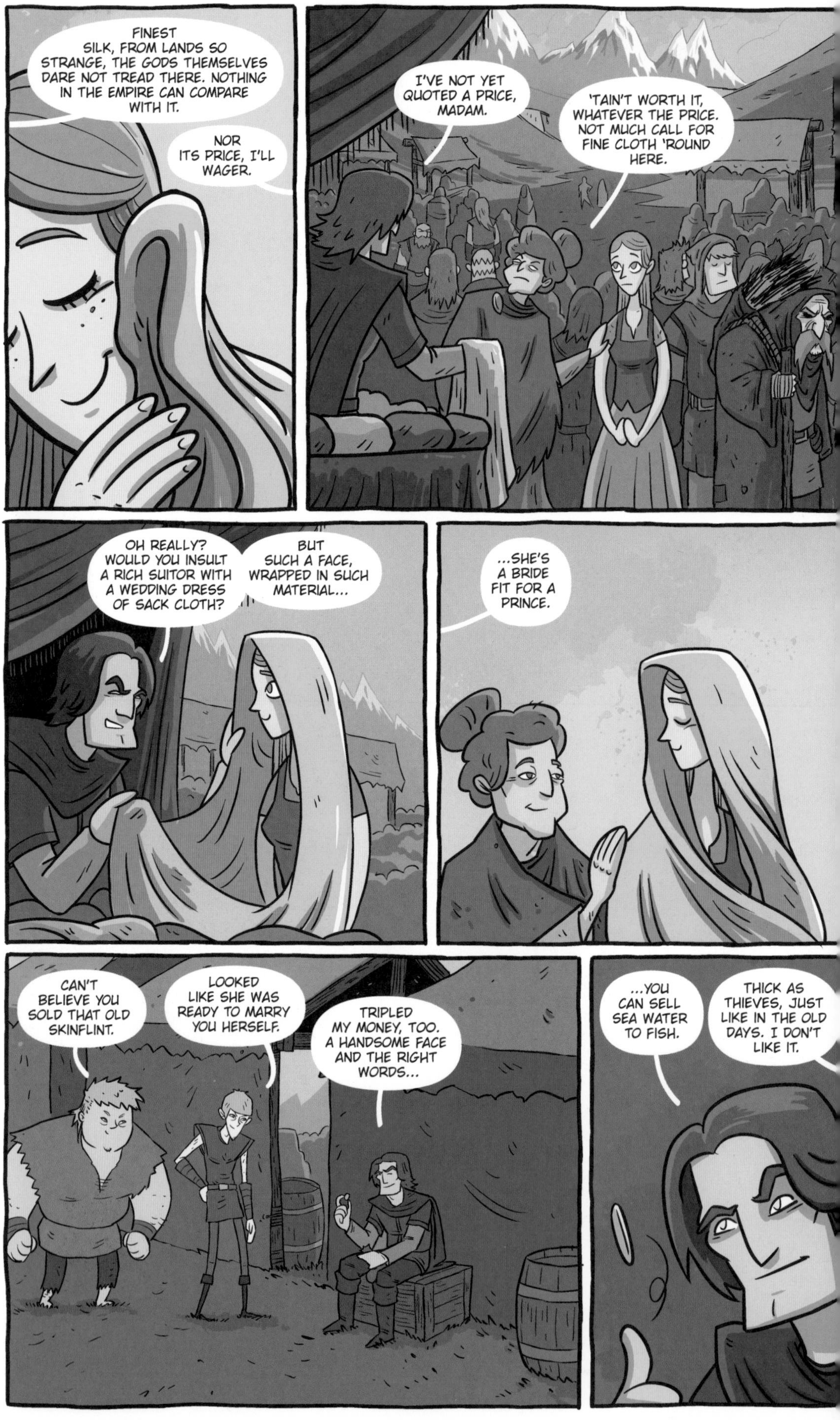
FINEST SILK, FROM LANDS SO STRANGE, THE GODS THEMSELVES DARE NOT TREAD THERE. NOTHING IN THE EMPIRE CAN COMPARE WITH IT.
NOR ITS PRICE, I'LL WAGER.
I'VE NOT YET QUOTED A PRICE, MADAM.
'TAIN'T WORTH IT, WHATEVER THE PRICE. NOT MUCH CALL FOR FINE CLOTH 'ROUND HERE.
OH REALLY? WOULD YOU INSULT A RICH SUITOR WITH A WEDDING DRESS OF SACK CLOTH?
BUT SUCH A FACE, WRAPPED IN SUCH MATERIAL...
...SHE'S A BRIDE FIT FOR A PRINCE.
CAN'T BELIEVE YOU SOLD THAT OLD SKINFLINT.
LOOKED LIKE SHE WAS READY TO MARRY YOU HERSELF.
TRIPLED MY MONEY, TOO. A HANDSOME FACE AND THE RIGHT WORDS...
...YOU CAN SELL SEA WATER TO FISH.
THICK AS THIEVES, JUST LIKE IN THE OLD DAYS. I DON'T LIKE IT.

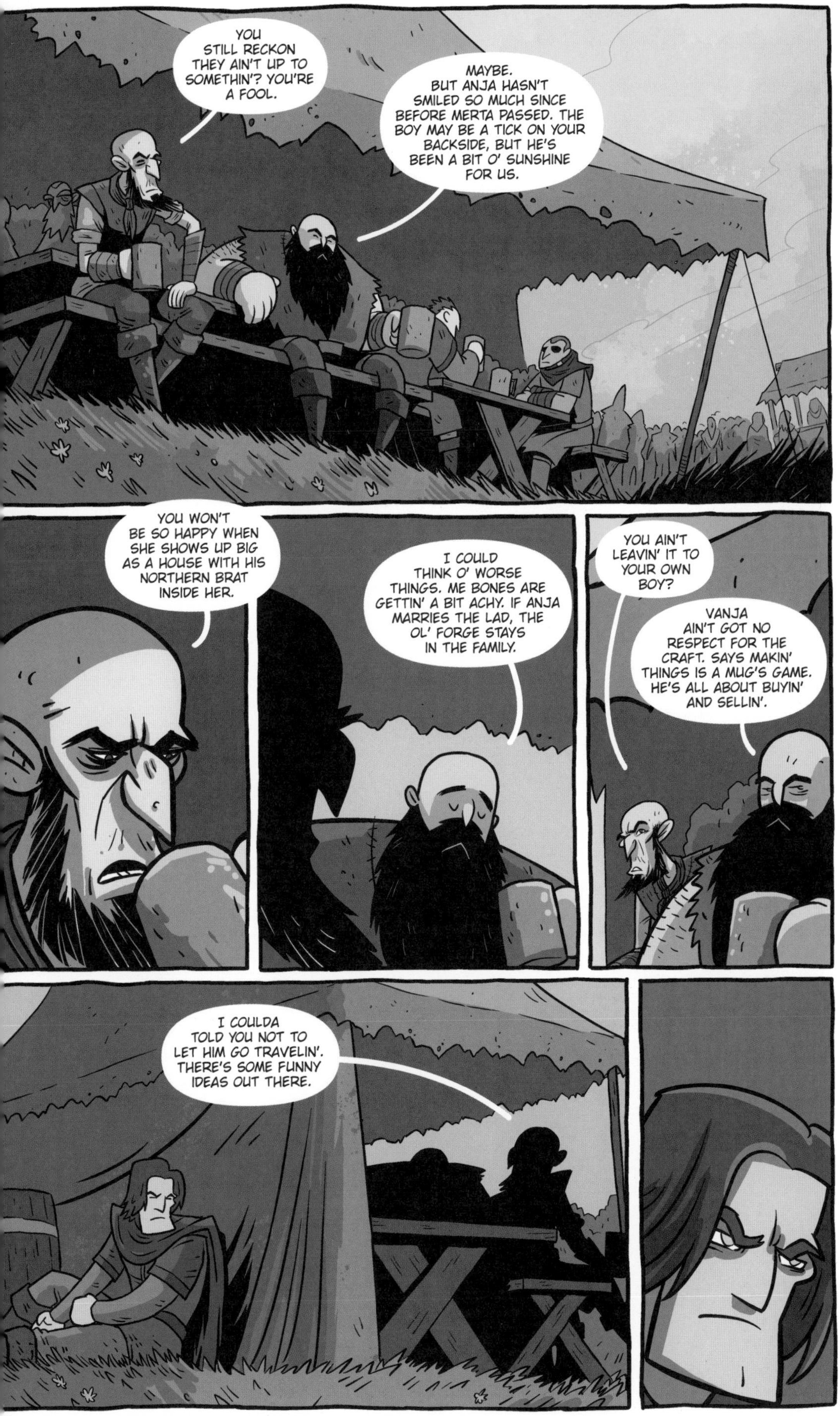
YOU STILL RECKON THEY AIN'T UP TO SOMETHIN'? YOU'RE A FOOL.
MAYBE. BUT ANJA HASN'T SMILED SO MUCH SINCE BEFORE MERTA PASSED. THE BOY MAY BE A TICK ON YOUR BACKSIDE, BUT HE'S BEEN A BIT O' SUNSHINE FOR US.
YOU WON'T BE SO HAPPY WHEN SHE SHOWS UP BIG AS A HOUSE WITH HIS NORTHERN BRAT INSIDE HER.
I COULD THINK O' WORSE THINGS. ME BONES ARE GETTIN' A BIT ACHY. IF ANJA MARRIES THE LAD, THE OL' FORGE STAYS IN THE FAMILY.
YOU AIN'T LEAVIN' IT TO YOUR OWN BOY?
VANJA AIN'T GOT NO RESPECT FOR THE CRAFT. SAYS MAKIN' THINGS IS A MUG'S GAME. HE'S ALL ABOUT BUYIN' AND SELLIN'.
I COULDA TOLD YOU NOT TO LET HIM GO TRAVELIN'. THERE'S SOME FUNNY IDEAS OUT THERE.

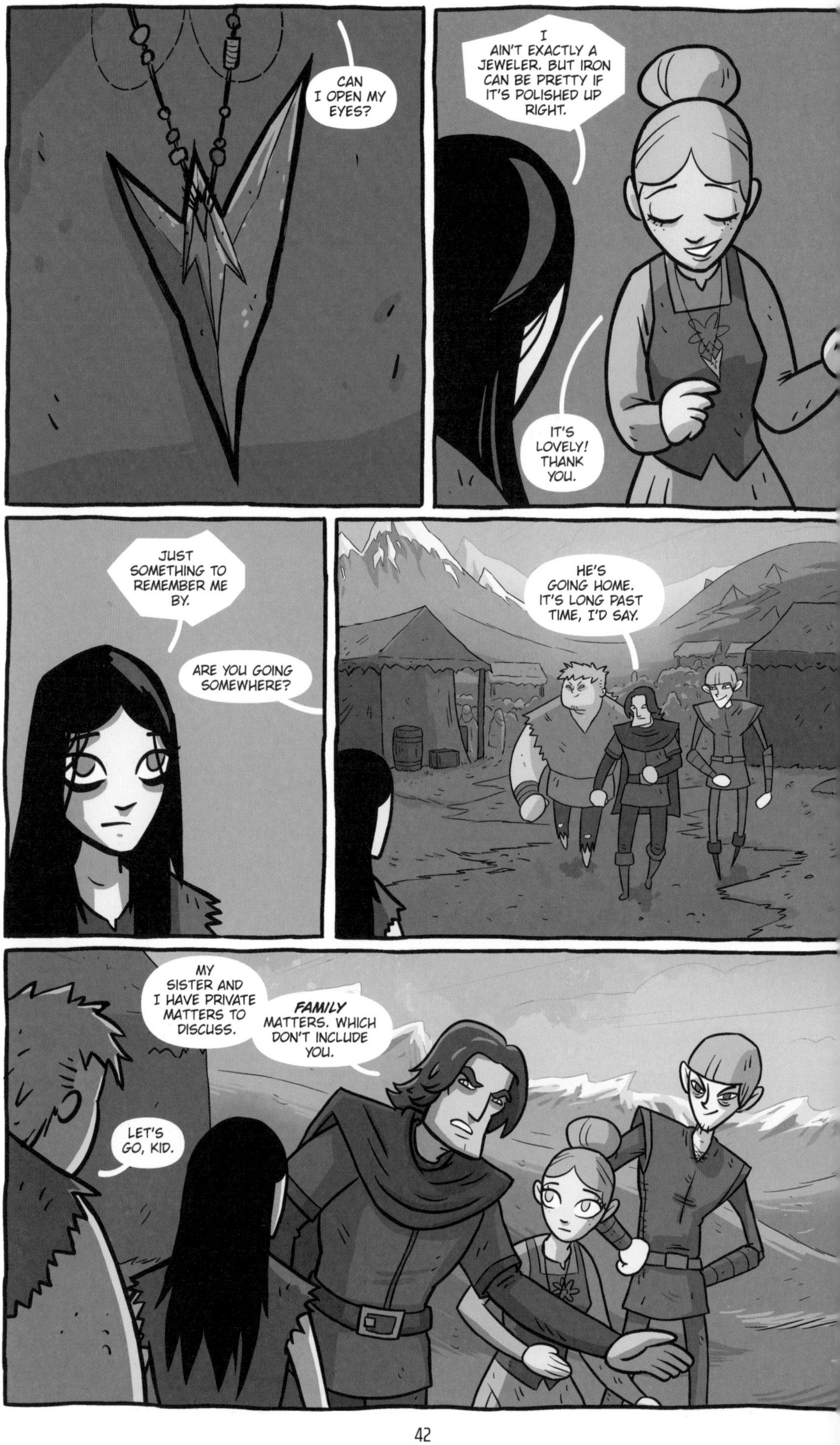
CAN I OPEN MY EYES?
I AIN'T EXACTLY A JEWELER. BUT IRON CAN BE PRETTY IF IT'S POLISHED UP RIGHT.
IT'S LOVELY! THANK YOU.
JUST SOMETHING TO REMEMBER ME BY.
ARE YOU GOING SOMEWHERE?
HE'S GOING HOME. IT'S LONG PAST TIME, I'D SAY.
MY SISTER AND I HAVE PRIVATE MATTERS TO DISCUSS.
FAMILY MATTERS. WHICH DON'T INCLUDE YOU.
LET'S GO, KID.

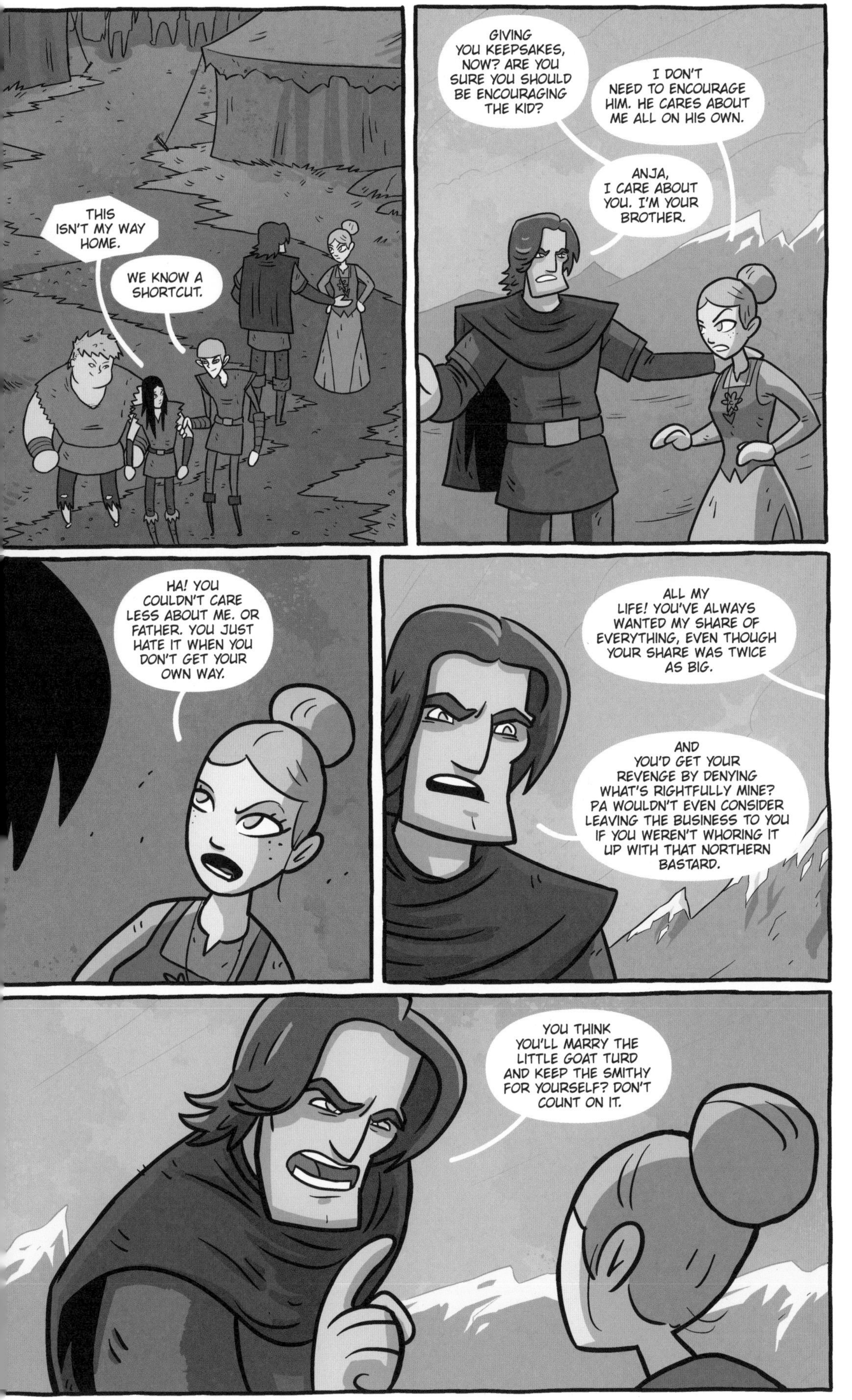
THIS ISN'T MY WAY HOME.
WE KNOW A SHORTCUT.
GIVING YOU KEEPSAKES, NOW? ARE YOU SURE YOU SHOULD BE ENCOURAGING THE KID?
I DON'T NEED TO ENCOURAGE HIM. HE CARES ABOUT ME ALL ON HIS OWN.
ANJA, I CARE ABOUT YOU. I'M YOUR BROTHER.
HA! YOU COULDN'T CARE LESS ABOUT ME. OR FATHER. YOU JUST HATE IT WHEN YOU DON'T GET YOUR OWN WAY.
ALL MY LIFE! YOU'VE ALWAYS WANTED MY SHARE OF EVERYTHING, EVEN THOUGH YOUR SHARE WAS TWICE AS BIG.
AND YOU'D GET YOUR REVENGE BY DENYING WHAT'S RIGHTFULLY MINE? PA WOULDN'T EVEN CONSIDER LEAVING THE BUSINESS TO YOU IF YOU WEREN'T WHORING IT UP WITH THAT NORTHERN BASTARD.
YOU THINK YOU'LL MARRY THE LITTLE GOAT TURD AND KEEP THE SMITHY FOR YOURSELF? DON'T COUNT ON IT.

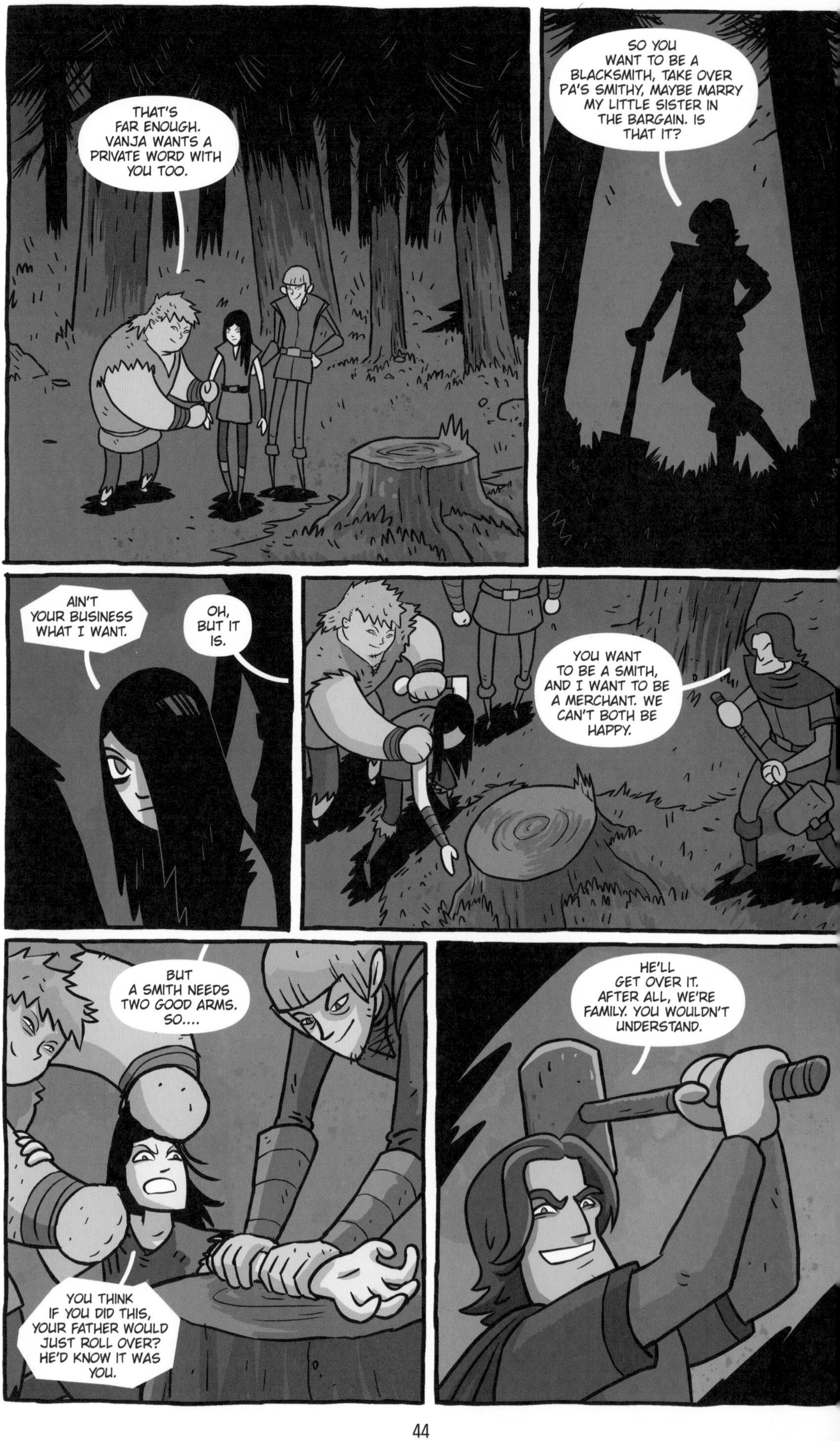
THAT'S FAR ENOUGH. VANJA WANTS A PRIVATE WORD WITH YOU TOO.
SO YOU WANT TO BE A BLACKSMITH, TAKE OVER PA'S SMITHY, MAYBE MARRY MY LITTLE SISTER IN THE BARGAIN. IS THAT IT?
AIN'T YOUR BUSINESS WHAT I WANT.
OH, BUT IT IS.
YOU WANT TO BE A SMITH, AND I WANT TO BE A MERCHANT. WE CAN'T BOTH BE HAPPY.
BUT A SMITH NEEDS TWO GOOD ARMS. SO....
YOU THINK IF YOU DID THIS, YOUR FATHER WOULD JUST ROLL OVER? HE'D KNOW IT WAS YOU.
HE'LL GET OVER IT. AFTER ALL, WE'RE FAMILY. YOU WOULDN'T UNDERSTAND.

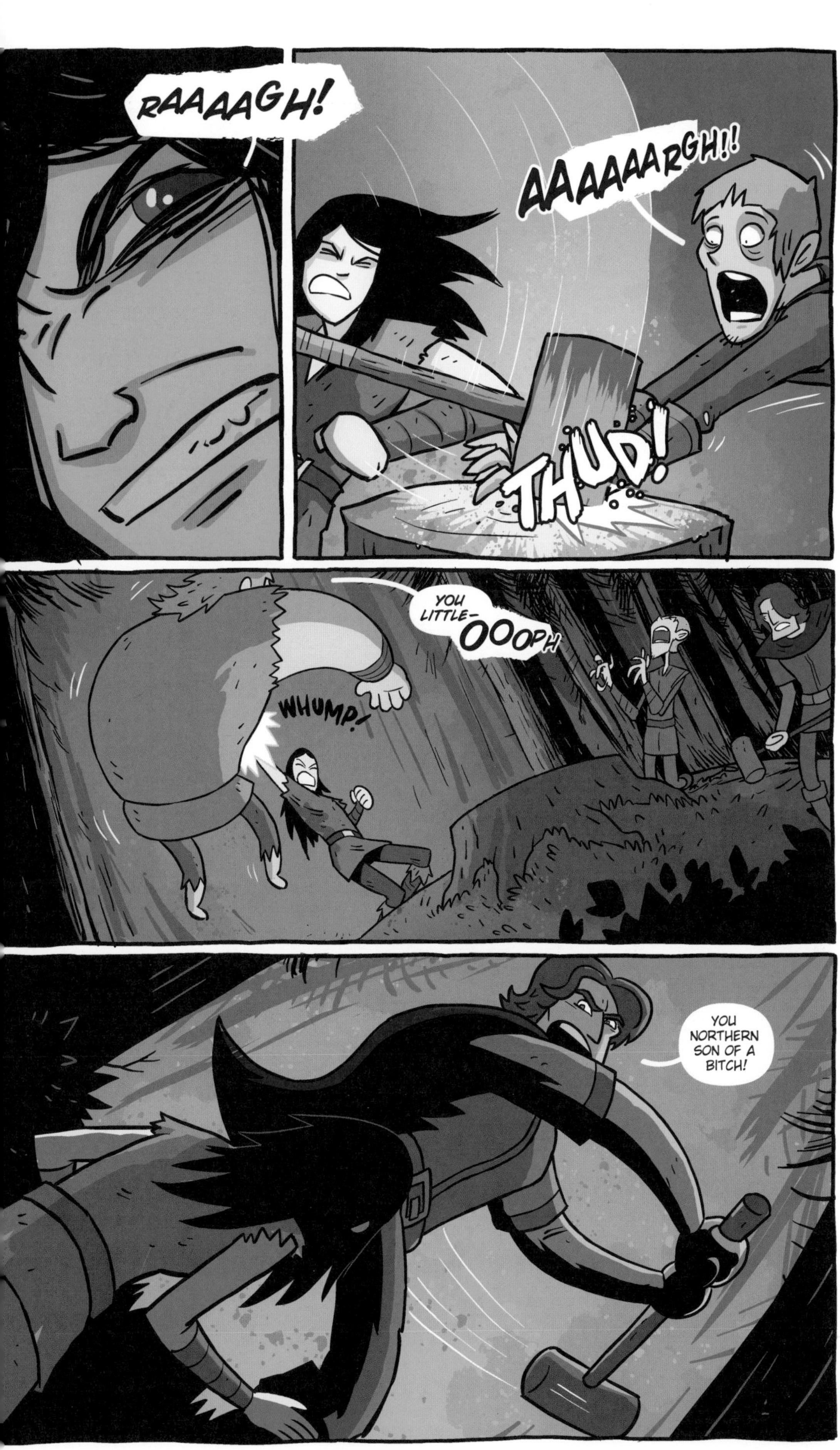
RAAAAGH!
AAAAAARGH!!
THUD!
YOU LITTLE- OOOPH
WHUMP!
YOU NORTHERN SON OF A BITCH!

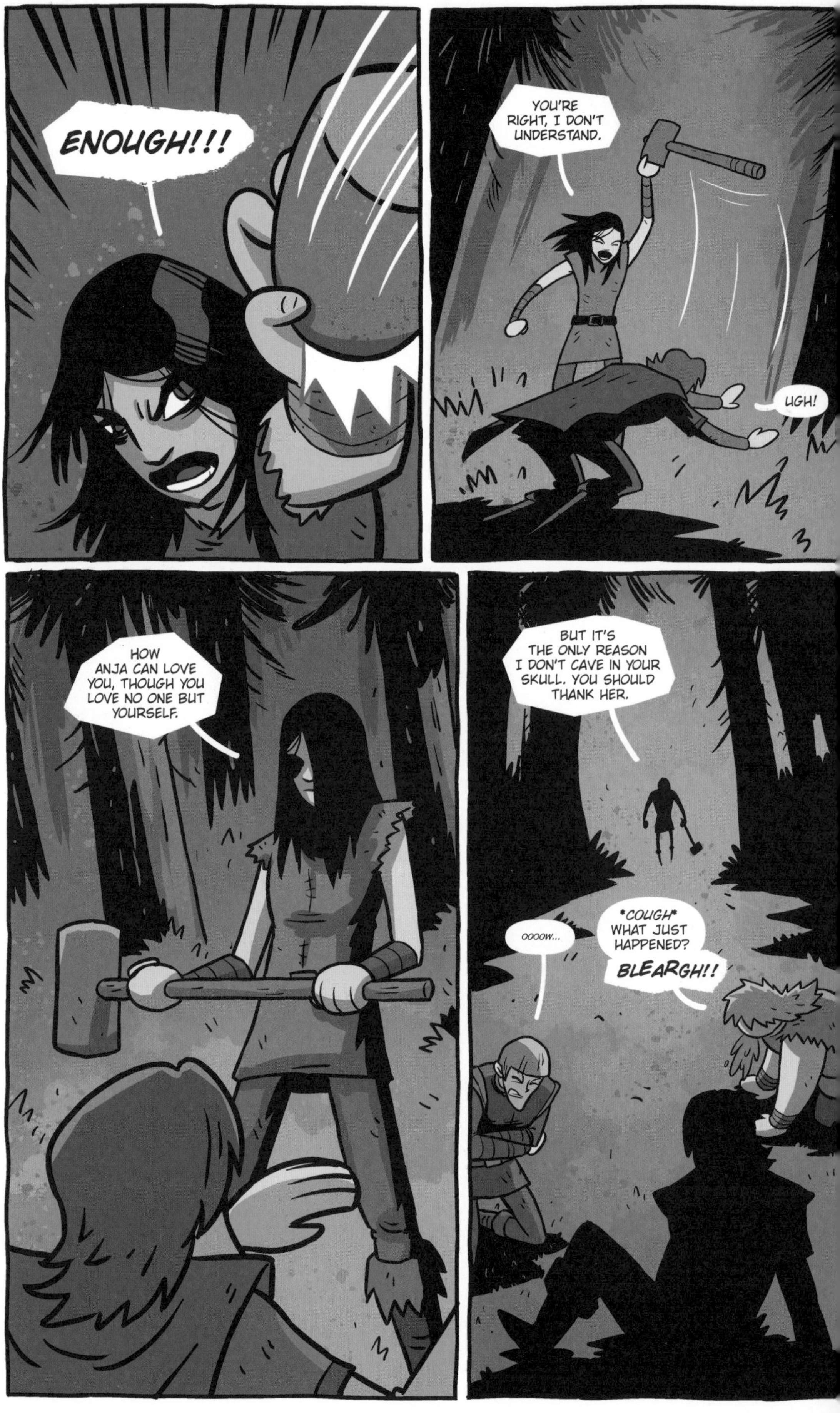
ENOUGH!!!
YOU'RE RIGHT, I DON'T UNDERSTAND.
UGH!
HOW ANJA CAN LOVE YOU, THOUGH YOU LOVE NO ONE BUT YOURSELF.
BUT IT'S THE ONLY REASON I DON'T CAVE IN YOUR SKULL. YOU SHOULD THANK HER.
OOOOW...
COUGH WHAT JUST HAPPENED?
BLEARGH!!

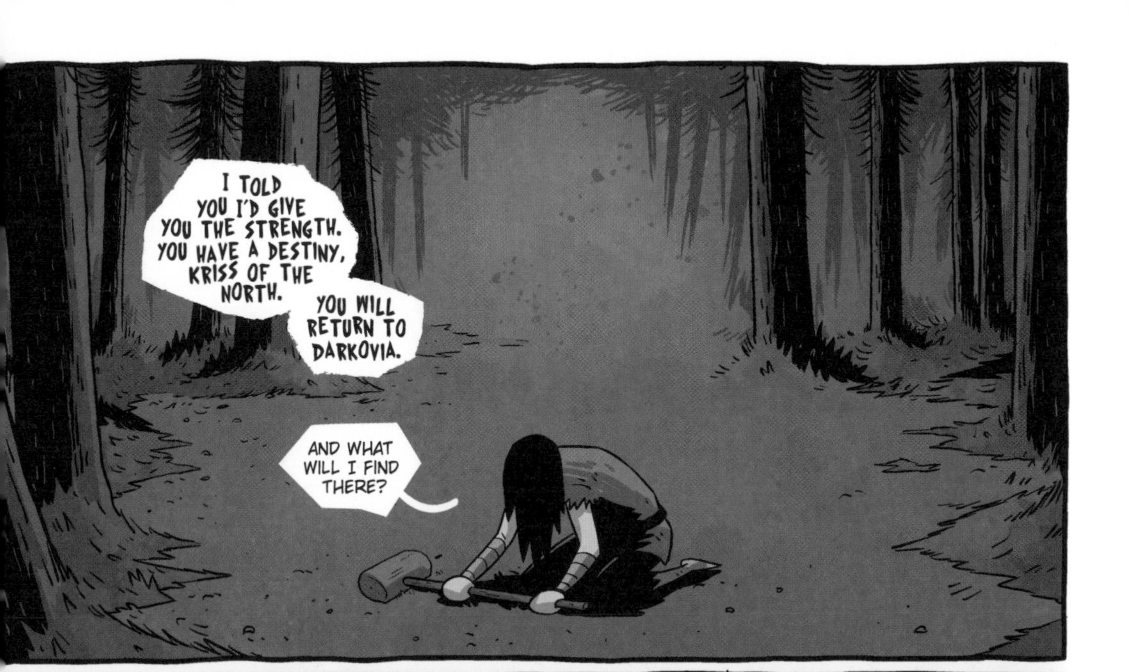
I TOLD YOU I'D GIVE YOU THE STRENGTH. YOU HAVE A DESTINY, KRISS OF THE NORTH.
YOU WILL RETURN TO DARKOVIA.
AND WHAT WILL I FIND THERE?

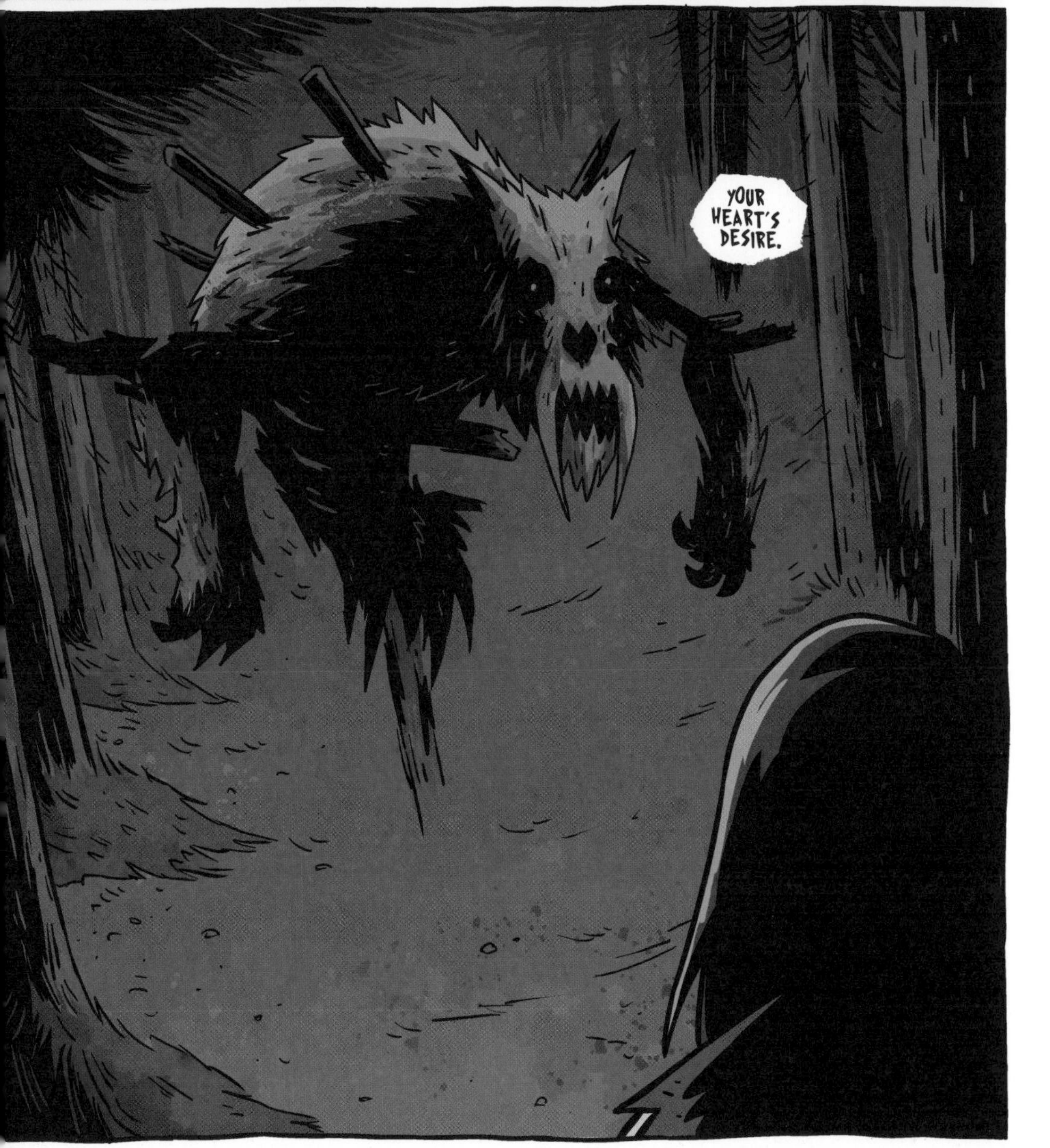
YOUR HEART'S DESIRE.

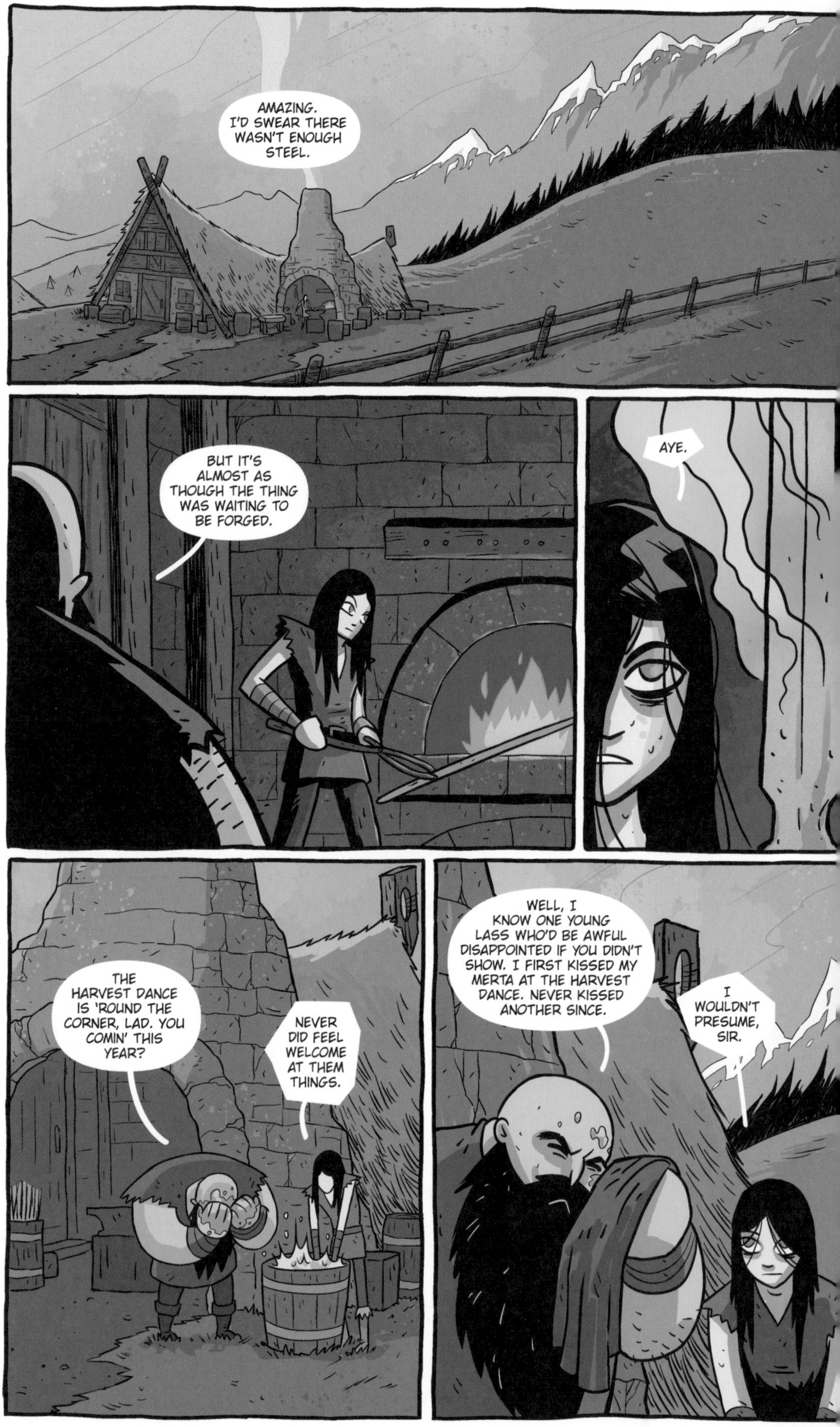
AMAZING. I'D SWEAR THERE WASN'T ENOUGH STEEL.
BUT IT'S ALMOST AS THOUGH THE THING WAS WAITING TO BE FORGED.
AYE.
THE HARVEST DANCE IS 'ROUND THE CORNER, LAD. YOU COMIN' THIS YEAR?
NEVER DID FEEL WELCOME AT THEM THINGS.
WELL, I KNOW ONE YOUNG LASS WHO'D BE AWFUL DISAPPOINTED IF YOU DIDN'T SHOW. I FIRST KISSED MY MERTA AT THE HARVEST DANCE. NEVER KISSED ANOTHER SINCE.
I WOULDN'T PRESUME, SIR.

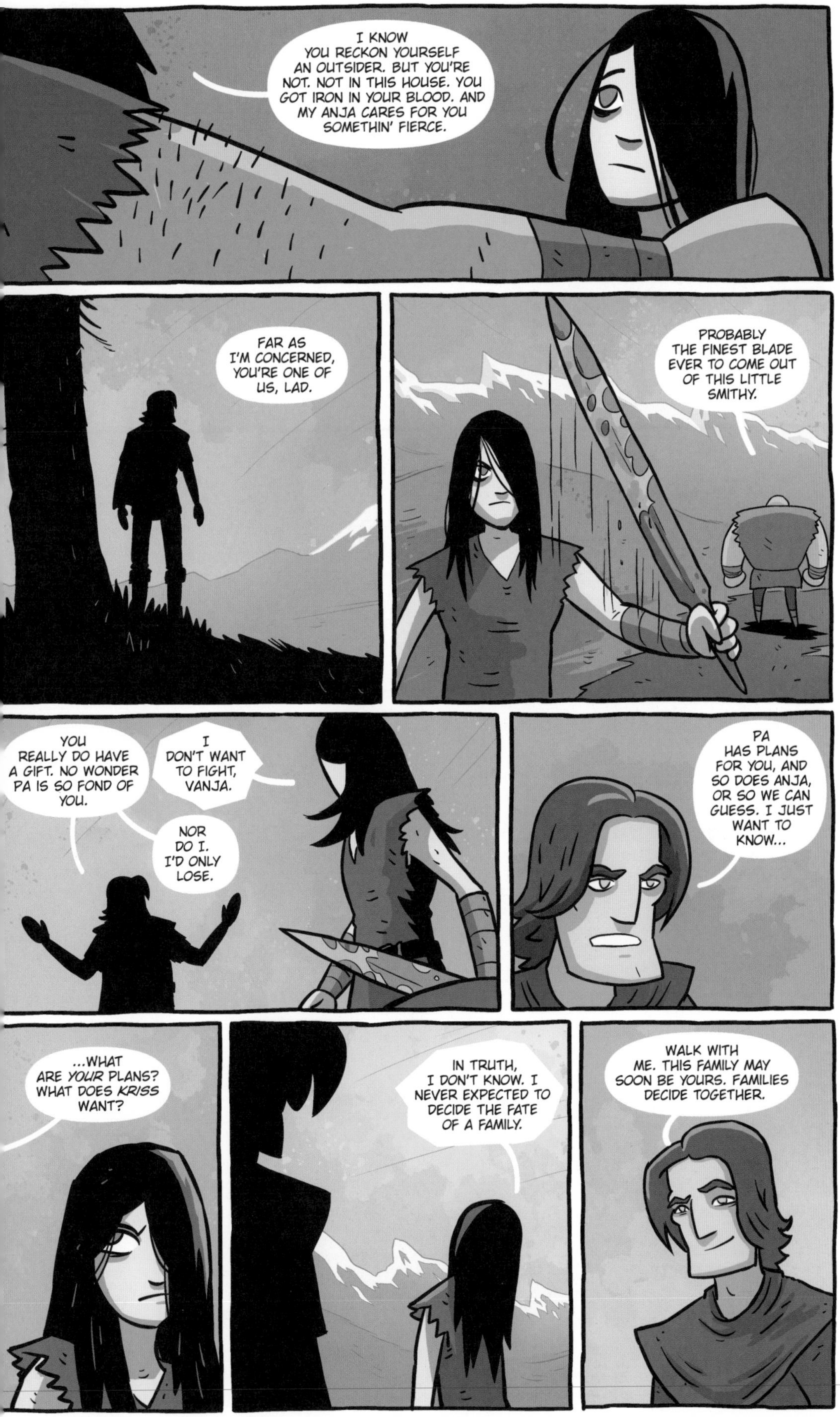
I KNOW YOU RECKON YOURSELF AN OUTSIDER. BUT YOU'RE NOT. NOT IN THIS HOUSE. YOU GOT IRON IN YOUR BLOOD. AND MY ANJA CARES FOR YOU SOMETHIN' FIERCE.
FAR AS I'M CONCERNED, YOU'RE ONE OF US, LAD.
PROBABLY THE FINEST BLADE EVER TO COME OUT OF THIS LITTLE SMITHY.
YOU REALLY DO HAVE A GIFT. NO WONDER PA IS SO FOND OF YOU.
I DON'T WANT TO FIGHT, VANJA.
NOR DO I. I'D ONLY LOSE.
PA HAS PLANS FOR YOU, AND SO DOES ANJA, OR SO WE CAN GUESS. I JUST WANT TO KNOW...
...WHAT ARE *YOUR* PLANS? WHAT DOES *KRISS* WANT?
IN TRUTH, I DON'T KNOW. I NEVER EXPECTED TO DECIDE THE FATE OF A FAMILY.
WALK WITH ME. THIS FAMILY MAY SOON BE YOURS. FAMILIES DECIDE TOGETHER.

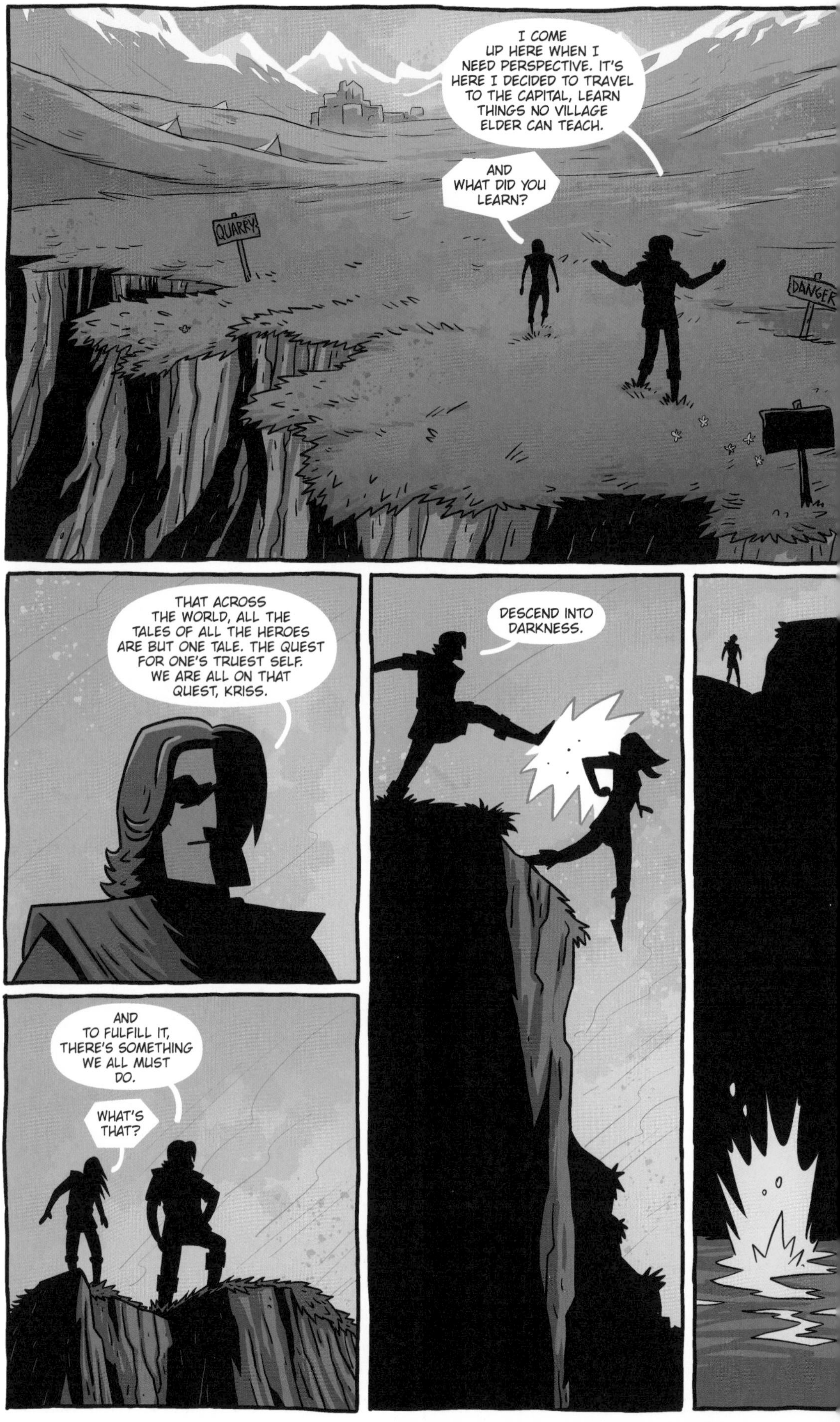
I COME UP HERE WHEN I NEED PERSPECTIVE. IT'S HERE I DECIDED TO TRAVEL TO THE CAPITAL, LEARN THINGS NO VILLAGE ELDER CAN TEACH.
AND WHAT DID YOU LEARN?
QUARRY
DANGER
THAT ACROSS THE WORLD, ALL THE TALES OF ALL THE HEROES ARE BUT ONE TALE. THE QUEST FOR ONE'S TRUEST SELF. WE ARE ALL ON THAT QUEST, KRISS.
AND TO FULFILL IT, THERE'S SOMETHING WE ALL MUST DO.
WHAT'S THAT?
DESCEND INTO DARKNESS.

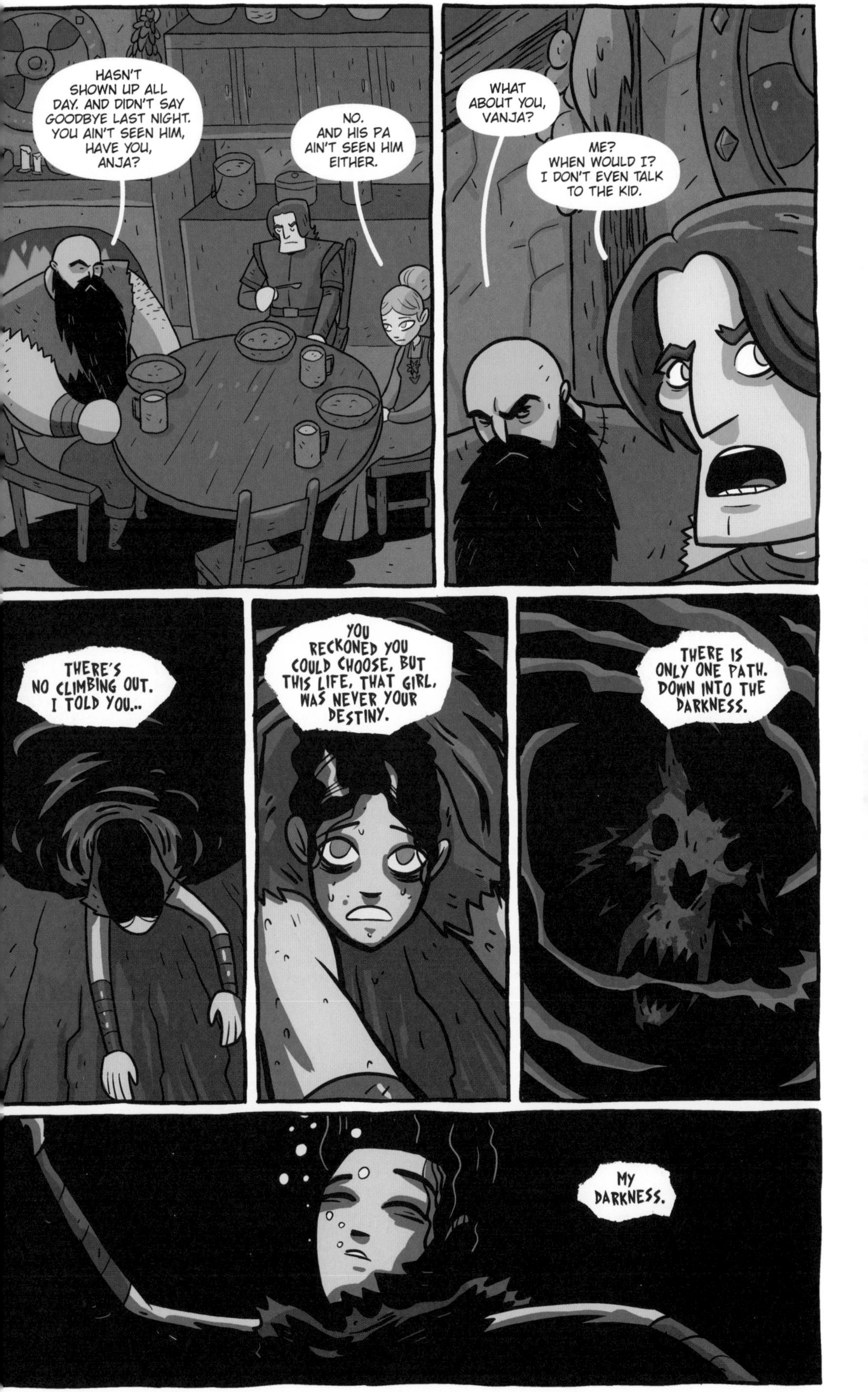
HASN'T SHOWN UP ALL DAY. AND DIDN'T SAY GOODBYE LAST NIGHT. YOU AIN'T SEEN HIM, HAVE YOU, ANJA?
NO. AND HIS PA AIN'T SEEN HIM EITHER.
WHAT ABOUT YOU, VANJA?
ME? WHEN WOULD I? I DON'T EVEN TALK TO THE KID.
THERE'S NO CLIMBING OUT. I TOLD YOU...
YOU RECKONED YOU COULD CHOOSE, BUT THIS LIFE, THAT GIRL, WAS NEVER YOUR DESTINY.
THERE IS ONLY ONE PATH. DOWN INTO THE DARKNESS.
MY DARKNESS.

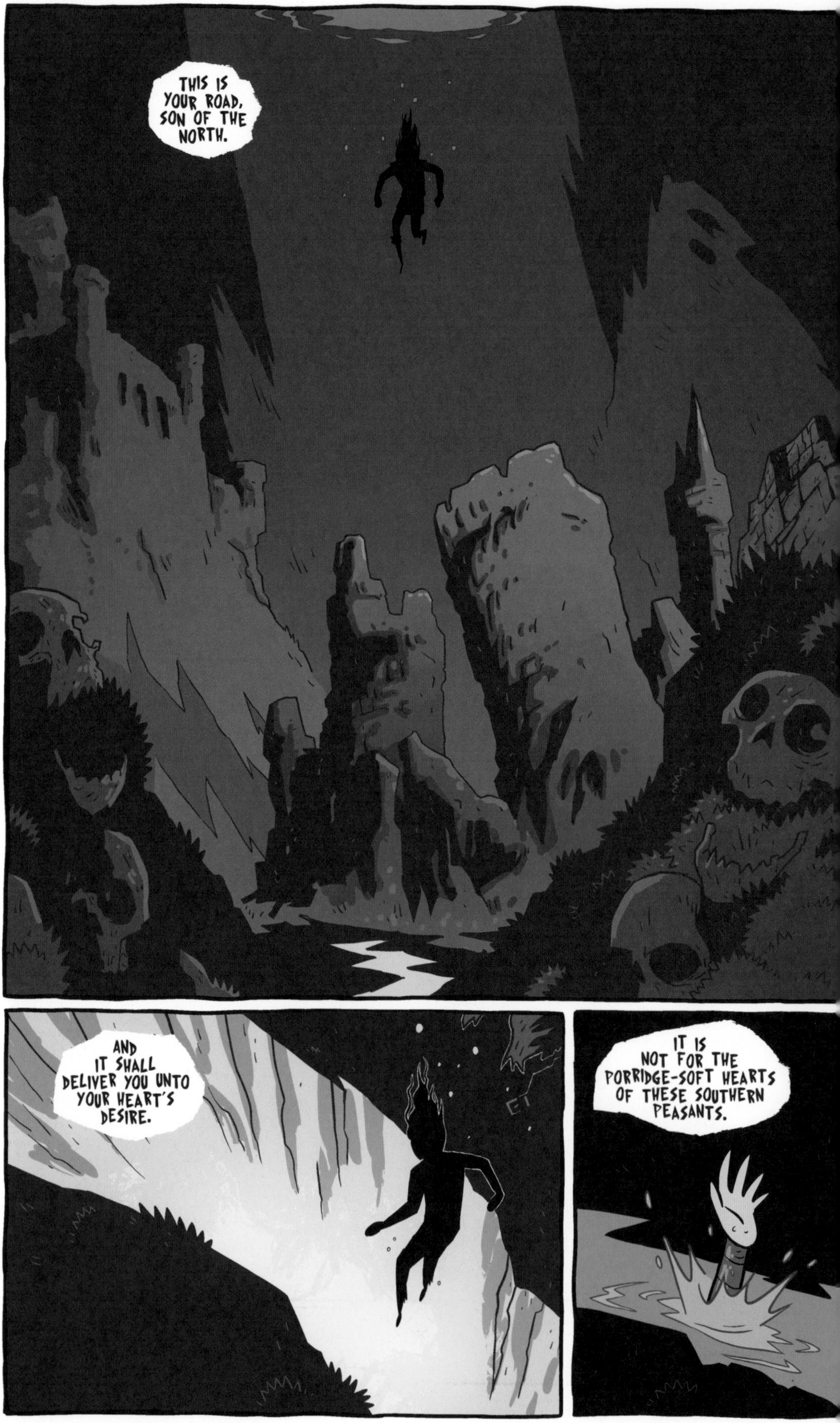
THIS IS YOUR ROAD, SON OF THE NORTH.
AND IT SHALL DELIVER YOU UNTO YOUR HEART'S DESIRE.
IT IS NOT FOR THE PORRIDGE-SOFT HEARTS OF THESE SOUTHERN PEASANTS.

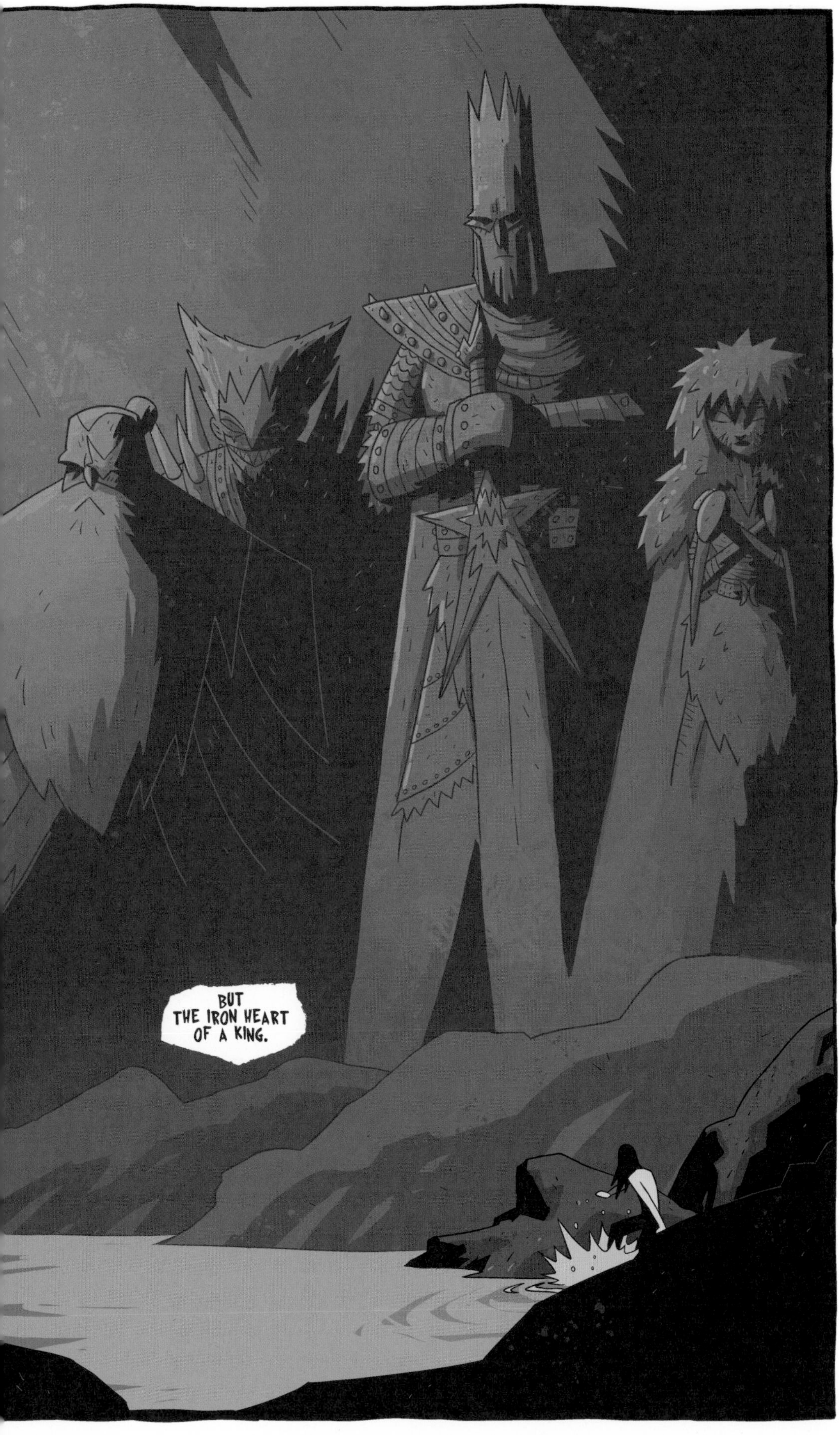
BUT THE IRON HEART OF A KING.

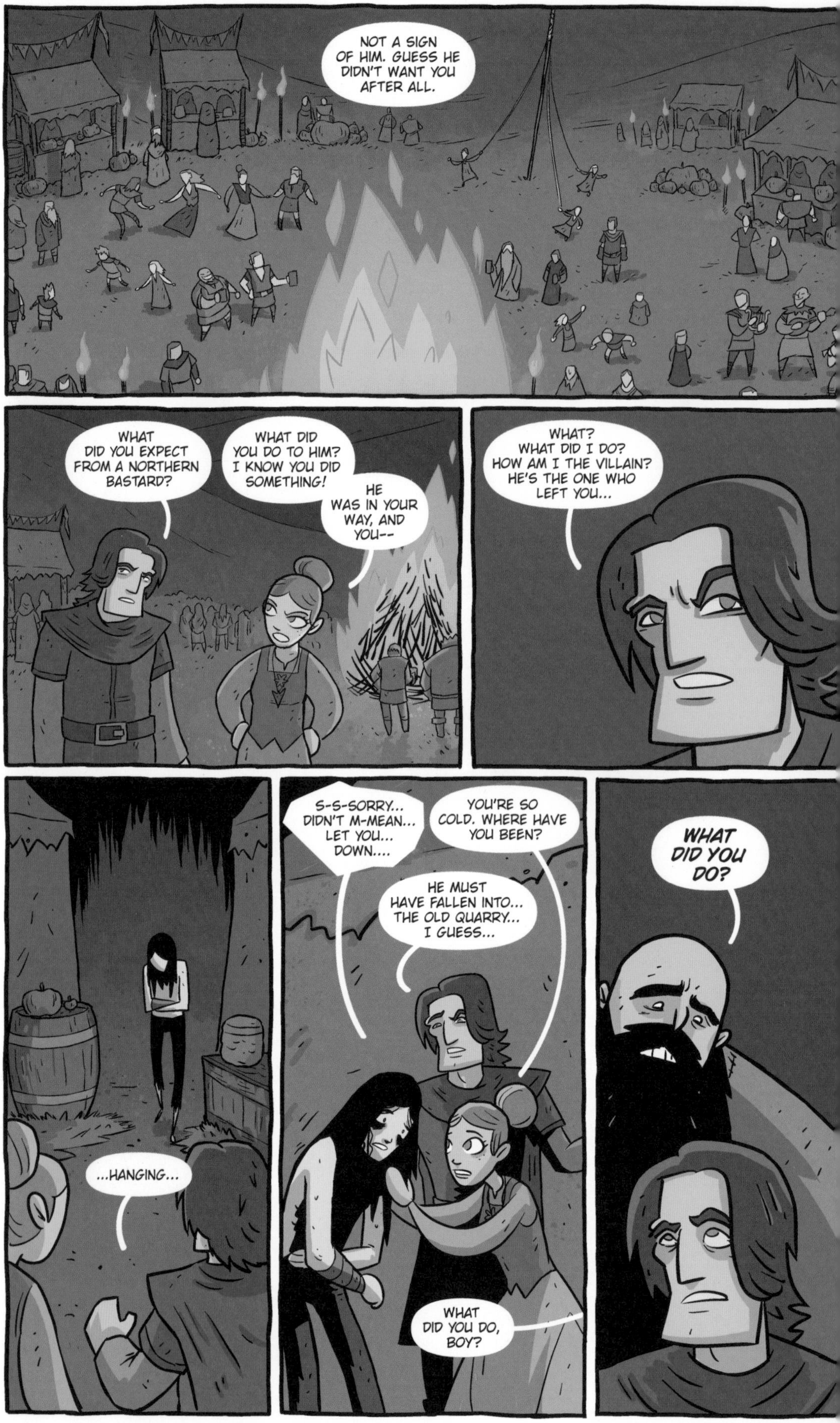
NOT A SIGN OF HIM. GUESS HE DIDN'T WANT YOU AFTER ALL.
WHAT DID YOU EXPECT FROM A NORTHERN BASTARD?
WHAT DID YOU DO TO HIM? I KNOW YOU DID SOMETHING!
HE WAS IN YOUR WAY, AND YOU--
WHAT? WHAT DID I DO? HOW AM I THE VILLAIN? HE'S THE ONE WHO LEFT YOU...
...HANGING...
S-S-SORRY... DIDN'T M-MEAN... LET YOU... DOWN....
YOU'RE SO COLD. WHERE HAVE YOU BEEN?
HE MUST HAVE FALLEN INTO... THE OLD QUARRY... I GUESS...
WHAT DID YOU DO, BOY?
WHAT DID YOU DO?

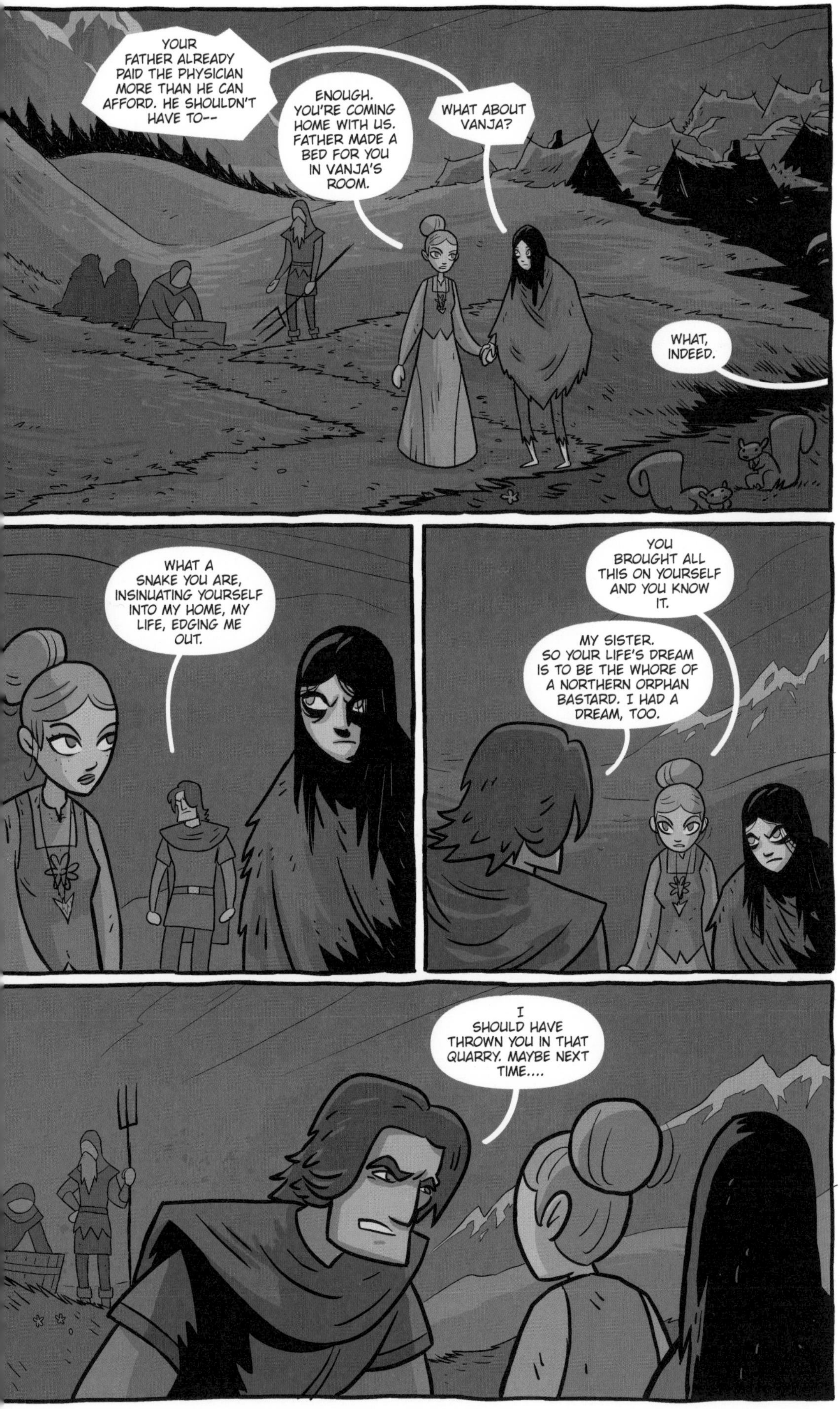
YOUR FATHER ALREADY PAID THE PHYSICIAN MORE THAN HE CAN AFFORD. HE SHOULDN'T HAVE TO--
ENOUGH. YOU'RE COMING HOME WITH US. FATHER MADE A BED FOR YOU IN VANJA'S ROOM.
WHAT ABOUT VANJA?
WHAT, INDEED.
WHAT A SNAKE YOU ARE, INSINUATING YOURSELF INTO MY HOME, MY LIFE, EDGING ME OUT.
YOU BROUGHT ALL THIS ON YOURSELF AND YOU KNOW IT.
MY SISTER. SO YOUR LIFE'S DREAM IS TO BE THE WHORE OF A NORTHERN ORPHAN BASTARD. I HAD A DREAM, TOO.
I SHOULD HAVE THROWN YOU IN THAT QUARRY. MAYBE NEXT TIME....

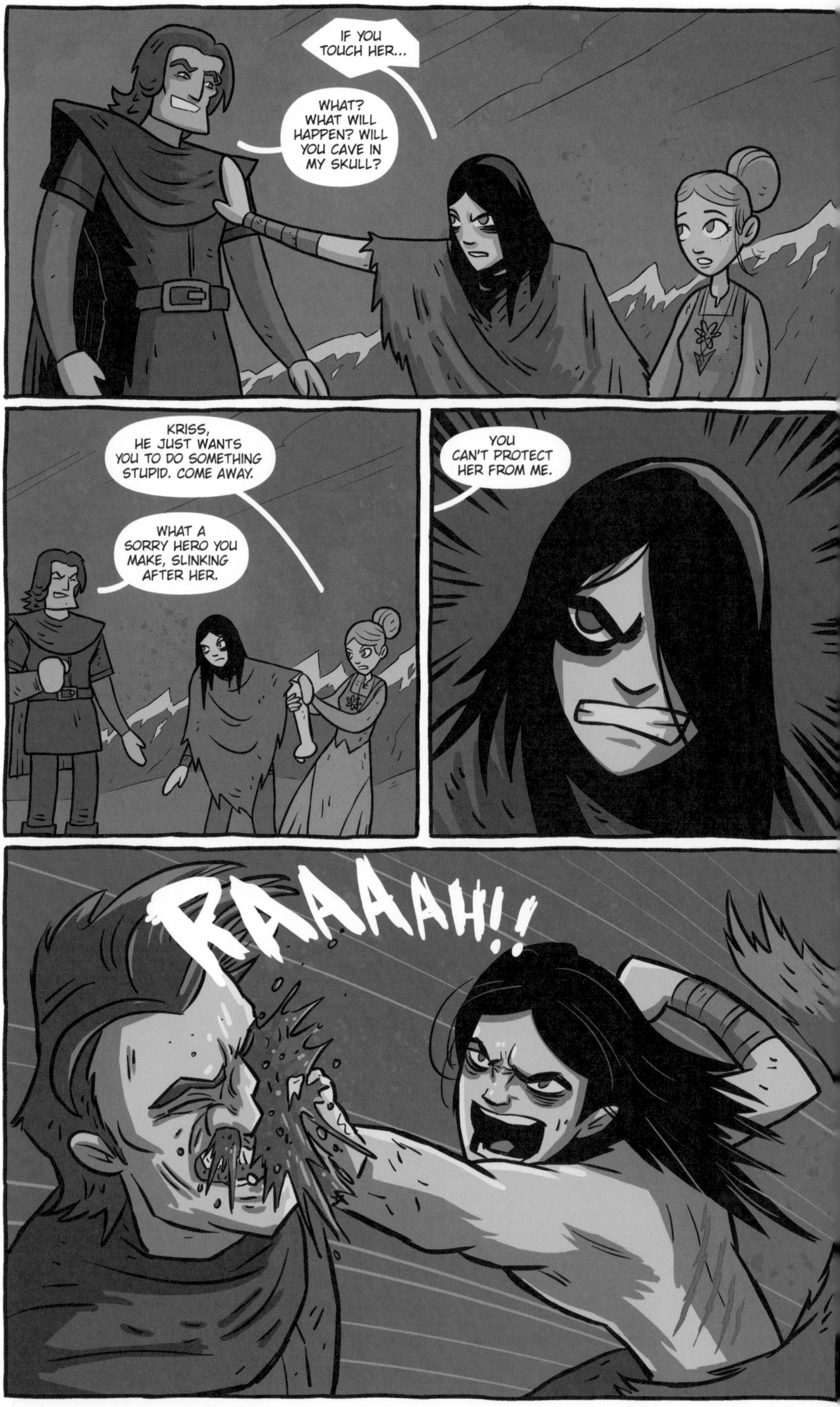
IF YOU TOUCH HER...
WHAT? WHAT WILL HAPPEN? WILL YOU CAVE IN MY SKULL?
KRISS, HE JUST WANTS YOU TO DO SOMETHING STUPID. COME AWAY.
WHAT A SORRY HERO YOU MAKE, SLINKING AFTER HER.
YOU CAN'T PROTECT HER FROM ME.
RAAAAH!!

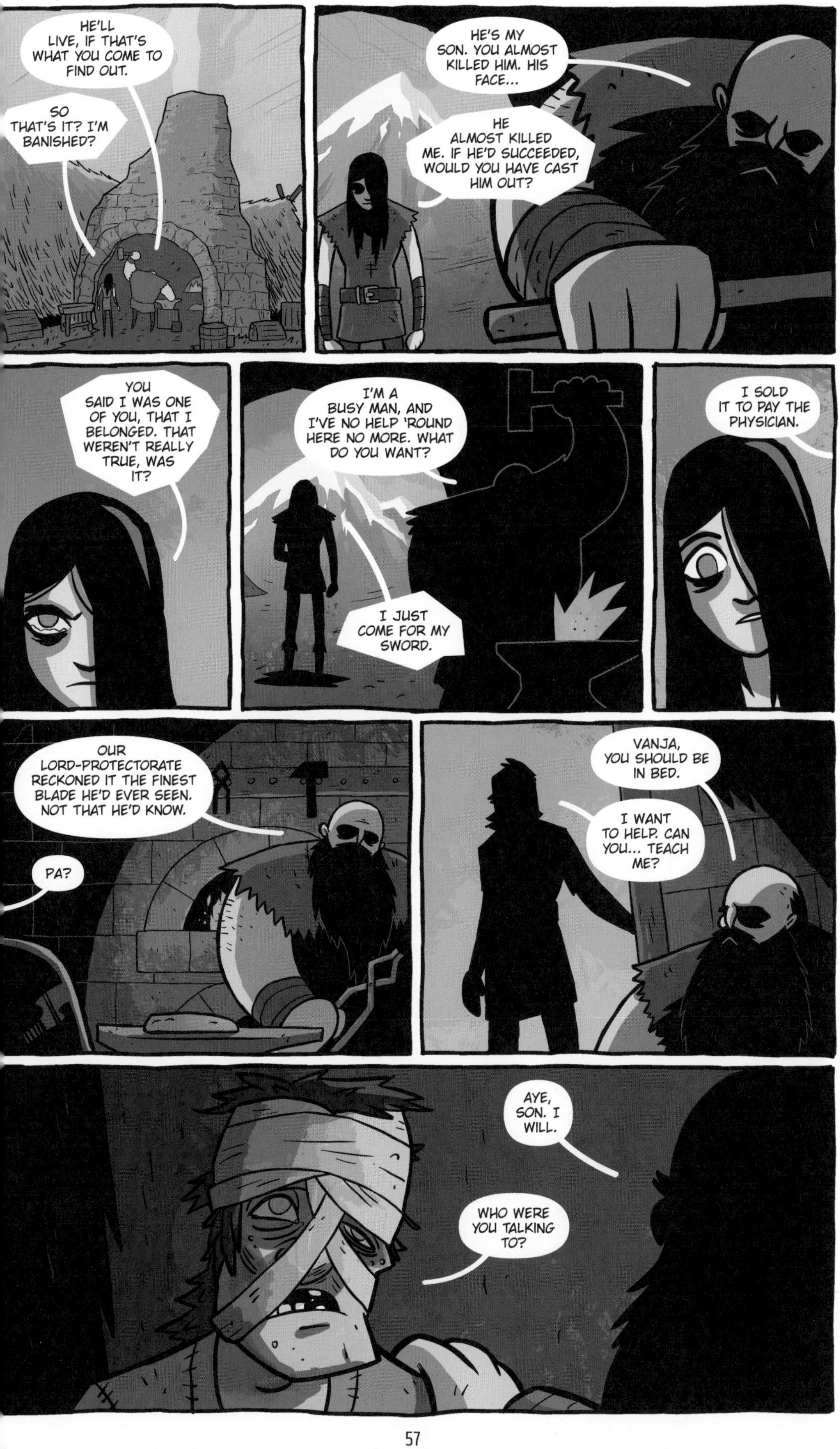
HE'LL LIVE, IF THAT'S WHAT YOU COME TO FIND OUT.
SO THAT'S IT? I'M BANISHED?
HE'S MY SON. YOU ALMOST KILLED HIM. HIS FACE...
HE ALMOST KILLED ME. IF HE'D SUCCEEDED, WOULD YOU HAVE CAST HIM OUT?
YOU SAID I WAS ONE OF YOU, THAT I BELONGED. THAT WEREN'T REALLY TRUE, WAS IT?
I'M A BUSY MAN, AND I'VE NO HELP 'ROUND HERE NO MORE. WHAT DO YOU WANT?
I JUST COME FOR MY SWORD.
I SOLD IT TO PAY THE PHYSICIAN.
OUR LORD-PROTECTORATE RECKONED IT THE FINEST BLADE HE'D EVER SEEN. NOT THAT HE'D KNOW.
PA?
VANJA, YOU SHOULD BE IN BED.
I WANT TO HELP. CAN YOU... TEACH ME?
AYE, SON. I WILL.
WHO WERE YOU TALKING TO?

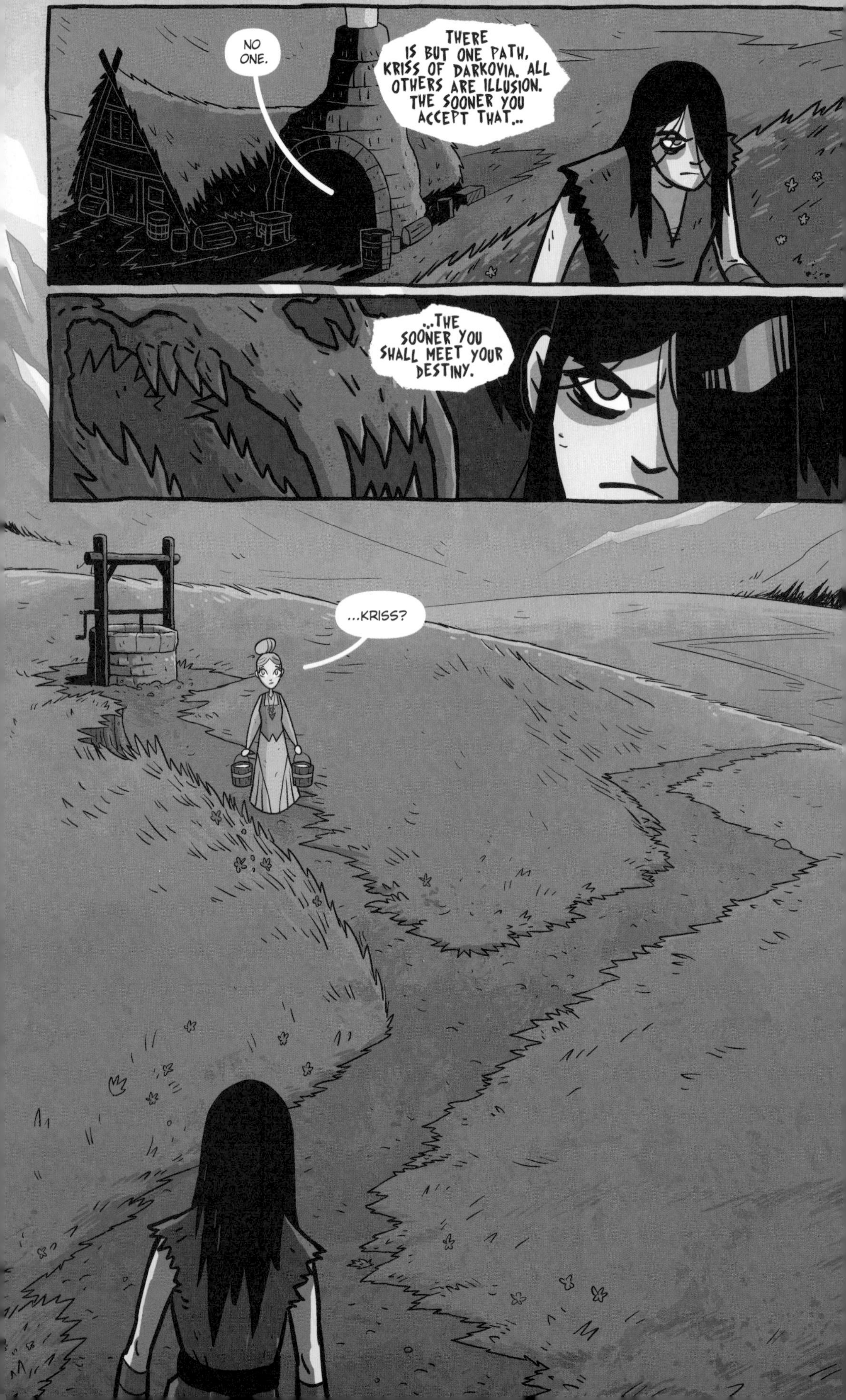
NO ONE.
THERE IS BUT ONE PATH, KRISS OF DARKOVIA. ALL OTHERS ARE ILLUSION. THE SOONER YOU ACCEPT THAT...
...THE SOONER YOU SHALL MEET YOUR DESTINY.
...KRISS?

CHAPTER THREE

THE ONLY GAME THAT MATTERS

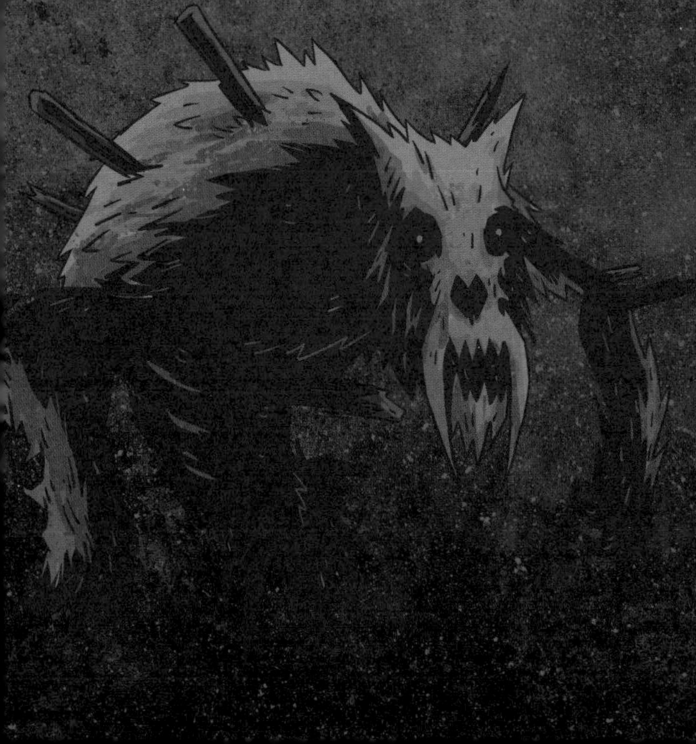

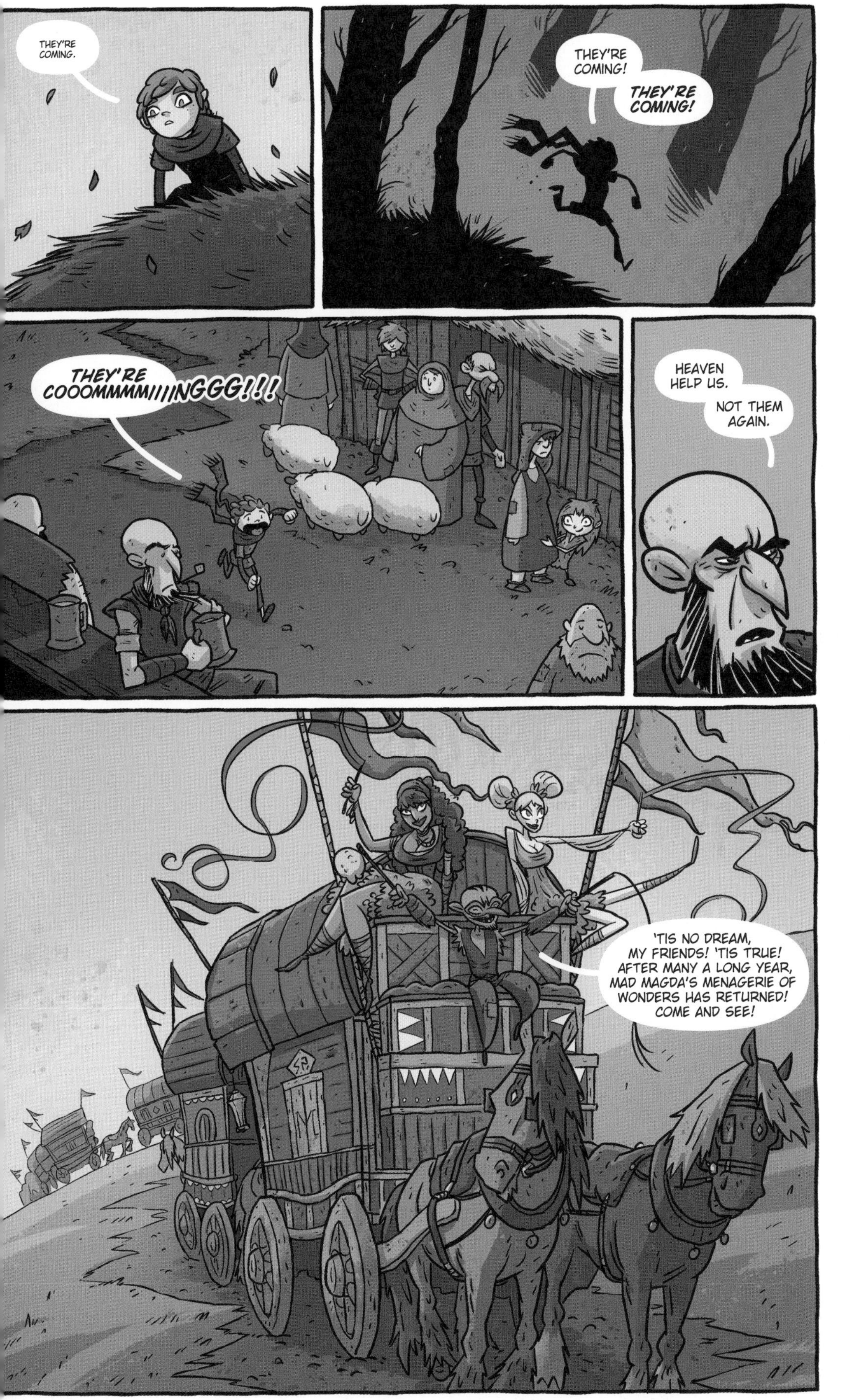
THEY'RE COMING.
THEY'RE COMING!
THEY'RE COMING!
THEY'RE COOOMMMMIIIINGGG!!!
HEAVEN HELP US.
NOT THEM AGAIN.
'TIS NO DREAM, MY FRIENDS! 'TIS TRUE! AFTER MANY A LONG YEAR, MAD MAGDA'S MENAGERIE OF WONDERS HAS RETURNED! COME AND SEE!

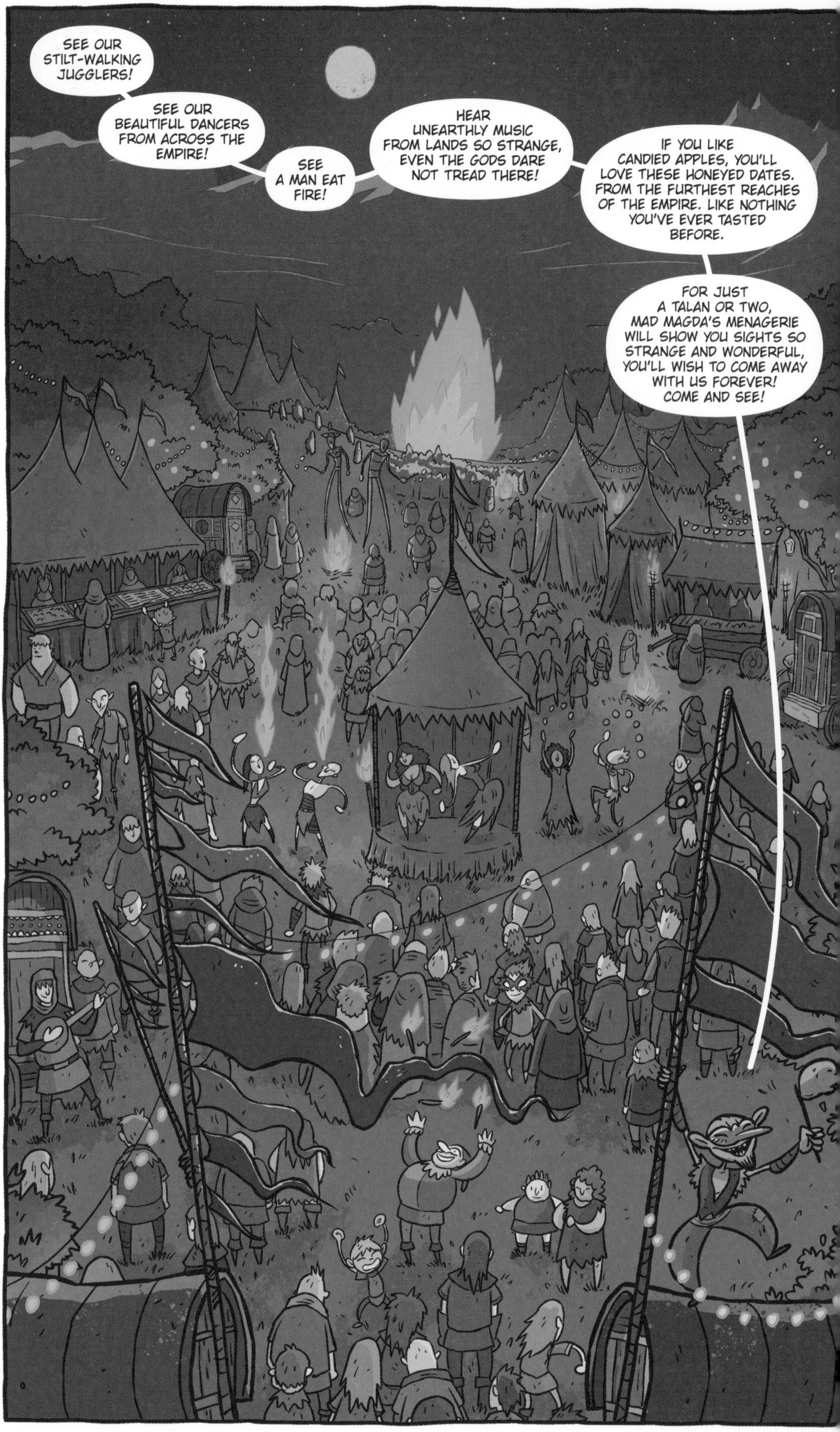
SEE OUR STILT-WALKING JUGGLERS!
SEE OUR BEAUTIFUL DANCERS FROM ACROSS THE EMPIRE!
SEE A MAN EAT FIRE!
HEAR UNEARTHLY MUSIC FROM LANDS SO STRANGE, EVEN THE GODS DARE NOT TREAD THERE!
IF YOU LIKE CANDIED APPLES, YOU'LL LOVE THESE HONEYED DATES. FROM THE FURTHEST REACHES OF THE EMPIRE. LIKE NOTHING YOU'VE EVER TASTED BEFORE.
FOR JUST A TALAN OR TWO, MAD MAGDA'S MENAGERIE WILL SHOW YOU SIGHTS SO STRANGE AND WONDERFUL, YOU'LL WISH TO COME AWAY WITH US FOREVER! COME AND SEE!

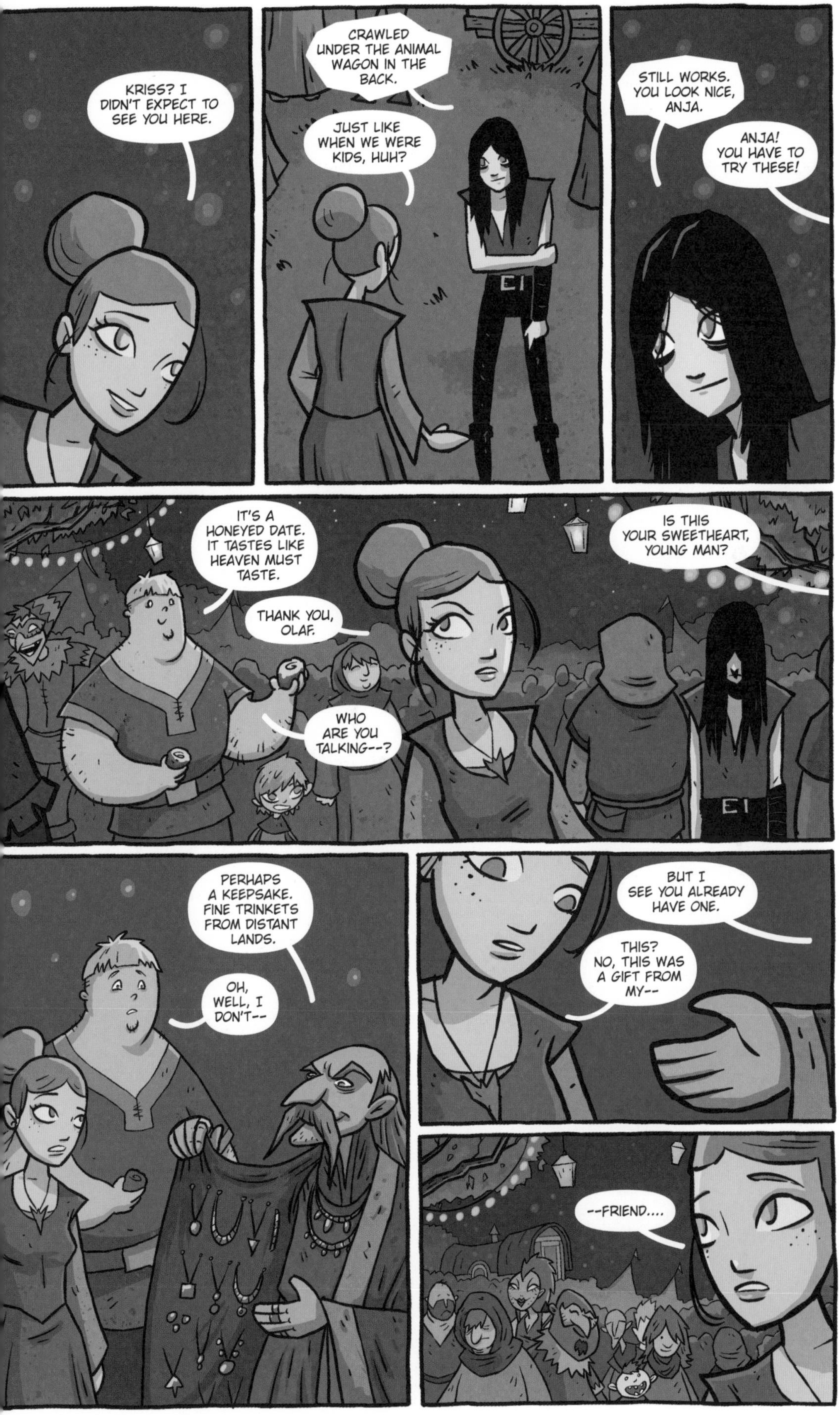
KRISS? I DIDN'T EXPECT TO SEE YOU HERE.
CRAWLED UNDER THE ANIMAL WAGON IN THE BACK.
JUST LIKE WHEN WE WERE KIDS, HUH?
STILL WORKS. YOU LOOK NICE, ANJA.
ANJA! YOU HAVE TO TRY THESE!
IT'S A HONEYED DATE. IT TASTES LIKE HEAVEN MUST TASTE.
THANK YOU, OLAF.
IS THIS YOUR SWEETHEART, YOUNG MAN?
WHO ARE YOU TALKING--?
PERHAPS A KEEPSAKE. FINE TRINKETS FROM DISTANT LANDS.
OH, WELL, I DON'T--
BUT I SEE YOU ALREADY HAVE ONE.
THIS? NO, THIS WAS A GIFT FROM MY--
--FRIEND....

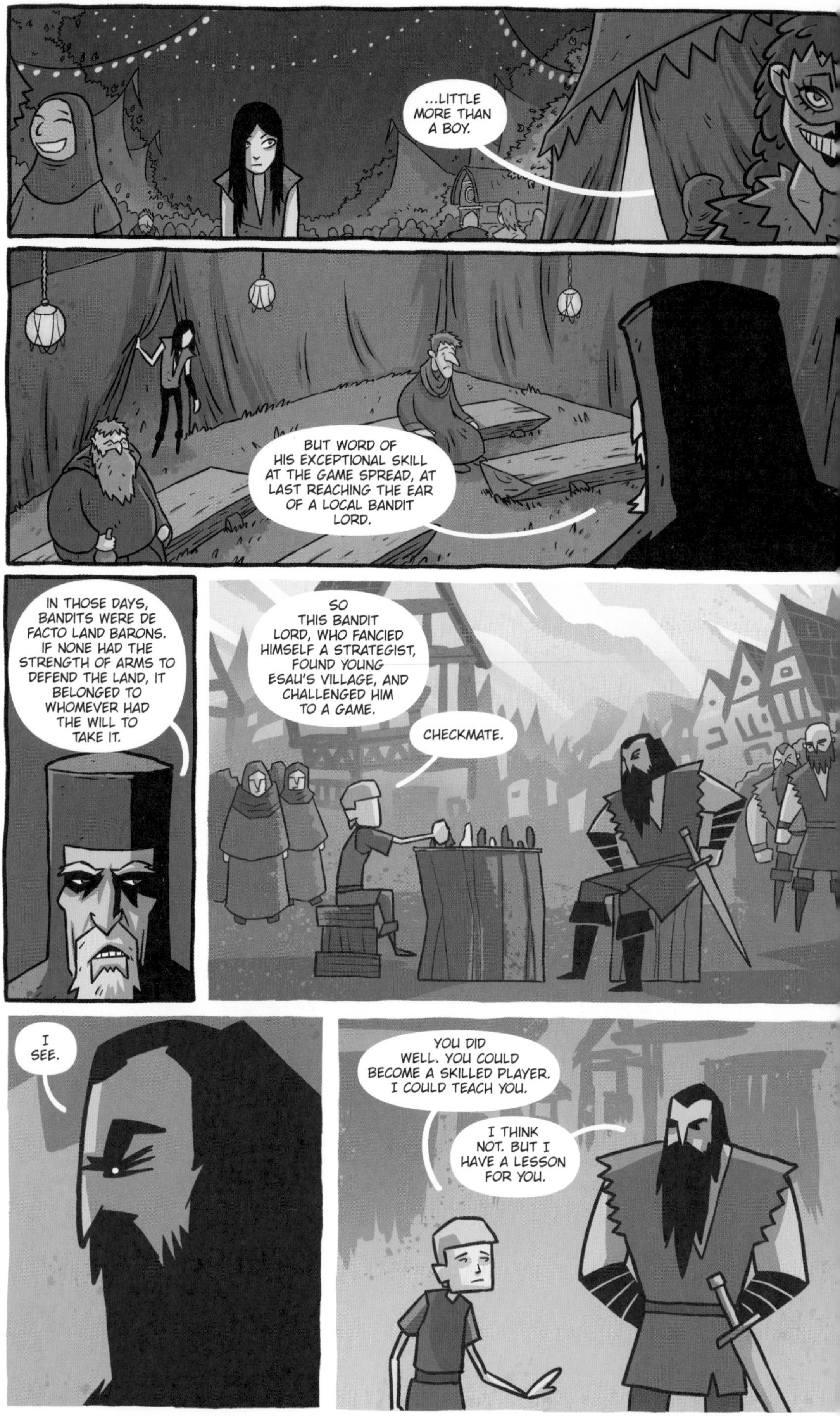

...LITTLE MORE THAN A BOY.
BUT WORD OF HIS EXCEPTIONAL SKILL AT THE GAME SPREAD, AT LAST REACHING THE EAR OF A LOCAL BANDIT LORD.
IN THOSE DAYS, BANDITS WERE DE FACTO LAND BARONS. IF NONE HAD THE STRENGTH OF ARMS TO DEFEND THE LAND, IT BELONGED TO WHOMEVER HAD THE WILL TO TAKE IT.
SO THIS BANDIT LORD, WHO FANCIED HIMSELF A STRATEGIST, FOUND YOUNG ESAU'S VILLAGE, AND CHALLENGED HIM TO A GAME.
CHECKMATE.
I SEE.
YOU DID WELL. YOU COULD BECOME A SKILLED PLAYER. I COULD TEACH YOU.
I THINK NOT. BUT I HAVE A LESSON FOR YOU.

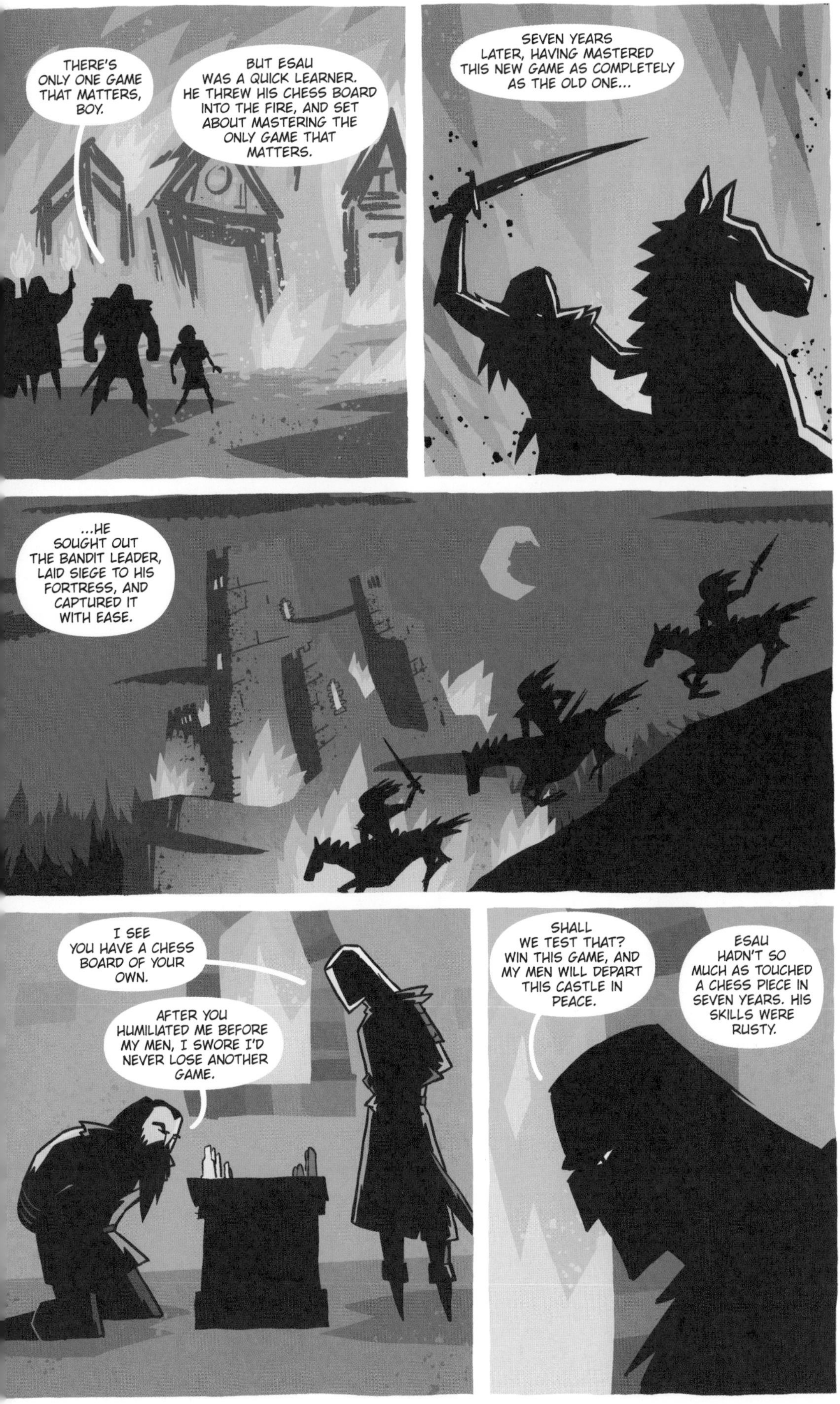
THERE'S ONLY ONE GAME THAT MATTERS, BOY.
BUT ESAU WAS A QUICK LEARNER. HE THREW HIS CHESS BOARD INTO THE FIRE, AND SET ABOUT MASTERING THE ONLY GAME THAT MATTERS.
SEVEN YEARS LATER, HAVING MASTERED THIS NEW GAME AS COMPLETELY AS THE OLD ONE...
...HE SOUGHT OUT THE BANDIT LEADER, LAID SIEGE TO HIS FORTRESS, AND CAPTURED IT WITH EASE.
I SEE YOU HAVE A CHESS BOARD OF YOUR OWN.
AFTER YOU HUMILIATED ME BEFORE MY MEN, I SWORE I'D NEVER LOSE ANOTHER GAME.
SHALL WE TEST THAT? WIN THIS GAME, AND MY MEN WILL DEPART THIS CASTLE IN PEACE.
ESAU HADN'T SO MUCH AS TOUCHED A CHESS PIECE IN SEVEN YEARS. HIS SKILLS WERE RUSTY.

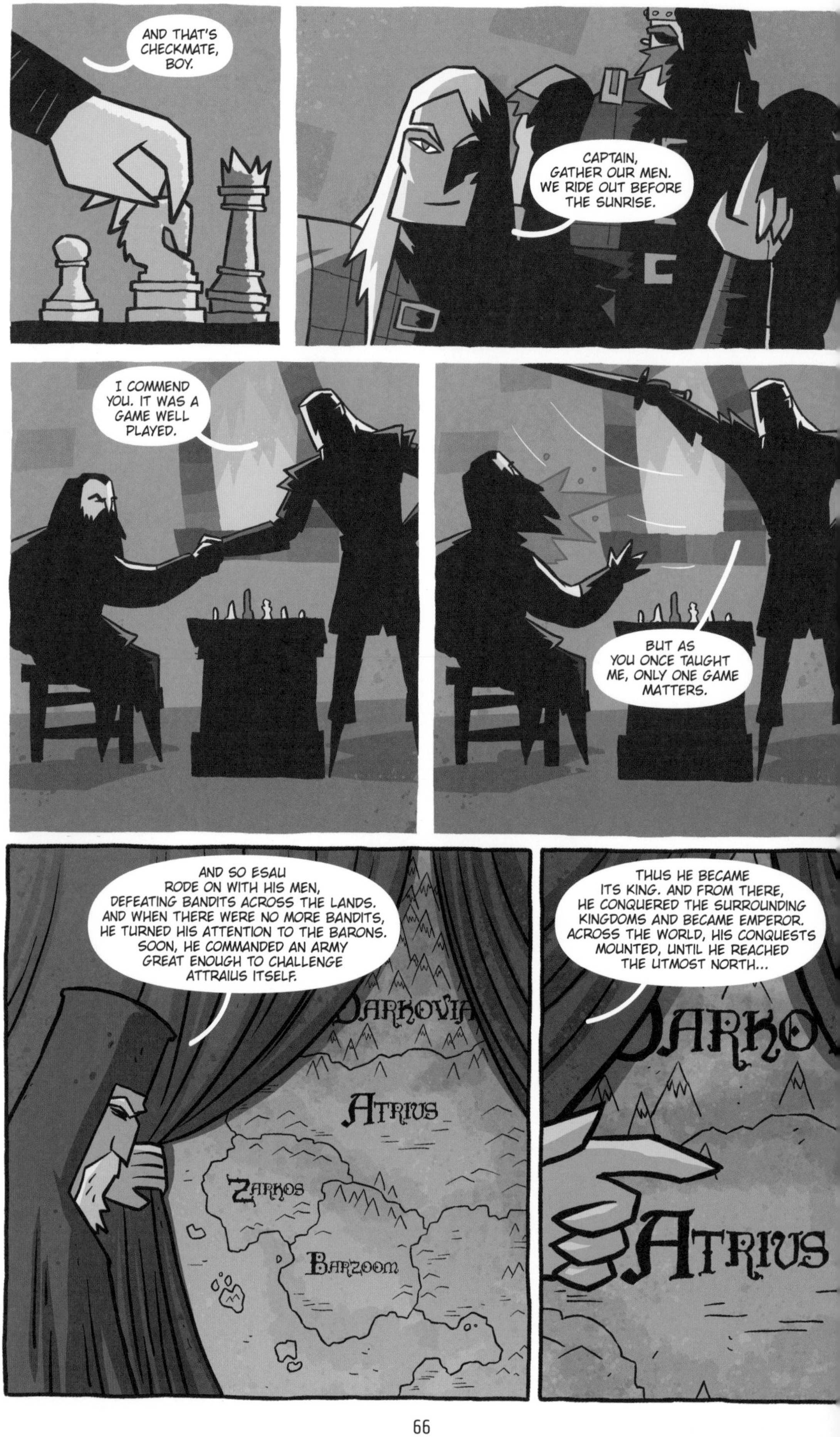
AND THAT'S CHECKMATE, BOY.
CAPTAIN, GATHER OUR MEN. WE RIDE OUT BEFORE THE SUNRISE.
I COMMEND YOU. IT WAS A GAME WELL PLAYED.
BUT AS YOU ONCE TAUGHT ME, ONLY ONE GAME MATTERS.
AND SO ESAU RODE ON WITH HIS MEN, DEFEATING BANDITS ACROSS THE LANDS. AND WHEN THERE WERE NO MORE BANDITS, HE TURNED HIS ATTENTION TO THE BARONS. SOON, HE COMMANDED AN ARMY GREAT ENOUGH TO CHALLENGE ATTRAIUS ITSELF.
DARKOVIA
ATRIUS
ZARKOS
BARZOOM
THUS HE BECAME ITS KING. AND FROM THERE, HE CONQUERED THE SURROUNDING KINGDOMS AND BECAME EMPEROR. ACROSS THE WORLD, HIS CONQUESTS MOUNTED, UNTIL HE REACHED THE UTMOST NORTH...
ATRIUS

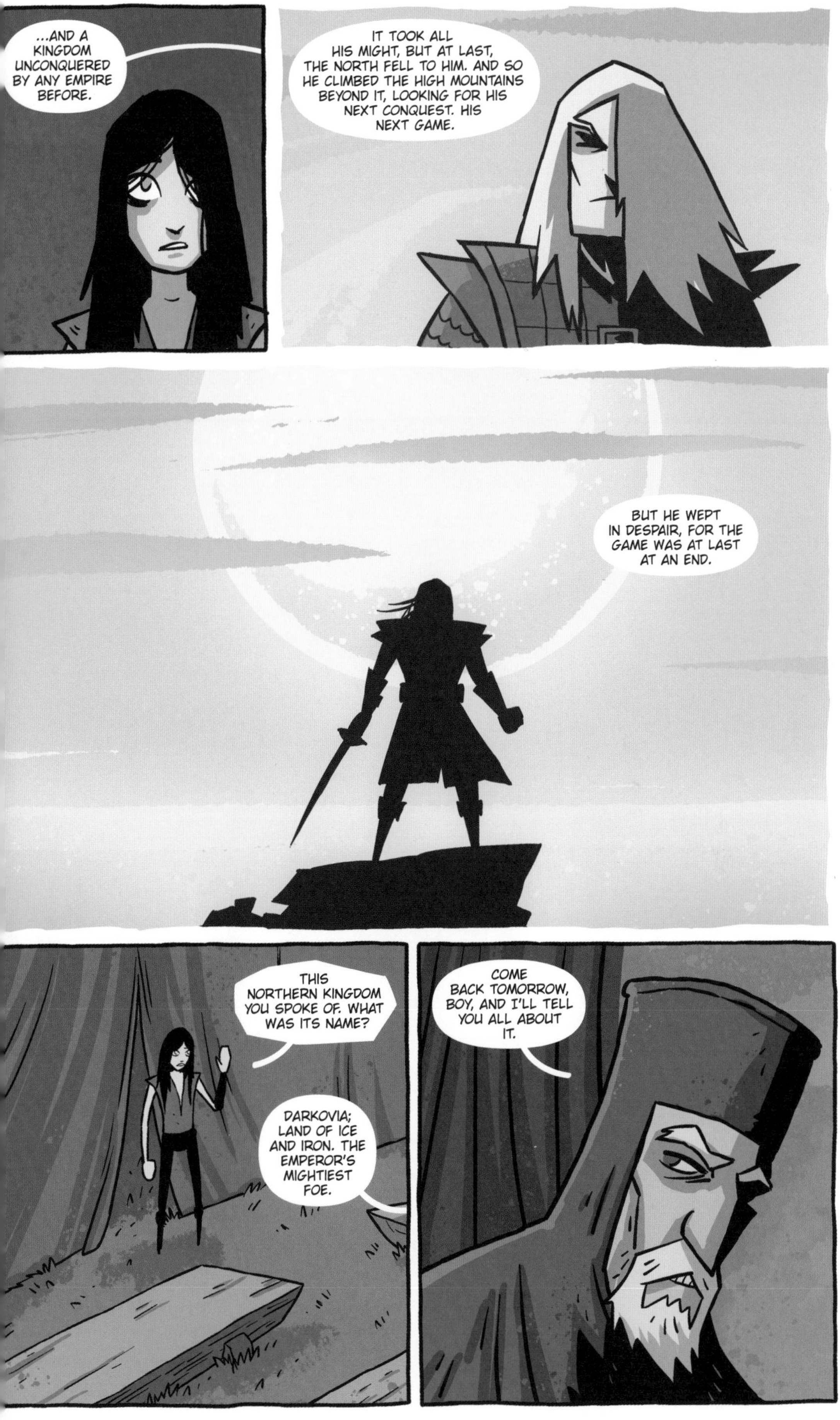
...AND A KINGDOM UNCONQUERED BY ANY EMPIRE BEFORE.
IT TOOK ALL HIS MIGHT, BUT AT LAST, THE NORTH FELL TO HIM. AND SO HE CLIMBED THE HIGH MOUNTAINS BEYOND IT, LOOKING FOR HIS NEXT CONQUEST. HIS NEXT GAME.
BUT HE WEPT IN DESPAIR, FOR THE GAME WAS AT LAST AT AN END.
THIS NORTHERN KINGDOM YOU SPOKE OF. WHAT WAS ITS NAME?
DARKOVIA; LAND OF ICE AND IRON. THE EMPEROR'S MIGHTIEST FOE.
COME BACK TOMORROW, BOY, AND I'LL TELL YOU ALL ABOUT IT.

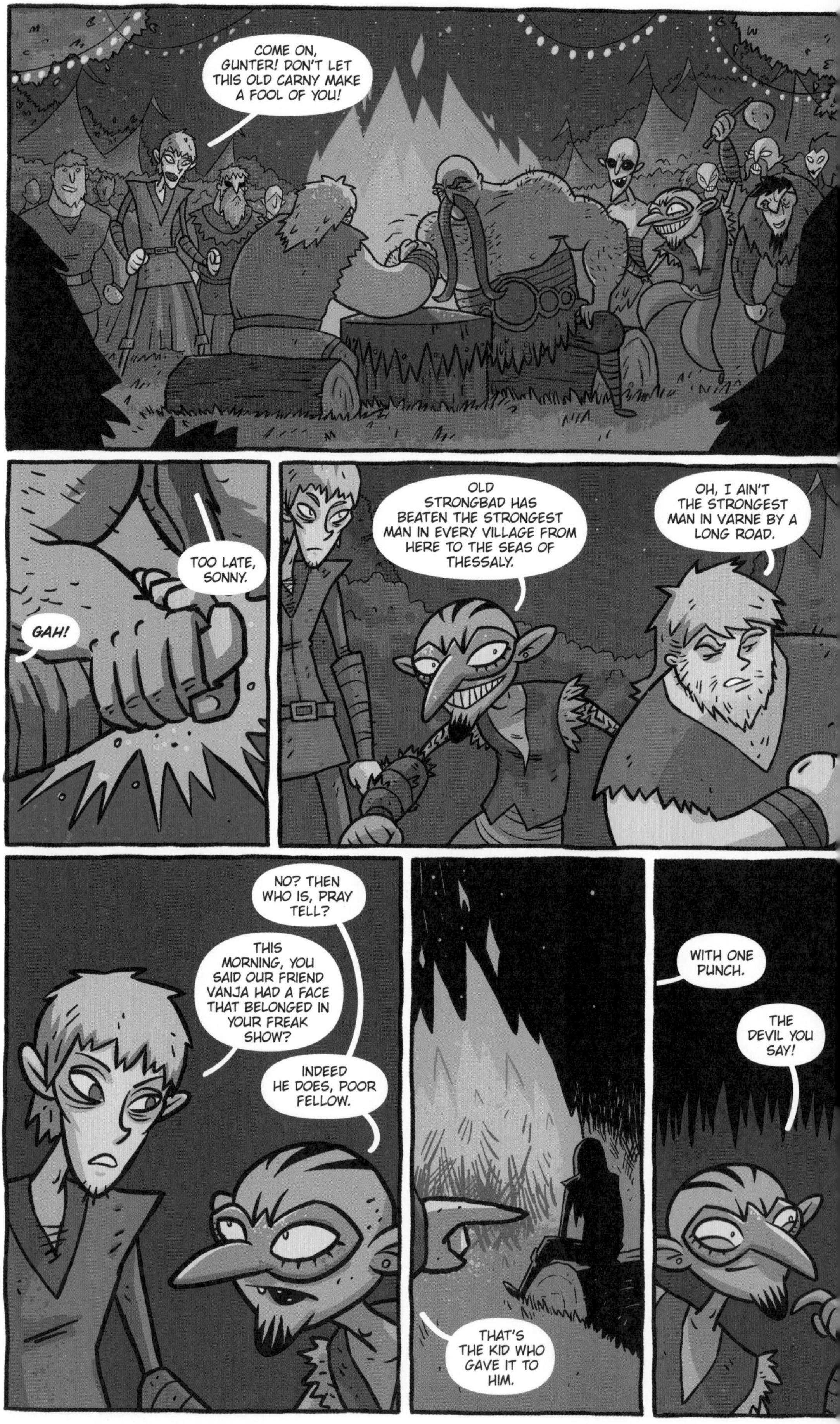
COME ON, GUNTER! DON'T LET THIS OLD CARNY MAKE A FOOL OF YOU!
TOO LATE, SONNY.
GAH!
OLD STRONGBAD HAS BEATEN THE STRONGEST MAN IN EVERY VILLAGE FROM HERE TO THE SEAS OF THESSALY.
OH, I AIN'T THE STRONGEST MAN IN VARNE BY A LONG ROAD.
NO? THEN WHO IS, PRAY TELL?
THIS MORNING, YOU SAID OUR FRIEND VANJA HAD A FACE THAT BELONGED IN YOUR FREAK SHOW?
INDEED HE DOES, POOR FELLOW.
THAT'S THE KID WHO GAVE IT TO HIM.
WITH ONE PUNCH.
THE DEVIL YOU SAY!

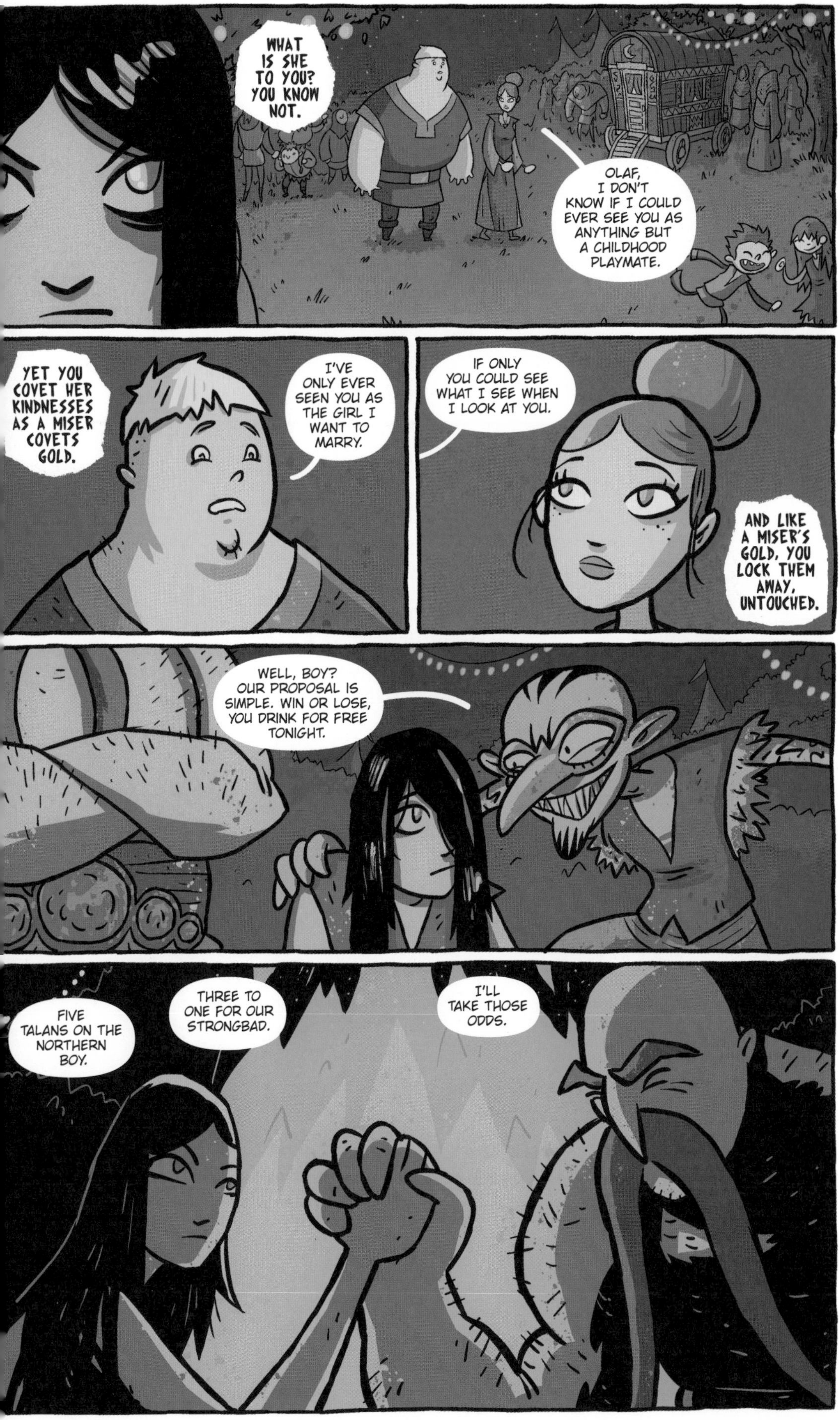

WHAT IS SHE TO YOU? YOU KNOW NOT.
OLAF, I DON'T KNOW IF I COULD EVER SEE YOU AS ANYTHING BUT A CHILDHOOD PLAYMATE.
YET YOU COVET HER KINDNESSES AS A MISER COVETS GOLD.
I'VE ONLY EVER SEEN YOU AS THE GIRL I WANT TO MARRY.
IF ONLY YOU COULD SEE WHAT I SEE WHEN I LOOK AT YOU.
AND LIKE A MISER'S GOLD, YOU LOCK THEM AWAY, UNTOUCHED.
WELL, BOY? OUR PROPOSAL IS SIMPLE. WIN OR LOSE, YOU DRINK FOR FREE TONIGHT.
FIVE TALANS ON THE NORTHERN BOY.
THREE TO ONE FOR OUR STRONGBAD.
I'LL TAKE THOSE ODDS.

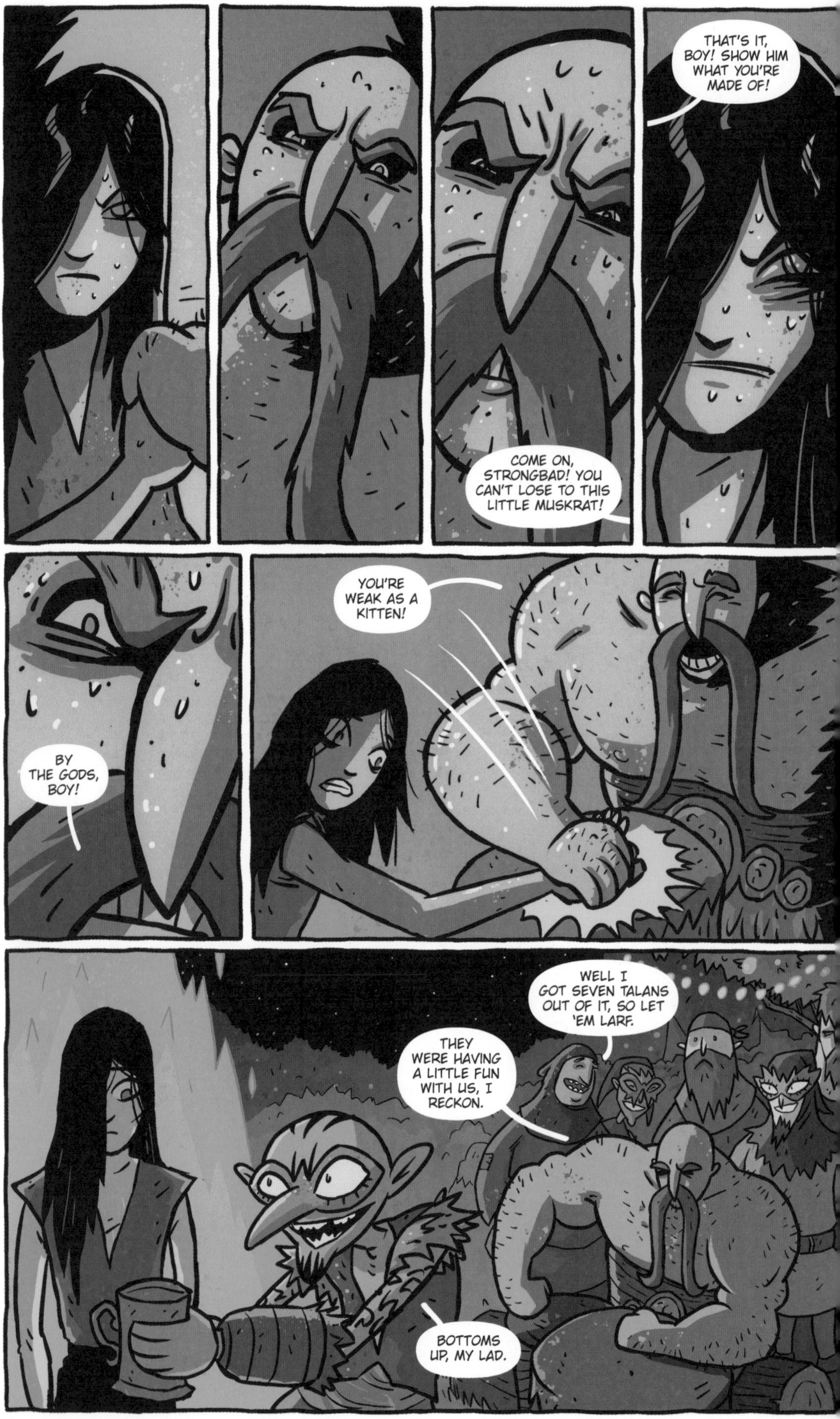
THAT'S IT, BOY! SHOW HIM WHAT YOU'RE MADE OF!
COME ON, STRONGBAD! YOU CAN'T LOSE TO THIS LITTLE MUSKRAT!
BY THE GODS, BOY!
YOU'RE WEAK AS A KITTEN!
WELL I GOT SEVEN TALANS OUT OF IT, SO LET 'EM LARF.
THEY WERE HAVING A LITTLE FUN WITH US, I RECKON.
BOTTOMS UP, MY LAD.

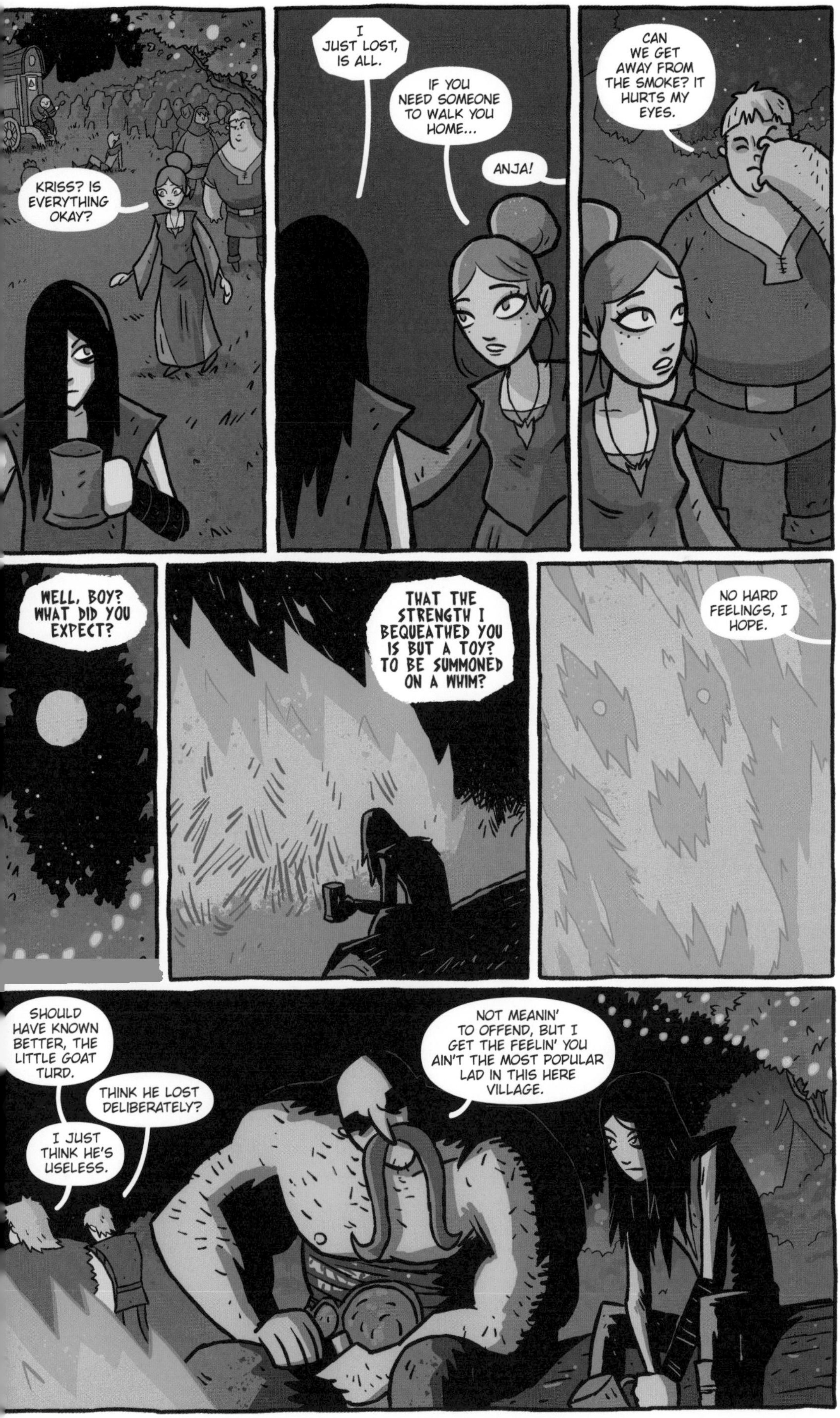
KRISS? IS EVERYTHING OKAY?
I JUST LOST, IS ALL.
IF YOU NEED SOMEONE TO WALK YOU HOME...
ANJA!
CAN WE GET AWAY FROM THE SMOKE? IT HURTS MY EYES.
WELL, BOY? WHAT DID YOU EXPECT?
THAT THE STRENGTH I BEQUEATHED YOU IS BUT A TOY? TO BE SUMMONED ON A WHIM?
NO HARD FEELINGS, I HOPE.
SHOULD HAVE KNOWN BETTER, THE LITTLE GOAT TURD.
THINK HE LOST DELIBERATELY?
I JUST THINK HE'S USELESS.
NOT MEANIN' TO OFFEND, BUT I GET THE FEELIN' YOU AIN'T THE MOST POPULAR LAD IN THIS HERE VILLAGE.

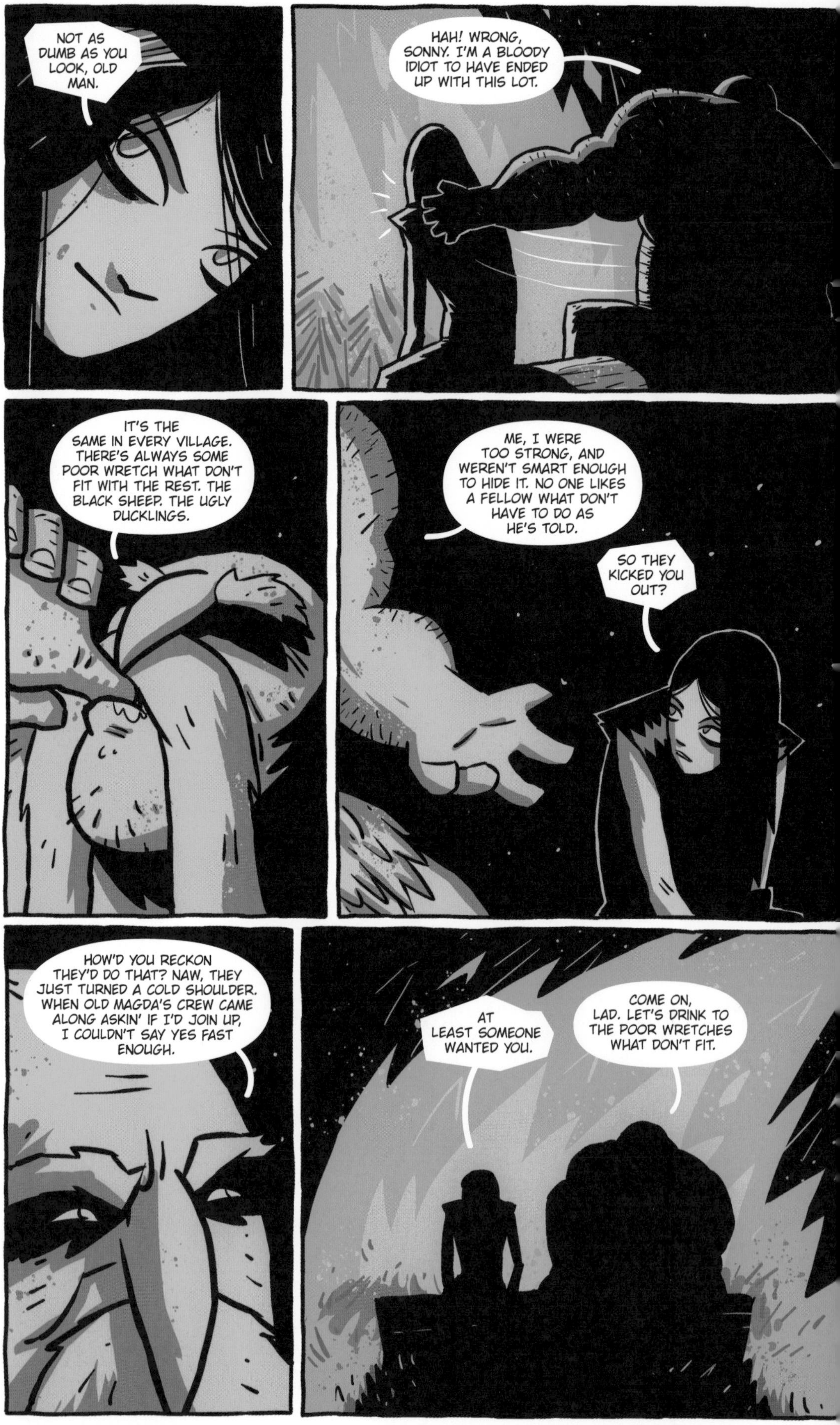
NOT AS DUMB AS YOU LOOK, OLD MAN.
HAH! WRONG, SONNY. I'M A BLOODY IDIOT TO HAVE ENDED UP WITH THIS LOT.
IT'S THE SAME IN EVERY VILLAGE. THERE'S ALWAYS SOME POOR WRETCH WHAT DON'T FIT WITH THE REST. THE BLACK SHEEP. THE UGLY DUCKLINGS.
ME, I WERE TOO STRONG, AND WEREN'T SMART ENOUGH TO HIDE IT. NO ONE LIKES A FELLOW WHAT DON'T HAVE TO DO AS HE'S TOLD.
SO THEY KICKED YOU OUT?
HOW'D YOU RECKON THEY'D DO THAT? NAW, THEY JUST TURNED A COLD SHOULDER. WHEN OLD MAGDA'S CREW CAME ALONG ASKIN' IF I'D JOIN UP, I COULDN'T SAY YES FAST ENOUGH.
AT LEAST SOMEONE WANTED YOU.
COME ON, LAD. LET'S DRINK TO THE POOR WRETCHES WHAT DON'T FIT.

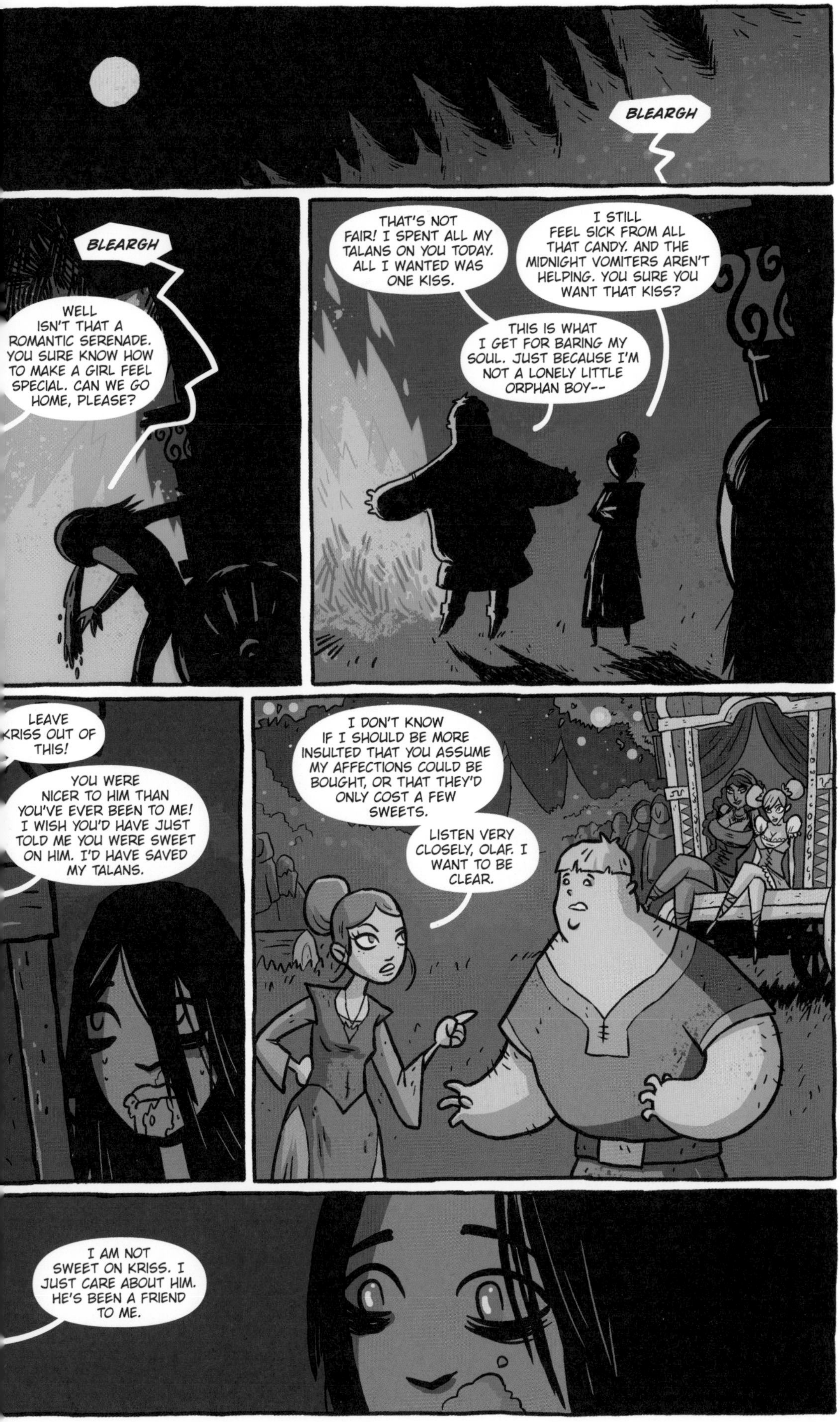
BLEARGH
BLEARGH
WELL ISN'T THAT A ROMANTIC SERENADE. YOU SURE KNOW HOW TO MAKE A GIRL FEEL SPECIAL. CAN WE GO HOME, PLEASE?
THAT'S NOT FAIR! I SPENT ALL MY TALANS ON YOU TODAY. ALL I WANTED WAS ONE KISS.
I STILL FEEL SICK FROM ALL THAT CANDY. AND THE MIDNIGHT VOMITERS AREN'T HELPING. YOU SURE YOU WANT THAT KISS?
THIS IS WHAT I GET FOR BARING MY SOUL. JUST BECAUSE I'M NOT A LONELY LITTLE ORPHAN BOY--
LEAVE KRISS OUT OF THIS!
YOU WERE NICER TO HIM THAN YOU'VE EVER BEEN TO ME! I WISH YOU'D HAVE JUST TOLD ME YOU WERE SWEET ON HIM. I'D HAVE SAVED MY TALANS.
I DON'T KNOW IF I SHOULD BE MORE INSULTED THAT YOU ASSUME MY AFFECTIONS COULD BE BOUGHT, OR THAT THEY'D ONLY COST A FEW SWEETS.
LISTEN VERY CLOSELY, OLAF. I WANT TO BE CLEAR.
I AM NOT SWEET ON KRISS. I JUST CARE ABOUT HIM. HE'S BEEN A FRIEND TO ME.

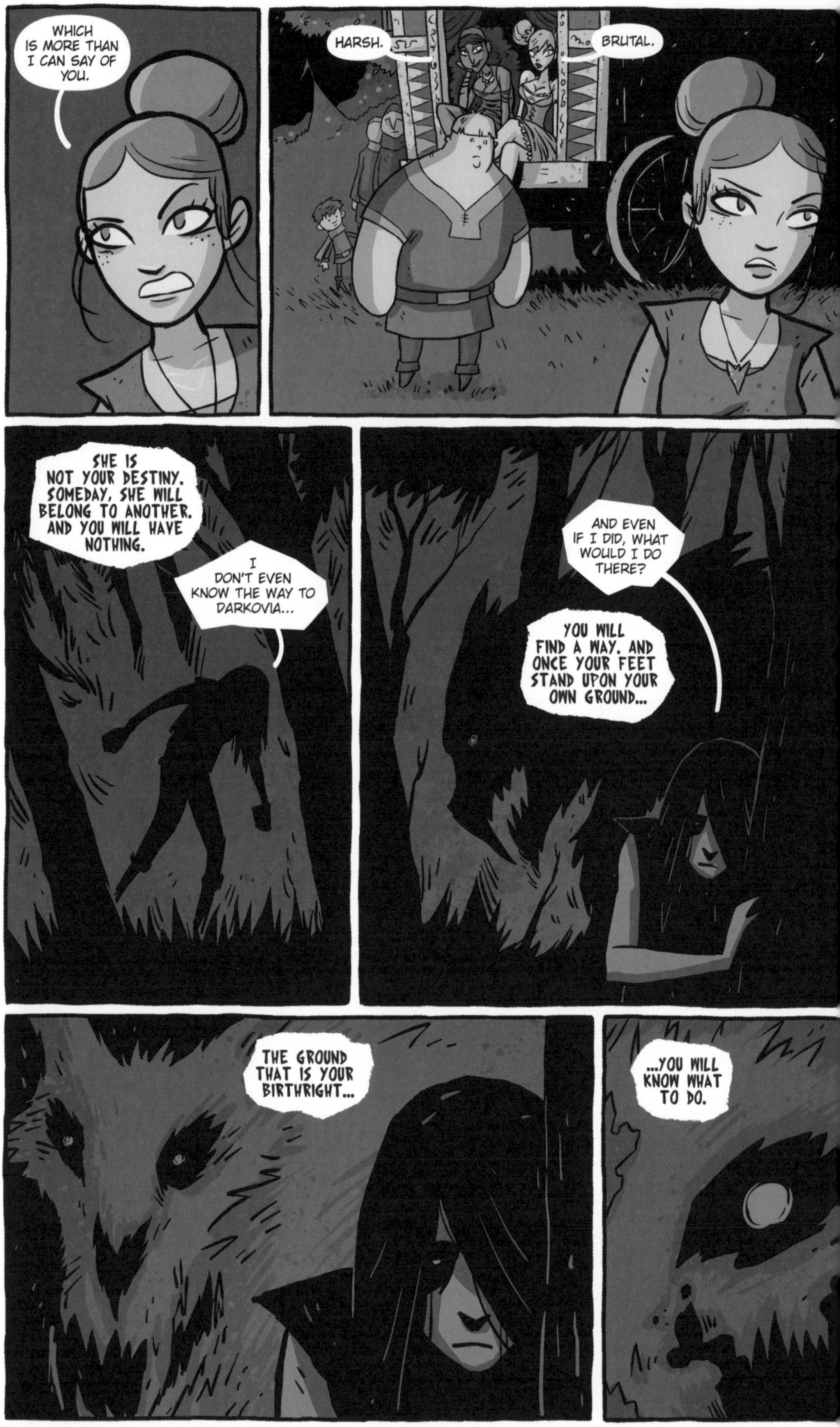
WHICH IS MORE THAN I CAN SAY OF YOU.
HARSH.
BRUTAL.
SHE IS NOT YOUR DESTINY. SOMEDAY, SHE WILL BELONG TO ANOTHER. AND YOU WILL HAVE NOTHING.
I DON'T EVEN KNOW THE WAY TO DARKOVIA...
AND EVEN IF I DID, WHAT WOULD I DO THERE?
YOU WILL FIND A WAY. AND ONCE YOUR FEET STAND UPON YOUR OWN GROUND...
THE GROUND THAT IS YOUR BIRTHRIGHT...
...YOU WILL KNOW WHAT TO DO.

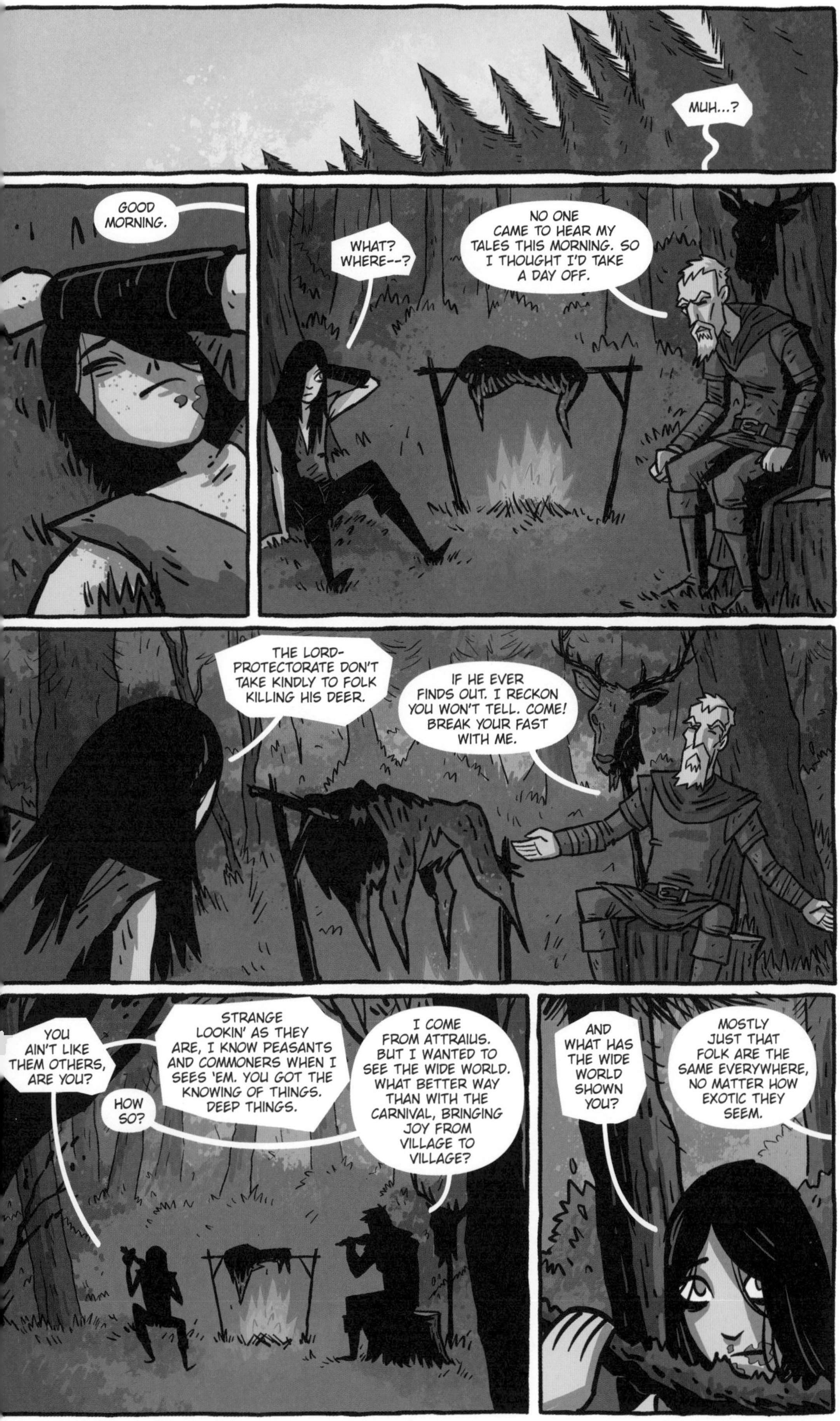
MUH...?
GOOD MORNING.
WHAT? WHERE--?
NO ONE CAME TO HEAR MY TALES THIS MORNING. SO I THOUGHT I'D TAKE A DAY OFF.
THE LORD-PROTECTORATE DON'T TAKE KINDLY TO FOLK KILLING HIS DEER.
IF HE EVER FINDS OUT. I RECKON YOU WON'T TELL. COME! BREAK YOUR FAST WITH ME.
YOU AIN'T LIKE THEM OTHERS, ARE YOU?
HOW SO?
STRANGE LOOKIN' AS THEY ARE, I KNOW PEASANTS AND COMMONERS WHEN I SEES 'EM. YOU GOT THE KNOWING OF THINGS. DEEP THINGS.
I COME FROM ATTRAIUS. BUT I WANTED TO SEE THE WIDE WORLD. WHAT BETTER WAY THAN WITH THE CARNIVAL, BRINGING JOY FROM VILLAGE TO VILLAGE?
AND WHAT HAS THE WIDE WORLD SHOWN YOU?
MOSTLY JUST THAT FOLK ARE THE SAME EVERYWHERE, NO MATTER HOW EXOTIC THEY SEEM.

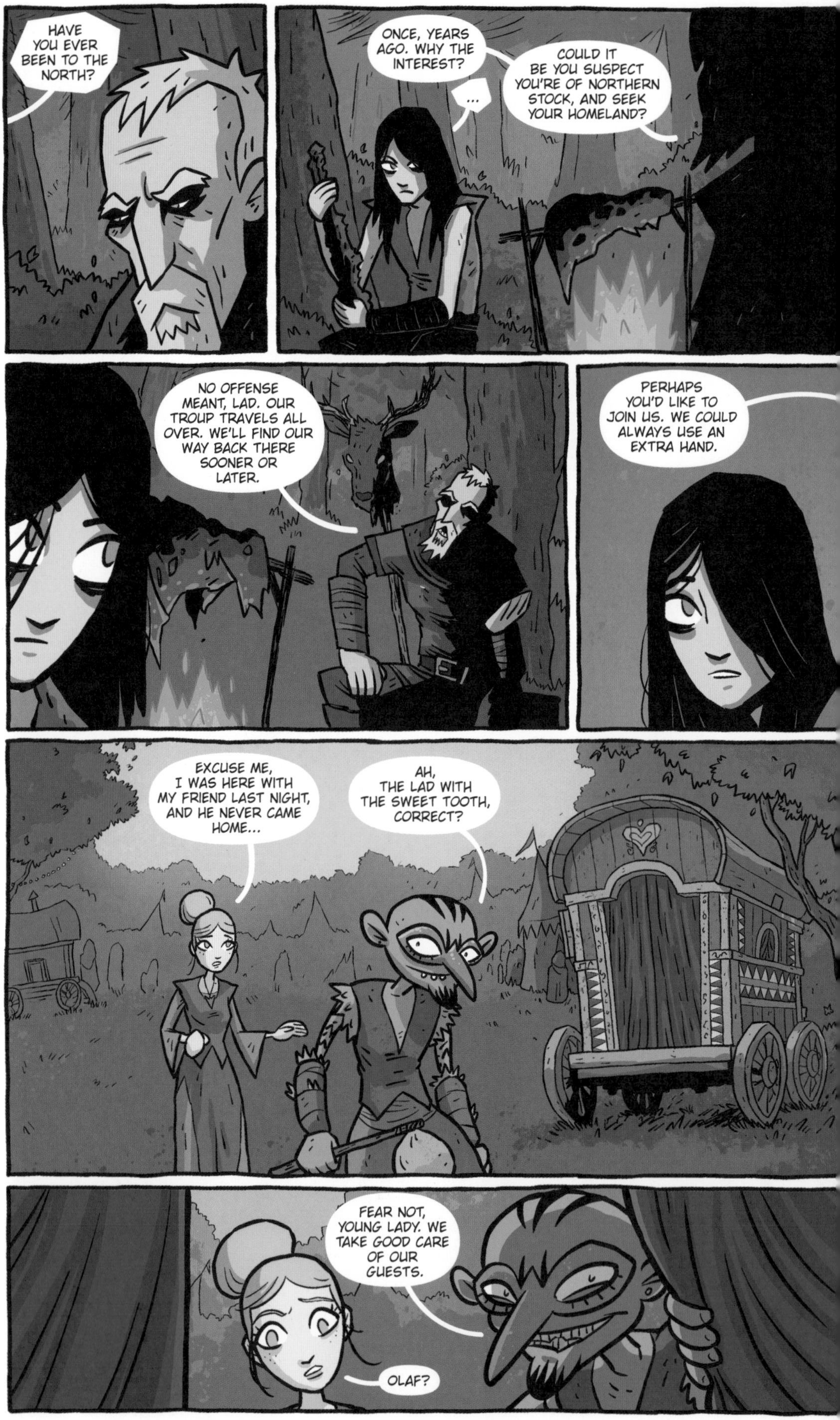
HAVE YOU EVER BEEN TO THE NORTH?
ONCE, YEARS AGO. WHY THE INTEREST?
...
COULD IT BE YOU SUSPECT YOU'RE OF NORTHERN STOCK, AND SEEK YOUR HOMELAND?
NO OFFENSE MEANT, LAD. OUR TROUP TRAVELS ALL OVER. WE'LL FIND OUR WAY BACK THERE SOONER OR LATER.
PERHAPS YOU'D LIKE TO JOIN US. WE COULD ALWAYS USE AN EXTRA HAND.
EXCUSE ME, I WAS HERE WITH MY FRIEND LAST NIGHT, AND HE NEVER CAME HOME...
AH, THE LAD WITH THE SWEET TOOTH, CORRECT?
FEAR NOT, YOUNG LADY. WE TAKE GOOD CARE OF OUR GUESTS.
OLAF?

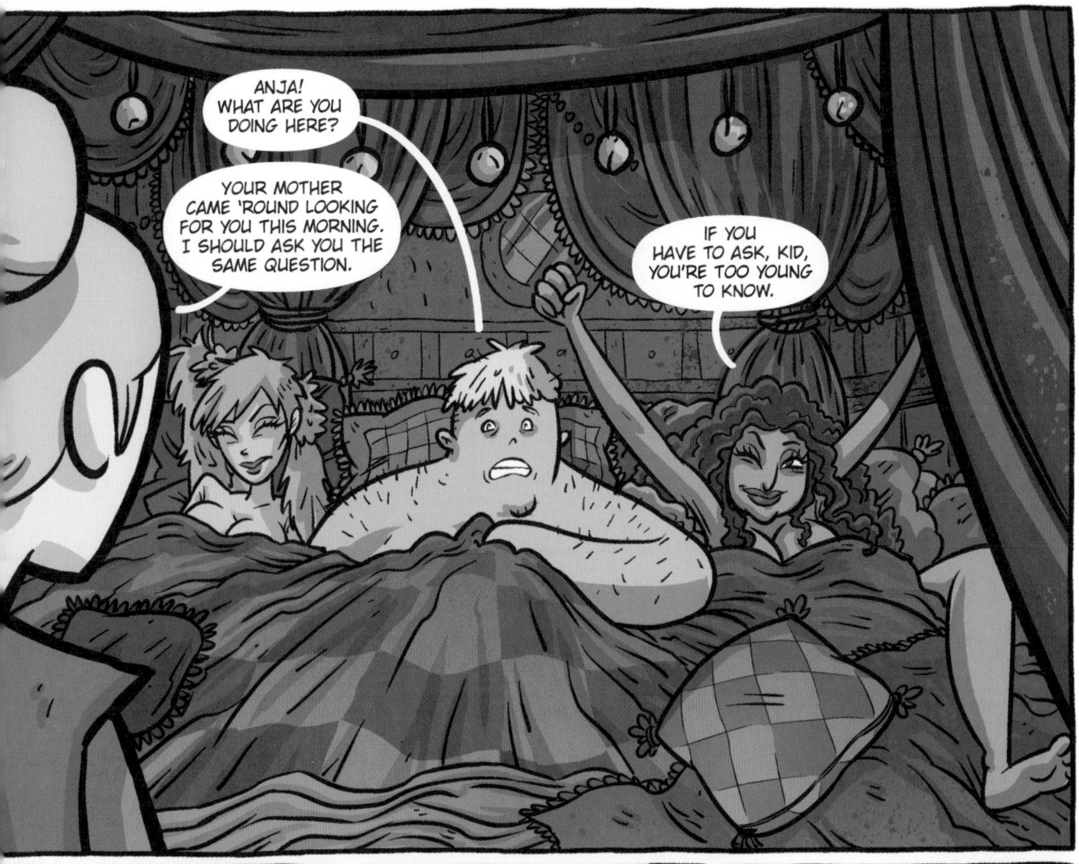
ANJA! WHAT ARE YOU DOING HERE?
YOUR MOTHER CAME 'ROUND LOOKING FOR YOU THIS MORNING. I SHOULD ASK YOU THE SAME QUESTION.
IF YOU HAVE TO ASK, KID, YOU'RE TOO YOUNG TO KNOW.

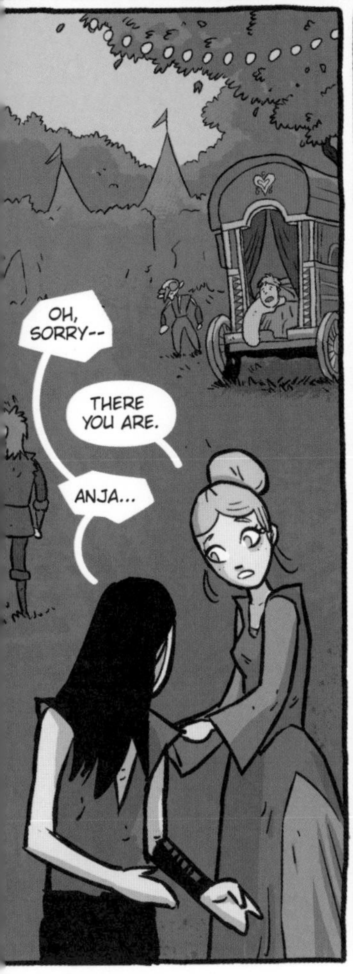
OH, SORRY--
THERE YOU ARE.
ANJA...

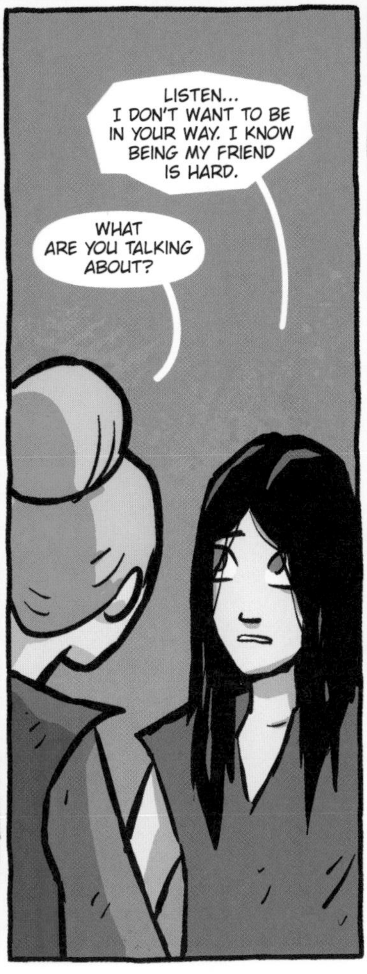
LISTEN... I DON'T WANT TO BE IN YOUR WAY. I KNOW BEING MY FRIEND IS HARD.
WHAT ARE YOU TALKING ABOUT?

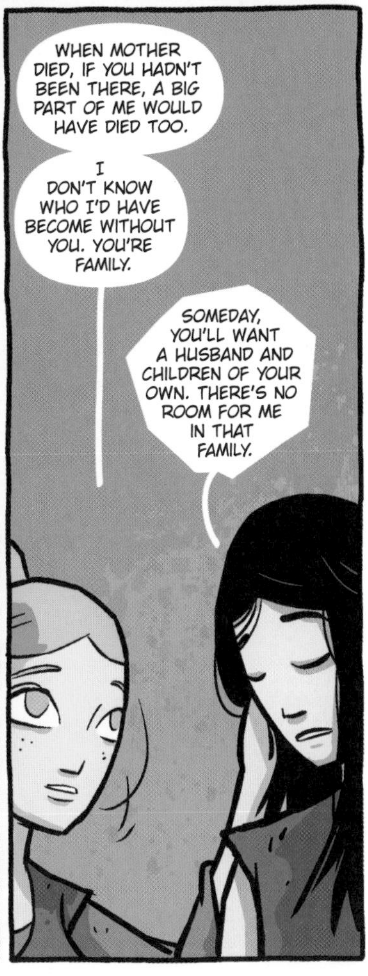
WHEN MOTHER DIED, IF YOU HADN'T BEEN THERE, A BIG PART OF ME WOULD HAVE DIED TOO.
I DON'T KNOW WHO I'D HAVE BECOME WITHOUT YOU. YOU'RE FAMILY.
SOMEDAY, YOU'LL WANT A HUSBAND AND CHILDREN OF YOUR OWN. THERE'S NO ROOM FOR ME IN THAT FAMILY.

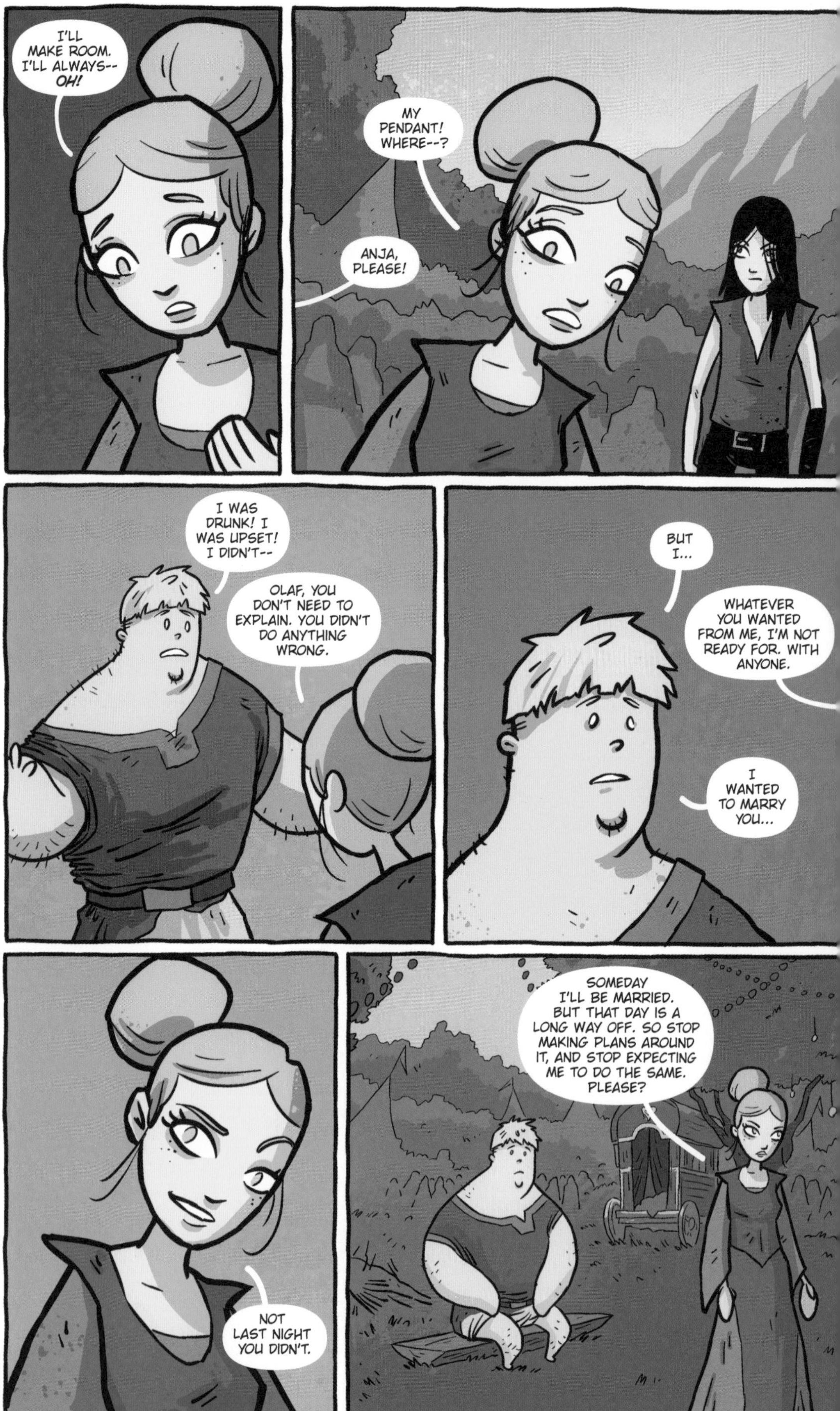
I'LL MAKE ROOM. I'LL ALWAYS-- OH!
MY PENDANT! WHERE--?
ANJA, PLEASE!
I WAS DRUNK! I WAS UPSET! I DIDN'T--
OLAF, YOU DON'T NEED TO EXPLAIN. YOU DIDN'T DO ANYTHING WRONG.
BUT I...
WHATEVER YOU WANTED FROM ME, I'M NOT READY FOR. WITH ANYONE.
I WANTED TO MARRY YOU...
NOT LAST NIGHT YOU DIDN'T.
SOMEDAY I'LL BE MARRIED. BUT THAT DAY IS A LONG WAY OFF. SO STOP MAKING PLANS AROUND IT, AND STOP EXPECTING ME TO DO THE SAME. PLEASE?

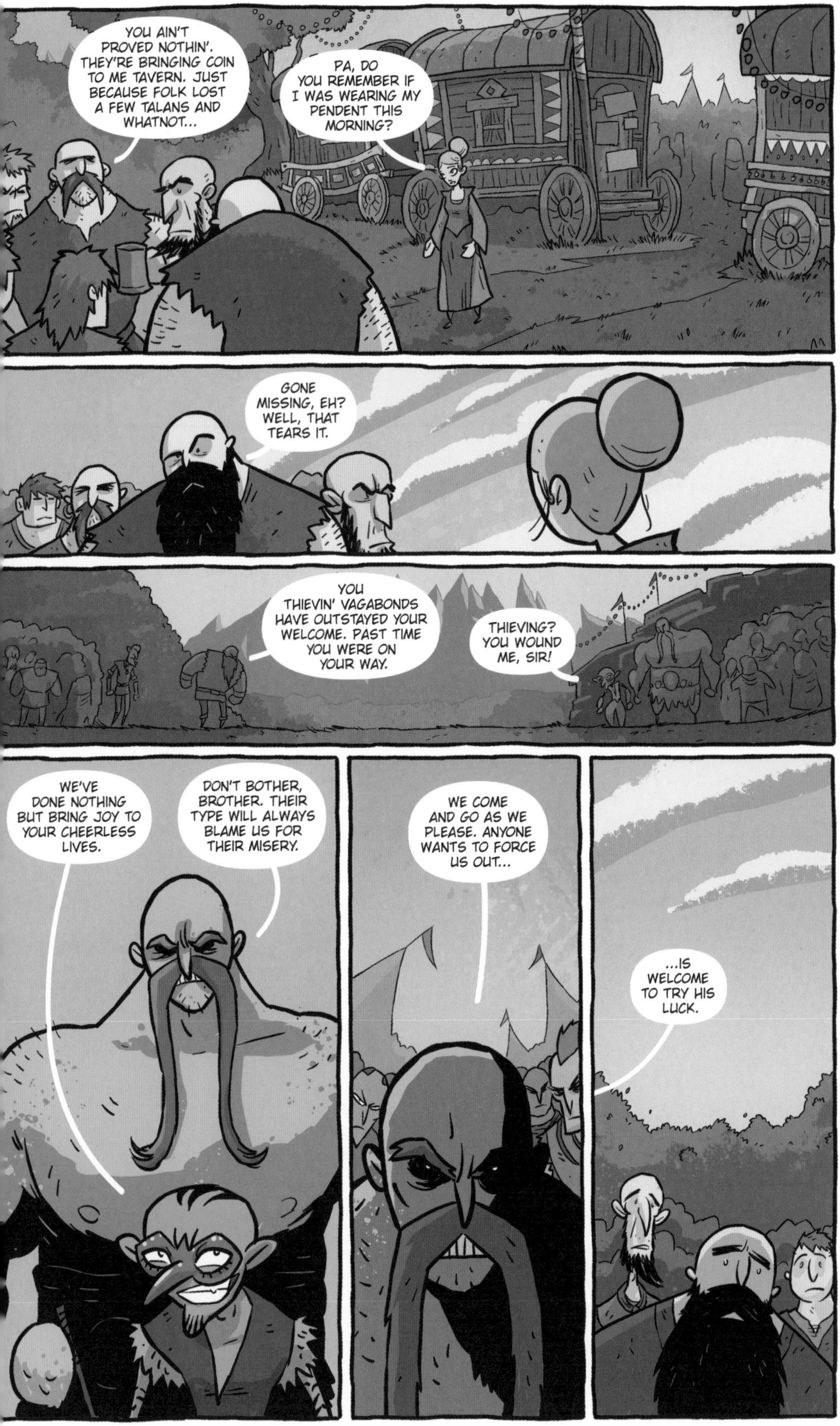
YOU AIN'T PROVED NOTHIN'. THEY'RE BRINGING COIN TO ME TAVERN. JUST BECAUSE FOLK LOST A FEW TALANS AND WHATNOT...
PA, DO YOU REMEMBER IF I WAS WEARING MY PENDENT THIS MORNING?
GONE MISSING, EH? WELL, THAT TEARS IT.
YOU THIEVIN' VAGABONDS HAVE OUTSTAYED YOUR WELCOME. PAST TIME YOU WERE ON YOUR WAY.
THIEVING? YOU WOUND ME, SIR!
WE'VE DONE NOTHING BUT BRING JOY TO YOUR CHEERLESS LIVES.
DON'T BOTHER, BROTHER. THEIR TYPE WILL ALWAYS BLAME US FOR THEIR MISERY.
WE COME AND GO AS WE PLEASE. ANYONE WANTS TO FORCE US OUT...
...IS WELCOME TO TRY HIS LUCK.

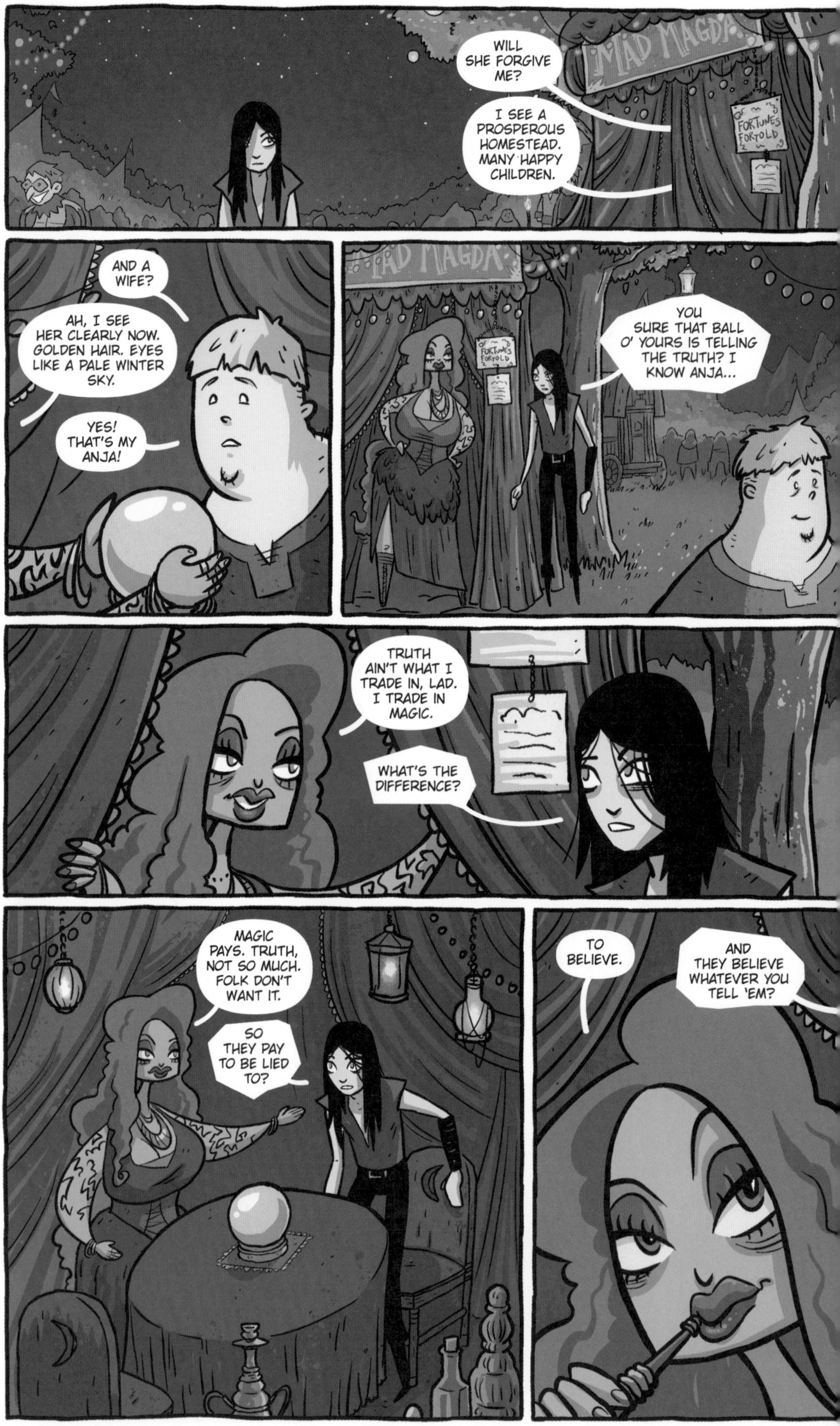

MAD MAGDA
FORTUNES FORTOLD
WILL SHE FORGIVE ME?
I SEE A PROSPEROUS HOMESTEAD. MANY HAPPY CHILDREN.
AND A WIFE?
AH, I SEE HER CLEARLY NOW. GOLDEN HAIR. EYES LIKE A PALE WINTER SKY.
YES! THAT'S MY ANJA!
MAD MAGDA
FORTUNES FORTOLD
YOU SURE THAT BALL O' YOURS IS TELLING THE TRUTH? I KNOW ANJA...
TRUTH AIN'T WHAT I TRADE IN, LAD. I TRADE IN MAGIC.
WHAT'S THE DIFFERENCE?
MAGIC PAYS. TRUTH, NOT SO MUCH. FOLK DON'T WANT IT.
SO THEY PAY TO BE LIED TO?
AND THEY BELIEVE WHATEVER YOU TELL 'EM?
TO BELIEVE.

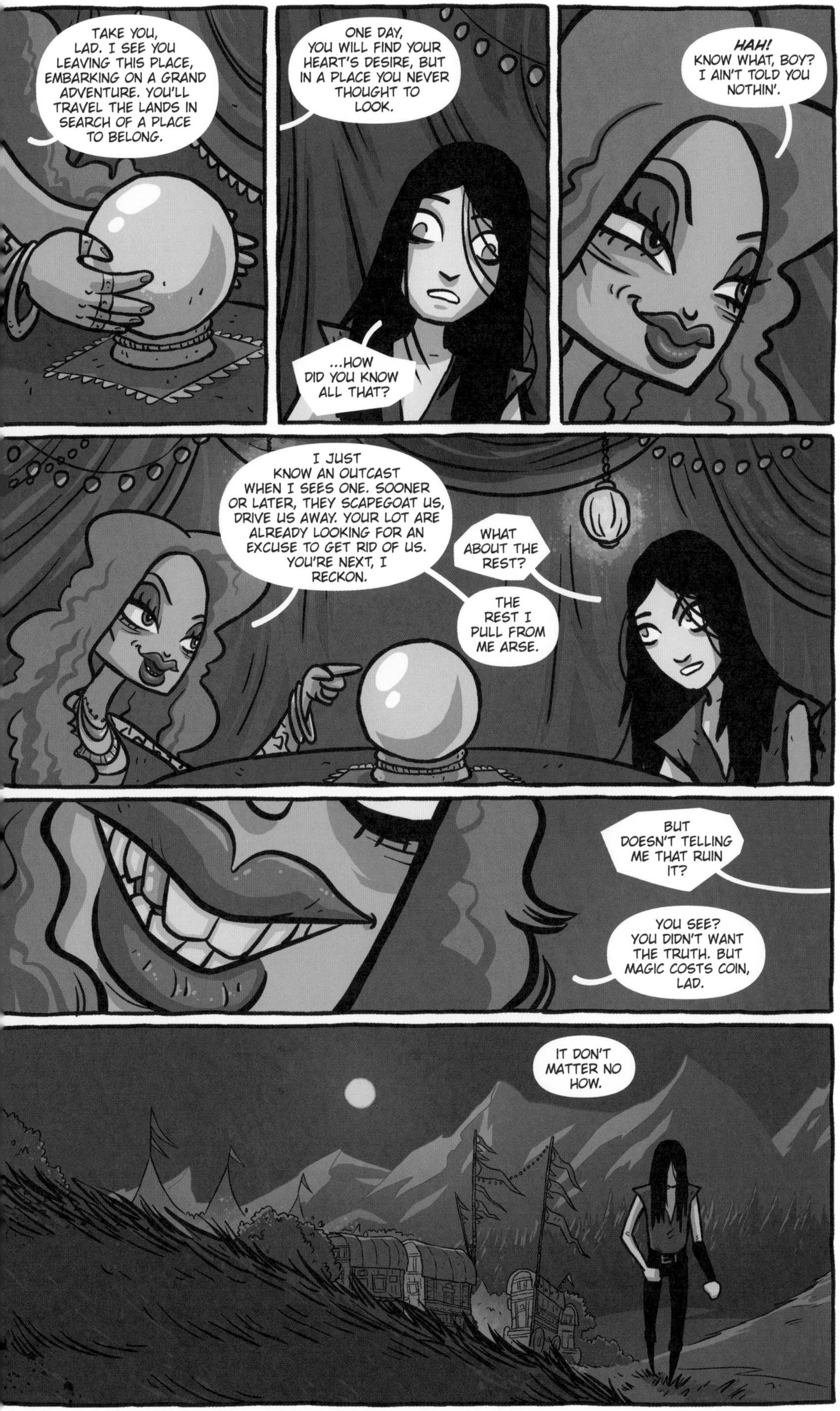
TAKE YOU, LAD. I SEE YOU LEAVING THIS PLACE, EMBARKING ON A GRAND ADVENTURE. YOU'LL TRAVEL THE LANDS IN SEARCH OF A PLACE TO BELONG.
ONE DAY, YOU WILL FIND YOUR HEART'S DESIRE, BUT IN A PLACE YOU NEVER THOUGHT TO LOOK.
...HOW DID YOU KNOW ALL THAT?
HAH! KNOW WHAT, BOY? I AIN'T TOLD YOU NOTHIN'.
I JUST KNOW AN OUTCAST WHEN I SEES ONE. SOONER OR LATER, THEY SCAPEGOAT US, DRIVE US AWAY. YOUR LOT ARE ALREADY LOOKING FOR AN EXCUSE TO GET RID OF US. YOU'RE NEXT, I RECKON.
WHAT ABOUT THE REST?
THE REST I PULL FROM ME ARSE.
BUT DOESN'T TELLING ME THAT RUIN IT?
YOU SEE? YOU DIDN'T WANT THE TRUTH. BUT MAGIC COSTS COIN, LAD.
IT DON'T MATTER NO HOW.

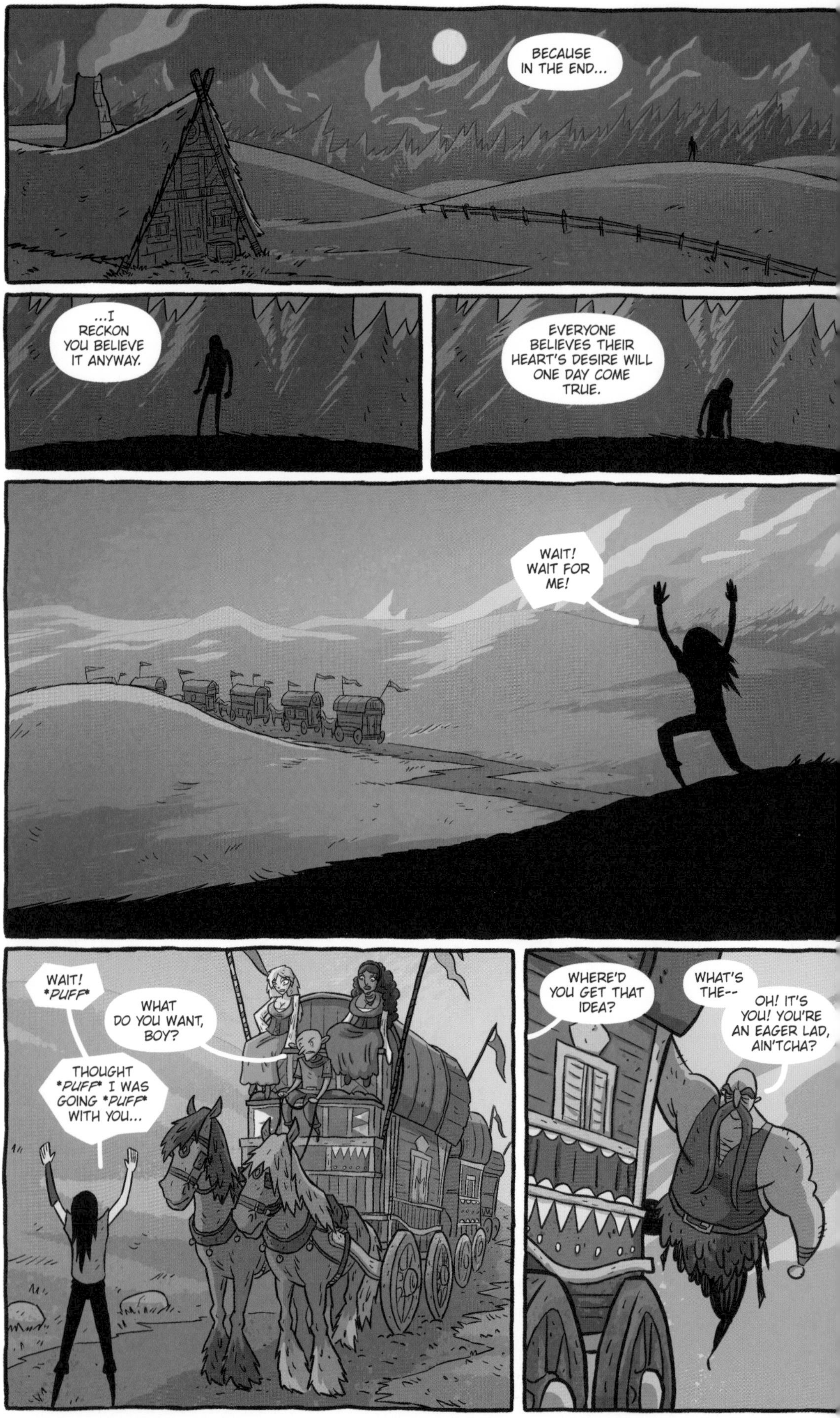
BECAUSE IN THE END...
...I RECKON YOU BELIEVE IT ANYWAY.
EVERYONE BELIEVES THEIR HEART'S DESIRE WILL ONE DAY COME TRUE.
WAIT! WAIT FOR ME!
WAIT! *PUFF*
THOUGHT *PUFF* I WAS GOING *PUFF* WITH YOU...
WHAT DO YOU WANT, BOY?
WHERE'D YOU GET THAT IDEA?
WHAT'S THE--
OH! IT'S YOU! YOU'RE AN EAGER LAD, AIN'TCHA?

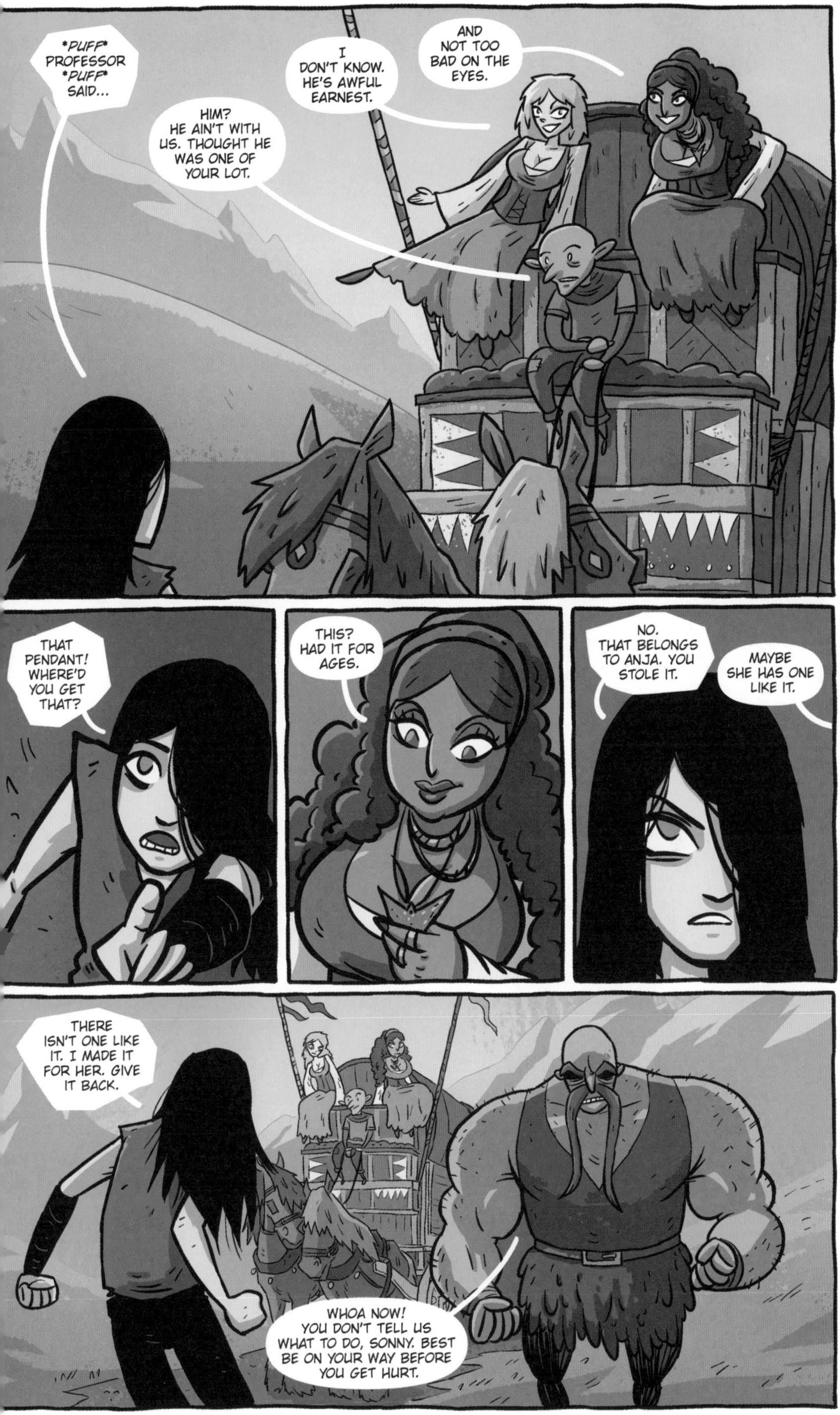
PUFF PROFESSOR *PUFF* SAID...
HIM? HE AIN'T WITH US. THOUGHT HE WAS ONE OF YOUR LOT.
I DON'T KNOW. HE'S AWFUL EARNEST.
AND NOT TOO BAD ON THE EYES.
THAT PENDANT! WHERE'D YOU GET THAT?
THIS? HAD IT FOR AGES.
NO. THAT BELONGS TO ANJA. YOU STOLE IT.
MAYBE SHE HAS ONE LIKE IT.
THERE ISN'T ONE LIKE IT. I MADE IT FOR HER. GIVE IT BACK.
WHOA NOW! YOU DON'T TELL US WHAT TO DO, SONNY. BEST BE ON YOUR WAY BEFORE YOU GET HURT.

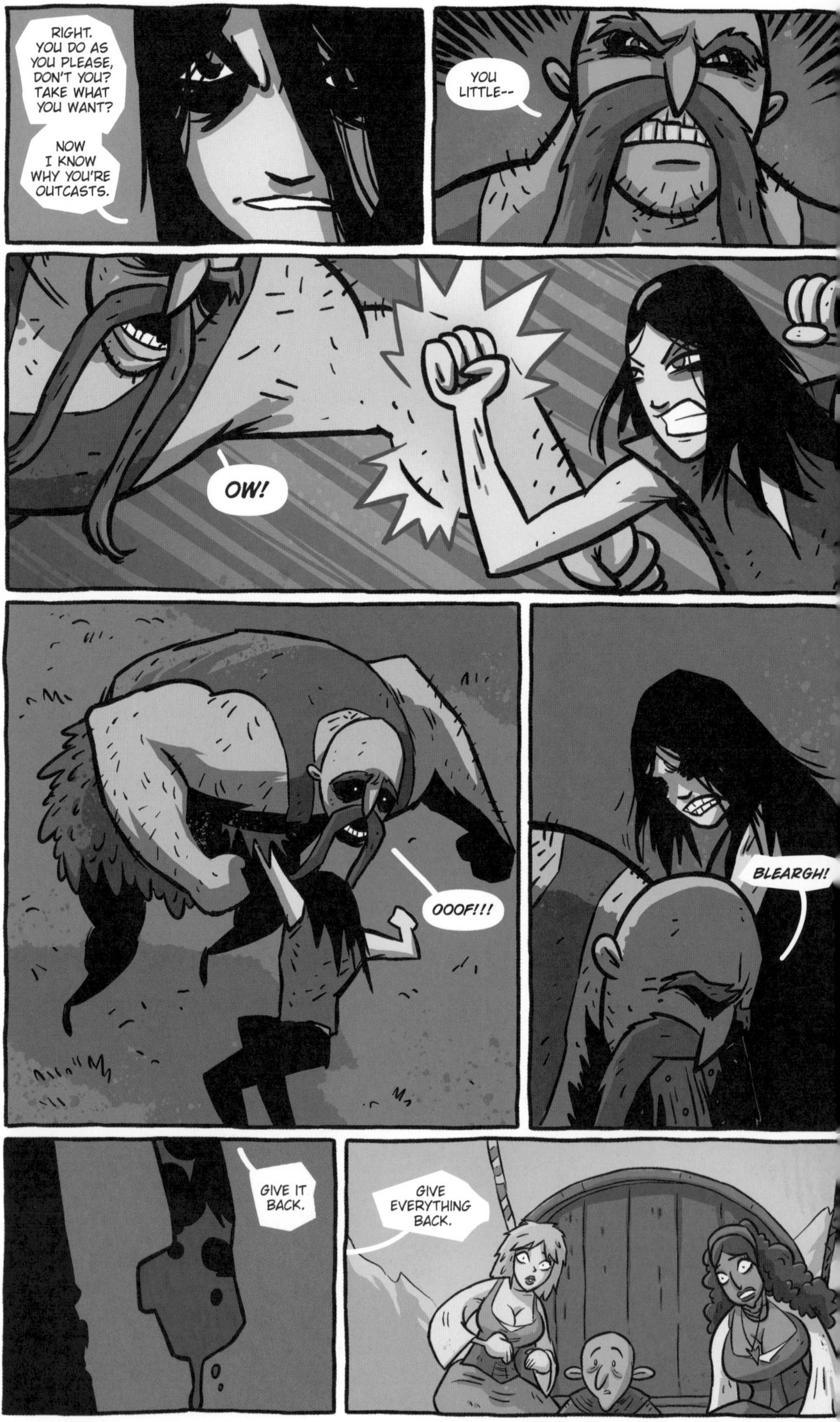
RIGHT. YOU DO AS YOU PLEASE, DON'T YOU? TAKE WHAT YOU WANT?
NOW I KNOW WHY YOU'RE OUTCASTS.
YOU LITTLE--
OW!
OOOF!!!
BLEARGH!
GIVE IT BACK.
GIVE EVERYTHING BACK.

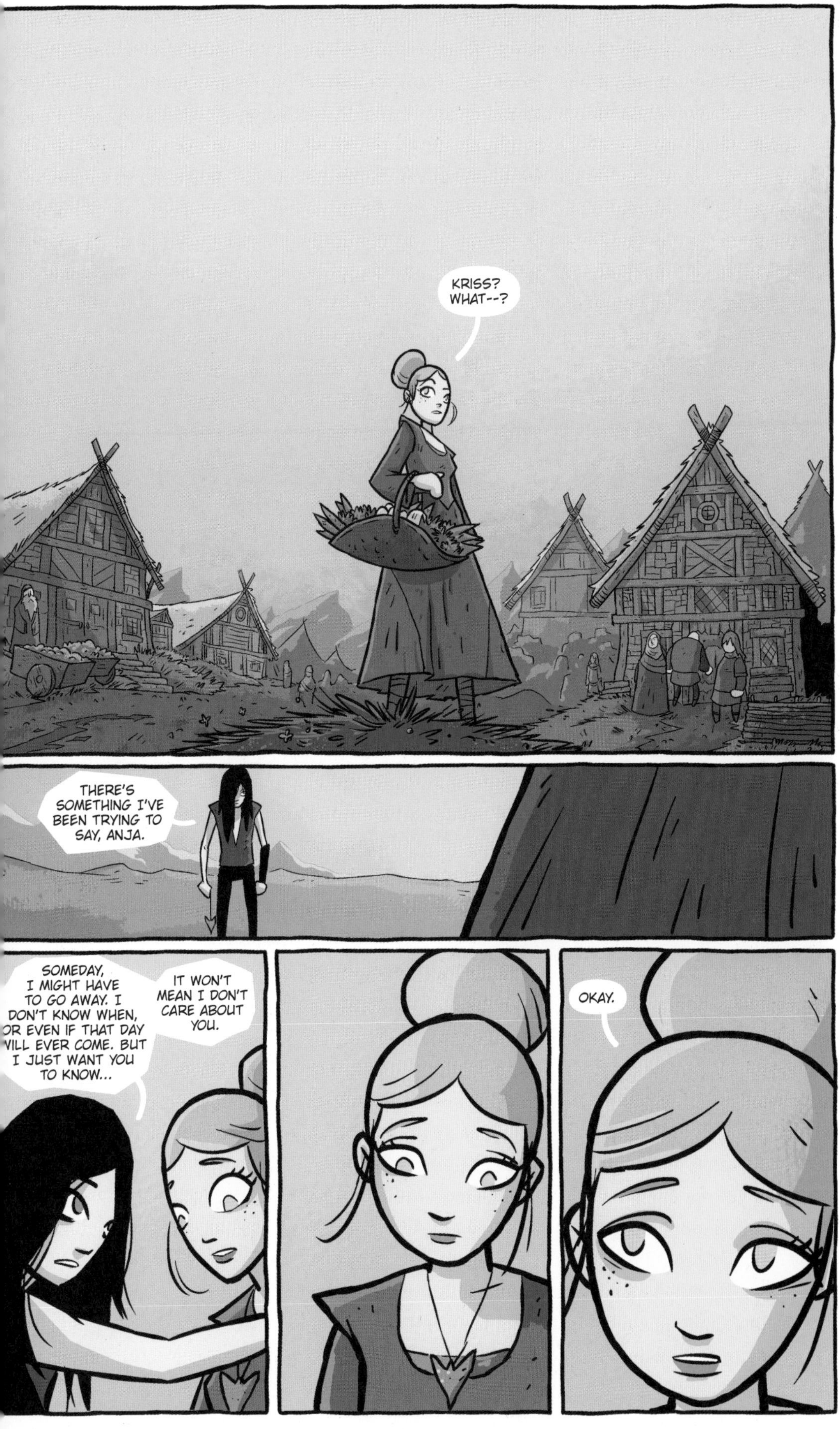
KRISS? WHAT--?
THERE'S SOMETHING I'VE BEEN TRYING TO SAY, ANJA.
SOMEDAY, I MIGHT HAVE TO GO AWAY. I DON'T KNOW WHEN, OR EVEN IF THAT DAY WILL EVER COME. BUT I JUST WANT YOU TO KNOW...
IT WON'T MEAN I DON'T CARE ABOUT YOU.
OKAY.

CHAPTER FOUR

ALL THAT YOU HOLD DEAR

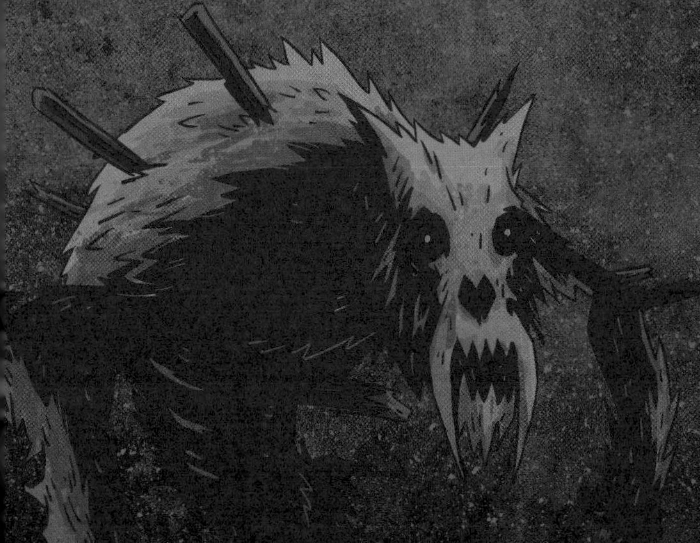

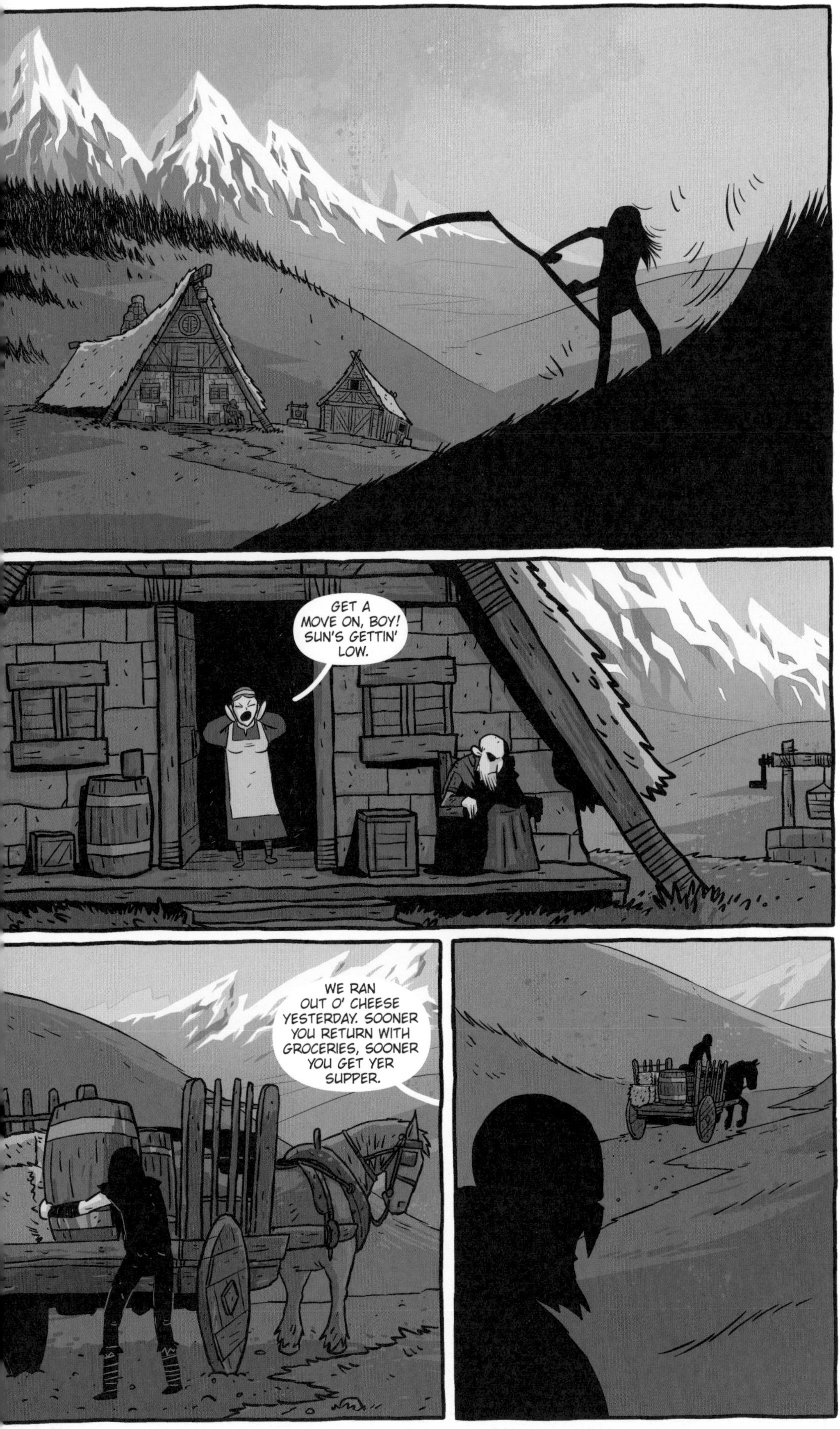
GET A MOVE ON, BOY! SUN'S GETTIN' LOW.
WE RAN OUT O' CHEESE YESTERDAY. SOONER YOU RETURN WITH GROCERIES, SOONER YOU GET YER SUPPER.

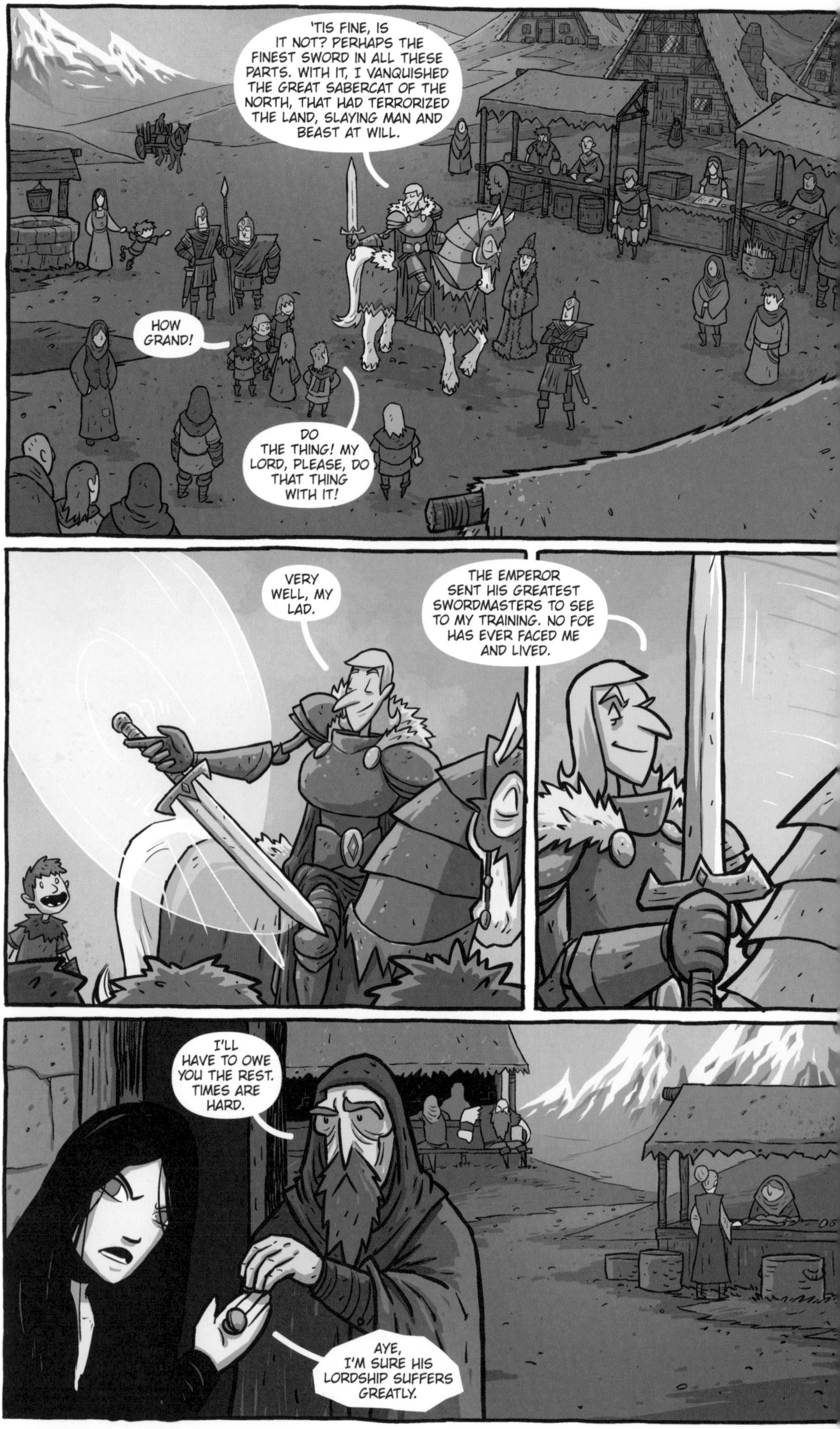
'TIS FINE, IS IT NOT? PERHAPS THE FINEST SWORD IN ALL THESE PARTS. WITH IT, I VANQUISHED THE GREAT SABERCAT OF THE NORTH, THAT HAD TERRORIZED THE LAND, SLAYING MAN AND BEAST AT WILL.
HOW GRAND!
DO THE THING! MY LORD, PLEASE, DO THAT THING WITH IT!
VERY WELL, MY LAD.
THE EMPEROR SENT HIS GREATEST SWORDMASTERS TO SEE TO MY TRAINING. NO FOE HAS EVER FACED ME AND LIVED.
I'LL HAVE TO OWE YOU THE REST. TIMES ARE HARD.
AYE, I'M SURE HIS LORDSHIP SUFFERS GREATLY.

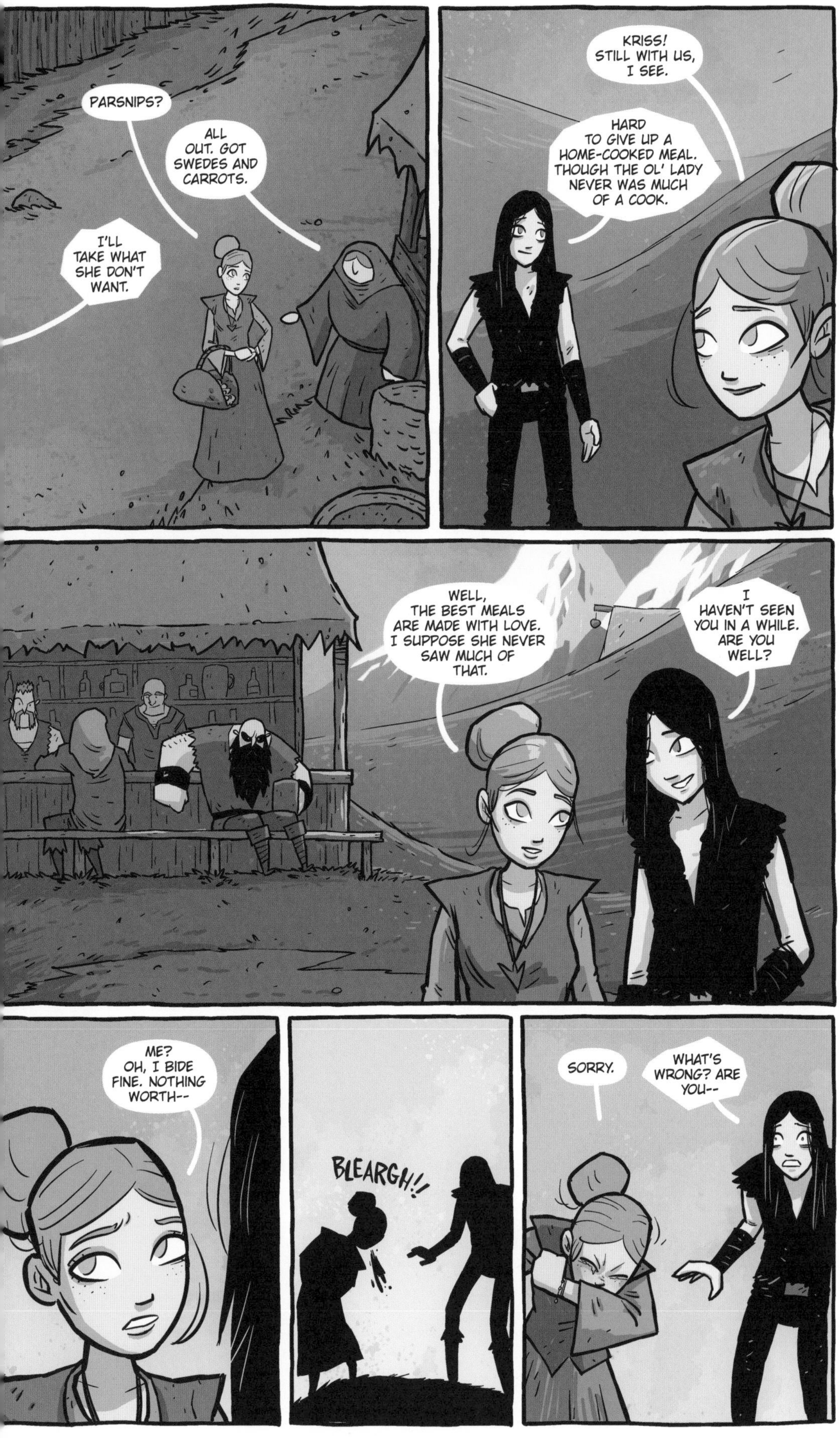
PARSNIPS?
ALL OUT. GOT SWEDES AND CARROTS.
I'LL TAKE WHAT SHE DON'T WANT.
KRISS! STILL WITH US, I SEE.
HARD TO GIVE UP A HOME-COOKED MEAL. THOUGH THE OL' LADY NEVER WAS MUCH OF A COOK.
WELL, THE BEST MEALS ARE MADE WITH LOVE. I SUPPOSE SHE NEVER SAW MUCH OF THAT.
I HAVEN'T SEEN YOU IN A WHILE. ARE YOU WELL?
ME? OH, I BIDE FINE. NOTHING WORTH--
BLEARGH!!
SORRY.
WHAT'S WRONG? ARE YOU--

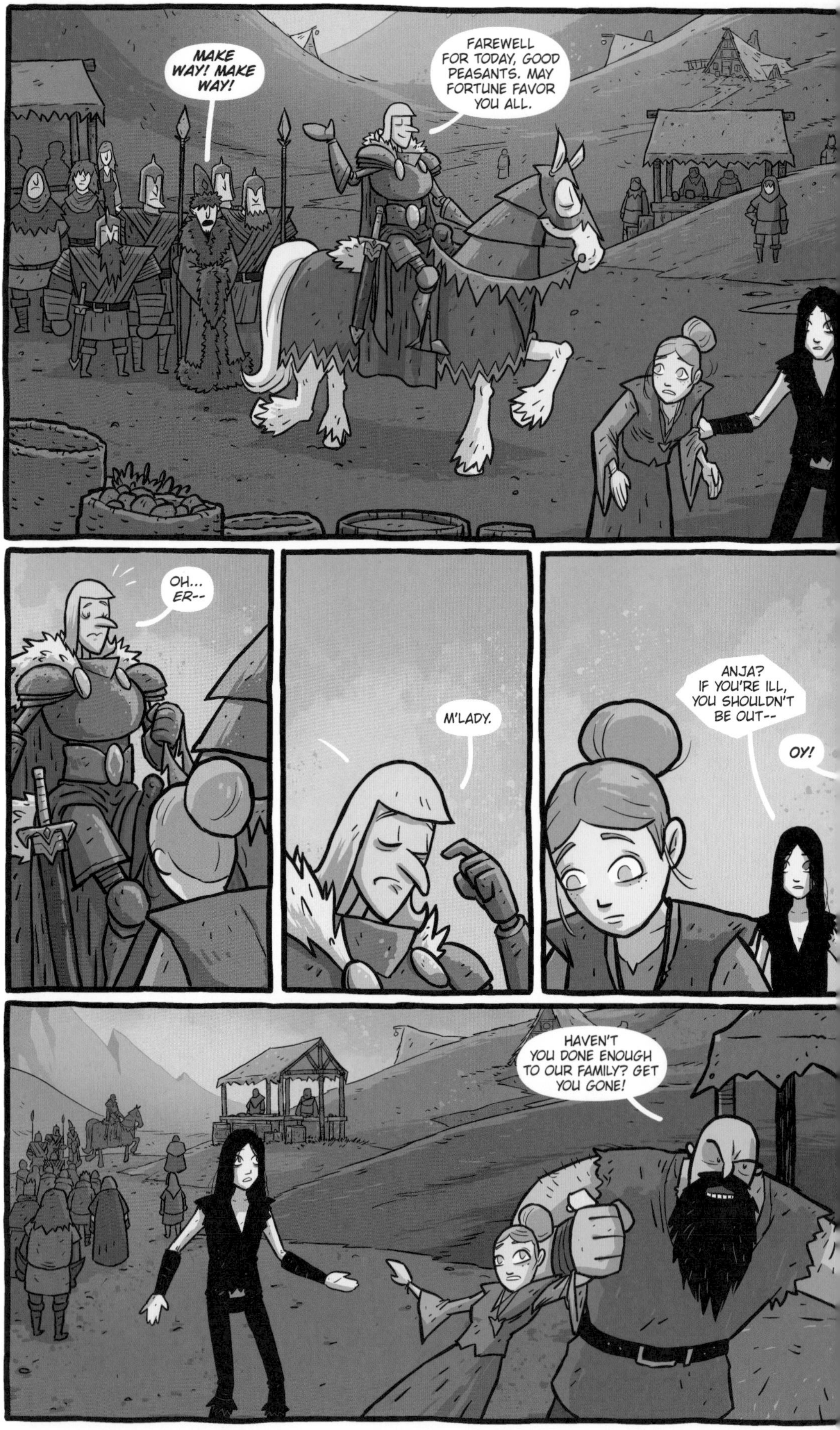
MAKE WAY! MAKE WAY!
FAREWELL FOR TODAY, GOOD PEASANTS. MAY FORTUNE FAVOR YOU ALL.
OH... ER--
M'LADY.
ANJA? IF YOU'RE ILL, YOU SHOULDN'T BE OUT--
OY!
HAVEN'T YOU DONE ENOUGH TO OUR FAMILY? GET YOU GONE!

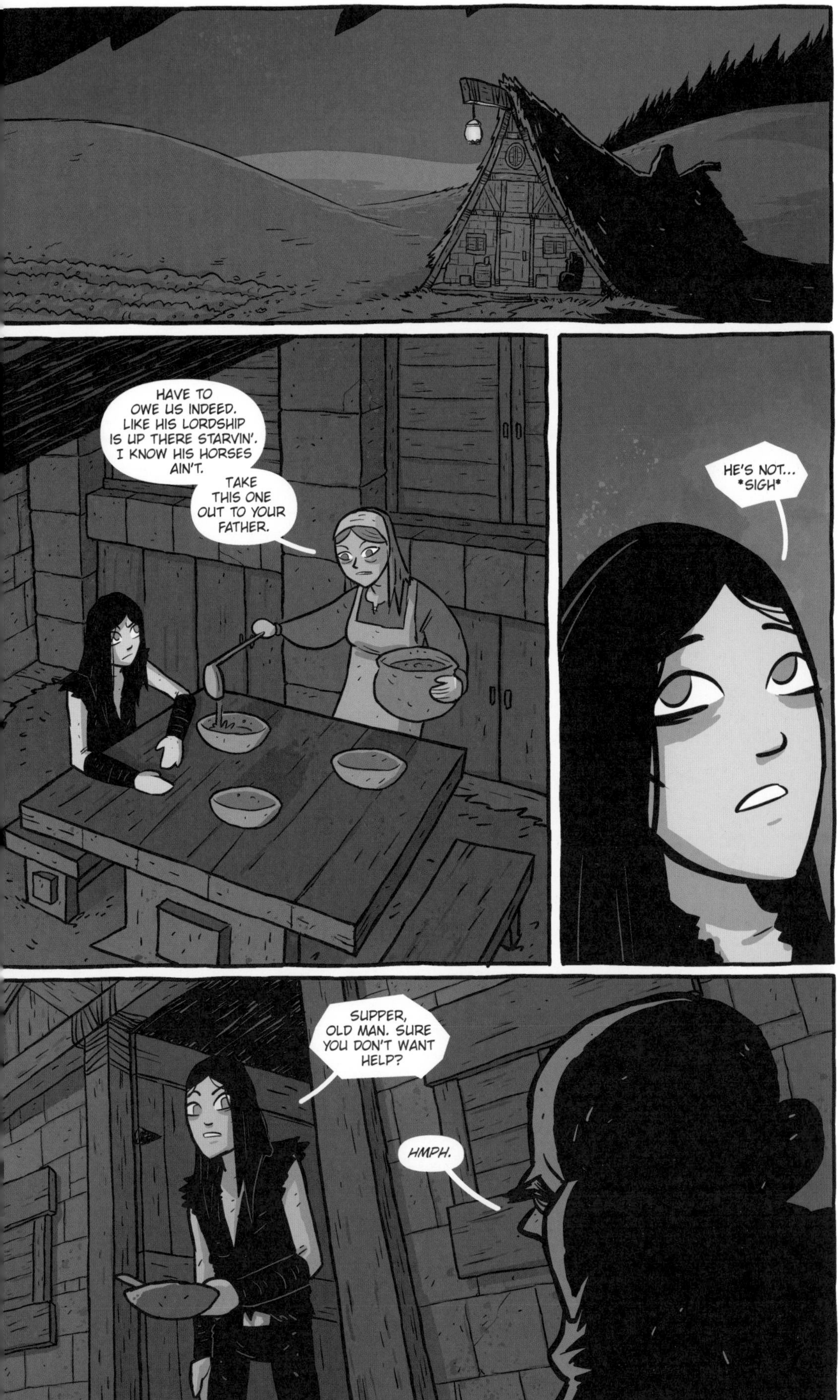
HAVE TO OWE US INDEED. LIKE HIS LORDSHIP IS UP THERE STARVIN'. I KNOW HIS HORSES AIN'T.
TAKE THIS ONE OUT TO YOUR FATHER.
HE'S NOT... *SIGH*
SUPPER, OLD MAN. SURE YOU DON'T WANT HELP?
HMPH.

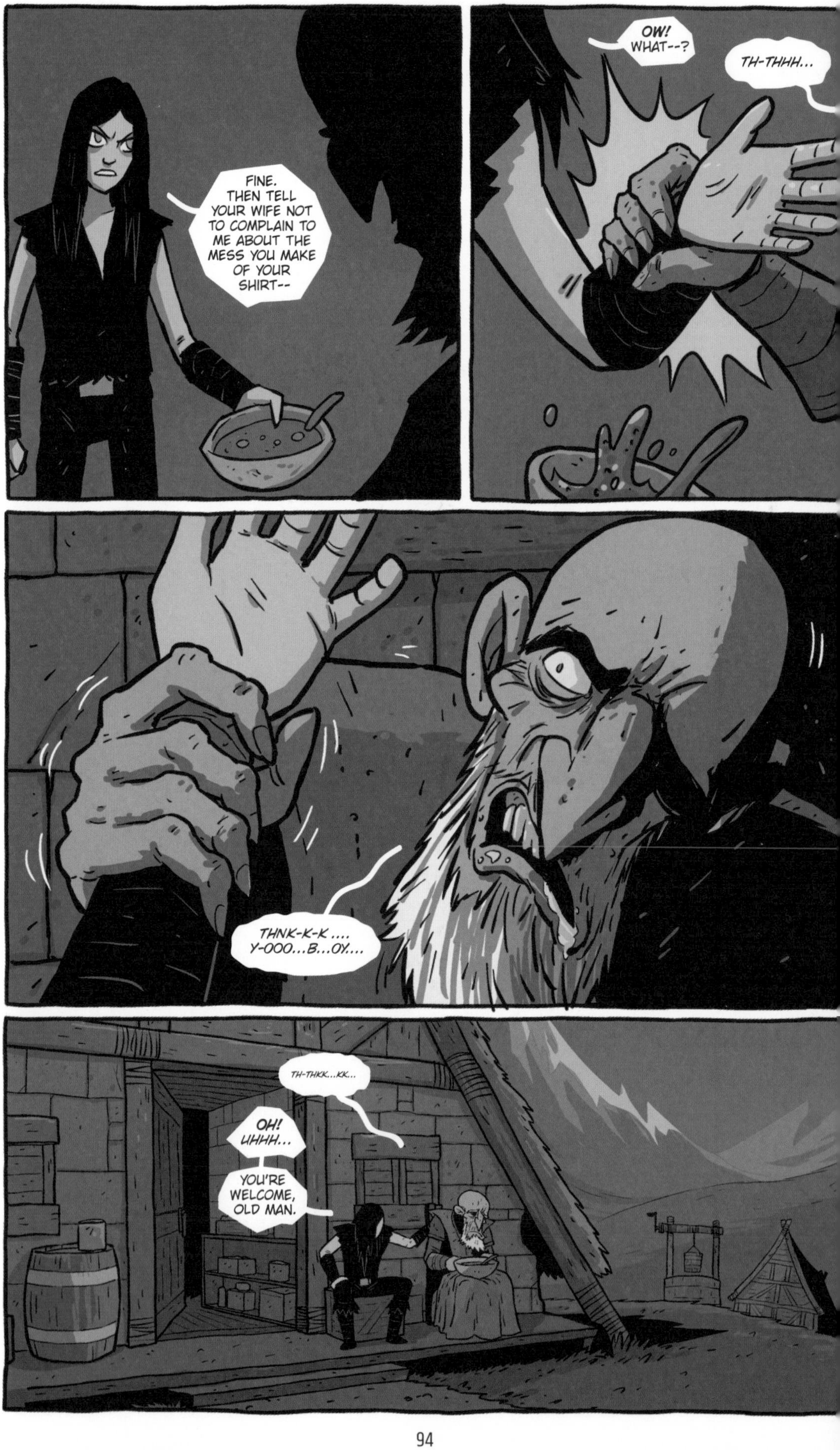
FINE. THEN TELL YOUR WIFE NOT TO COMPLAIN TO ME ABOUT THE MESS YOU MAKE OF YOUR SHIRT--
OW! WHAT--?
TH-THHH...
THNK-K-K.... Y-OOO...B...OY....
TH-THKK...KK...
OH! UHHH...
YOU'RE WELCOME, OLD MAN.

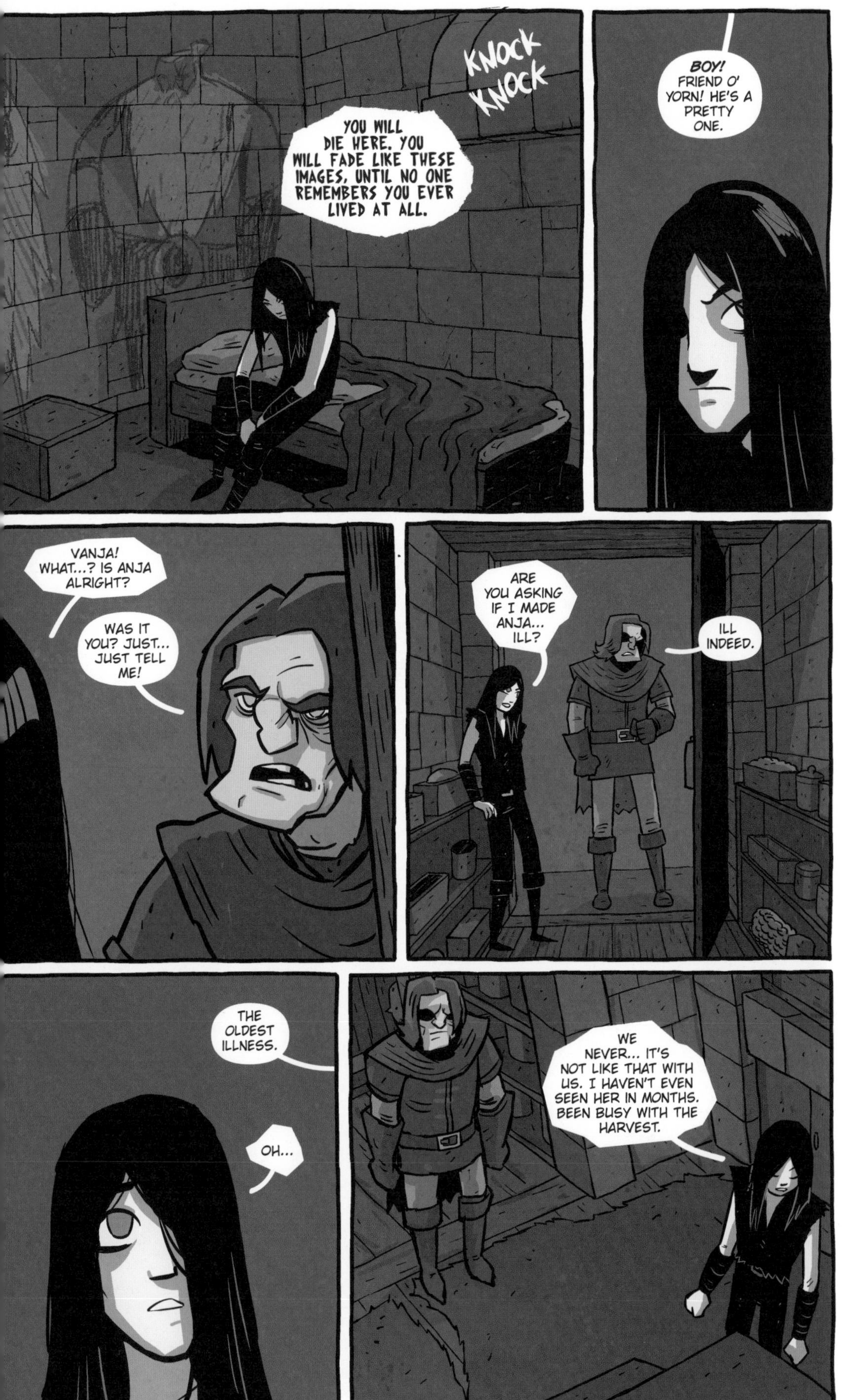
KNOCK KNOCK
YOU WILL DIE HERE. YOU WILL FADE LIKE THESE IMAGES, UNTIL NO ONE REMEMBERS YOU EVER LIVED AT ALL.
BOY! FRIEND O' YORN! HE'S A PRETTY ONE.
VANJA! WHAT...? IS ANJA ALRIGHT?
WAS IT YOU? JUST... JUST TELL ME!
ARE YOU ASKING IF I MADE ANJA... ILL?
ILL INDEED.
THE OLDEST ILLNESS.
OH...
WE NEVER... IT'S NOT LIKE THAT WITH US. I HAVEN'T EVEN SEEN HER IN MONTHS. BEEN BUSY WITH THE HARVEST.

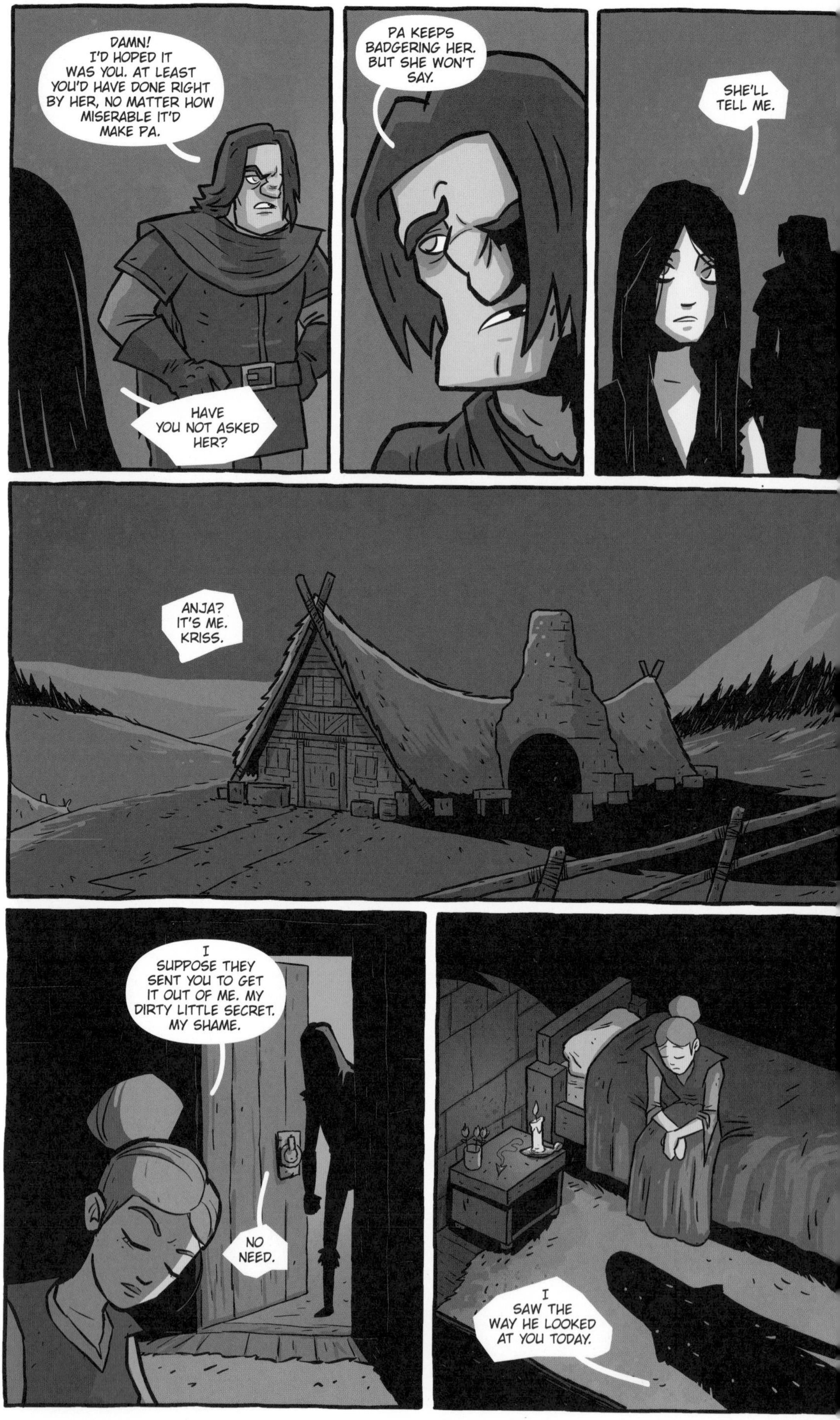
DAMN! I'D HOPED IT WAS YOU. AT LEAST YOU'D HAVE DONE RIGHT BY HER, NO MATTER HOW MISERABLE IT'D MAKE PA.
HAVE YOU NOT ASKED HER?
PA KEEPS BADGERING HER. BUT SHE WON'T SAY.
SHE'LL TELL ME.
ANJA? IT'S ME. KRISS.
I SUPPOSE THEY SENT YOU TO GET IT OUT OF ME. MY DIRTY LITTLE SECRET. MY SHAME.
NO NEED.
I SAW THE WAY HE LOOKED AT YOU TODAY.

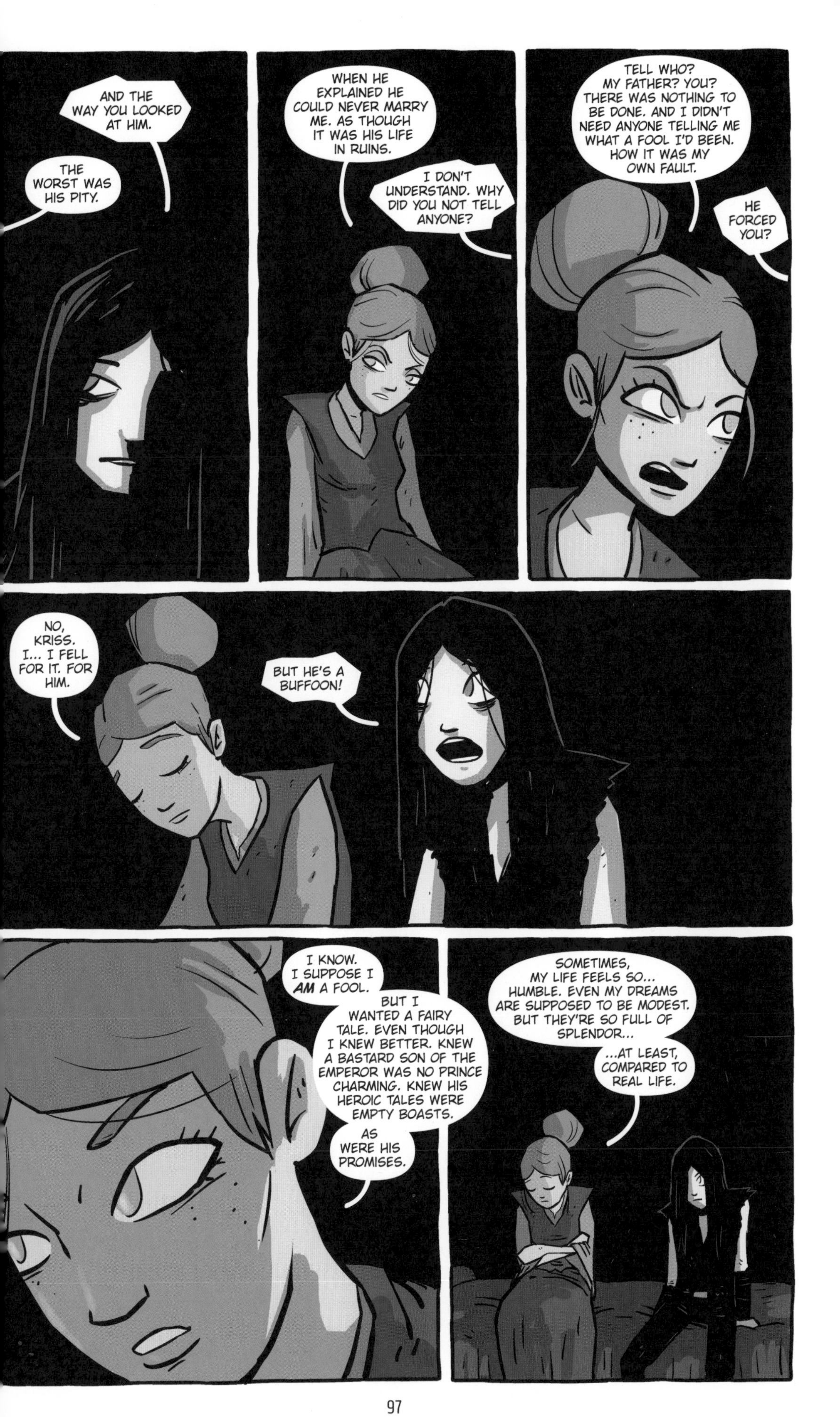
AND THE WAY YOU LOOKED AT HIM.
THE WORST WAS HIS PITY.
WHEN HE EXPLAINED HE COULD NEVER MARRY ME. AS THOUGH IT WAS HIS LIFE IN RUINS.
I DON'T UNDERSTAND. WHY DID YOU NOT TELL ANYONE?
TELL WHO? MY FATHER? YOU? THERE WAS NOTHING TO BE DONE. AND I DIDN'T NEED ANYONE TELLING ME WHAT A FOOL I'D BEEN. HOW IT WAS MY OWN FAULT.
HE FORCED YOU?
NO, KRISS. I... I FELL FOR IT. FOR HIM.
BUT HE'S A BUFFOON!
I KNOW. I SUPPOSE I ***AM*** A FOOL.
BUT I WANTED A FAIRY TALE. EVEN THOUGH I KNEW BETTER. KNEW A BASTARD SON OF THE EMPEROR WAS NO PRINCE CHARMING. KNEW HIS HEROIC TALES WERE EMPTY BOASTS.
AS WERE HIS PROMISES.
SOMETIMES, MY LIFE FEELS SO... HUMBLE. EVEN MY DREAMS ARE SUPPOSED TO BE MODEST. BUT THEY'RE SO FULL OF SPLENDOR...
...AT LEAST, COMPARED TO REAL LIFE.

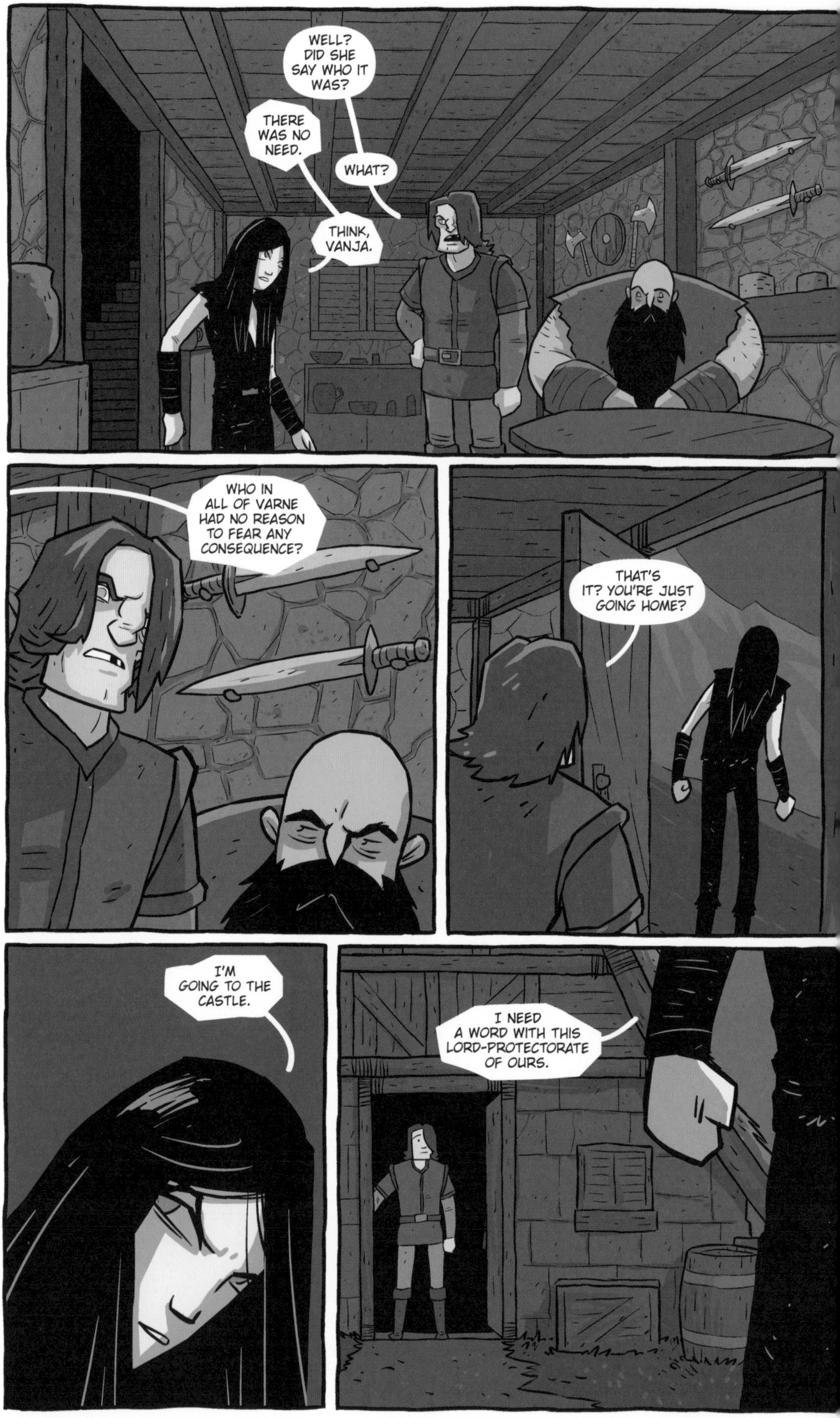
WELL? DID SHE SAY WHO IT WAS?
THERE WAS NO NEED.
WHAT?
THINK, VANJA.
WHO IN ALL OF VARNE HAD NO REASON TO FEAR ANY CONSEQUENCE?
THAT'S IT? YOU'RE JUST GOING HOME?
I'M GOING TO THE CASTLE.
I NEED A WORD WITH THIS LORD-PROTECTORATE OF OURS.

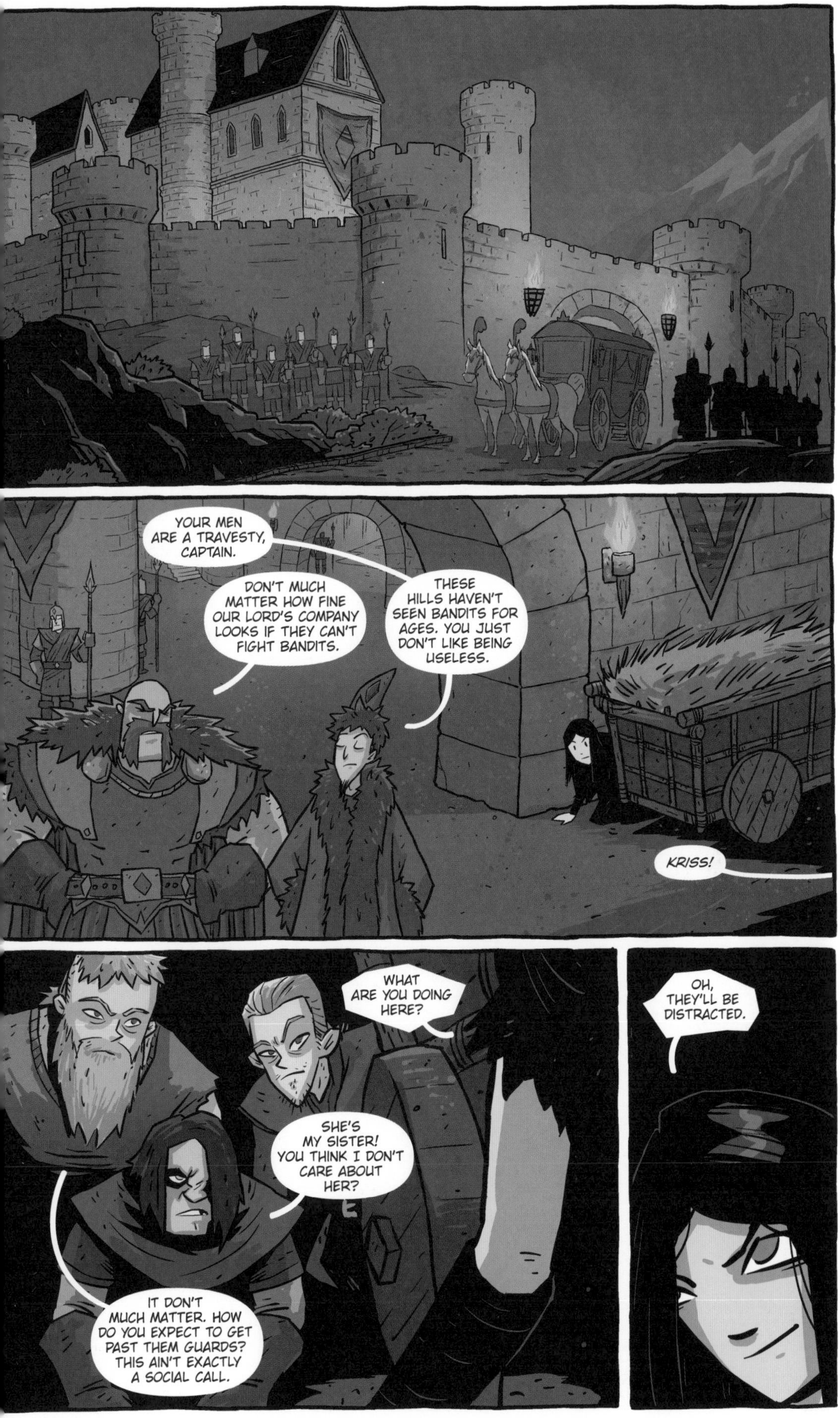
YOUR MEN ARE A TRAVESTY, CAPTAIN.
DON'T MUCH MATTER HOW FINE OUR LORD'S COMPANY LOOKS IF THEY CAN'T FIGHT BANDITS.
THESE HILLS HAVEN'T SEEN BANDITS FOR AGES. YOU JUST DON'T LIKE BEING USELESS.
KRISS!
WHAT ARE YOU DOING HERE?
SHE'S MY SISTER! YOU THINK I DON'T CARE ABOUT HER?
IT DON'T MUCH MATTER. HOW DO YOU EXPECT TO GET PAST THEM GUARDS? THIS AIN'T EXACTLY A SOCIAL CALL.
OH, THEY'LL BE DISTRACTED.

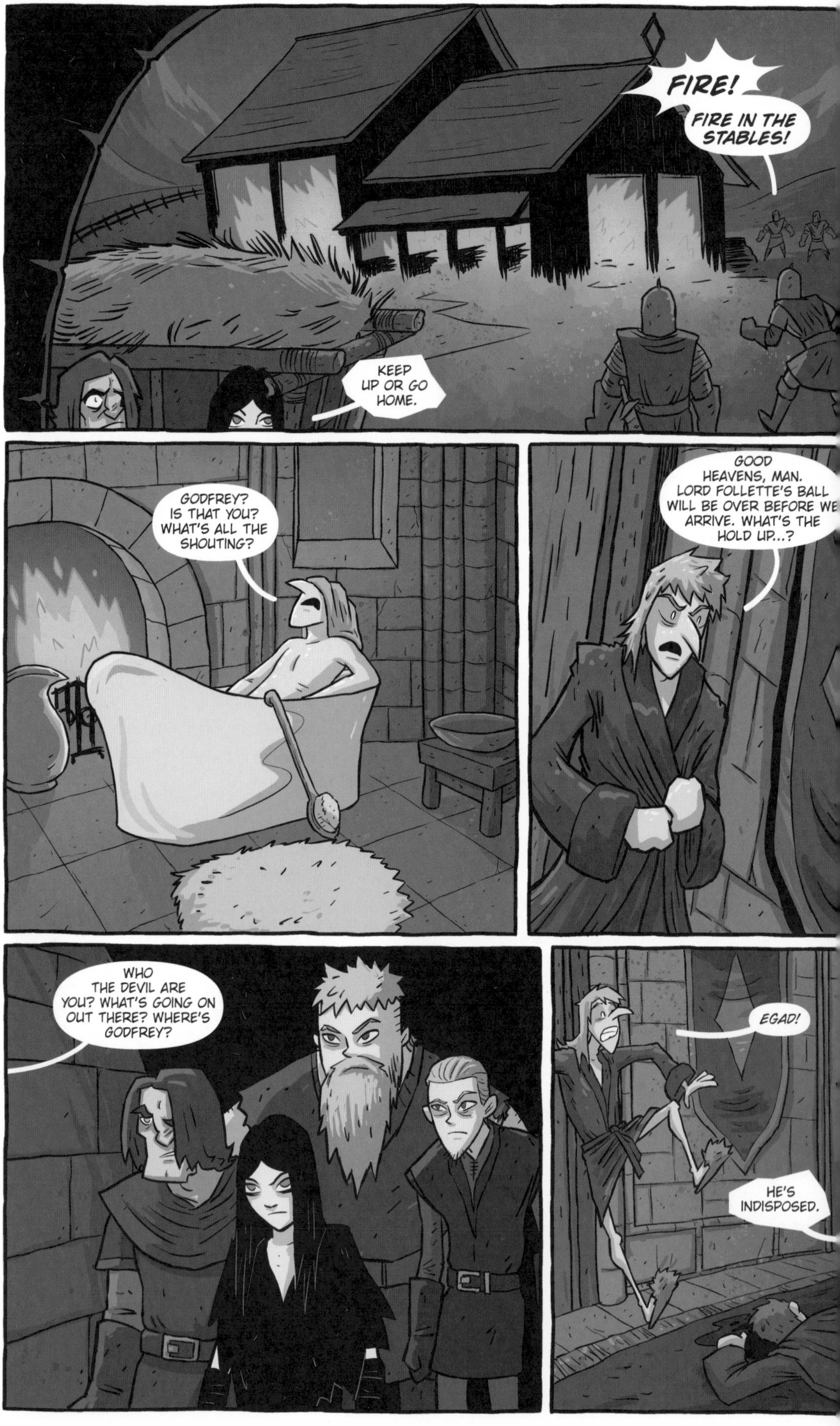
FIRE!
FIRE IN THE STABLES!
KEEP UP OR GO HOME.
GODFREY? IS THAT YOU? WHAT'S ALL THE SHOUTING?
GOOD HEAVENS, MAN. LORD FOLLETTE'S BALL WILL BE OVER BEFORE WE ARRIVE. WHAT'S THE HOLD UP...?
WHO THE DEVIL ARE YOU? WHAT'S GOING ON OUT THERE? WHERE'S GODFREY?
EGAD!
HE'S INDISPOSED.

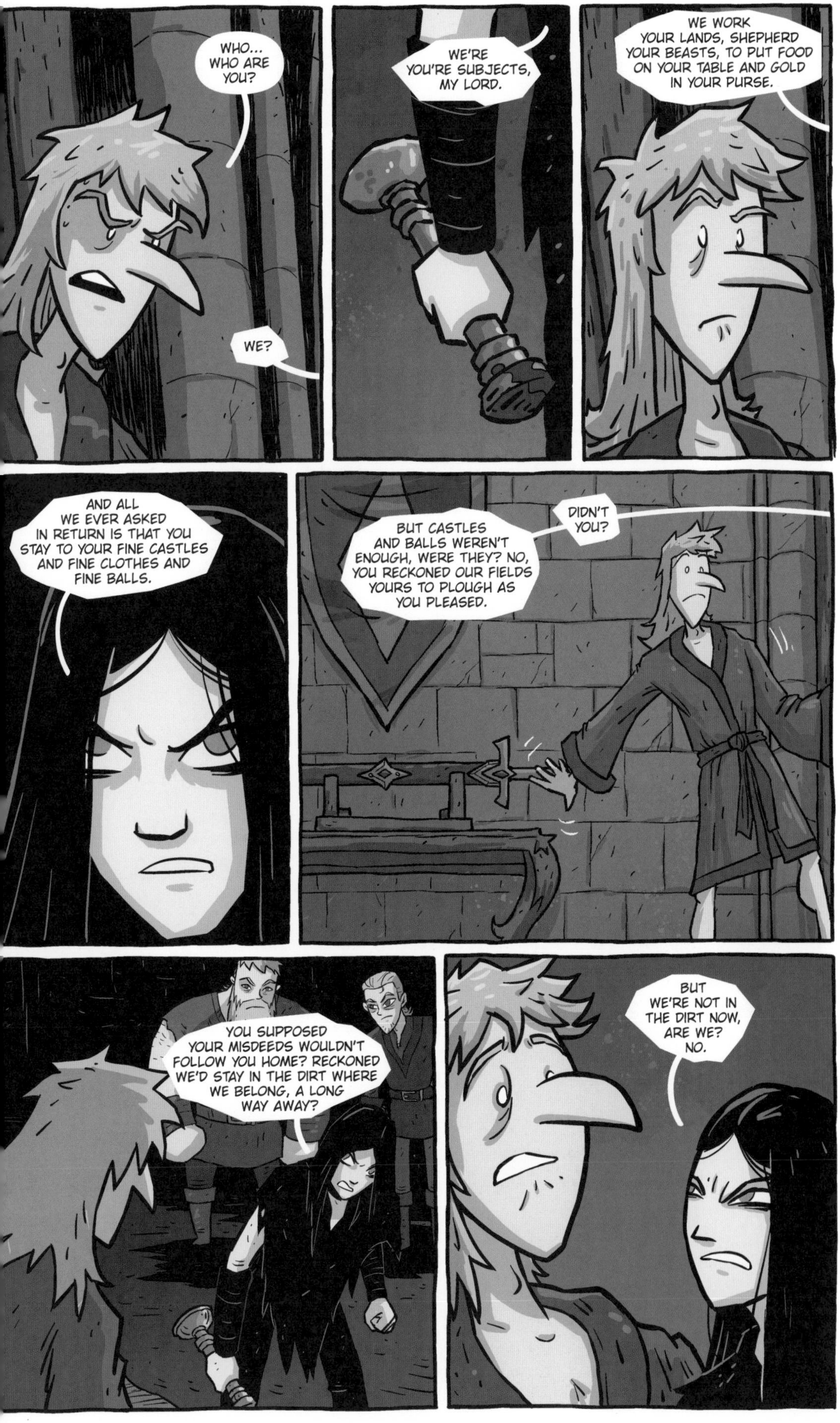
WHO... WHO ARE YOU?
WE?
WE'RE YOU'RE SUBJECTS, MY LORD.
WE WORK YOUR LANDS, SHEPHERD YOUR BEASTS, TO PUT FOOD ON YOUR TABLE AND GOLD IN YOUR PURSE.
AND ALL WE EVER ASKED IN RETURN IS THAT YOU STAY TO YOUR FINE CASTLES AND FINE CLOTHES AND FINE BALLS.
BUT CASTLES AND BALLS WEREN'T ENOUGH, WERE THEY? NO, YOU RECKONED OUR FIELDS YOURS TO PLOUGH AS YOU PLEASED.
DIDN'T YOU?
YOU SUPPOSED YOUR MISDEEDS WOULDN'T FOLLOW YOU HOME? RECKONED WE'D STAY IN THE DIRT WHERE WE BELONG, A LONG WAY AWAY?
BUT WE'RE NOT IN THE DIRT NOW, ARE WE? NO.

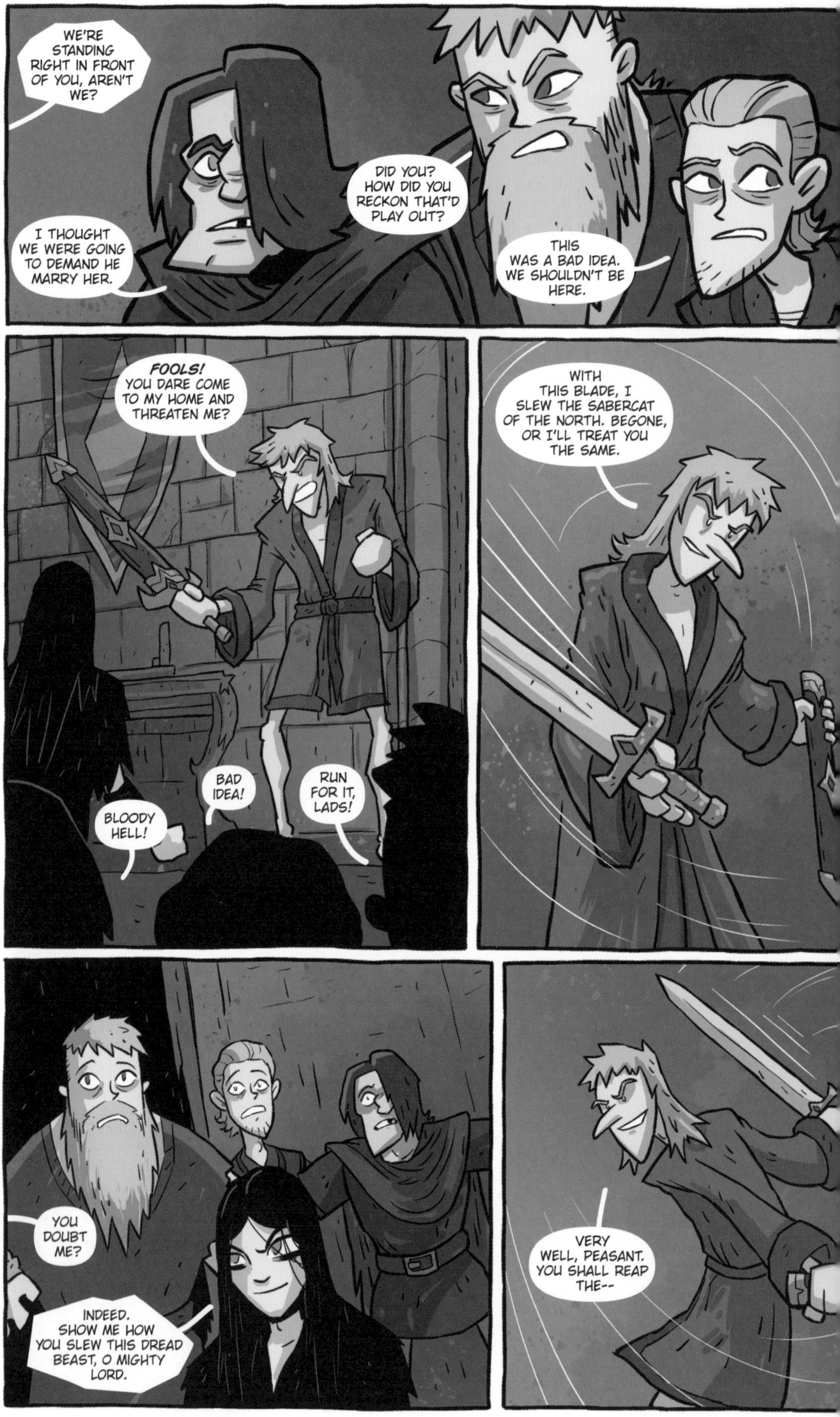
WE'RE STANDING RIGHT IN FRONT OF YOU, AREN'T WE?
I THOUGHT WE WERE GOING TO DEMAND HE MARRY HER.
DID YOU? HOW DID YOU RECKON THAT'D PLAY OUT?
THIS WAS A BAD IDEA. WE SHOULDN'T BE HERE.
FOOLS! YOU DARE COME TO MY HOME AND THREATEN ME?
BLOODY HELL!
BAD IDEA!
RUN FOR IT, LADS!
WITH THIS BLADE, I SLEW THE SABERCAT OF THE NORTH. BEGONE, OR I'LL TREAT YOU THE SAME.
YOU DOUBT ME?
INDEED. SHOW ME HOW YOU SLEW THIS DREAD BEAST, O MIGHTY LORD.
VERY WELL, PEASANT. YOU SHALL REAP THE--

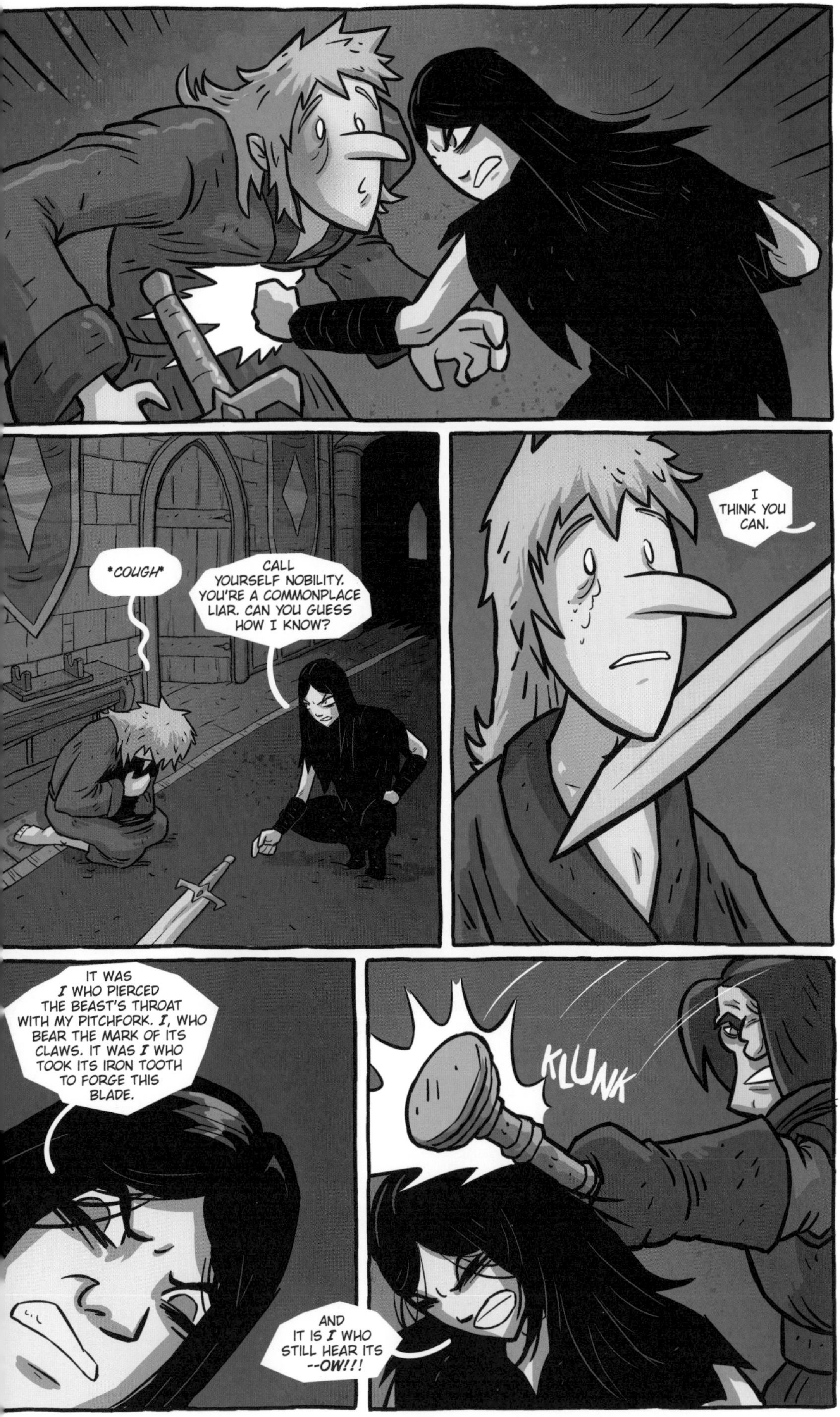
COUGH
CALL YOURSELF NOBILITY. YOU'RE A COMMONPLACE LIAR. CAN YOU GUESS HOW I KNOW?
I THINK YOU CAN.
IT WAS I WHO PIERCED THE BEAST'S THROAT WITH MY PITCHFORK. I, WHO BEAR THE MARK OF ITS CLAWS. IT WAS I WHO TOOK ITS IRON TOOTH TO FORGE THIS BLADE.
KLUNK
AND IT IS I WHO STILL HEAR ITS --OW!!!

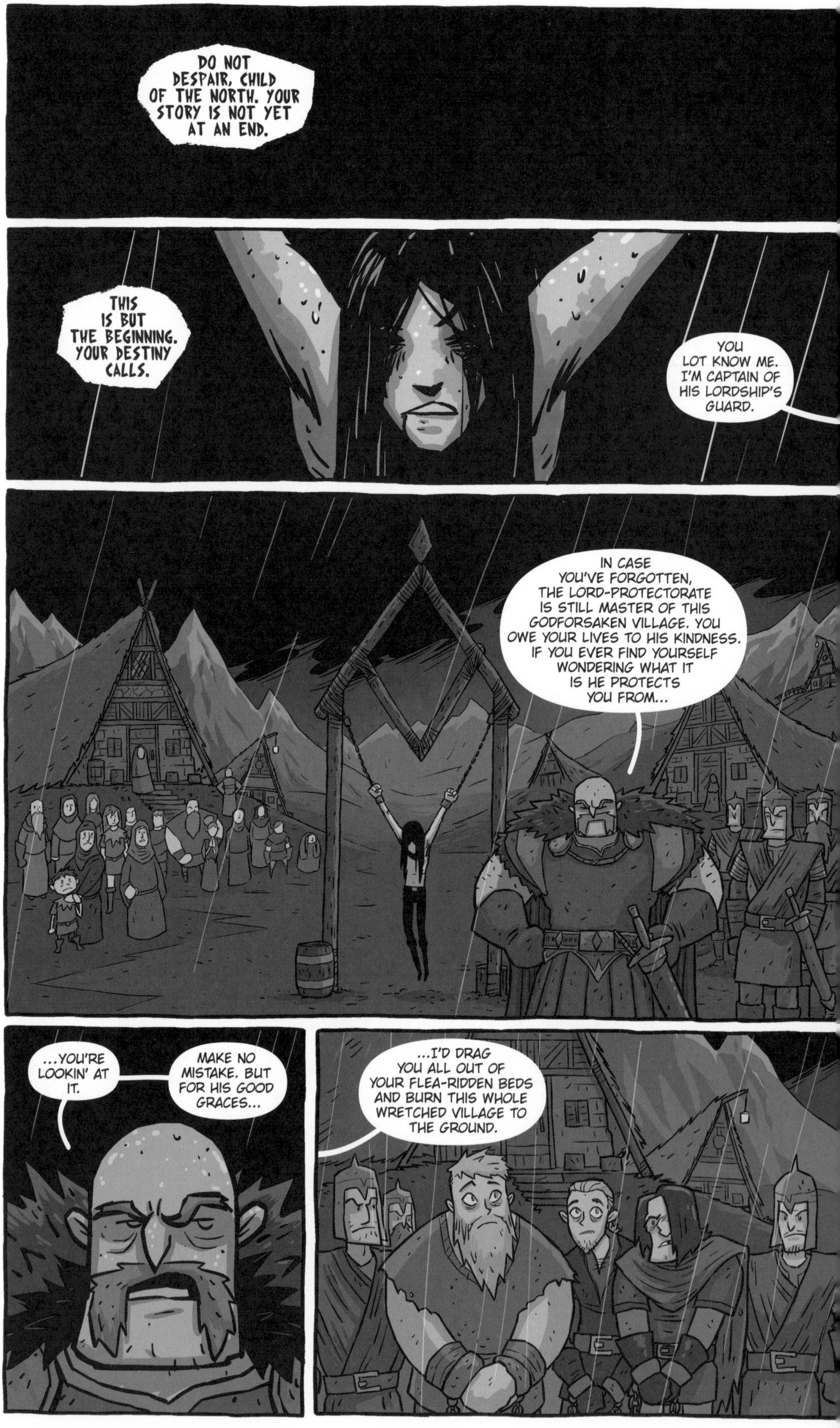
DO NOT DESPAIR, CHILD OF THE NORTH. YOUR STORY IS NOT YET AT AN END.
THIS IS BUT THE BEGINNING. YOUR DESTINY CALLS.
YOU LOT KNOW ME. I'M CAPTAIN OF HIS LORDSHIP'S GUARD.
IN CASE YOU'VE FORGOTTEN, THE LORD-PROTECTORATE IS STILL MASTER OF THIS GODFORSAKEN VILLAGE. YOU OWE YOUR LIVES TO HIS KINDNESS. IF YOU EVER FIND YOURSELF WONDERING WHAT IT IS HE PROTECTS YOU FROM...
...YOU'RE LOOKIN' AT IT.
MAKE NO MISTAKE. BUT FOR HIS GOOD GRACES...
...I'D DRAG YOU ALL OUT OF YOUR FLEA-RIDDEN BEDS AND BURN THIS WHOLE WRETCHED VILLAGE TO THE GROUND.

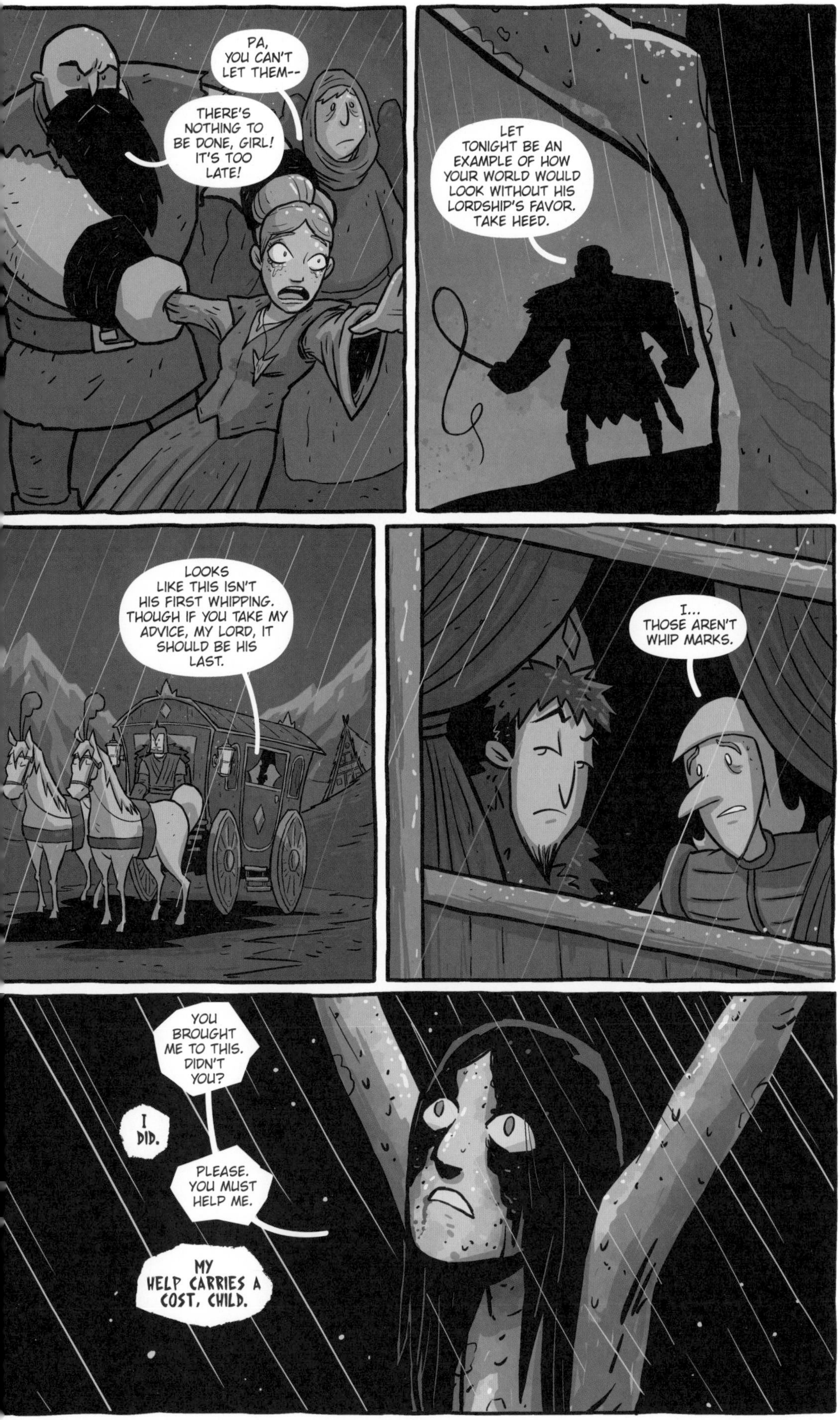
PA, YOU CAN'T LET THEM--
THERE'S NOTHING TO BE DONE, GIRL! IT'S TOO LATE!
LET TONIGHT BE AN EXAMPLE OF HOW YOUR WORLD WOULD LOOK WITHOUT HIS LORDSHIP'S FAVOR. TAKE HEED.
LOOKS LIKE THIS ISN'T HIS FIRST WHIPPING. THOUGH IF YOU TAKE MY ADVICE, MY LORD, IT SHOULD BE HIS LAST.
I... THOSE AREN'T WHIP MARKS.
YOU BROUGHT ME TO THIS. DIDN'T YOU?
I DID.
PLEASE. YOU MUST HELP ME.
MY HELP CARRIES A COST, CHILD.

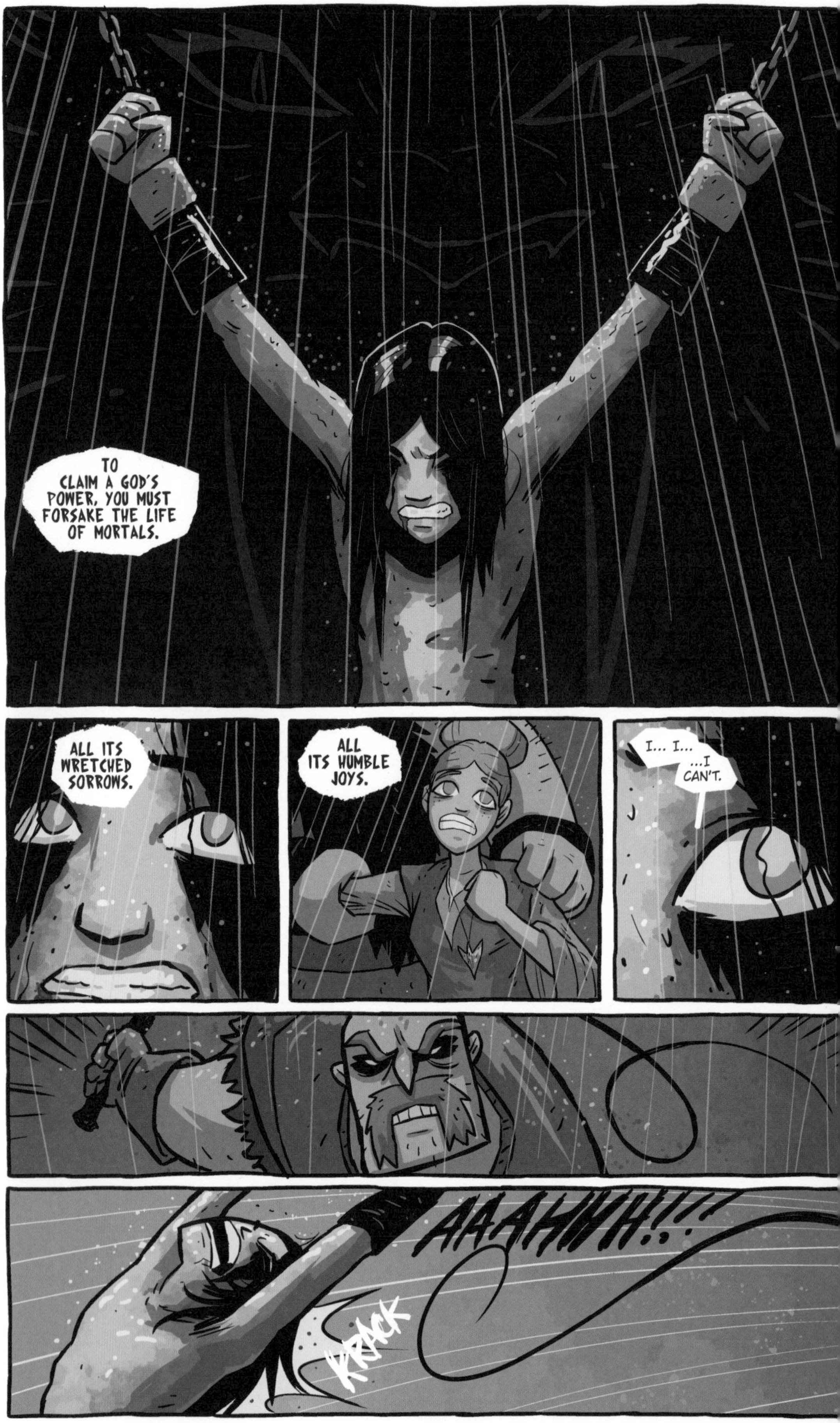
TO CLAIM A GOD'S POWER, YOU MUST FORSAKE THE LIFE OF MORTALS.
ALL ITS WRETCHED SORROWS.
ALL ITS HUMBLE JOYS.
I... I...
...I CAN'T.
AAAHHH!!!
KRACK

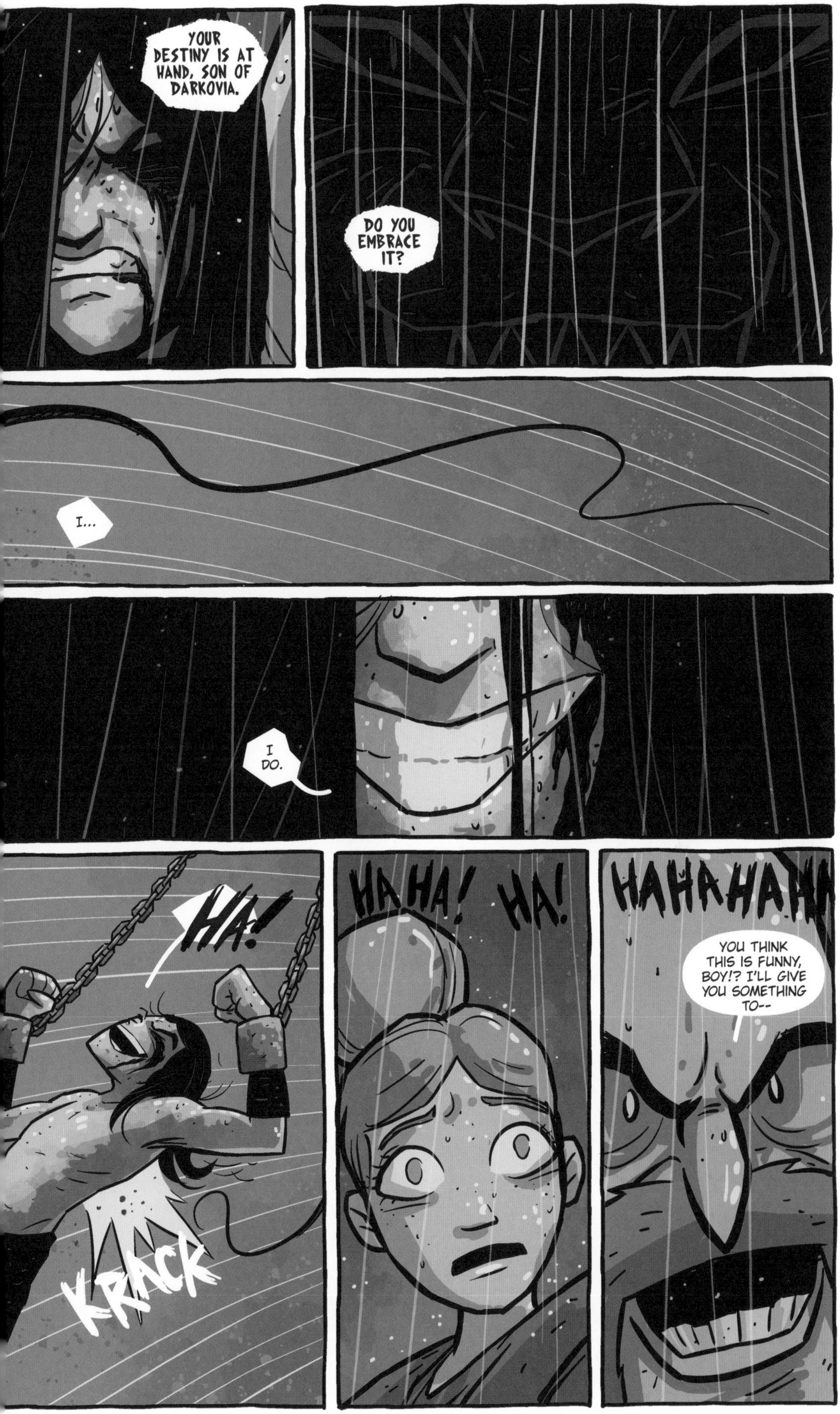
YOUR DESTINY IS AT HAND, SON OF DARKOVIA.
DO YOU EMBRACE IT?
I...
I DO.
HA!
KRACK
HAHA! HA!
HAHAHAHA
YOU THINK THIS IS FUNNY, BOY!? I'LL GIVE YOU SOMETHING TO--

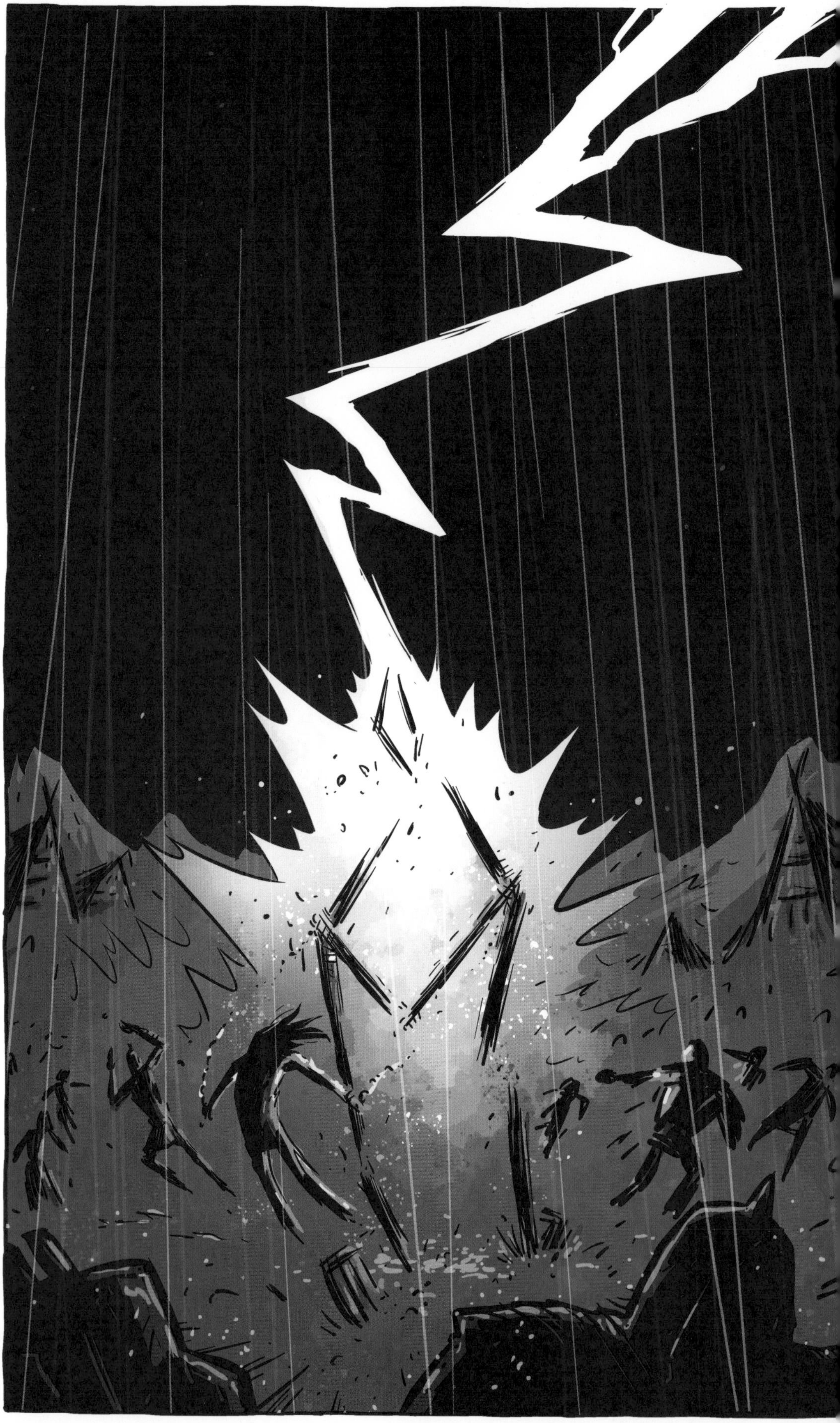

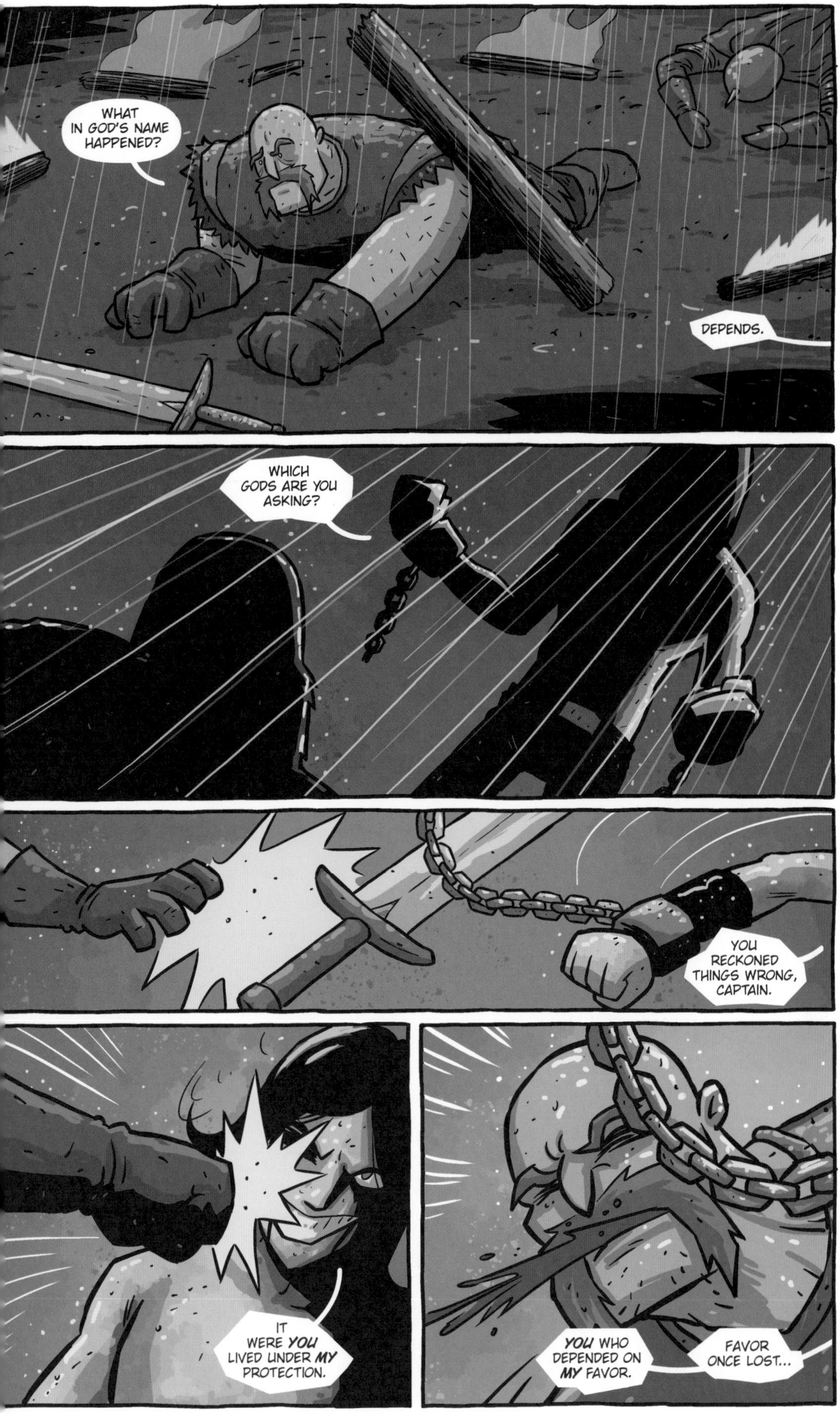
WHAT IN GOD'S NAME HAPPENED?
DEPENDS.
WHICH GODS ARE YOU ASKING?
YOU RECKONED THINGS WRONG, CAPTAIN.
IT WERE *YOU* LIVED UNDER *MY* PROTECTION.
YOU WHO DEPENDED ON *MY* FAVOR.
FAVOR ONCE LOST...

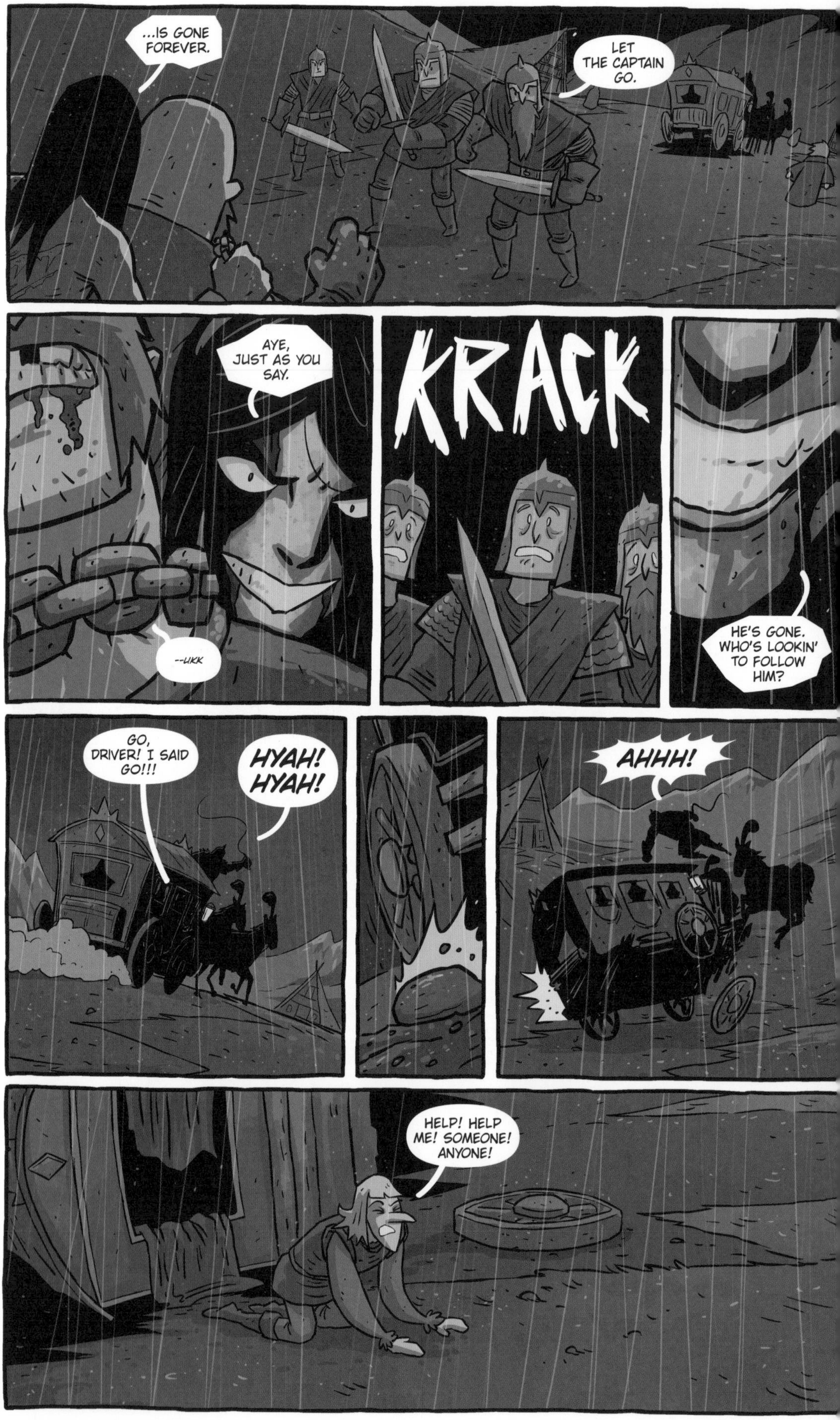
...IS GONE FOREVER.
LET THE CAPTAIN GO.
AYE, JUST AS YOU SAY.
--UKK
KRACK
HE'S GONE. WHO'S LOOKIN' TO FOLLOW HIM?
GO, DRIVER! I SAID GO!!!
HYAH! HYAH!
AHHH!
HELP! HELP ME! SOMEONE! ANYONE!

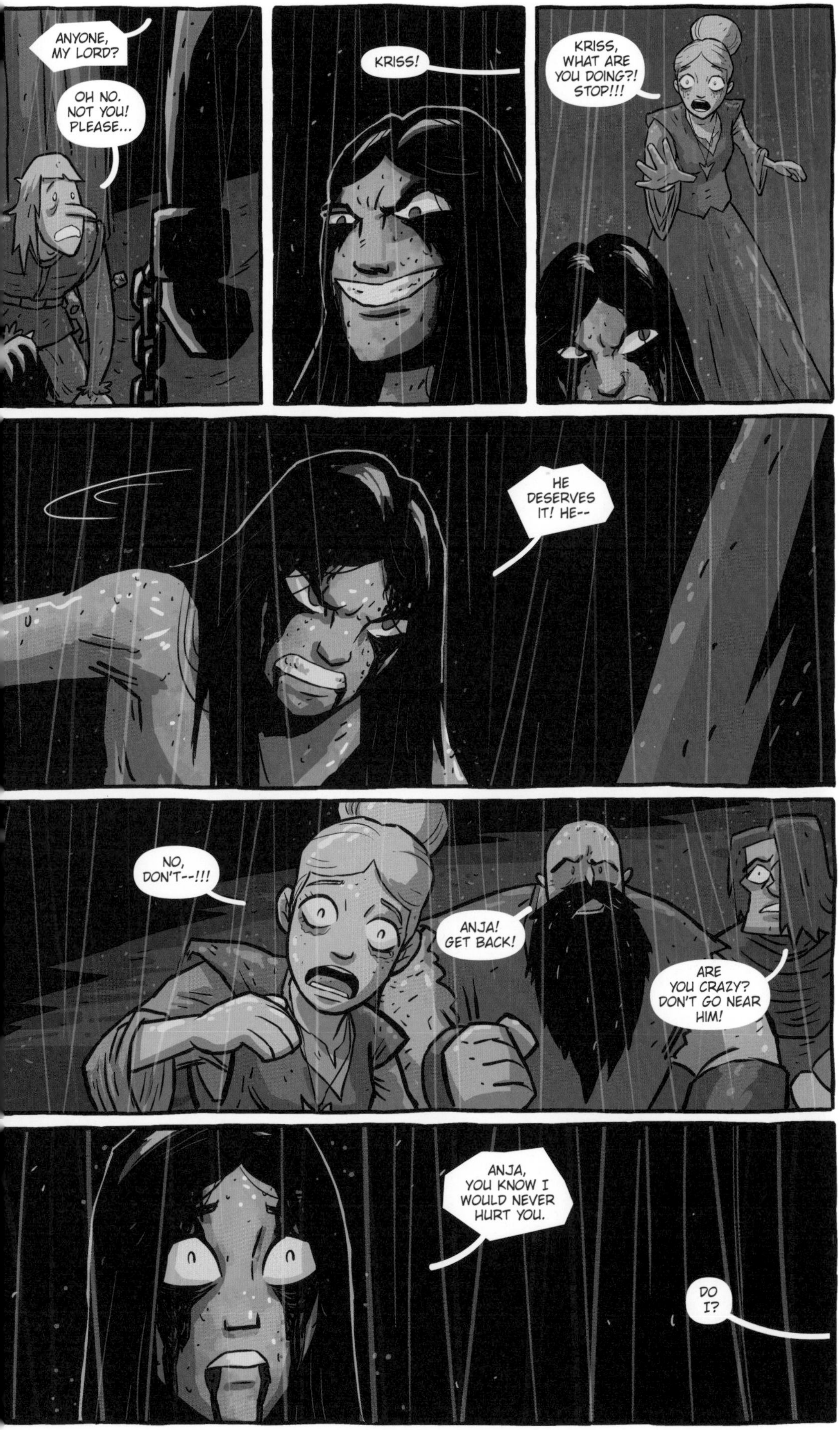
ANYONE, MY LORD?
OH NO. NOT YOU! PLEASE...
KRISS!
KRISS, WHAT ARE YOU DOING?! STOP!!!
HE DESERVES IT! HE--
NO, DON'T--!!!
ANJA! GET BACK!
ARE YOU CRAZY? DON'T GO NEAR HIM!
ANJA, YOU KNOW I WOULD NEVER HURT YOU.
DO I?

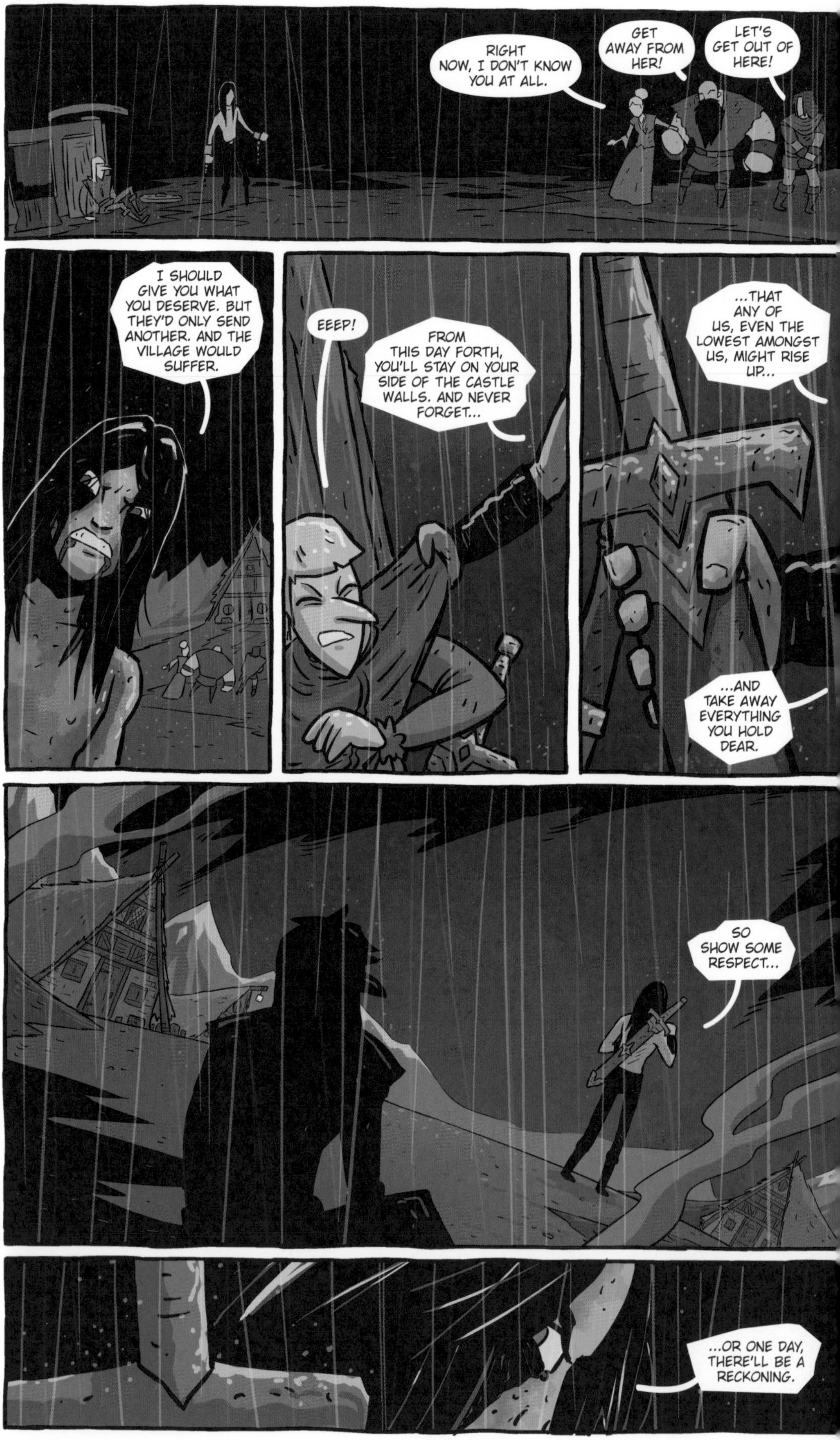
RIGHT NOW, I DON'T KNOW YOU AT ALL.
GET AWAY FROM HER!
LET'S GET OUT OF HERE!
I SHOULD GIVE YOU WHAT YOU DESERVE. BUT THEY'D ONLY SEND ANOTHER. AND THE VILLAGE WOULD SUFFER.
EEEP!
FROM THIS DAY FORTH, YOU'LL STAY ON YOUR SIDE OF THE CASTLE WALLS. AND NEVER FORGET...
...THAT ANY OF US, EVEN THE LOWEST AMONGST US, MIGHT RISE UP...
...AND TAKE AWAY EVERYTHING YOU HOLD DEAR.
SO SHOW SOME RESPECT...
...OR ONE DAY, THERE'LL BE A RECKONING.

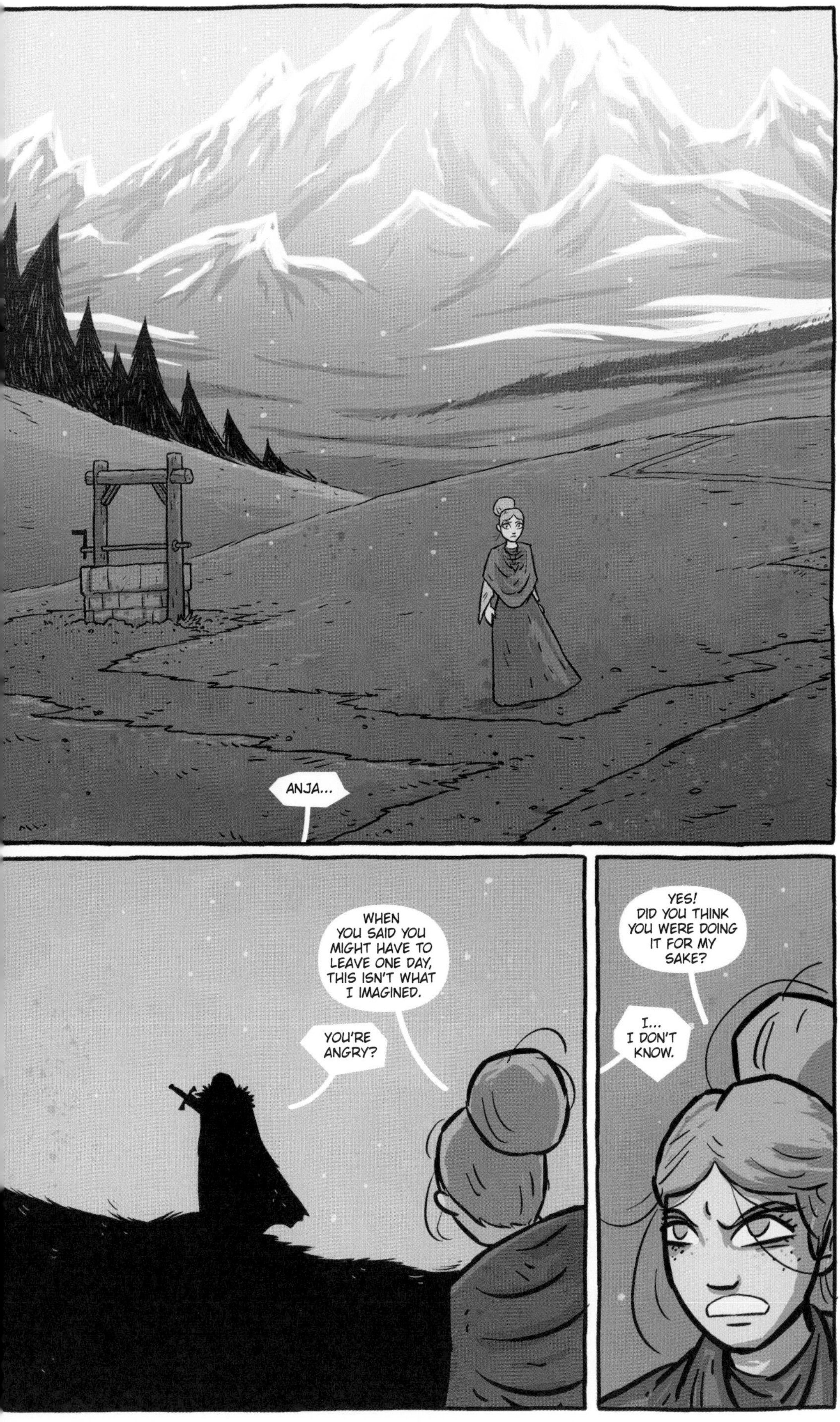
ANJA...
WHEN YOU SAID YOU MIGHT HAVE TO LEAVE ONE DAY, THIS ISN'T WHAT I IMAGINED.
YOU'RE ANGRY?
YES! DID YOU THINK YOU WERE DOING IT FOR MY SAKE?
I... I DON'T KNOW.

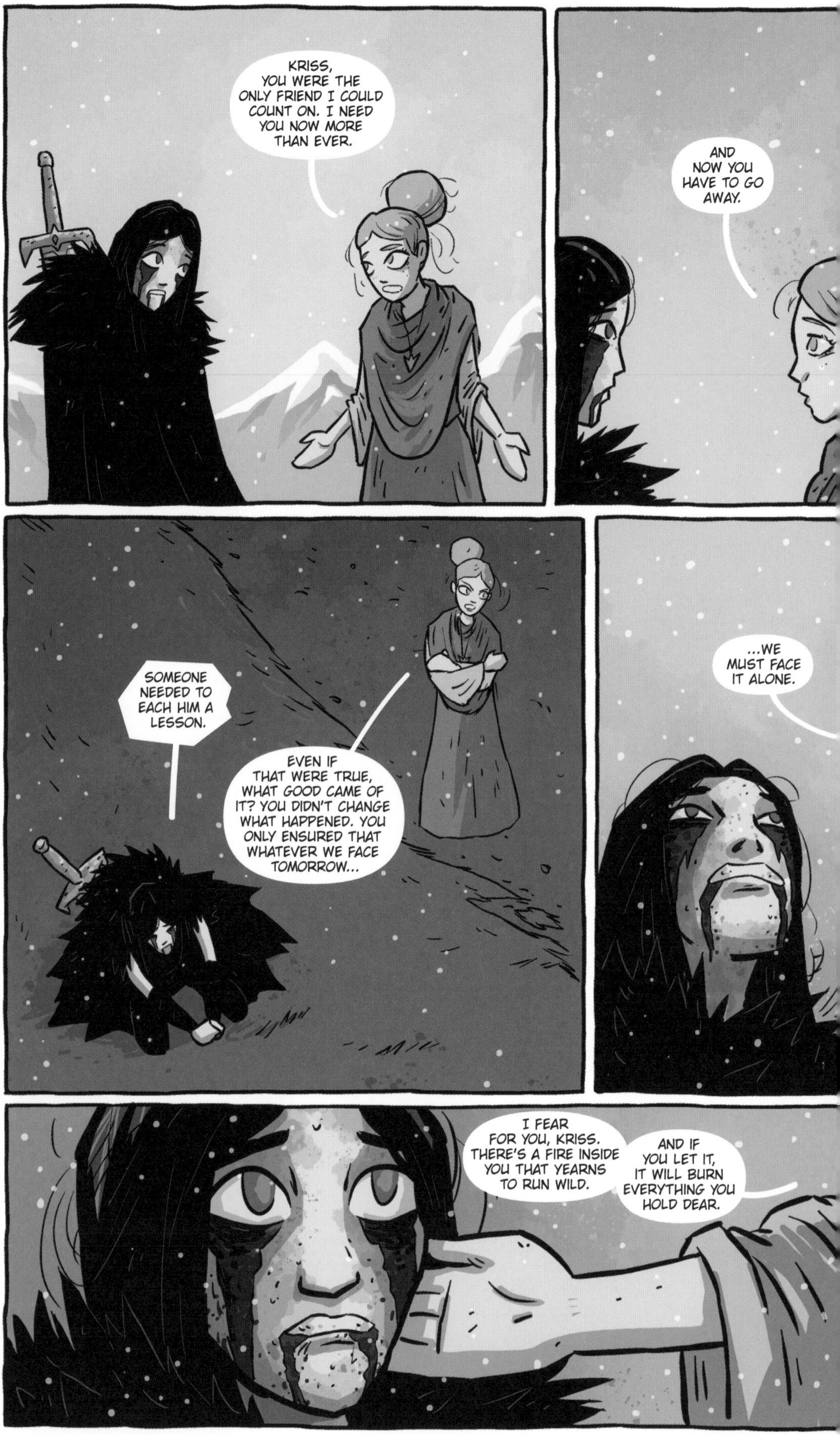
KRISS, YOU WERE THE ONLY FRIEND I COULD COUNT ON. I NEED YOU NOW MORE THAN EVER.
AND NOW YOU HAVE TO GO AWAY.
SOMEONE NEEDED TO EACH HIM A LESSON.
EVEN IF THAT WERE TRUE, WHAT GOOD CAME OF IT? YOU DIDN'T CHANGE WHAT HAPPENED. YOU ONLY ENSURED THAT WHATEVER WE FACE TOMORROW...
...WE MUST FACE IT ALONE.
I FEAR FOR YOU, KRISS. THERE'S A FIRE INSIDE YOU THAT YEARNS TO RUN WILD.
AND IF YOU LET IT, IT WILL BURN EVERYTHING YOU HOLD DEAR.

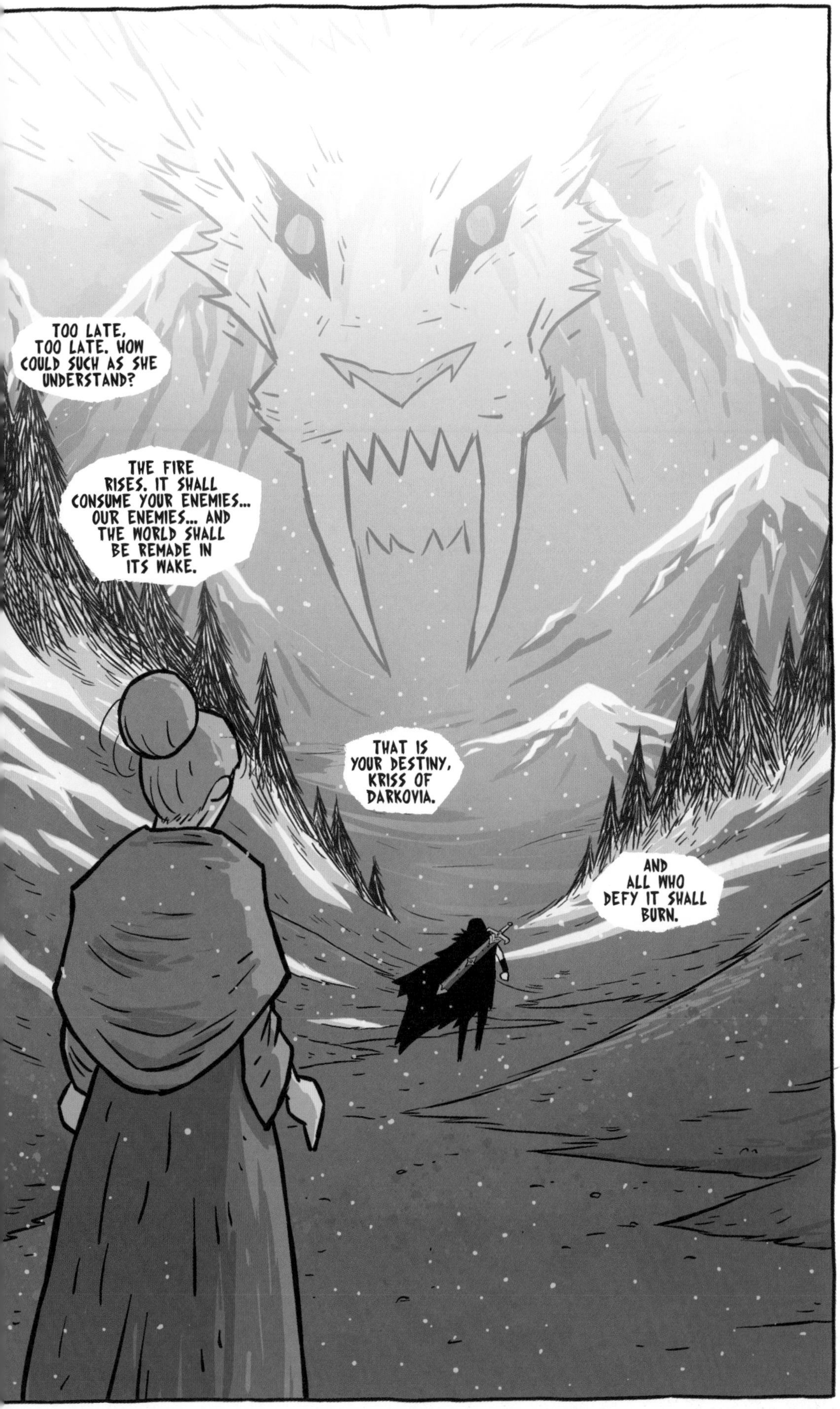
TOO LATE, TOO LATE. HOW COULD SUCH AS SHE UNDERSTAND?
THE FIRE RISES. IT SHALL CONSUME YOUR ENEMIES... OUR ENEMIES... AND THE WORLD SHALL BE REMADE IN ITS WAKE.
THAT IS YOUR DESTINY, KRISS OF DARKOVIA.
AND ALL WHO DEFY IT SHALL BURN.

SKETCH GALLERY

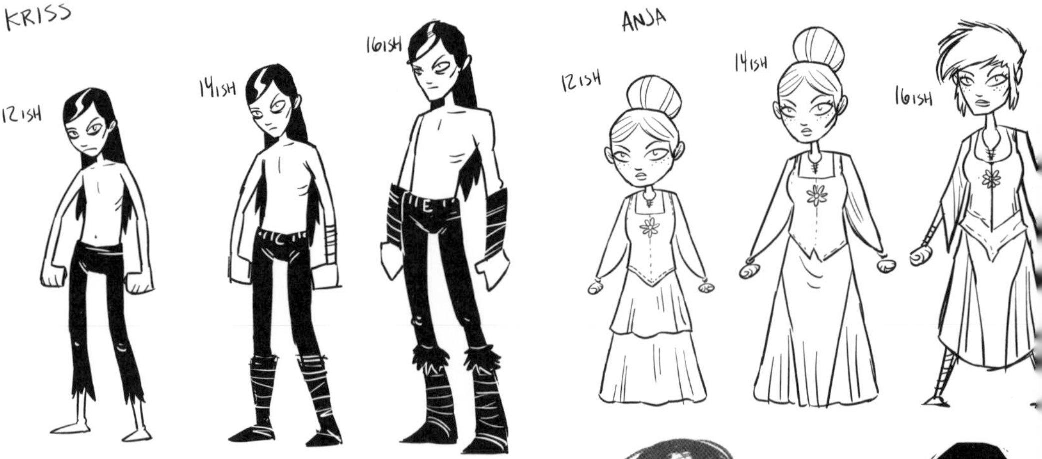
KRISS
12ISH
14ISH
16ISH
ANJA
12ISH
14ISH
16ISH

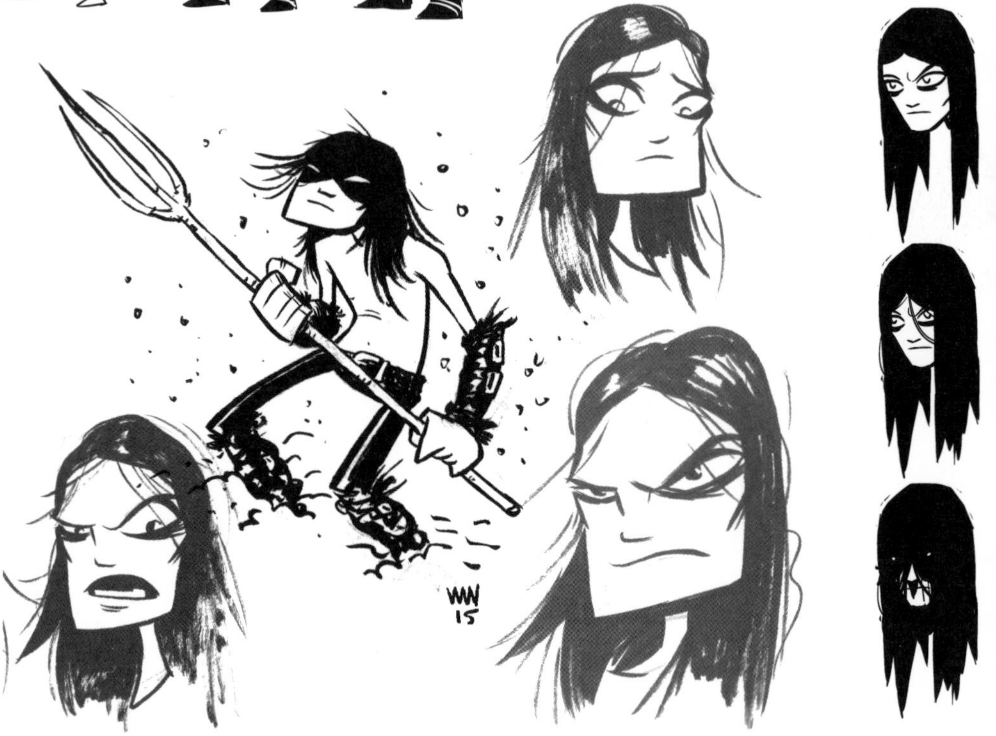

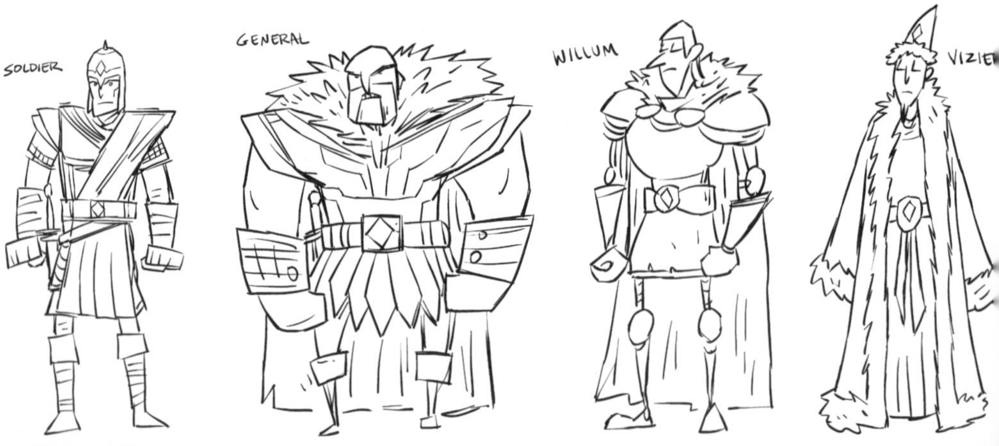
SOLDIER
GENERAL
WILLUM
VIZIE

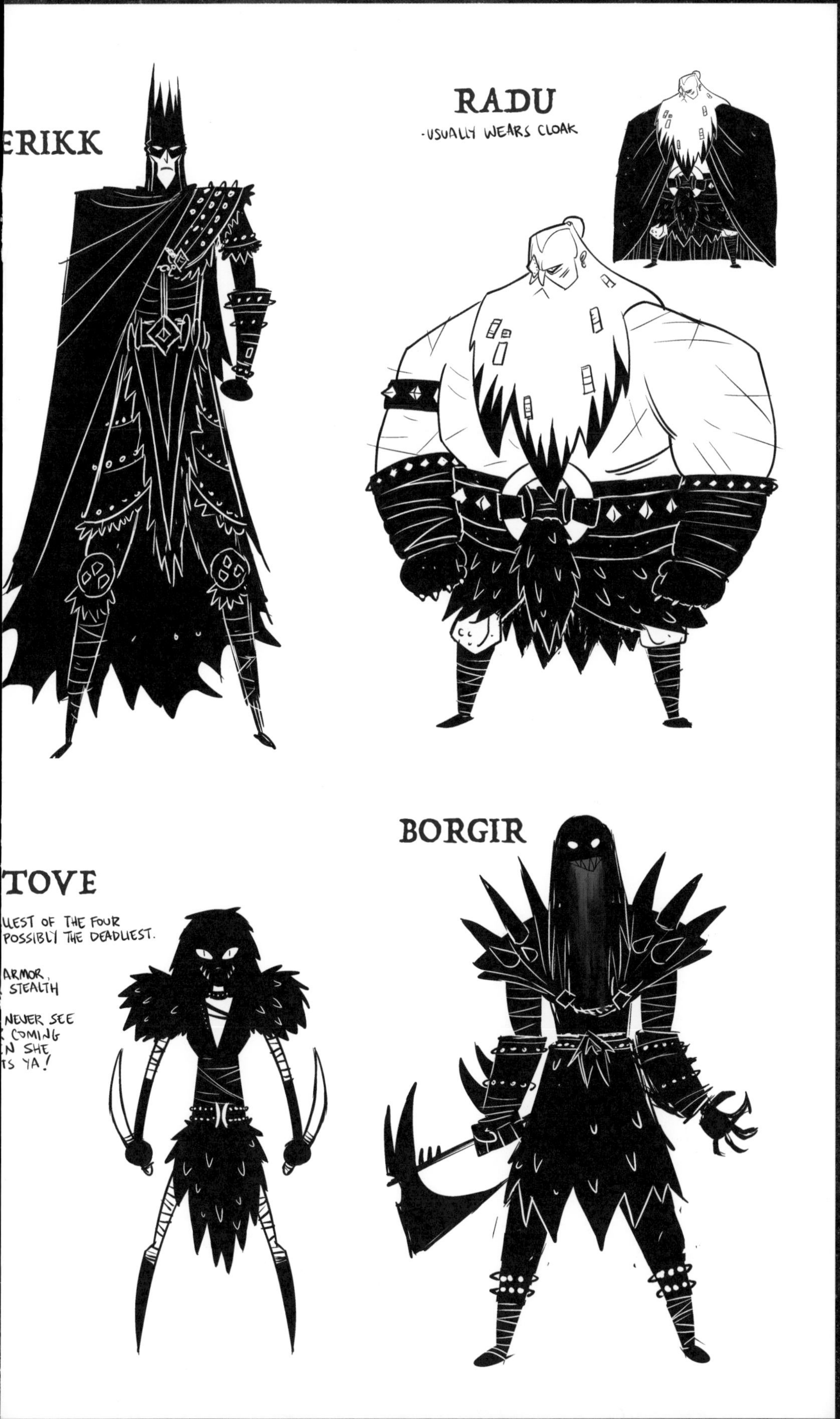

ERIKK
RADU
-USUALLY WEARS CLOAK
BORGIR
TOVE
LLEST OF THE FOUR
POSSIBLY THE DEADLIEST.
ARMOR,
STEALTH
NEVER SEE
COMING
N SHE
TS YA!

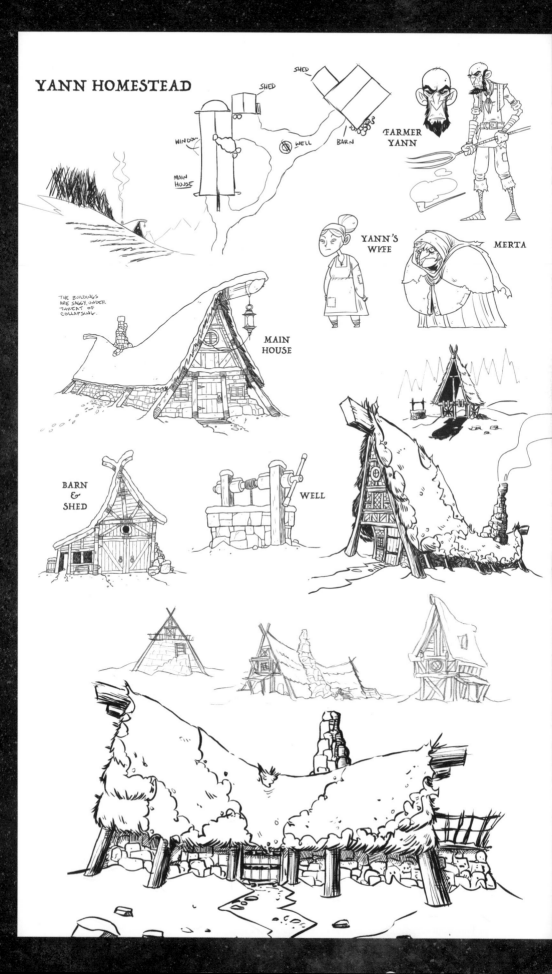

YANN HOMESTEAD

SHED

SHED

WINDOW

MAIN HOUSE

WELL

BARN

FARMER YANN

YANN'S WIFE

MERTA

THE BUILDINGS ARE SAGGY, UNDER THREAT OF COLLAPSING.

MAIN HOUSE

BARN & SHED

WELL

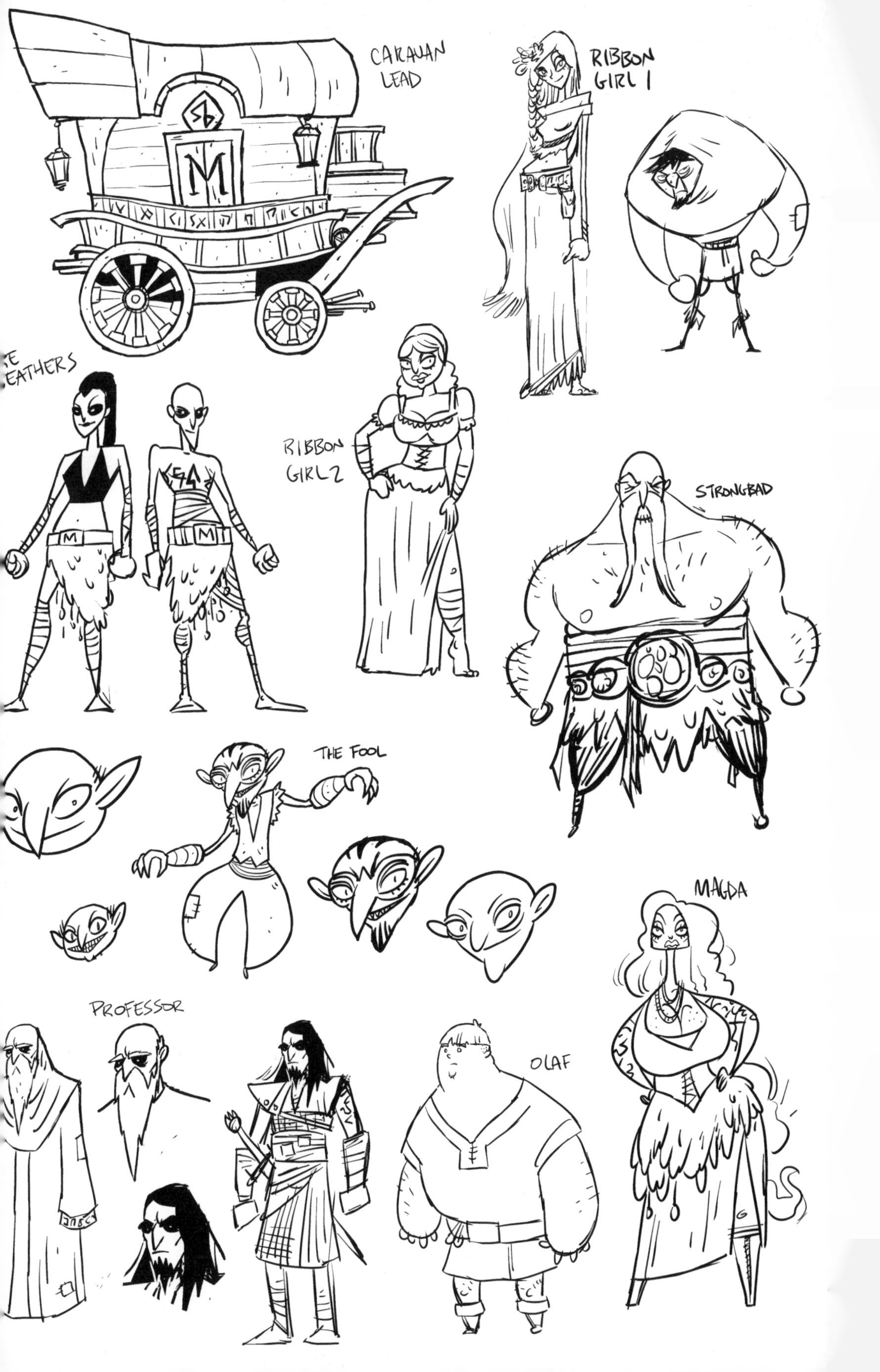
CARAVAN LEAD
RIBBON GIRL 1
E
EATHERS
RIBBON GIRL 2
STRONGBAD
THE FOOL
MAGDA
PROFESSOR
OLAF

CREATOR BIOS

Grim are the words and grimmer the deeds of the one known as **TED NAIFEH**, for it was he who brought darkness unto tween readers in the form of *Courtney Crumrin*. Seven volumes did this tale of magic and grumpiness span in the telling. When one story ends, another begins, and thus did Ted Naifeh forge the saga of *Princess Ugg*, a mighty warrior on a quest for education. This tale was followed by *Night's Dominion*, a burning crucible in which heroes were forged in fire and blood.

Little else is known of Ted Naifeh, save that he dwells in the war-torn land of San Francisco, which, like ancient Pompeii, trembles in the shadow of impending doom.

WARREN WUCINICH has been working steadily in the comic book field since 2009. Among the many Oni Press titles he has contributed to, Warren has served as colorist on the totally tubular *Pizzasaurus Rex* by Justin Wagner and has illustrated over a dozen issues of *Invader ZIM*.

Before Warren and Ted created *Kriss*, Warren colored Ted's highly acclaimed series *Courtney Crumrin* and *Princess Ugg*.

He currently resides in Durham, NC where he spends most of his time making comics, bingeing 80s cartoons, eating pie, and complaining about mosquitoes.